Another Life

and

The House

on the Embankment

by *Yuri Trifonov*

Translated from the Russian

by Michael Glenny

SIMON AND SCHUSTER · NEW YORK

Library of Congress Cataloging in Publication Data

Trifonov, IUrii Valentinovich, 1925–
Another life; and, The House on the Embankment.

Translation of: Drugaia zhizn' and Dom na
naberezhnoï.
I. Trifonov, IUrii Valentinovich, 1925–
Dom na naberezhnoi. English. 1983.
II. Title: Another life.
III. Title: House on the embankment.
PG3489.R5D713 1983   891.73'44   83-17576

Another Life

"I dedicate this to my wife, Alla"—Y.T.

Again she woke up in the middle of the night, just as she had lately been waking up every night, as though someone had roused her with a familiar, malicious nudge: "Think, think, try and understand!" She could not. Her mind was capable of nothing but self-torture. Yet whatever it was that woke her demanded obstinately that she try to make sense of everything: there must be a meaning; somebody must be guilty, it's always the family who are guilty; she shouldn't go on living, she ought to die herself. If only she could discover how she was guilty. And there was another thought, secret and shameful: "Was death really the end of everything?" And then she would reprimand herself: "What a fool I am. How can I think about death when I have a daughter?"

Yet she found it easy enough to think about death; it was something unpleasant but inevitable that had to be gone through—like, for instance, having to go to hospital for an operation. Thoughts about death were much easier to bear than memories; they caused pain, while thoughts of death caused nothing but a passing mood of reflection.

Now it was starting again. Long ago he used to come home from the museum on payday slightly drunk, usually from the Sevan, a bar next door to the museum, or else Fyodorov would take him back to his place, where they would stay up drinking much too late. Then when he came home he would go straight to bed and fall asleep immediately. He invariably woke up in the middle of the night, however, at three or four o'clock, just as she was doing now. He would keep her from sleep by shuffling into the kitchen for a glass of water or some food out of the refrigerator, while she would curse him angrily, half asleep. When he woke her up at those times she hated him: "What a selfish child you are!"

At other times, behaving with great resourcefulness and cunning, he would hide the fact that he had been drinking; he was a very clever actor. She noticed neither the smell nor his reddened eyes, believed him when he said, "I'm dog-tired," pitied him, and quickly turned down the bedclothes. He would collapse into bed and start to snore, but later that night he would always give himself away by waking up long before morning. Now the same thing was happening with her. For her the equivalents of alcohol were memory and pain. By day she concealed them. No one must notice: at work, at home, her daughter Irinka, her mother-in-law—most of all her mother-in-law, because if she were to notice, the pain would be worse. So in the daytime she kept up the camouflage by exerting all her strength, but at night she had none left.

Sometimes he would wake up at night when he hadn't been drinking at all—just like that, for no apparent reason other than mere whim. It wasn't as if he were old; insomnia is something old men suffer from. It irritated her, because she was a light sleeper and would wake up as soon as he started sighing or tossing about, and particularly when he looked at his watch. He had a habit of picking up his watch from the lid of the blanket chest to peer at it, and the metal watch-strap would always clink against the chest. There had been many rows about that clinking noise. She would get furious. It was so stupid. The wretched man tried hard to handle the watch without making a noise, but somehow it never worked: invariably something, usually the metal strap would brush against the lid of the chest—and a metallic "clink" would ring out, sharp and clear in the nighttime silence, and she would wince, having already awakened and lying there tensely waiting for the noise.

Her mother-in-law had continued living with her in the apartment. Where else could she go?

This woman firmly believed that the death of her son, in November of the previous year from a heart attack at the age of forty-two, was the fault of his wife. Living with his mother was difficult; they would have liked to break up the arrangement and part forever but were constrained because the old woman was lonely and if she were to part from her granddaughter, sixteen-year-old Irinka, she would be condemned to ending her life among strangers (her sister and niece showed no great enthusiasm for inviting her to live with them, and in any case she, Alexandra Prokofievna, would never have accepted such an offer). Furthermore, Olga Vasilievna had to think of her daughter, who loved her grandmother and without whom she would have been deprived of care when her mother was at work. All this had tightened itself into such a stone-hard, indissoluble knot that there seemed to be no way to undo it.

So she was waking up in the middle of the night and racking her brains in despair while by day her only relief was in leaving the house, scuttling away, disappearing. Nowadays she seized the opportunity thankfully whenever her work took her away from Moscow. She realized that this was wrong, that it was weakness, that Irinka needed her now more than ever— and she needed Irinka. Away on her trips she missed her daughter painfully, always hastened to come back, spent at least five rubles every evening talking to her by telephone, and on returning would discover that her daughter, absorbed in her own little concerns, had managed perfectly well without her. Far from comforting Olga, this only increased the pain, so that she would once more feel the urge to get away again, to escape, knowing in advance that it wouldn't help. Oh, how she would have pitied, how she would have appreciated the old woman if only she lived somewhere far away! But in these little rooms, in that tiny little hallway, the years they had all spent together stood crammed tightly one against another, blatant and unadorned, like the patched carpet slippers in the crude wooden box that Sergei had knocked together and that still stood under the coatrack. Here, in all this overcrowded muddle, there was no room for pity. Her mother-in-law might say, "You used not to buy cookies like these before. Where did you get them? On Kirovskaya Street?" That one sentence instantly destroyed all the sympathy for her mother-in-law which Olga had been scraping together crumb by crumb. It meant: You never treated *him* to cookies, but now, for yourself, you've started buying them. Trivial things like this, so petty and stupid as to be ridiculous, wounded her like a blow from an iron bar—because they were deliberately spiteful and meant to hurt.

As painful as the cookies had been the business of the television set. Long ago, while Sergei was still alive, they had wanted to buy a new, big one in place of their little old set with its antediluvian screen and had put aside the money. Yet Sergei's TV watching had often infuriated Olga—perhaps it was wrong of her to have been so annoyed, so unfairly and stupidly irritated (though to be frank, she had good reason for it), because of the way he used to sit for hours, oblivious to everything else, watching endless sports programs. He would collapse into the green armchair, legs crossed, cigarette between his teeth, the round ashtray with a little fish on it beside him on the floor—and then stay there as though glued to the TV, deaf to questioning or even shouting. But why *all* the programs one after another? Surely they can't all be equally interesting? "I'm relaxing! I have a right to rest and relaxation, haven't I?" His anger was slightly calculated, put on to make sure that everyone realized how incredibly tiring his work was.

In fact, he really did get tired at work, and he had troubles there too. But then so did everyone. He lacked the necessary coolness and stamina. What's more, he would often cover up and keep quiet about his problems, many of which she heard about only much later. When she had difficulties at work she always told him about them and it made her feel better, but he concealed his, ashamed of his failures. And then, slouched in front of the television, he would complain, half genuinely and half acting the fool: "Gentlemen, my nerve cells need rest. Dogs eat grass, intellectuals listen to music, and I watch sports—it's my therapy, my bromide, my vacation, damn your lack of perceptiveness, gentlemen. . . ."

Just the usual buffoonery, but his mother, Alexandra Prokofievna, felt impelled to intervene in her son's defense. Sometimes, to support him, she would sit down beside him and watch ice hockey or volleyball—it didn't matter to her what it was—and exchange comments with him that made Olga almost burst out laughing. On occasion, subtly and covertly but always so that Olga realized it, he would make fun of Alexandra Prokofievna during these conversations in front of the television, but the old woman obstinately pretended that sports greatly interested her. Ah yes, thirty or forty years ago she had been a keen hiker. And not long since, she had donned an ancient pair of khaki-colored pants and an outlandish jacket dating from the days of "war communism" in the early twenties, shrugged into an old knapsack that had once been used for collecting scrap metal, and set off quite alone by train out into the country. She had, it seems, been taking a trip to the places where long ago she had gone walking with her husband, Sergei's father, a mathematics professor who had been a passionate hiker, tourist, and photographer. (Sergei's father had joined the Volunteer Reserve in 1941 and had been killed that fall in the defense of Moscow.) Alexandra's bizarre hiking gear dating from the twenties gave her a tragicomic look. Sergei took it all calmly—he allowed no one else to make fun of his mother, or even to smirk at her behind her back—but Olga found herself upset by the whole thing. If people were able to understand and forgive the old woman's pathetic eccentricities, why could they not understand her, Olga Vasilievna? Why couldn't they see her grief? There seemed to be absolutely no way of making her mother-in-law—a woman by no means stupid, with a law degree—acknowledge Olga Vasilievna's right to suffering.

"But of course buy a new TV, buy it, don't hesitate!" she said when Olga stupidly decided to ask her advice.

Irinka was desperate for a bigger television. Olga didn't care about it, but in a nearby store, in the next-door building in fact, where Irinka was always popping in for this and that, they were selling a very good brand of TV set which was rarely available, and a decision had to be made.

"I tell you: Buy it. Why deny yourself the pleasure?"

Olga said that she was not in a mood for pleasures.

"I understand, but on the other hand you're not planning to shut yourself up in a convent."

"No, I don't want to go into a convent, that's true."

Olga purposely gave the older woman a sour reply, in order to hurt her—after all, it was she who had meant to cause Olga pain with her remark about pleasure.

"So don't upset yourself, take out the money, Sergei put it aside for that purpose, it's what he would have wanted. . . ."

The kind smile froze on Alexandra Prokofievna's flat, high-cheekboned, Tartar-like face, and her eyes—narrow, bright-blue slits, Sergei's eyes—stared at her coldly and without pity.

Embittered by these malicious digs, Olga decided not to buy the television, just to spite the old woman. She shouted at Irinka, who burst into tears. But later, still more embittered, Olga changed her mind and bought it. For four months her mother-in-law never once watched television. She explained that she was sparing her eyes and was afraid of radiation, but it was also meant as a demonstration. One of Olga's friends tried to reassure her: You must find a *modus vivendi*, be tolerant; you both share the same grief and you both love the same little girl. Olga also thought that things would somehow settle themselves, but after a certain incident she realized that it was no good, it would never work out.

It happened less than two months after the TV incident, in January, when her anguish became intolerable. It was at such moments that she no longer wanted to go on living. One night, tortured by insomnia, Olga got up and went into the kitchen, where she burst into helpless tears. She took a sedative, then drank some cold tea from the teapot. Suddenly she heard Alexandra Prokofievna shuffling into the kitchen; she couldn't sleep either. That shuffling sound pierced Olga Vasilievna to the core because it was so familiar: Sergei had shuffled along exactly like that in those same backless slippers, which the old woman had for some reason taken to wearing around the house. And it seemed to Olga that it was Sergei walking in them. He used to come into the kitchen when all three of the others were sitting there, stand in the doorway wearing a hat made out of newspaper, raise his hand and say, "I greet ye, my people!" Irinka, of course, would collapse with laughter. He was always trying to bring them all together, make them feel closer, united, even if only for a minute, even if only by jokes and clowning. And now, suddenly, the shuffling sound brought it all rushing back to her and she sobbed aloud, unable to control herself. It was terrible, unforgivable, because no one should ever see her tears.

Alexandra Prokofievna came in wearing a nightgown, her gray hair unkempt, her face yellow and disagreeable-looking.

She glanced at Olga, walked over to the cabinet, took down a cup, and filled it with water. No, she was not going to give the water to Olga; she needed the water herself.

She acted as if she could neither see nor hear Olga Vasilievna sobbing, and merely asked in her usual querulous voice, "Where do we keep the bicarbonate of soda?"

Without answering, Olga went out of the kitchen.

She could not forget the question about the bicarbonate, the unseeing eyes—because something that was kept concealed in daytime had suddenly come out into the open. The truth is laid bare at night. Olga was crying; yet the old woman had looked at her with hatred.

It had happened in the past that Olga and Sergei had some of their bitterest rows at night. He had said one night that if it weren't for Irinka he would leave Olga, and that seemed to her such a lethal truth that she had hardly been able to live through till dawn. Yet the next morning he was making jokes and talking nonsense, having remembered nothing, and their nighttime argument evaporated without a trace, like a nightmare.

A few months later he suddenly announced that he intended to go away alone for a vacation at New Year's. This frightened Olga. She refused to let him go by himself and demanded to be taken along. In those days it was easy enough to get ten days' unpaid leave, but there was a problem about leaving Irinka, because Sergei's mother was slightly unwell. It was nothing serious, and if Sergei had needed a vacation she would have let them go without hesitation. But on this occasion, realizing she was doing it mostly for the benefit of her daughter-in-law, she flatly refused to be left alone with Irinka. As part of an outright conspiracy, Alexandra Prokofievna invited her sister Vera over, along with Vera's daughter, Sergei's cousin Tamara, who was a neurologist at an exclusive clinic.

Olga had never liked Tamara and did not believe a word of her long, pedantic explanation of Alexandra Prokofievna's illness at the dinner table; she was obviously exaggerating things in order to confuse everyone. Not wishing to start an unpleasant argument, Olga said nothing and took it all impassively, even though it was an obvious plot. But that night she could restrain herself no longer and woke Sergei with a question—only to experience that same nightmarish feeling that everything was collapsing, the ground sliding away under her feet.

"Come on, admit it—there's someone else you want to be with, just the two of you, isn't there?"

"Yes, there is, there is," he said in a whisper, instantly awake. "That someone is myself. I want to be alone with myself. I want a rest from you, from mother, from all of you, all of you."

For a moment she believed it—she was used to trusting him—but then she had second thoughts: Did he really need to be alone? She could think of no reasons why he should want to go, all alone, hundreds of miles away from Moscow. So although she was usually inclined to take him at his word and was easily reassured, this time she did not altogether accept his reason. In her heart of hearts she was nagged by a doubt that provoked the sickening thought: "He's got someone else!"

He liked small blond women. She found this out one day quite by chance. He had a penchant for miniature women that he could cradle in his arms. One day he had said tenderly to Olga, "What a pity you're so solidly built. I would like to be able to carry you in my arms."

Yet all his women were on the large side. Pure coincidence; it just happened that way, he used to say. He had had five women, four before Olga; she was the fifth. Maybe there had been others as well—in fact almost definitely, it was indubitable—but she knew for certain about those four and could only guess and suspect there were others. About the four, though, she had gradually wormed all the details out of him and could name them all—Valka, Svetlana, and so on—and never missed an opportunity to say something cutting, to make some sarcastic gibe about them and about him simultaneously. She hated them, these she-devils, these sluts, two of whom had been older than he was and had taught him all kinds of disgusting things; one had been the same age as Sergei and had fancied herself as a high-minded intellectual, although in fact she was an oversexed bitch who had schemed by fair means or foul to make him marry her. He, thank God, had resisted her wiles and had treated her firmly although maybe not entirely decently, but she deserved it, the bitch. Then there had been a pudgy pink-and-white creature with whom he had worked in the museum, empty-headed and affected but very beautiful, who was always running away from him while he chased after her. One day he got fed up with this: she ran out of the house where they were meeting; this time he didn't chase her, and it all came to an end.

Despite her hysterical behavior, this fourth woman was generously built and he called her Brünnhilde. He used to say that her breasts were as heavy and round as soup plates. Olga felt a special hatred for her. She hated them all even now, all four, because Sergei still caused her pain and continued to do so. And so, she thought, he never did have any tiny little blondes, and that was perhaps why he had a longing for them. Once he went away on a twelve-day vacation without her, to a place called Peresvetovo, between Moscow and Gorky. She found this unforgivable, not simply because she thought he was bound to be unfaithful to her in Peresvetovo but because he had gone in spite of her desperate plea. Yet three days later came a telegram: "Lovely here. Bring Irinka." She asked for a day off work, took the train with Irinka to Peresvetovo, and, of course, he was forgiven. They went sledding down the hills on a Finnish sled, and next morning, seeing them off on the train, he mumbled, "What a silly, silly woman you are!"— and kissed her, scratching her mouth with his unshaven face. And not long ago, when they were applying for a vacation at a spa, the doctor had pronounced Sergei "Effectively healthy." Everything had been fine—blood tests, heart, blood pressure. And then what had happened? No one could understand. And she could not understand how she was to live without him. Yet somehow she had managed it thus far—thus far for five months and twenty-five days! She could not conceive how she had done it: the time had just passed, senselessly, dragging; she had simply kept going. . . .

The alarm clock would ring at seven. For another hour and a half she would lie sunk in oblivion, not the oblivion of sleep but the oblivion of a vanished life. Then slowly she would get up, put on her quilted nylon robe, Sergei's present to her on her last birthday; or sometimes without even her robe, just in her nightdress, uncombed, because she no longer bothered about her appearance. She would wander into the kitchen, put on the kettle for tea, a saucepan of water for kasha and another for eggs, and take the cottage cheese and yogurt from the refrigerator, so that while she and Irinka were washing and getting dressed the cottage cheese and yogurt would warm up a little in the heat of the kitchen. She would switch on the radio, which stood on top of the cabinet. And all the time, no matter what she was doing or what she was thinking about, she could feel an emptiness and coldness behind her back.

There had been a boy called Vlad, good, kind, boring, hopeless, but intellectually gifted; he had a broad, pockmarked face and was slightly popeyed, which gave him a look of earnestness and devotion. He wore spectacles in a tortoiseshell frame. Whenever he laughed—which happened rarely and always unexpectedly—he would cover his mouth with his hand, because his upper lip had slightly more of a cleft in it than was normal. It was not a real harelip, rather a kind of hint at a harelip. Vlad was a medical student, and even then people were predicting a great career for him in medicine. Olga Vasilievna's mother (for whom all *externals*—whether a person's looks, an overcoat, a bookshelf, curtains, even a bunch of flowers—were of absolutely no significance at all, and who was influenced only by a rather vague, debatable quality that she claimed to detect with her inner eye and which she called *essence*) very much wanted her daughter to marry Vlad. But Olga simply could not accept this idea, even though she was as aware of Vlad's qualities as her mother was. Just think—to have to spend the rest of your life looking at that vast, pockmarked face. . . .

And so it dragged on, half feeble courtship, half childlike friendship, hopeless for Vlad, joyless for Olga, lasting two or three years (she was simultaneously being bored by the attentions of another young man, called Gendlin, an engineer and a total nonentity, even though her mother approved of him too), until the fateful moment of graduation, the start of real life, a job teaching school on Pulikha Street. She was twenty-four, with no line of retreat; all her girl friends, damn them, were already married. And suddenly Vlad appeared with another young man, named Sergei. They had met the previous winter at a student camp in Zvenigorod and had instantly become friends. Vlad was in general a lover of his fellow man: he developed great enthusiasms for people, although it must also be said that his judgment of them was often less than brilliant. He regarded Sergei's mother, for instance, as a paragon among women; he trembled before her, tried to ingratiate himself with her, and all because Alexandra Prokofievna had once been a typist in the Political Department of the Red Army during the civil war. But that, of course, came later; before Sergei, he had first befriended some flier in the Air Force, then a wrestling champion who looked like an ape, then a secondhand bookseller who dealt in very old detective novels and who was a garrulous know-it-all and a morphine addict. Vlad's new friend Sergei was a historian who had recently graduated and now worked in some obscure institution in a job that was not in his field. In addition, as Vlad announced when he introduced him, Sergei was the undisputed champion of the Zvenigorod region at various word games, such as saying words backward.

In fact, on that first evening he had amazed Olga with this bizarre skill. Vlad would shout excitedly, "Dining room," and his friend would reply, "Moorgninid." "Glance" cried Vlad, and immediately came the response: "Ecnalg." "Briefcase," Vlad suggested slyly, secretly rejoicing at his friend's inevitably successful retort. And with only a moment's hesitation Sergei answered, "Esac . . . feirb." "What was that?" cried Vlad. "Say it again, please! We must check it." They checked it, and it was faultless. It produced an enormous impression. Vlad added to the excitement by announcing, "But he's a genius. A plain, ordinary genius."

In those days Sergei was slim and well built, with a shock of thick hair and a spring in his walk; he had an odd but infectiously cheerful way of talking, and he was unlike anyone else

Olga knew. She felt that something had happened. Suppressing her nervous excitement, she joined in the game and asked, "Earthquake?" "Ah!" cried Vlad. "That's a very difficult one." The new visitor looked at her for a second as though agreeing—yes, that's difficult—then said quietly but firmly, "Ekauqhtrae."

This mysterious word pierced her like a needle. It was, perhaps, the uttering of a password that heralded a complete change in her life. A crazy, unheard-of, unwritten word: "Ekauqhtrae," but it was a mirror image of another, a real word, in which she had always believed—"earthquake." That game, that funny, absurd first meeting and the nonsense they talked as they drank vodka and ate sardines, stuck in her memory forever, because it had given her an inward shock and was the omen of a change in her destiny.

Added to this, it was at the beginning of spring, a vaguely unsettling time whose meaning had to be guessed, like the word "ekauqhtrae," a time when all the people around her, holding their breath in expectation and conjecture, were constantly whispering and arguing about something. The new guest, however, displeased Olga's mother because on that first visit he rushed out of the house to buy a bottle of vodka. When she came to know him better, Olga guessed that it had not been fondness for liquor but plain shyness and a particular, excessive nervousness that made him do the stupidest things. For years her mother could not forget Sergei's *faux pas*. "And do you remember," she would say whenever her son-in-law did something wrong, "how he ran out for a bottle of vodka the very first evening he was here?" Her mother, who strove so hard to grasp the "essence" of things, was incapable of perceiving that this silly behavior did not represent the "essence" of Sergei's character at all. She was firmly convinced that Vlad was the most suitable for her daughter: that, for her, was the essence of the situation. Poor mother—for all her love for her daughter, she could never rise above the naïve egotism that was so characteristic of her—naïve because it never entered her head to detect a trace of egotism in herself. Quite the reverse: she saw herself as enveloped in a positive cloud of altruism; in her own eyes she lived only for others. There was a certain truth in this, except that on closer examination it was plain that "others" meant only one person—Georgii Maximovich. At any rate, she insisted that Vlad was the better one for Olga, imagining that she was concerned about her daughter, whereas in fact she was really concerned about herself; Vlad was more suitable from *her* point of view. She had also disliked the word games that first evening, and Sergei's story of how he and Vlad visited a mental hospital. And Sergei was brilliant at telling stories. Georgii Maximovich, who came into the studio for a cup of tea while Sergei was telling that story, also looked at him disapprovingly.

There was a remarkable synchronism between Olga's mother and Georgii Maximovich. Whenever her mother pronounced some opinion, Georgii Maximovich would nod in confirmation, accompanying his nods with such phrases as "I guess that's so" or "I'm afraid you're right." Olga's real father had died long ago, when she was six. Her mother had met Georgii Maximovich during the wartime evacuation, when they were both working in the same factory, she in the planning department and Georgii Maximovich as decorator and painter in the workers' club. He was an artist who had studied before the revolution under some famous Greek, had traveled and taken part in exhibitions abroad. He was arrested and "reeducated," and after his release could not reestablish himself as an artist; gradually he lost heart altogether, so that by the time he was evacuated to a remote little town in the Urals he had degenerated into a mere starving sign-painter.

But when Georgii returned to Moscow with his new family, Olga and her mother, he was given a studio and a room in an artists' cooperative. He began to be recognized again; he was mentioned in the press and given commissions. He had not, it seemed, wasted his time during his wartime evacuation to the Urals but had worked like an ox—because art is made by oxen, according to Jules Renard, who was Georgii Maximovich's favorite author—and had drawn a whole gallery full of studies of industrial workers entitled "Urals Steel"; these drawings were exhibited several times, were reproduced as prints and even made into postcards—and Georgii Maximovich underwent a kind of renaissance, a second youth, or as he put it, "my rosy period." All would have continued to go well had Georgii Maximovich not become ill just then, in the late forties. He had headaches, then something went wrong with his eyes. He was forbidden to work and went away to a sanitarium. After that he developed heart trouble, and shortly before Sergei appeared, Georgii Maximovich had a heart attack. How old was he then? Olga's mother was seventeen years younger than he; she was forty-three when Sergei came on the scene, so Georgii Maximovich was sixty.

He still walked with a straight back and his handshake was firm. When meeting someone for the first time, he had a habit of looking hard and intently into the person's face and unceremoniously staring them up and down. New acquaintances found this disconcerting. Sergei admitted later that he had been slightly taken aback by his first encounter with Georgii Maximovich: "He looked at me as if I had stolen something."

Georgii Maximovich, however, also had another habit: having thoroughly studied a new person he would announce that he had "an interesting face" and that he would be "very interesting to paint." In the tone of these remarks there was undoubtedly something of the slightly patronizing attitude of the artist standing above the rest of humanity, but they were at the same time an innocent flattery that everyone enjoyed hearing. Georgii Maximovich never made these comments to Sergei, however. He was on his guard from the first. Of course Georgii Maximovich's reactions on such occasions were not really his own: like a sensitive membrane, he simply picked up the vibrations given out by Olga's mother. She and he were, in fact, perfectly attuned to each other. And a very good thing too—"Thank God for it," thought Olga.

She had never been jealous; she hardly remembered her father, and Georgii Maximovich treated her mother well. He obviously loved her, while she, poor woman, positively adored him, and over the years they had grown to have the same tastes, the same opinions about people, about art, books, money, everything. Her mother was constantly absorbed in his problems and his illnesses. She simply had no time for anyone else's life.

When Irinka was born, Olga's mother was at first torn between her granddaughter and her husband; she wanted to be useful, to be everywhere at once, but she lacked the strength for it and gave in, surrendering her role to the child's other grandmother. Olga forgave her. For some time they lived with neighbors in the apartment next door to the studio on Sushchevskaya Street, where her mother and Georgii Maximovich lived; next they lived with her mother and Georgii; then Sergei's mother suffered a grievous blow—the death of Sergei's sister, her unmarried daughter, a sick, unhappy girl whom she greatly loved—and they decided to move in with her in her two-room apartment on Shabolovka.

It was here that Sergei had spent his childhood. Everything in the place was familiar to him and much loved, and although Olga sensed at once that living with her mother-in-law was not going to be easy, Sergei very much wanted it and said they ought to meet the old woman halfway—although, incidentally, she was hardly an old woman but a noisy, bustling middle-aged lady. They could at least give her a granddaughter. It was sad for Olga to leave her mother, but there was nothing to be done about it. All this had happened of its own momentum, beginning that evening when Sergei first arrived—tousle-headed, wearing his lumberjack shirt and a jacket with padded shoulders—and said words backward.

After that first evening came spring, meetings in backyards, doorways, cafés, bars; then summer, Vlad still totally unaware of what was happening, scraping together the money for a trip south—heat, cool sea, liberation. Four of them went together: Olga and Rita, her friend of those days who later vanished without a trace, and Vlad and Sergei. Vlad had a friend—or rather, a friend of his father's—a general in the army medical corps, who owned a house at Gagra, on the eastern shore of the Black Sea. He had promised to rent them rooms. They needed two: one for Rita and Olga, one for Sergei and Vlad, but there turned out not to be room enough for them all in the house. The summer was burning hot and Gagra suffocatingly humid. In the end, Vlad's friend—whose name was apparently Porfiry Nikolaevich, or it might have been Parfenty Mikhailovich, a vague man who had once worked in some important institution in Moscow but was now living on a pension in his house in Gagra—could rent out only one small and rather unpleasant room; he also offered them a summerhouse in his garden. The boys were given the room and the girls took the summerhouse, right by the beach. It was a flimsy, shacklike structure that would nowadays be called a bungalow and has become the fashion all along the Black Sea coast. At first everything was fine, but then certain disadvantages came to light. The girls, for instance, had to go through the garden and into the house to go to the bathroom. Apart from that, the other house guests, Porfiry Mikhailovich's relatives, friends, and acquaintances, who were many and of whom more were constantly arriving by car, led a noisy, hectic kind of life. They spent all day and every day drinking, horsing around, shouting songs, playing records loudly and dancing on the veranda, barbecuing kebabs in the garden; in the evening they would all flock down to the sea for a swim—down the garden path, through the gate in the fence and out onto the pebbly beach. The house stood just above the shoreline.

Parfenty Nikolaevich's rowdy guests would invite Vlad, Sergei, and the girls to join them. The boys never refused, since they had no money, Gagra was an expensive place, and the wine and Georgian brandy flowed freely. Rita, an unattractive, scheming girl, fed up with her lonely life in Moscow, also plunged into this whirlpool, which looked dangerous but tempting.

Olga, however, said firmly, "No." There were occasional roughnecks among the people who wandered through the garden in the evening, and once someone tried to break into the shack at a late hour; the door shook, stupid Rita giggled, but Olga guessed that it wasn't Rita they wanted. "Hey, Miss High-and-Mighty," they shouted from outside. "Come for a swim with us." In a stern voice Olga threatened them with the police.

Next morning she complained to Vlad, who ran into the house to fetch Porfiry Parfentievich's wife, a graceful lady who always wore white; her black hair was streaked with gray, and she had gold on her fingers, gold in her ears, and when she opened her large purple lips she revealed a great deal of gold in her mouth as well: "Please forgive my hooligans, girls. They are children of the South. The sun is in their blood. The sun makes people crazy."

Sergei was brilliant at swimming and diving. He and Rita would swim far out beyond the line of buoys, while Olga and Vlad splashed about near the shore. For all his clumsiness or shyness in practical matters and in personal relations, Sergei was physically very brave. He could never bring himself to ask Porfiry how much rent they should pay for the shack, or to tell him about the bathroom, which the house guests often kept occupied in a long, continuous succession, thereby putting Rita and Olga in an embarrassing situation; afraid of causing offense, he would postpone any encounter with their host in a cowardly fashion, but at the same time he never turned down the offer of a drink, or an invitation to join the other guests on the veranda, and she detected with annoyance a vacillating and unmanly streak in his character. Yet he was always ready to get involved if there was a fight on the beach, and he thought nothing of diving into the water from a height of thirty-five feet. Each day she became more aware that she was hooked.

Never before had she fallen for anyone quite so hopelessly, or desperately. Nothing else existed any longer. All other thoughts vanished. Only a few days had passed—what could have changed in such a short time?—yet everything around her seemed to have altered: the color of the sky, the smell of the sea, the taste of kebab. It was as if a needle on some inward dial had moved forward: everything inside her was churning much more rapidly than before. She also felt something new and disturbing, as though some extra, superfluous source of gravitational pull was causing her torment and discomfort. She couldn't bear it, for instance, when he went into the house and stayed there for a long time. Of course it was nonsense to feel like that; yet she went through agonies: Why is he in there? Who is he with? Whose laughter is that coming from the veranda? Male laughter upset her as much as female. It meant that he was enjoying himself more in there than out here with her. These torments were strange, divorced from reason, born of pure instinct. After all, he wasn't her husband, they hadn't even made love yet; that idea, in fact, was only just beginning to take shape in her secret fantasies; yet from her feelings and the pain she experienced they might as well have been lovers.

One day she could stand it no longer and walked up to the veranda to call him. Vlad and Rita were getting ready to go to the beach, but Sergei had taken the chess set indoors with him. She had started learning to play chess, wanting to do everything that he did (one day, overcoming her fear, she had even dived off the ten-foot springboard), and as she opened the glass door she saw several people, men and women, sitting around a table drinking. They were all looking at Sergei, who was standing a little apart so that everyone could see him, and doing a piece of mimicry. He was an excellent mimic; two of his best acts were "the old druggist" and "the soccer fan." He had, in fact, many talents—he could draw, he sang well, and he had taught himself to play the guitar.

At that moment on the veranda she suddenly felt a fierce wave of revulsion toward him, like an attack of nausea, and toward the people around the table staring at him with cheerful, boozy amiability. As they clapped, shouted "Bravo!" and raised their glasses to toast him in Georgian—*"Allaverdi, Sergo!"*—she completely lost her temper and said angrily, "All right, now you can say a word backward—'buffoon,' for instance—and then say goodbye. They're waiting for us on the beach."

He stared at her in amazement with his narrow blue eyes and actually opened his mouth to say something in protest, or maybe even to say "buffoon" backward, but she took him by the hand, he silently obeyed, and they went out.

On the way to the beach she gave him a lecture, deriving keen pleasure from the fact that he took it in silence while she scolded him with motherly severity: "Don't you see how shameful, how disgusting it is to demean yourself in front of those drunken fools? You, an intellectual, clowning to amuse those rich, idle ne'er-do-wells."

He defended himself good-naturedly. "You're too much of an extremist. Take it from me as an historian—extremism never leads to good results."

Yet he seemed to enjoy being held by the hand, to enjoy her indignation on his account. It was perhaps at that moment that her mind created the model which for years she was to keep before her as the ideal form of their relationship, toward which she would strive with her utmost strength, and to which he cunningly pretended to submit while remaining in fact remote and uninvolved: to lead him by the hand and teach him what was right, no matter what the cost in pain and heartache. On the beach, when Vlad heard her attacking him, he rushed to his friend's defense: "You don't know the local customs. Here, if they offer you a drink or invite you to join a party, you can't refuse."

Rita, who had long been nursing a grudge (even her little mind had finally grasped that neither Vlad nor Sergei was interested in her, and she was gradually starting to hate Olga), said that Olga was, as usual, making a mountain out of a molehill. As for Parfenty and his house guests, in Rita's opinion they were perfectly normal, decent people and Olga was wrong to despise them. "There's no need to look down your nose at them" was her expression. But what did these people do for a living, for God's sake? Where did they get the money for such fabulous generosity? It's rude, it's bad form to ask questions about other people's money. They're obviously not crooks, because if they were they would be in prison. Thus ran the logic of this stupid creature, with whom Olga had inexplicably struck up a short-lived friendship. Rita was a thin girl with reddish-blond hair, freckled white skin, blue eyes, and a sharp little nose. She had never lost the firm belief that she was beautiful, and the years passed for her in a state of unremitting perplexity: Why did no one else ever notice it?

Although they were an ill-assorted foursome, they went everywhere together: to the bazaar; to the movies; to the little smoke-filled snack bar where Datiko, a fat man with a tiny head, served them wine and small, fat-soaked Georgian meat pies called *chebureki;* along the promenade; among the white-clad crowd sauntering up and down the main street; to the tennis courts to watch the good players, whom Sergei and Vlad watched with jealous fascination. Later in the day they too were allowed to leap around the court for a bit. Both of them were only just starting to learn, taking lessons from the professional, Otto Janovich. Vlad was useless at tennis, but Sergei showed promise, and every evening he got better at it; if he had wanted to, he could have become a real tennis player—with his natural talent he could have become a real anything: a real swimmer, musician, draftsman, even a nuclear physicist. Otto Janovich said that his movement was "excellent," but the boys couldn't afford rackets of their own and pay for lessons too, for they had to economize to pay the fare home.

Olga and Rita sat on long benches in the shade of a row of poplar trees and watched them play. The sight of Sergei in his white T-shirt and white peaked cap, his thin sunburned face, his powerful well-rounded legs in the short socks that he had brought from Moscow specially to wear with his sneakers (he had no idea he would be playing tennis but thought he would be playing volleyball, for which he was a fanatic), made her heart thump with happiness. It gave her a warmth to watch him when he couldn't see her, to see his enthusiasm, his exertion, his irritation, his delight—it was all laid bare for her. One day Otto Janovich, a gnomelike little man with a beard, surreptitiously passed her a note. Unfolding it carefully so that Rita wouldn't see, she read: "Come tomorrow at nine o'clock in the morning. I will teach you free of charge and for as long as you like." The little gnome charged a high rate for an hour's instruction, and he was said to be a rich man. She smiled at him and shook her head. Otto Janovich made a face expressing profound disappointment. And there were many others that summer who wanted to teach her free of charge and for as long as she liked!

No doubt about it, she was pretty then. She had not yet started to put on weight. Everything about her was in harmony, coordinated, her body smooth and firm, and although she couldn't swim, she ran fast, played volleyball, and could turn a perfect cartwheel. She couldn't possibly do it now, but in those days it was nothing for her to turn ten cartwheels in succession without a trace of strain. Men stared at her on the beach. At that age she tanned very evenly and quickly, an ability that she later somehow lost. Foolishly, she would lie in the scorching sun for hours, regardless of the effect on her. She wore her hair shoulder length, in the way that was fashionable at the time, loose and unkempt. Sergei used to call it "the head of the Medusa." But it greatly suited her—that thick, luxuriant, dark-auburn mass of hair above her clear, rounded, pure forehead, as yet without a wrinkle. It was probably the best year of her life, the year of her prime. She realized this from the way men watched her; the Georgians would stare at her as she came out of the water, insolently clicking their tongues and smacking their lips. And of course they pestered her shamelessly, always trying to make friends, to strike up a conversation or share the book she was reading, and inviting her to play volleyball. Sergei and Vlad spent their time in constant expectation of a fight.

Her admirers included a bunch of men from Leningrad, a naval captain staying with Porfiry called Tsnakis, and some actors, tanned almost black, with one of whom Sergei had a scene in which he hit the actor with an inflatable rubber dolphin, inflicting a minor scratch that led to much fuss and shouting. The police appeared, and only Porfiry saved Sergei from getting into trouble. And then there was someone else who made a pass at Olga in the forest when they all drove out on a trip to Lake Ritsa. There was also a funny little middle-aged creature with an olive complexion, one of Porfiry's house guests, who made a simultaneous play for both Rita and Olga. Thoughtful and obliging, he went every morning to the bazaar and bought them salad, buttermilk, and fruit. He treated Vlad and Sergei with paternal benevolence, apparently not regarding them as serious rivals. He would follow them down to the beach and exasperate them with his boring conversation, from which it was all the harder to escape because the little man himself had such good manners. One day, under an oath of secrecy, he showed Rita a medical certificate that stated that So-and-So, while possessing normal sexual potency, was incapable of procreation owing to inadequate fertility, confirmed and signed by Dr. Such-and-Such, medical director of a polyclinic. Naturally Rita divulged this news to the others, which provoked much hilarity. The little olive-skinned man vanished soon afterward and did not reappear.

Sergei taught Olga to swim. How they enjoyed those lessons!

It would have been boring if she had been able to swim as well as he could. He held her with his arms, she floundered, clinging to his neck, laughed, sank, surfaced again blinded by spray, all the time feeling his hands, which in the water were very bold.

Vlad watched them, straining his eyes—he could not wear his spectacles in the water—trying to make out what was going on over there among all the laughter and the splashing, and sometimes he would offer, "I could teach you too, if you like. If Sergei gets bored . . ."

Ever gallant, poor Vlad was not much better in the water than Olga was. He was misled by the brusque and apparently irritated way that Sergei shouted at her: "Won't you ever understand, woman? Move your legs like a frog!" He loved calling her "woman," as though they had spent a lifetime together. There were other terms of affection, such as "elephant child" and "elephant cow." People who knew them found it odd that she put up with being called such unflattering names, but she liked it: she knew what was happening when he used them. Vlad would bob alongside, trying to teach her, and they couldn't help laughing because it all seemed so funny. Puffing out his cheeks in his conscientious efforts to help, Vlad never realized that he was an unwanted intruder. Rita, who understood this and the reason for it very well, grew quietly furious; she was under the impression that Sergei had been invited for her, so she interpreted these developments as treachery. Sergei and Olga regarded each other as a joyous fount of mutual pleasure and fun; every word, every childish joke, set off peals of laughter.

One night Rita started a quarrel by demanding to have the window shut. Olga protested; the shack was very stuffy.

"But I'm cold," Rita asserted obstinately.

"It's stifling."

"I don't intend to catch a chill just to please you."

"We won't be able to sleep with the window shut."

"You'll sleep perfectly well. I'm not worried about you."

They bickered like this for a long time and Rita, of course, won: the window was shut. Olga felt self-assured and happy. Rita's animosity did not subside; she began accusing Olga of selfishness.

"What a fool I was to agree to come with you. All you ever think of is yourself. Living with you for even ten days is intolerable, you're such a complete egotist."

Listening to this tirade, Olga felt no hostility and no urge to answer back: deep in her heart she actually pitied Rita. But how could she help her? It would be wonderful if only Vlad would show even a faint sexual interest in Rita, but Vlad persisted in treating her with nothing but comradely good nature, which was not at all what she needed.

"I don't know why I'm an egotist," said Olga, yawning and smiling through her drowsiness. "Let's go to sleep, I'm tired."

"Of course *you're* sleepy—you've been rushing around and shrieking your head off all day," grumbled Rita. "The reason why you're an egotist is because you think of yourself the whole time. You never give a thought for other people. I've never had a worse vacation in my life. It's been hell, like a nightmare."

Then, to crown it all, Rita threw a fit. Olga ran indoors for Rita's pills and water and woke up the others. Lying there in the shack with a wet towel around her head, Rita cursed her fate in a pathetic voice and begged for a ticket back to Moscow. Olga murmured some nonsense to calm her down, but she was thinking: "Tomorrow, in the sea . . ." No one else's tears or heartaches could dim her happiness.

Rita found a woman friend who was vacationing in nearby Akhali and moved out to join her. One day they saw her walking arm-in-arm with this friend, a middle-aged straw blonde, accompanied by two men in pajamas—in those days it was the fashion in the South for men to stroll around town wearing striped pajamas as if they were summer suits. All four were talking noisily. Rita glanced at Olga in passing and walked on with barely a nod.

At first, sleeping alone in the shack made Olga uneasy. She did not fall asleep until dawn, listening to the roar of the surf, suffering alternate agonies of elation and depression and of something else incomprehensible: the unknown. There were sounds of people walking through the garden; the rasp of cicadas; a car honking; someone driving out through the gates. Where, Olga wondered, could they be going at this hour of the night? To the bar for some wine, perhaps? In the morning she would complain to the boys that fear had kept her awake all night. She was not telling the truth: her restlessness had been caused by unbearable expectation, a welter of confused thoughts.

In fact, from her first night alone in the shack she was waiting for him to come. Then one morning the boys promised they would stand guard over her. And they would all go swimming that night.

The night was pitch black: nothing could be seen beyond two paces; a starless, southern night. The clouds hung low in the sky and breathing was difficult. On the beach were sounds of talk, of footsteps on the pebbles; many other people were sensible enough to swim at night. They conversed in undertones, some in whispers; the air was charged with a certain mystery, of which Olga was thrillingly aware, although she thought it was her imagination and the mystery was within herself. Then she discovered that people really were whispering, that the mysteriousness was genuine and had nothing to do with her feelings. After a while her head began to reel and her legs felt weak from the sultry humidity, from the thick darkness and a premonition of mystery. The darkness was so thick that you could bathe naked. Olga walked toward the sea, unable to see the water. Never in her life, neither before nor after that night, had she bathed in such warm water; its temperature must have been at least a hundred degrees. There were no waves, only a flat, quiet calm, as though this were not the sea but merely a mass of warm water as in a swimming pool, with only gentle splashing sounds and an indistinct murmur of voices to be heard amid the utter blackness.

She sensed there was something unusual about tonight. Vlad had disappeared. Though he might be nearby, he was silent, not giving away his whereabouts. She could not see Sergei when he took her by the hand and led her into the deeper water. They stopped when the water was up to her shoulders. He said it was like a sacred rite, like bathing in the holy waters of the Ganges or the Jordan, or in tropical rivers where the water was like steaming milk. Vladimir, grand duke of Russia, had been baptized in the Dnieper—although it must have been a great deal colder.

She laughed at him: "Don't you know a lot!"

He asked, "Would you like me to teach you to swim?"

She was surprised: he had been doing nothing else all day. She waded close to him and clasped him around the neck, and they stood and kissed for a long, long while. It was the first time, but it was as good as if they had kissed many times before; the only strange thing was that there were people all around but no one could see them. Vlad called out to them from far away. She felt embarrassed and started to pull away; they struggled, then ran out of the water and collapsed onto the rocks.

The rocks were warm; yet she soon felt cold and started to shiver.

"Hey, where the hell are you?" Vlad shouted.

Sergei closed her mouth with his hand. Unable to contain themselves, they both burst into giggles and rolled off the rocks on which they were sitting.

"Ah, there you are . . . hiding in the dark." Vlad sat ponderously down beside them. "Well, I've fixed up my ticket."

Chilled to the bone, Olga was afraid to ask "What ticket?" lest her voice betray how much she was shivering. It was ridiculous to be shivering on such a sultry night, but she didn't want Vlad to guess what was happening to her. He explained that he had made arrangements with one of the clinics of the First Moscow School of Medicine to work there during August. He was still a medical student then, in his fifth year, even though he was three years older than Olga and Sergei; he had started university later than they had.

She realized from his voice that he had guessed. She felt very sorry for him. Tongue-tied, he mumbled some nonsense —pathetic instructions about what they had to do before his departure. The conversation on the beach continued painfully until about two in the morning; then she announced that she wanted to go to bed. It was not that she really wanted to sleep—her brain was wide awake and racing—but something made her say it; it was simply impossible for the three of them to go on sitting there any longer.

Always the gentleman despite everything, Vlad asked whether she needed anyone to stand guard. What an excellent husband he would have made, if only . . . Olga's mother thought there was "a little bit" of Pierre Bezuhov in Vlad. Since Pierre in *War and Peace* was her favorite hero, coming from her "a little bit" meant a great deal. Georgii Maximovich used to say that Vlad had a face like the Mordovian god Keremet, that it would be interesting to paint him (he did paint him, in several long sittings that caused Vlad much discomfort) and that he very much wished everything would work out between Olga and Vlad: "Don't play hard to get; you'll never find a better husband." Now he's a professor, chairman of his department. He has three children and a wife —a kindhearted shapeless cow of a woman with a broad, fat bottom; she is a doctor too, a radiologist. But that night he was crushed, miserable, and could only ask in a defeated voice, "Do you need anyone to stand guard?"

Both men went away, leaving her alone, her wet bathing suit spread out on the wooden sill to await the sun. She couldn't sleep, but not because she was afraid; that night there were no footsteps, no voices, nothing. She lay with open eyes, her heart thumping; she knew it would not stay dark much longer: he must come soon. After about twenty minutes he came. Again the thought of Vlad worried her: suppose he had noticed Sergei leaving their room and had guessed where he was going? She asked him why he hadn't waited until tomorrow, when Vlad would be gone.

In reply he asked, "What's Vlad to you?"

In truth Vlad meant nothing to her.

"I couldn't wait till tomorrow."

There was no talk—no promises, no vows; she simply entrusted herself to him forever.

Later there were many, countless other nights, in Moscow and in the country, in the summer, in wet weather, in the chill of the fall when the heat was not yet on and the room was warmed by a portable electric heater; they made love almost every night. Theirs was a rare gift; her girl friends sometimes exchanged intimate details of their love life, but Olga never did. If she had told them about it, they wouldn't have believed her and would have thought Olga was telling the same sort of lies that they themselves invented, but the secret was very simple: what one of them lacked, the other possessed, and what they both possessed was merged jointly and fully into a wholeness—although of course this didn't happen all at once; it didn't happen on the first night, not even in their first year. Then she realized that with anyone else it could never be as it was with him. What was it like that night in the shack? A sultry, airless night, long forgotten . . .

The superfluous Vlad hung around their necks for one more day. In the water Sergei never once came near her. He spent all the time with Vlad, even seemed to be avoiding her. This alarmed her; then she calmed herself with the thought that he was cunningly acting this way on purpose; after all, he knew and she knew that he would come to her again that night. Then some man invited Vlad to go swimming; they swam away from the shore and the man gave Vlad some news. At that time all kinds of rumors and snatches of news were going around. She had forgotten what this particular piece of information was; she remembered only that Vlad and Sergei became unusually excited and were going to run to find Porfiry, but their host, the man said, had left for Moscow, that his wife was sick and couldn't see anyone, and that all the other guests had also left and gone home. Not a single car remained in the driveway.

They went into town to wander around the bazaar and the little shops. Whenever Vlad moved away or turned aside from them, Sergei would take her hand and squeeze her fingers, contrive to touch her or press up against her. Vlad and Sergei argued a lot that day, talking very noisily, but she could think of nothing but what would happen that night. In the bazaar, they were selling the first grapes of the season. She realized, of course, that the news might be interesting, but she was obsessed with another event and also slightly perplexed: On *this* day of all days, how could Sergei be so absorbed by something else, and how could he, for instance, even fail to hear her when she asked him a question?

The Greek maid, who had a pronounced mustache, was puttering around the garden with a rake, while Titan, the German shepherd, lay sprawled miserably on the porch, his head on his paws. The family and guests had all dispersed, vanished; even Porfiry's wife, the elegant lady with the blue lips, looking like a Gogolesque corpse, had disappeared somewhere.

How good they were, those few days when Olga and Sergei had the house virtually to themselves. The Greek maid was frightened of sleeping in the house alone and had invited them to share the second-floor verandah. They spent five days there. Everything in the house was built to gigantic proportions; the divan on the verandah was apparently designed to accommodate an orgy. The rooms, as yet unaired, were still full of the sour, stale fumes of wine mixed with a faint smell of dog, but out on the verandah the sea air blew, at once enervating and bracing. They talked steadily day and night, insatiably learning about each other. For them, everything was already settled. Yet in October, Vlad was amazed when he was invited to their wedding. It had, apparently, never occurred to him that things were going so far or so fast.

After all, they had only just met—and already they had lived through an idyll on a verandah over the sea, no secrets between them, closer to each other than they had ever been to anyone else. August brought difficult encounters with his mother, but it changed nothing. Perkhushkovo in the fall, electric trains in the evening, meeting at suburban stations; it was then that Svetlana had shown up, a nightmare that for a long time would not go away and that almost suffocated her.

When did she first hear about Svetlana? Was it from his mother?

No, when his mother spoke the name, Olga had shuddered: it was already known to her, already embedded in her mind like a tiny splinter, inflaming the surrounding tissue, causing a slow, painful swelling. Sergei was open, thoughtless and indiscreet and blabbed a great deal about his past, so she had heard about the bespectacled Svetlana who would stop at nothing to hold on to him. At first Olga had not taken her too seriously, because everybody had a past, including herself: there had been Gendlin, for instance. He had been totally ousted from her life, buried several millennia ago, like Pharaoh Tutankhamen. They had met, she seemed to remember, at a recital at the Conservatory. He was an engineer or some other variety of technician, tall, with a rather odd walk that at every step made him seem about to sit down. Her mother's reproachful voice saying "Gendlin called again" always made her feel guilty—not because of Gendlin but because of her mother. Getting rid of Gendlin had been no problem; he had quietly dropped away of his own accord like an autumn leaf falling off a branch, but she had nevertheless said to Sergei proudly and somewhat didactically, "So I told him absolutely straight that he must stop calling me up, because it was pointless. He understood, and that was that. You have to break it off with one good sharp tug, like pulling out an aching tooth."

Sergei had agreed—yes, yes, of course. Like an aching tooth. Since she was still unacquainted with his capricious and unstable character, his submissive nods and his instant unforced agreement with whatever she said gave her a sense of ease and security. This did not, however, last very long; it lasted only until her first meeting with her future mother-in-law.

The room in that house on Shabolovka amazed her; hexagonal in shape, with an unusually high ceiling, it had been sliced out of what had once been a much larger room, leaving several plaster cupids ruthlessly cut in half through their rumps. One foot and a little wing adorned the cornice of the hexagonal room, while the other foot and a small hand, holding a bow, projected into the hall. None of the cupids had any heads; these were now on the other side of the partition that divided the apartments. The walls, papered in dark-cherry-red wallpaper, ornamented with a white basketwork pattern, were hung with innumerable photographs. Sergei at once drew her attention to one of them: a pyramid of bewhiskered men in military tunics, fur hats, and greatcoats, and, barely noticeable in one corner, a small figure in a white head-scarf with indistinguishable features.

"That's my mother in the Red Army Political Department. In 1920."

It was emphasized from the very beginning that his mother was not to be compared with other, ordinary mothers; she was not an aging lady but someone who had Made History. Olga Vasilievna, however, had approached this woman—very wrinkled and thin-lipped, with narrow eyes and prominent cheekbones—with enormous sympathy and a sincere desire to love her, not because she had Made History (she was indifferent to all relics, ruins, and witnesses to the past) but because she was Sergei's mother. They drank tea out of small and very cheap cups that might almost have belonged to a child's tea set. His sister came, wrapped in an old-womanish shawl, a fat, ungainly girl, completely unlike Sergei, with a vaguely wistful, enigmatic smile. Whenever she talked, she would assume this lopsided smile and look away to one side. She was three years older than Sergei.

Everything in the house—the walls, the ceiling, the china, the furniture, and the people who lived in it—was distinguished by a peculiar kind of incoherence. Yet how she loved it all! He ran out to the store for a bottle of Georgian red wine—they had developed a passion for red wine in Gagra. And then, when Sergei's sister went into the next room and Olga was left alone with her future mother-in-law, the old woman suddenly asked, "Do you know anything about Svetlana?"

Olga admitted that she did know about her, but only vaguely.

"Well, I've news for you, and there's nothing vague about it." Her eyes, narrow blue slits with steely pupils, bored into Olga's eyes. "This Svetlana, whom I had never heard of until the day before yesterday, is expecting Sergei's child."

This creature, it transpired, had come to the house and told them her story, with much hysterical embroidery (later it was proved to be a very ordinary attempt at blackmail; she was relying on their credulity), and now Olga was being put on trial to see how she reacted. The shabby little living room was suddenly transformed into the setting for a kangaroo court; the only things missing were the commissar's leather tunic with a Mauser in its wooden holster.

"Are you sure you can be happy at the cost of another person's unhappiness?"

Olga stammered, "I don't know. . . . Are you sure this is true?"

The woman with the steely eyes nodded coldly.

"But we love each other. They will have to give each other

up. . . ." In a miserable voice Olga tried to resist the on-slaught.

"You're speaking of the way scoundrels behave. My son is not a scoundrel. He's simply irresponsible."

Suddenly the sister reappeared, having heard everything. Twisting her mouth into a smile, she said tensely and force-fully, "Don't pay any attention to her. As usual she is distort-ing and oversimplifying everything." Turning to her mother, she angrily spat out, "You're talking nonsense again. It makes me sick to listen to you."

The old woman subsided. Sergei came running in with the wine, and Olga summoned up all her strength to stop herself from bursting into tears. Sergei understood completely and began to cross-question his mother. It was impossible to dis-cover what he and his mother and sister really thought about this snake, Svetlana, because she did not seem to exist: what mattered to them was a principle, over which all three quar-reled fiercely, each insisting that he or she was in the right.

Olga could make no sense of it all. One thing, however, she did understand, or so she thought: *They did not want her.* In-consistency lay in the very nature of these people, and to draw any hasty conclusions from what they said or did was likely to be a mistake. Sergei said that Svetlana was lying. She be-lieved him. Yet somehow he found it very difficult to break with Svetlana: she threatened suicide, he was tormented with guilt, visited her relatives, and had several meetings with Svetlana's brother, a boxer. He went to see doctors and she had pregnancy tests done at a laboratory, but they were nega-tive. It was quite obvious from Svetlana's behavior that she was pulling a con trick; unfortunately Sergei's mother was easily influenced by persistent liars, even though—so Olga guessed—the old lady wanted Svetlana even less than Olga as a daughter-in-law.

The whole nightmare lasted for three weeks of September, and at a certain moment it looked as if Svetlana had suc-ceeded in her aim of pulling Sergei, if not over to her side, at least away from Olga. So lethal was the blow delivered by this scheming bitch that Olga actually decided to break it off with him. Something stayed her hand, however, and she held on.

A ring on the doorbell at midnight. There stood a drab-looking, disheveled, bespectacled girl on little bandy legs. Are you Olga? Yes, I am. Olga at once realized who it was and felt the blood rush to her face. Her hatred for this female was terrifying: she wanted to pick her up, throw her downstairs and break every bone in her body. Instead, of course, she politely asked her to come in, and they talked in the foyer. Svetlana tried to convince Olga that Sergei did not love her, could never love her. It was no use for Olga to try to deceive herself: he couldn't abide "women like her"; it was just a temporary thing on his part, an aberration that would pass; they would be "very unhappy," and more hysterical nonsense of the same sort. Olga felt as if something were squeezing her guts. Speechless, she stared at the thin, triangular little face with its sharp, trembling chin and huge eyes, the magnified pupils quivering behind thick lenses as though Svetlana were in pain. To prove she was telling the truth—this was her reason for coming—she announced that Sergei had recently spent two nights with her, in August—after he had come back from the South.

Olga responded firmly, "You're lying!"

She did not believe it for a moment, even though Svetlana took great pleasure in mentioning a particular detail that she could not have known if she had been lying.

Olga still did not believe this naïve little fool. Next day, as she ran through the rain to the bookstore near the Hotel Metropole, where they had agreed to meet—her intention being to tell him, finally, to go to hell—in her heart she felt absurdly calm and secure. She secretly believed he would be indignant, would explain, try to vindicate himself, and dispel the horror of this sudden threat. Never in her life had she experienced anything like this. She had confided nothing to her mother or her stepfather; she was fighting this battle on her own. Now she had to reach a decision within a matter of seconds.

Sergei, his features darkening into a scowl—it was at this moment that she began to notice a strange side to his character—said, "She's a little slut, but she's telling the truth. Except that I spent one night at her place, not two."

My God, but why, why? Why did he do it? Why tell her about it even if it was the truth?

"I felt sorry for her. I knew I was going to leave her, and I pitied her."

He took pity on *her;* yet he was quite ready to make a casual admission that caused extreme pain to the woman he loved. There, in the rain, outside the Metropole, they wandered up and down like lunatics, bumping into people— something large and impressive was under construction there, the building was covered in scaffolding, and now and again when it started to rain harder they would huddle under the projecting boards for shelter—and talking, talking, talking as they tried to work out how to go on living, whether they should stay together or part, perhaps forever. She wavered from one alternative to the other, but with every minute her resolution to leave him weakened. Suddenly it occurred to her that this had been sent by fate to test her and that if she could only fight back she would be happy. It ended with their going into the Metropole restaurant and eating a good lunch; he had received his pay from the museum that day, and they spent half of it on the meal.

The wedding took place a month later. It was the end of October, cold but sunny; they sealed the windows with newspaper to keep the guests from getting chilled and borrowed a record player and some records from their neighbors. It was not so much a wedding reception as an ordinary party, with vodka, snacks, and chicken à la Kiev brought in from a nearby restaurant. Sergei composed and typed out some hilarious invitation cards, along the lines of:

Dear Friend!
    If your soul longs for respite and you wish to forget for a while the cares of family/bachelor/factory/school (delete whichever is inapplicable) life, come to our domestic wedding and/or concert . . .

The program of the "concert" was a farrago of delightful nonsense (Sergei was brilliant at such things) made up of the bridegroom's party pieces—impressions, saying words backward, songs, a lecture by Dr. Polysaev on the benefits of starvation, and God knows what else, but it was all forgotten now, vanished—no, there was one thing:

Gastronomic orgasms.
By kind permission of the bride's mother, henceforth referred to as mother-in-law.

She remembered this because it had been the cause of a minor quarrel that broke out late that night when they were washing the dishes—Olga, her mother, and another woman who came in to help, with Georgii Maximovich doing the drying. Sergei, dead drunk, was snoring in another room.

Georgii Maximovich announced that he was puzzled: What were gastronomic orgasms? If it was meant to be a joke, then it was in rather dubious taste. If it wasn't a joke, then what, he would like to know, was it supposed to mean? Did it refer to some sort of disease, or what? And why the reference to the "mother-in-law"? All the jokes about mothers-in-law had been played out about the year 1900. Olga's mother smiled ironically and said that she wasn't in the least offended by that sort of humor, and as far as she was concerned they could go on making such jokes. Even if she had felt offended, she would never have admitted it. Later it emerged that Olga's mother detested the idea of playing the role of mother-in-law and she did not like the word; least of all did she make any claims to excellence in matters gastronomic.

No marriage is simply a union of two individuals, as people think, but a merger or a collision between two clans, two worlds. Every marriage is bipolar: two systems collide in space and are fused into a dual entity forever. Who will dominate whom? Who wants what? How will they get it? His world, his relatives, arrived and opened their eyes in wild curiosity at the sight of her relatives, her world; and although there was never again in the whole seventeen years of their married life such a full-scale meeting, such a frank, unshuttered encounter, the collision of the two worlds began then and persisted all those years, often unseen and unheeded by any of them. And now Sergei was dead—but the old war still went on.

There was not, of course, any actual warfare. Everything was settled calmly and peacefully, if one didn't count a few mild subterranean tremors. Nevertheless, Olga felt nervous:

she sensed that her future mother-in-law could be awkward and prickly, and that Sergei's slightly eccentric sister was the sort of girl who might easily do something unpredictable. She was worried, too, about her mother's brother, Uncle Petya; he and his family were apt to be loud and tactless.

Before they sat down at the table, Georgii Maximovich invited all the guests to see his studio. To get there they had to go down a long corridor; along the right-hand side was a row of doors leading into other studios, while on the left were the communal bathroom, the communal kitchen, and the communal lavatory shared by all the inhabitants of the third floor. The house was a typically bad design of the 1920s. The guests proceeded, shuffling, along the corridor, while other, inquisitive tenants stood in the doorways of the communal kitchen and bathroom—the wives, mothers, and children of the artists who shared the house—and the artists themselves opened the doors of their studios and stared out at the crowd. The artists' wives and mothers were not exactly well disposed toward Olga and her mother, although the two women had been living in the house for eight years, a period in which it would have been perfectly possible to get used to them and accept them. But for some reason the artists' wives and mothers had fond memories of Georgii Maximovich's first wife and his son Slava, from both of whom Georgii Maximovich was separated several years before the war.

The procession of guests moved in total silence, and at first there were several rather embarrassing minutes—clouds of soapy steam billowed out of the bathroom, where someone was doing his or her laundry, the toilet in the communal lavatory gurgled incessantly—then suddenly Sergei squeezed Olga's fingers and started singing Mendelssohn's wedding march in a loud, raucous voice: "Póm, pom, pa-pá-pa-pom, póm-pom . . ." Someone else joined in, people laughed, began talking, and the awkwardness vanished. At that moment the red-haired Zika, wife of an artist called Vasin, appeared with a bunch of roses. Without a word she pushed the bouquet into Olga's hands and bent forward—she was tall and clumsy—to kiss Olga on the cheek. Olga hardly knew Zika, but later she came to know her well.

Georgii Maximovich's studio was unusually tidy, which no

one, of course, noticed. Everybody crowded into the middle of the large room under a 200-watt lamp, where Georgii Maximovich displayed his paintings, one after another, on an armchair that served as a temporary easel. Olga had never liked these pictures very much, but no doubt the fault was in her own lack of understanding, because all the other artists in the house spoke of Georgii Maximovich with respect, showed him their efforts and asked his advice. Yet Olga felt that all these oil paintings of ponds, birch groves, streams, and ravines, all these old men, children, dogs, hands, and heads drawn in sanguine on large sheets of paper, were exactly like countless other paintings and drawings done long ago by other artists, and she could not see the point of repeating what already existed in the world.

Evidently, though, there was some point to it, because Georgii Maximovich's works were accepted by an art-purchasing commission, people bought them and Georgii Maximovich was no pauper. A kind, well-educated man, he had studied in Paris, had known Modigliani and Chagall, and he loved to pepper his conversation with French words, even though he read and spoke French very badly. At one time he had been called "the Russian Van Gogh," but Olga couldn't help wondering how he managed to understand so much about other people's work while he had so little insight into his own. It was said that as a young man he had painted quite differently, but for some reason none of his works from that period had survived.

Georgii Maximovich loved to invite people into his studio and baffle them, overwhelm them with a display of his work. Clearly he was quite genuinely proud of all these ponds and birch groves, and it was forgivable in an old man who had never enjoyed a surfeit of either fame or prosperity, and in any case Olga's mother loved him so much—but to drag everybody into his studio on her wedding day was really going a bit too far, and Olga felt more than a little angry with her stepfather. He had no qualms, for instance, about showing them a series of drawings of a nude woman on a divan, a woman with broad hips, a pronounced waist, and disheveled hair, although her face wasn't visible. No one knew that this was her mother; yet it made Olga feel uncomfortable, and she tried not to look at the drawings. Everything would have been fine, the guests were nodding appreciatively and saying, "Ah, yes . . ." as they sighed gently, when suddenly Sergei's mother asked a tactless question, unconnected with Georgii Maximovich's work.

"Er, please tell me," she said, "what is that picture?"

"That's the famous *Guernica*," Georgii Maximovich replied hurriedly, not wishing the attention of the others to be distracted from his own works. "It's a reproduction, not an original picture."

"Why is it famous? This is the first I seem to have heard of it."

Later that remark of Alexandra Prokofievna's—"This is the first I seem to have heard of it"—became a sort of byword, a family joke that summed up Alexandra Prokofievna's "system." Now and again Olga and her mother would exchange glances and whisper to each other, "This is the first I seem to have heard of it," and burst out laughing. But that evening it was far from being a laughing matter; reluctantly turning aside from his pictures, Georgii Maximovich began conscientiously to explain why *Guernica* was a great and famous picture. The guests were perplexed. Georgii Maximovich explained enthusiastically and painstakingly. Most of them gradually bowed to his authority and at least pretended to understand what Picasso had tried to express, but Alexandra Prokofievna obstinately stuck to her guns.

"No, I find your arguments unconvincing. I can see nothing there except some broken skulls and scraps of newspaper."

"Mother, this is your personal problem," said Sergei's sister.

"I'll work on her; she'll straighten herself out and see reason, don't worry," said Sergei.

Alexandra Prokofievna answered her son quite sharply, and suddenly she received some unexpected support from Uncle Petya, who was already several drinks ahead of the others.

"You're absolutely right, my dear," he declared, raising a didactic forefinger. "They gave you a bashing for formalism, Georgii, but it seems you haven't learned your lesson. Why do you hang that junk in your studio?"

Alexandra Prokofievna went on: "You yourself are a realistic painter, Georgii Maximovich. When you paint a woman, it's a woman. A head is a head, a leg is a leg, and so on." As she spoke, Alexandra Prokofievna boldly pointed at the drawing of Olga's mother in the nude. "Everything in your pictures is in its right place. So why do you preach one thing and practice another?"

Georgii Maximovich was in an awkward situation. He turned pale, took out a large violet-colored handkerchief and blew his nose. What could he explain to the guests in the five short minutes before the food, the vodka, and the toasts? Could he tell them the story of his life? Olga began to feel sorry for him, but before she could open her mouth to come to her stepfather's rescue, her mother flung herself into the breach.

"Petya, my dear," she said, "you have spent all your life making machine tools, haven't you? What would you have said if Georgii had taken it into his head to teach you how to build machine tools?"

"What would I have said? I'd have ground him into powder." Uncle Petya roared with laughter, shaking his curly gray head. "I'd have made mincemeat out of him. I'd have chopped him into shreds, like sauerkraut, if he'd had the cheek to tell me how to do my job."

Everybody laughed surreptitiously, glancing as they did at Alexandra Prokofievna. Then Sergei's sister said, "Still, I think life would be very boring if nobody ever gave an opinion except about his own work."

On that, it seemed, the discussion ended, and at last came the solemn moment for which they had all been invited into the studio, when Georgii Maximovich produced from the storage area a large painting in a heavy gilded frame—his wedding present to the bride and bridegroom. It was an original by the French artist Duvernois, a view of old St. Petersburg. Later, when they were in financial difficulties, they more than once cast mercenary glances at the Duvernois; one day they even called in an appraiser from the state auctioneers, but, disappointed by the low figure he quoted (it was not a small amount, but considerably less than the figure which for years they had cherished in their thoughts), they decided not to sell it, and it hung there still.

As the guests were filing out of the studio, politely elbowing one another into the hall, Alexandra Prokofievna remarked in a low voice to Georgii Maximovich (her tone was triumphant, and as Olga overheard it her heart missed a beat): "You may say what you like, my dear man, but I can't agree with you. . . ."

That night, as they washed the dishes in the communal kitchen, trying not to make a noise, Georgii Maximovich whispered to Olga, "That mother-in-law of yours—oy-oy-oy! Quite a character . . . It's lucky for you you're going to start your married life living here." Then, after a few moments' silence, he added magnanimously: "She has an interesting face. It would be a challenge to paint her." He and Alexandra Prokofievna were totally different people, sprung from different strata of the earth.

The only occasion on which Georgii Maximovich showed intransigence and reminded everyone that he was the "responsible leaseholder" of the apartment was in May: the fate of Irinka was decided then.

It was the first spring of their married life. Nothing had yet become fixed, everything was fluid and precarious. Olga was still working as a teacher but was looking for another job. The work in school was hard and the daily journey to get there was a long one. Some university friends of hers had promised to find her something better, but nothing had materialized, and so she still got up every morning at half-past six to trek across to the other side of Moscow.

Having managed to get on bad terms with the director of the museum, Sergei was also thinking of changing jobs. Money was tight. And then it turned out that Olga was pregnant. They did not tell their mothers. They decided to take urgent measures, because to have a child in their circumstances was simply unthinkable. They knew no doctors who did that sort of thing; in fact they knew no medical people at all except Vlad, and they had not seen him for six months. He had already graduated and was now an intern in a hospital.

Sergei didn't like asking Vlad. Olga hesitated too, but since she had always regarded Vlad as one of the world's good guys —a very faithful, old, tried and tested good guy—she made up her mind to ignore Sergei's reluctance (she herself had no scruples; she even had an obscure feeling that Vlad would actually be pleased), and called up her old friend. To her astonishment Vlad, far from being pleased, sounded upset and confused, but then he went zealously and rapidly into action. They went over to his place and he gave her an injection. Sergei stood beside the couch, holding her hand and looking away.

He later confessed that at a certain moment he felt hatred for their friend: Vlad should have refused to do it. But Vlad, with his dogged conscientiousness . . . The injection did no good. Vlad recommended a doctor of his acquaintance, an old man who was prepared to do abortions even though it was illegal in those days. It would have to be done at home, behind closed doors and drawn curtains.

They had to tell Olga's mother, who told Georgii Maximovich—there was no hiding it any longer, and her mother was terrified and helpless. She had never had an abortion. She thought of the operation as utterly shameful, criminal, and probably fatal. She stared at Olga with eyes full of panic, tearful, and whispered, "Oh, my little girl, what are we going to do?"

In many things she remained naïve to the end of her days, even when she had turned into an old woman. In later years Olga had several abortions, both at home and in a hospital, and realized that it was not the worst pain in the world, if only because it was a pain that came to an end.

But back then, in that May, she knew none of this. Georgii Maximovich suddenly stunned everybody by saying, "As the responsible leaseholder, I forbid it. . . ." They never did discover whether he was really afraid of breaking the law or whether he just gave in to her mother's mood of panic.

In any event, Irinka came into the world thanks to Georgii Maximovich's phrase "As the responsible leaseholder . . ." Later there were to be times when Olga was tormented by unbearable memories. Her daughter never knew that she had been unwanted. Everybody managed to forget it—Sergei, her mother, Georgii Maximovich, and, no doubt, Vlad. But Olga knew and remembered it. And when on a slushy day in the fall she was hurrying along Gogol Boulevard toward the Arbat, to go to a store, and suddenly felt such a violent pain in her belly that she staggered and would have fallen had not a passer-by helped her to a bench on the boulevard, she at once thought, "This is my punishment for . . ."

Irinka was born at seven months. When they had just come home from the maternity hospital, Sergei wanted to look at the baby and Olga shrieked, screening the child with her body, "Don't look! Don't look! Later! Go away!" She couldn't bear having him see such a miserable, puny little creature. Only after three days did she show him the little body, which had begun to look like a real baby. Now Irinka was the tallest girl in her class. And Sergei was no longer on this earth.

How quickly it had all passed.

Their life together had, after all, been long, far beyond the power of memory to recall in full—why had it passed so quickly? Everything was muddled. It had been both quick and short. Times that had gone slowly now seemed like a moment, while the present moment dragged on without end and without meaning.

In December, soon after the day that had smashed their life into fragments, she said to her daughter—it was a moment of despair, Irinka was the person closest to her, and Olga wanted only one little drop of comfort although it was foolish to expect that comfort from a child (what's more, she said it more for herself and for someone who couldn't hear)—"What a good life we had when your father was alive."

Not all was truth, of course, in that sigh. There was falsehood in it too. Her point was that mere life itself—no matter whether it was good, bad, or horrible—meant everything. There was life and there was nonlife; there was nothing in between. Everything in the world belonged to one or the other, and therein alone, perhaps, lay hidden not only the source of Olga's suffering but also of her hope. She had not understood this at the time; even now she could but guess at it, and then only vaguely.

The girl sensed the falsity in the remark, spoken as it was

"for someone who couldn't hear," and looking askance, she said, "It wasn't all that good."

Olga was crushed by this retort. She couldn't think what to say in reply. Faïna, a most intelligent woman, who had been her friend since their childhood days before the war, said, "Of course she's an incredibly selfish child—thanks to you and Sergei, and especially to Sergei's mother. But that's not the point. She's worried about you; she's warning you not to live in the past: 'It wasn't all that good.'"

Faïna thought Olga should start looking for another husband at once: "Don't be a fool. You can't bring Sergei back, and you're destroying yourself. Bear in mind that you don't have much time—a year or two, and after that you can forget it." Less than two months after that, Faïna invited her to a party, but Olga refused to go: Why should she go to parties when meeting strangers only made her depression worse? When Faïna invited her to Novgorod for Christmas, Olga again refused; instead she and Irinka went to stay in a *pension,* but there too she felt miserable and fled away, leaving Irinka with the other young people who were staying there. Faïna, however, would not give up; she was an obstinate girl, or rather forty-three-year-old woman—abandoned by her husband, her son in the army, her mother in a home for the aged. She invited Olga to a New Year's party given by some friends of hers who were architects—charming, intelligent people: "Don't be afraid, you fool; no one's going to make a grab for you or anything like that. You can just relax and listen to the music." But Olga didn't care whether they were charming or rude, intelligent or stupid; she just didn't want to see anyone.

Not for any good reason, not because it was against her principles; she simply didn't feel like it.

After Irinka's cruel remark, Faïna too, having hesitated a little, also uttered some of the unpalatable truth, no doubt thinking that although the medicine she was administering was very bitter, it was necessary: "Do you really believe that life with Sergei was so good?" Olga answered, "Yes." What else could she say? "I don't know"? "Wasn't it obvious"?

There was a vendor's stall on the corner of Chekhov Street and Sadovaya where she and Faïna loved to buy fresh bagels.

They had been on sale there even before the war, at six kopecks apiece, and the physical memory of that childhood
pleasure had persisted: one of the thrills of street life was to
push a coin into the little square window and from the deli-
cious-smelling depths a kindly hand was thrust out with a soft,
puffy, crusty bagel, newly born as from the womb. Then,
chewing and savoring life, to stroll along Sadovaya toward
Samotechnaya, then to Tsvetnoi Boulevard with its crowds
and bustle, the circus, the market, taxis, Gypsies, the secondhand store, a movie theater—whatever one's heart desired.
And the Narva Restaurant nearby. Whenever they felt the
need for mutual comfort, for a frank heart-to-heart talk (Faïna
in those days lived on Krasnogvardeiskaya in a communal
apartment that was like an ant heap, in which she shared one
room with her mother, her son, her husband, and an aged,
stale-smelling female relative who never spoke), they would go
to Tsvetnoi Boulevard, down the hill past the movie theater
or to the market to stare and jostle, to buy fruit, picking out
the sweetest pears or a watermelon, or just a glassful of fried
sunflower seeds, and then wander up and down the boulevard,
complaining to each other of their misfortunes—and life grew
more bearable.

The long years of closeness with this woman—her best
friend, her best counselor, her closest rival, the best-informed
spy on her short-lived triumphs and disasters—had taught her
that the most important rule when dealing with Faïna was to
put oneself in her place and try to see everything from Faïna's
point of view. Faïna, of course, was profoundly unhappy;
compared with her, Olga always regarded herself as shamefully, disgracefully lucky. At times it seemed to Olga that
there was a constant overflow of surplus goodness, prosperity,
and blatant female satisfaction pouring from her as if from
one vessel into another—or rather, to be more precise, she
felt this was what it must seem like to other people, and above
all to poor Faïna.

It now turned out that Faïna had always seen everything
quite differently, and thanks to these unexpected and hitherto
carefully concealed powers of insight, she was even daring to
cheer Olga up. This was too much! How could she say their

married life hadn't been happy? *Their life* had been a complete, living, pulsating organism that had now vanished from the face of the earth. It had had a heart, like a live creature; it had had lungs, genitals, sense organs, and it had developed, flourished, sickened, and worn out; it had died from neither old age nor illness but because the element that powered its bloodstream had disappeared. What a strange creature "their life" had been. No one else had been able to understand exactly what it was like. Other people could only guess, imagine various shapes in the air, fantasize, make vague assumptions that "their life" looked like this or that, consisted of this or that. And they themselves . . . they themselves had never been able to define it in words. Sometimes Olga thought quite sincerely that their life was good, sometimes it depressed her, and at other times—which lasted for hours, sometimes days on end—she thought it was terrible.

Now she simply could not believe that such thoughts had ever entered her head, that she had sometimes hated *their life.*

But she had, she had! Like that winter (they were still living in her mother's apartment) when she was tormented by the red-haired Zika, Vasin's wife. It had ended in Olga's humiliation and was now almost forgotten; memory had repressed the suffering and shame she had felt. But it had happened—fourteen years ago—and it had also been part of *their life.* She had realized that Sergei was not unaware of Zika's charms. The fact that Zika flirted with him and probably made a serious attempt to seduce him was natural. Women were attracted to him; she knew this and it upset her. But she also knew that he was indolent and hard to arouse, that he was bored by stupid, flirtatious women and greatly preferred male talk over vodka and dill pickles to female company. Once, when she was trying to get him to say whether he might ever be unfaithful to her, he said with a sigh, "Remember what Hemingway said? 'If only one didn't have to talk to them . . .'"

Zika was young and robust, with long arms and legs and muscular buttocks. The sculptors on the first floor were always asking her to pose for allegorical statues, such as discus throwers or collective-farm peasant women with baskets on their shoulders personifying abundance. Zika's powerful physique frightened Olga Vasilievna; she felt that Sergei was attracted to this type, that it reminded him of the forgotten Brünnhilde. Zika had an unremarkable face, round, fresh-complexioned, always wearing a faint smile, framed in reddish-blond curls: the face of a simpleton. She worked as an illustrator for a publisher of children's books, for whom she turned out feeble, unimaginative water colors. Vasin, by contrast, was frail, ugly, and old, at least he seemed old to Olga at the time; he must have been in his early forties, twice Zika's age. It all began with a friendly exchange of invitations, tea parties or drinks around the tape recorder—a pastime just becoming fashionable in those days. Vasin had bought a Dnieper tape recorder, a huge, clumsy thing that felt as heavy as a suitcase full of scrap iron, and he recorded everybody, telling them to sing, talk, or recite poetry, after which they would eagerly listen to all the nonsense as he played it back.

Vasin earned a great deal by painting official portraits, which he did jointly with his partner Arkasha. They would mark off the canvas in squares and paint rapidly and skillfully, as if it were a production-line job in a factory. Sometimes Zika helped them. Apart from potboiling in this way, Vasin also did some serious painting on his own. He would quote Sasha Chërny's poem that says that every artist needs two muses: the shopgirl for the needs of the body and the lady dentist for the good of the soul. "All next week," he would say, "I'm going to work for the shopgirl." Or: "I spent this afternoon with my lady dentist. She's so sweet, it was delightful." This meant that he had traveled out into the countryside on a commuter train with his sketchbook and had enjoyed himself all day painting, wet through and freezing. He painted landscapes, which were remarkably good. Georgii Maximovich thought he was gifted but dissolute and used to say that "artists like him never amount to a hill of beans." Vasin was a drunkard.

Altogether Olga felt sad about Valerii Vasin; eventually abandoned by Zika, he had drunk himself to death while still in his fifties. He was a true artist; he lived as though in a dream, did his potboiling as though in a dream, and awakened only when he was at his easel and doing the real painting that he loved. Indifferent to visitors, he would have been quite happy to live alone, to drink alone, but Zika was easily bored and forced him to lead a social life. He loved Zika very much and did everything she wanted.

And Zika was cunning; she played up to Olga, flattered her, insinuated herself into her favor. "Would you like me to take the baby out? Do you need any milk? I'm going to the store. . . ." And it was always said casually, naturally, like a real friend. One day she lent them some money. At first Olga acquiesced and accepted it; then she realized that it had been done with an ulterior motive. She began finding excuses to duck out of Zika's invitations and refused to let Sergei go to the Vasins'.

Sergei took offense. Why not? She could not explain, and he failed to guess that it was a case of wretched jealousy—so wretched and seemingly so unfounded that she felt ashamed to talk about it, but she could not fight it. "What's the matter? Why don't you want me to go and see Valerii?" "I don't want you to—and that's all." "I will not be dictated to." He flared up and ran out to the Vasins' apartment. He had always dreaded being turned into a henpecked husband. All this happened at the time when he had left the museum without first getting another job, and he was touchy and irritable. She was teaching school all day, while Sergei stayed at home, helped Olga's mother look after Irinka, went shopping in the market, hauled buckets of water—the water was kept in the kitchen and in the hallway, and the supply had to be replenished three times a day.

The domestic chores, the idleness, the lack of money and, above all, the uncertainty about his professional future continued to make Sergei depressed in the evenings. He would loaf around not knowing what to do with himself. It was this that made him easy prey for the tall, muscular Zika. The only puzzle was: Why did she need him?

Now he was dead and no one needed him.

One day Olga went into Vasin's studio and saw Sergei sitting at the table; a grubby cotton towel was draped around his neck, as though he were wearing a napkin in a restaurant, and Zika was cutting his hair. "What does this mean?" Olga inquired. The reply was a burst of laughter. Vasin and another man, one of his friends, were seized with such a paroxysm of laughter that they were speechless. It transpired that Sergei had bet his hair playing poker and had lost. In a thoroughly natural, cheerful tone of voice, Zika assured Olga, "Don't worry, Olga dear, I'll only snip off a tiny bit. Purely symbolic. It will even improve his looks."

Olga was amazed that Sergei was sitting there as obedient as a lamb.

She never knew whether there really was anything between them. Perhaps there was. And then perhaps there wasn't. Olga stopped speaking to Zika; she became an enemy. The change from close friendship to fierce hostility took place with unusual rapidity, in the space of two or three months. Today she had no recollection of how this quarrel had developed, or whether she had had any arguments with Zika before that encounter in the empty corridor. By the spring Olga had already begun to feel afraid of Zika. She would glare fixedly at Olga, and whenever they happened to meet in the kitchen or in the hallway she never made way for Olga but always walked straight toward her and tried to jostle her. At some point Olga must have made some very telling remark about Zika, and the other women must have passed it on; the hatred between them had probably begun with that. All the details had long since faded from her memory, but a vague recollection of that dispute with Sergei about the wretched Zika had remained. It was a dispute about nothing, a pure foolishness on her part; yet at the time it had seemed to Olga that her life depended on its outcome. Did he love her enough to give up—if she begged him to—the minor pleasure of a gossip over a glass of vodka in Vasin's studio? How she suffered—and how convinced she was that she was in the right. She thought: "What could be clearer? If he loves me, he'll give it up. If he doesn't love me, he'll keep on going to the Vasins'." An infallible test. But Sergei somehow didn't see it quite so clearly. He wanted proof. He demanded that she show him a warrant for his arrest, as it were.

"For the thousandth time: Why? Are you jealous of Zika—is that it? You must be crazy."

"I'm simply asking you," she would say, almost in tears. "I'm just asking, that's all. I beg you on my knees." And one day she really did fall on her knees, which so unnerved him that he promised to do whatever she asked. All right, he wouldn't go to the Vasins' any more. She loved him very much at such moments because they revealed an aspect of him that she longed to see. But an hour and a half later—it happened at dawn, after a sleepless night—he was insisting again: "No, it's the purest insanity, it's impossible. You're demanding obedience and blind faith, like the fathers of the church . . . *Credo, quia absurdum est . . .*" And her wave of joy was followed by misery, because she had browbeaten him with tears and sleepless nights into making a futile little concession. All that effort—just to stop him from going to see Vasin! And what about the future? Would she have to fall on her knees and sob every time? She might have much more important things to ask and he would be unmoved, like a rock.

She was also distressed by the thought that they were quarreling so desperately, to the point of tears, over a stupid, empty-headed woman who wasn't worth even a contemptuous glance. How Zika would have rejoiced if she had known what discord she aroused! Of course the whole thing was idiotic, and Olga had been stupid; unable to see what was important and what wasn't. She had caused herself agonies over nothing at all. . . .

Sergei continued to visit Vasin, doing so now out of obstinacy, as a matter of principle.

At the same time both of them were trying to prepare each other for their future life together. There were grim days when Olga longed to be alone with her mother, wanted to divorce Sergei; it was at such moments that she hated *their life,* when it had only just begun. She had completely forgotten whatever had preceded the encounter in the corridor with which the whole business had culminated. Maybe she had been careless enough to say something unnecessary, to pass on a bit of the gossip about Zika that was going around. Some people stopped seeing the Vasins. Everyone in the house knew of the enmity between Zika and Olga, which naturally extended to Olga's mother and Georgii Maximovich. As a member of an art-purchasing commission, Georgii Maximovich vetoed the purchase of two of Vasin's pictures. Vasin got drunk, stood outside their apartment, and shouted rude remarks through the door. Olga saw Zika on the street with a tear-stained face. It seemed impossible that Sergei should continue to see the Vasins.

She was walking down the big hall when Zika appeared around the corner. They were alone. Zika did not turn aside but headed straight toward Olga until they were staring at each other, eye to eye. She just had time to think, "The eyes of a madwoman . . ." before Zika came close to her and with white lips said, "I know everything, you mean little bitch. You're killing your husband. But to hell with him; just leave Valerii and me alone or I'll destroy you! Got it?" And she took a swing with her powerful arm.

Olga ran down the empty hall, fear gripping her entire body. It was too painful to remember.

Faïna said that Olga should go immediately to the District Prosecutor's office and at the same time to Zika's place of work, where she turned out her messy little water colors. Faïna had a friend who was a journalist, whom they immediately called up, then and there on the boulevard, from a pay phone, to ask him whether he could get a news item or a feature story printed about Zika's attack. Olga seethed with a passionate desire for revenge, wanting to take Zika to court and have her jailed for at least a couple of years for assault.

But when she returned home late that evening she felt nothing but a headache and a sort of jaded exhaustion all over her body, as though she had just survived a serious illness. She decided not to tell anyone else about the incident after all, because she felt so unbearably sorry for Sergei: what he would have suffered if she had told him about it. So in effect the whole affair never went beyond the walls of that empty hallway. And her mother never found out.

She must stop thinking about it. From then on, Olga couldn't bear the thought of seeing the Vasins, of meeting Zika in the hall again or in the communal kitchen. Zika, fortunately, began avoiding Olga—she never looked her in the eye any more and evaded any contact with her. Soon after the affair, Olga and Sergei moved over to live with his mother on

Shabolovka, where the old lady had been alone since the death of her daughter. Sergei asked Olga if she would make the move and she agreed with relief: there would be no more long corridors smelling of oil paint and turpentine, no more noisy gatherings in the evening to argue about color values, the French school, or suprematism, no hectic activity throughout the house on the days when the art purchasing commission was at work, no communal bathroom with a concrete floor and a notice on the wall that said: "It is categorically forbidden to wash paintbrushes in the bathtub!," no shared kitchen with four tables and four stoves, no mother, no Georgii Maximovich forever hoping to astound, if not the world, then the neighbors, no Vasin and no Zika. On the other hand, there would be her mother-in-law.

Faïna said, "If only you hadn't had to live with your mother-in-law, Sergei might be alive now."

That was not true, because living with his mother had not been nearly such an ordeal for him as for her. If the cause had lain with the old woman, Olga would have been the one to have a heart attack, not Sergei, though of course Alexandra Prokofievna's presence and her perpetual lecturing were an extra strain on top of something more fundamental. When men pass the age of forty, strange things start happening to them: they understand something about themselves of which they were previously unaware. There are some who come to terms with it and settle down forever, while others are gripped by a restlessness of the spirit. Sergei was one who fell under the spell of this unease.

It began imperceptibly after Praskukhin had arranged for his transfer to the institute. The job at the museum had been undemanding, badly paid and a dead end, but it had the advantage of being extremely peaceful, whereas at the institute things started happening: promises, hopes, plans, passions, cliques, dangers at every step—Praskukhin against Demchenko, Demchenko against Kislovsky, and then there was Klimuk, then the whole business about changing the topic of his dissertation. He dashed around, first to one thing, then to another, then to a third: at one moment it was the history of the streets of Moscow, next a subject so remote as scarcely to qualify as history. This constant restlessness was his undoing. At first he would be full of enthusiasm; then inevitably his interest would cool and he would fling himself into some new project. A perpetually restless failure, a "grasshopper mind."

But so what? She never reproached him, never demanded the unattainable. If they couldn't afford Yalta, they would spend their vacation with Aunty Pasha in Vasilkovo. When they hadn't enough for a TV set, they listened to the radio. Never once in their life together had she said to him, "Look at So-and-So, he's made it, and you're nowhere." She had never urged him to make an impossible effort or to strain himself; other people's success never worried her. On the contrary, she used to say to him, "We don't need your dissertation. We need you in good health. Stay a junior research fellow, but whatever happens don't kill yourself, don't push yourself too hard, don't try to knock down walls with your forehead—your head's not meant for that."

It was her mother-in-law who suffered most from the fact that her son's career was not flourishing as others' were. Alexandra Prokofievna greatly disliked certain of Sergei's friends from his schooldays who had made something of themselves, and she treated them coldly whenever they came to visit. In her view Sergei was exceptional and deserved a better fate, whereas Olga was unaffected by vanity or envy. She was worried by something else. Those seven years at the museum had been totally wasted. Of course, the fact that he had nothing to show for them, nothing in return, no reputation built, was his own fault: he had spent his time daydreaming, constantly chasing will-o'-the-wisps. But his colleagues were guilty too, and viciously so: they had not tried to prevent the waste of his talents, like wheels turning, racing endlessly to no effect.

Seven years! The years in which others of his age had made feverish efforts, displayed spurts of energy that got them further and further ahead while he had lived as though he had ninety years in which to prove himself. There had been plans of sorts: he had done archival research and had reached the stage of having talks with a publisher about the topic "Moscow in 1918." Someone named Ilya Vladimirovich had made promises and tried to push the plan forward a bit, but in the end it had all come to nothing. After countless meetings, telephone calls, discussions over meals and cups of tea, Ilya Vladimirovich had turned out to be a total nonentity. Alexandra Prokofievna asked Sergei indignantly, "Why do you get mixed up with such trash?" As was his habit, Sergei made excuses and defended those who had falsely raised his hopes: "But Ilya Vladimirovich doesn't run the publishing house— he's just another client, like me."

Those were the years in which Irinka reached the age when she started school; when the household moved to a new apartment—the new place was completely renovated and parquet flooring installed—and Olga was first promoted to senior research fellow and then put in charge of her own laboratory at the All-Union Institute of Scientific Research. Yet all Sergei's work of those years, all the lengthy fuss about his "Moscow in 1918" ended in failure and the book was never published. Admittedly some of the material from it was used for the first version of his dissertation, but then that version was abandoned. New topics were found: the February Revolution, the czarist secret police, and so on. But here too Sergei found himself up a blind alley, faced with an impenetrable wall. And there were other troubles: his quarrel with Klimuk, his sudden interest in that house on the embankment and everything connected with it, and Klimuk's treachery. . . .

How well Olga knew all the expressions of his face, his walk, the way his voice changed when the next disaster overwhelmed him or some new, fascinating but chimerical project floated into view.

When she had first met him, of course, he had been different.

Year after year of disappointments gradually wore him down, drained his strength; he began to stoop and to weaken; yet some central core remained untouched, like a thin steel rod that bent but did not break. And that was the root of the trouble: he refused to change his innermost nature. This meant that although he suffered agonies as a result of his many failures, lost faith in himself, frittered away his energies in enthusiasms so absurd they made people think he had taken leave of his senses, although he strained his poor heart

She thanked him and began to pour out the tea. Some money from the committee, no doubt. Drinking his tea in noiseless sips, Bezyazichny told her how everyone in the department grieved for Sergei and how much they missed him, because many people there had liked him. This remark stung Olga and brought her to life. Why did he say *"many people"* had liked him? According to the rules of this game he should have said "everybody liked him," or "people liked him at the institute," or at least "he was liked." But he had said *"many people* liked him," which implied that there had been—and still were, now that he was dead—*a few people* who hadn't liked him and still didn't. Of course there were such people. Olga had no doubts about the existence of those *few people,* but it was rather strange to hint about them to his widow in the very first minutes of this visit.

She looked hard at Bezyazichny, trying once again to recall what Sergei had said about him, but nothing came to mind.

"You talk as though Sergei Afanasievich had been working in peace and concord with everyone right up to the very last day. As though he hadn't submitted his request to resign," said Olga. "He practically regarded himself as already dismissed."

"But that's not so. You are profoundly mistaken." Bezyazichny clasped a hand to his chest. "I know about his request. But first, the matter remained undecided up to, so to speak, the tragic day. . . . The director was on vacation. And Gennadii Vitalevich Klimuk most definitely didn't want to make the decision."

"Gennadii Vitalevich didn't want to? Don't talk to me about Gennadii Vitalevich. More than any of the others he wanted to get rid of Sergei—but only if someone else would actually do it."

"I assure you—you're mistaken."

"No, I am not mistaken."

This man had had an ulterior motive in saying "many people liked him." He had shown his hand. It was now clear that he was one of Sergei's enemies, or perhaps sympathized with his enemies. Had they really sunk so low as to send this person on a visit that required such tact?

with the fury of his despair and self-reproach, he still refused to break that invisible, steely core within himself. And despite it all she loved him, forgave him, and never demanded anything of him.

It was two weeks after the funeral that Bezyazichny appeared. Olga had never met him before but had heard of his name from Sergei—in what connection she had forgotten. He had apparently taken part in the investigation of Sergei's "case," but Olga could not remember what his attitude had been. The people at the institute had been divided, according to Sergei, into three groups: the few absolute scoundrels, the few middle-of-the-roaders, and some who behaved impeccably. Olga felt nervous because she didn't know to which category Bezyazichny belonged and, consequently, how she should treat him. He came accompanied by an elderly woman named Sorokina.

"Do forgive me—I've just been to the delicatessen next door," said Sorokina, smiling guiltily and ingratiatingly as she showed Olga her shopping bag full of food.

For two or three seconds her eyes flickered around in search of a place to put down her bag, and she could find nowhere better than the shoebox. Silently Olga picked up the bag and transferred it to the little table under the telephone.

"What a marvelous delicatessen you have. They have 'doctor's' sausage and little Dutch cheeses, which we hardly ever see in the stores around us, even though our delicatessen is supposed to supply foods for special diets. . . ."

As she twittered away, the woman looked at Olga with great feeling and gave her voice an expression of profound compassion, as though the fact that Olga was lucky enough to live near such a good delicatessen might help in some little way to relieve her grief. When she realized that Olga was not interested in talking about the delicatessen, Sorokina took off her raincoat and hat and for a while uttered nothing more than an occasional sigh.

Olga had for some time been dreading this visit from Sergei's colleagues. They could only bring her pain. Everyone who had known Sergei, even if only slightly, caused her pain. Clearly, though, she had to put up with this visit, and the sooner they came and went, the better for her. Both these people were from the institute's trade union committee and, as far as Olga understood it, they were fulfilling some formal obligation. The funeral was over, the urn had been buried and the funeral committee had been dissolved; these two, however, belonged to the social affairs committee or something of the sort. They did not intend to stay for long. If the conversation dragged on, the food might go cold, but Olga did not propose to do anything about it. She was incapable of making any special effort for the occasion. Bezyazichny wiped his feet on the doormat and glanced around him, making vague mooing noises. Olga could not understand what he wanted until he suddenly took off his shoes and stood there in his socks. Aha, it was wet in the street and he did not want to mess up the floor. As though she cared about the floors at a moment like this.

Why didn't these people understand anything? She had to give him Sergei's slippers, which were lying near the door for all to see. She found it painful and tactless of him to take them.

Her mother-in-law was doing something in the kitchen when Olga went in to put on the kettle for tea; she had to make some gesture of hospitality. Alexandra Prokofievna refused to go out and meet them.

"I don't want to see anyone from the institute," said the old woman. "First they persecute him, then they come and express their sympathy. I have nothing to say to them."

The implication was that Olga could talk to them because she and they had somehow been engaged in the same activity—persecuting Sergei. She wanted to pretend she hadn't noticed but couldn't help saying, "Don't talk nonsense. These people didn't persecute Sergei. They haven't done anything wrong; they have simply come to express the usual official condolences. Nobody persecuted Sergei."

"Yes they did," said Alexandra Prokofievna and went out of the kitchen.

Olga sat down on a stool and for a minute was motionless—her heart was beating very hard. Sergei had not been perse-

cuted. The harm done to him had not been intentional; had simply happened because certain people had been pursu ing their own ends. That was a different matter. She hea Alexandra Prokofievna go into her room and lock the door.

Olga felt awkward in front of these strangers. Still, let the come—it meant nothing. She stood up, went into the livi room carrying something in a little bowl. The two from trade-union committee were sitting at the table, frozen in a tudes of profound dejection. The woman was just percept nodding her head and staring at the floor. Probably imagined that this pose and the faint nodding expressed cere sympathy. "What a fool she is," thought Olga. B zichny immediately leaped to his feet and began to say they had come literally only for a minute, she shouldn't gone to the trouble of making tea for them. He had shor a rosy complexion, a robust, young-looking face, gray h a short crew cut. It was impossible to tell his exact age; h perhaps around fifty. He wore a black suit, the jacket pled, with disproportionately broad, padded shoulder put it on specially to visit a widow," she thought w difference. "Black. Out of mothballs."

"Here are a few articles that belonged to Sergei A vich." He took out of his briefcase a tin box that ha held Czech cigarettes and in which something rattled; a folding hunter's knife that had obviously been opening cans and pulling corks during the parties t place fairly frequently in Sergei's department; three books; a comb with a long handle; a soccer calendar a copy of *Foreign Literature*; and an old noteboo telephone numbers with dogeared pages. He took object and placed it on the table with as much care a been made of glass.

With a fixed stare, Olga gazed at this trivial, ra lection of junk which for some reason they had brou and thought: "Don't they realize that it must be have to look at my dead husband's possessions? W doing it?" She wanted to pick it all up and thro Instead she gathered up the things and carried th the windowsill.

Bezyazichny said something and handed her a

"Sergei Afanasievich was working in the same field we do," said the woman in a quavering voice. Taking off her spectacles and pressing her fleshy chin into her chest, she began to polish the spectacles with a handkerchief. Her face took on a lachrymose expression and her voice was scarcely audible. "The revolution and the civil war . . . He and I worked together for six years. He was a fine man, extremely kind and responsive . . . a good man."

The fleshy chin quivered. Olga gave the woman a cold look. "It would be interesting to know how both of you voted at the hearing of Sergei's notorious 'case,'" she said.

The woman started; her eyes widened and described a momentary revolving movement. Olga had, of course, put the question rudely and no doubt placed her visitors in an awkward situation, but then they were making things just as awkward for her by simply sitting there, drinking tea and talking about Sergei.

"I didn't vote at all, because I was out of Moscow at the time. I was in Poland, on official business," said Bezyazichny with a contemptuous wave of the hand. "In any case, you know . . ." His gesture and tone of voice implied, "Is it really worth resurrecting all that nonsense?"

Sorokina said, "I, as it happens, voted for the whole thing to be brought out into the open." She blushed. "In the circumstances it was the only proper way . . ."

At that moment Irinka entered—or rather burst in unceremoniously, as she always did—and asked for a ruble and a half before the store closed. Having fired off this request, she noticed the visitors and said, "Oh, hello!"

Olga introduced her daughter, who smiled a very charming, welcoming smile, in the way she always did whenever she needed to wheedle money out of somebody.

Olga fumbled in her purse, looking for silver and copper.

"Oh, look!" Irinka shrieked with delight, rushing over to the windowsill. "I've been looking for it everywhere. How did it get here?"

She seized the long-handled comb.

"They brought it from your father's office. There's a ruble fifty for you."

"Oh . . ." Hesitating, Irinka put the comb back on the windowsill, then asked, "Mother, can I have it, please? You did buy it for me, remember?"

"Take it," said Olga.

Irinka ran out. Someone was obviously waiting for her in the hall; there was whispering, and then the door slammed. There was no more to talk about. It seemed the right moment for them to get up and go, but Bezyazichny started talking about Sergei's unfinished dissertation. The academic council, it seemed, was of the opinion—no decision had been taken yet, but the word was going around—that the institute should undertake the job of completing the dissertation and then publish a monograph. They would assign some special people to it. It would be incorporated into the official schedule, so the whole department would be involved. They would have to process a certain amount of unused source material and find what was still left in Sergei's papers in his desk. They were all counting on Olga Vasilievna's help. She felt irritation beginning to boil up inside her.

"I'll do it when I have the time and the energy," she said. "Right now I don't intend to go looking for anything."

"Of course, of course," mumbled Sorokina. "Only when Olga Vasilievna feels she is able to . . ."

"It will be entirely in Olga Vasilievna's own interest," said Bezyazichny.

Out in the foyer Bezyazichny said unexpectedly to Sorokina as he was helping her into her coat, "Excuse me, Paulina Ivanovna, but I won't be able to see you out. There is a little matter I have to discuss with Olga Vasilievna . . ."

They went back into the living room. Olga did not want to carry on the conversation in the hall, right outside her mother-in-law's door. She sensed that something unpleasant was impending. Bezyazichny said that he found it embarrassing to mention this, but he had no alternative because it was an official matter. He was chairman of the institute's staff credit union. Sergei Afanasievich had borrowed a hundred and sixty rubles with an undertaking to repay it within six months, but almost two years had passed, the money had not been paid back, and now a complication had arisen: the fund was empty, several requests for small loans were outstanding and they could not be met. The board of management had come to a unanimous decision . . . they felt . . . they were worried . . . the situation was . . .

Olga listened, stunned. The words reached her through a dense fog.

"I don't have that much money," she said.

"The fact of the matter is . . . You see, we haven't the right . . . If there were a general meeting of all the union's shareholders . . . but on the other hand if you were to make a voluntary . . ." Bezyazichny mumbled on, his heavy red face twitching as though he were sneezing, which no doubt indicated his extreme state of embarrassment. "Believe me, I find it very distasteful. But I am only carrying out . . ."

Olga said that there were a hundred rubles in Sergei's savings account, but it would be some time before she could get that money—not until the court had granted probate, in fact. As for the hundred and sixty rubles borrowed from the credit union, this was the first she had ever heard of it.

"When did he borrow this money?"

Bezyazichny produced a notebook from his pocket, leafed through it, and found the entry: the money had been advanced on March 5, 1971.

Where on earth had it all gone? Why had he needed so much? "A woman." This was the first thought that came into her head, and it made her temperature climb. Nevertheless she replied very calmly, "This is really the first I have heard of it. He usually told me everything about his expenses, his debts." This was not the complete truth, but it was true enough in broad terms.

"In that case it makes it even more embarrassing for me. I am sorry."

After a pause he said, "I'll do everything I can to persuade the members of the board of management, in view of the circumstances . . . You might perhaps care to write a statement. I'll do what I can." He clasped his hands to his chest and bowed his head. "Most of his colleagues were on good terms with him, so I hope . . . I'll have a preliminary word with one or two people . . ."

He went on muttering in this vein, pressing his hands to his chest and bowing, while he moved out of the room and into the hall. Everything had apparently been said. It was over for the time being. Why had they given her money in that envelope he gave her if they then demanded it back from her? It was all so confusing. Olga stared at this short, stocky, grizzled little man in his crumpled, old-fashioned black suit dating from the fifties and made some mechanical, meaningless remark.

As he was leaving he said, "So they'll phone you about the monograph. Do have a look around and collect whatever material you can find. The folder I mentioned is the one tied with pink ribbon."

In the past, whenever sudden troubles had arisen and she hadn't known what to do, she had always asked Sergei's advice—usually at night, before they went to sleep, when Irinka was already asleep and her mother-in-law had shut herself in her room. Although he was never very successful in solving his own problems, he always gave her sensible advice. He was good at soothing her when something had upset her. But now—who was there? Her mother-in-law mustn't know, because she would feel nothing but malicious satisfaction. She would regard it as confirmation of her belief that Olga and Sergei had never been really close and that he had led a separate life.

Olga was oppressed by a feeling that was not jealousy but something else, an emotion of a different quality—the burned-out remains of jealousy. It was as if she had been handed an urn containing these strange ashes, the ashes of a jealousy that was dead but whose remains she was holding in her hands, clutching them to her heart.

She was convinced that a woman was mixed up in this somewhere. Ashes, ashes, nothing but ashes. Yet her hands were trembling. In her own savings account she had two hundred and eighty rubles, which she and Sergei had put aside for a specific purpose—to buy a television set. To take money out of that account to pay off some questionable debt would be stupid.

Sergei used to say, "Don't fuss, old lady."

with the fury of his despair and self-reproach, he still refused to break that invisible, steely core within himself. And despite it all she loved him, forgave him, and never demanded anything of him.

It was two weeks after the funeral that Bezyazichny appeared. Olga had never met him before but had heard of his name from Sergei—in what connection she had forgotten. He had apparently taken part in the investigation of Sergei's "case," but Olga could not remember what his attitude had been. The people at the institute had been divided, according to Sergei, into three groups: the few absolute scoundrels, the few middle-of-the-roaders, and some who behaved impeccably. Olga felt nervous because she didn't know to which category Bezyazichny belonged and, consequently, how she should treat him. He came accompanied by an elderly woman named Sorokina.

"Do forgive me—I've just been to the delicatessen next door," said Sorokina, smiling guiltily and ingratiatingly as she showed Olga her shopping bag full of food.

For two or three seconds her eyes flickered around in search of a place to put down her bag, and she could find nowhere better than the shoebox. Silently Olga picked up the bag and transferred it to the little table under the telephone.

"What a marvelous delicatessen you have. They have 'doctor's' sausage and little Dutch cheeses, which we hardly ever see in the stores around us, even though our delicatessen is supposed to supply foods for special diets. . . ."

As she twittered away, the woman looked at Olga with great feeling and gave her voice an expression of profound compassion, as though the fact that Olga was lucky enough to live near such a good delicatessen might help in some little way to relieve her grief. When she realized that Olga was not interested in talking about the delicatessen, Sorokina took off her raincoat and hat and for a while uttered nothing more than an occasional sigh.

Olga had for some time been dreading this visit from Sergei's colleagues. They could only bring her pain. Everyone who had known Sergei, even if only slightly, caused her pain. Clearly, though, she had to put up with this visit, and the sooner they came and went, the better for her. Both these people were from the institute's trade union committee and, as far as Olga understood it, they were fulfilling some formal obligation. The funeral was over, the urn had been buried and the funeral committee had been dissolved; these two, however, belonged to the social affairs committee or something of the sort. They did not intend to stay for long. If the conversation dragged on, the food might go cold, but Olga did not propose to do anything about it. She was incapable of making any special effort for the occasion. Bezyazichny wiped his feet on the doormat and glanced around him, making vague mooing noises. Olga could not understand what he wanted until he suddenly took off his shoes and stood there in his socks. Aha, it was wet in the street and he did not want to mess up the floor. As though she cared about the floors at a moment like this.

Why didn't these people understand anything? She had to give him Sergei's slippers, which were lying near the door for all to see. She found it painful and tactless of him to take them.

Her mother-in-law was doing something in the kitchen when Olga went in to put on the kettle for tea; she had to make some gesture of hospitality. Alexandra Prokofievna refused to go out and meet them.

"I don't want to see anyone from the institute," said the old woman. "First they persecute him, then they come and express their sympathy. I have nothing to say to them."

The implication was that Olga could talk to them because she and they had somehow been engaged in the same activity—persecuting Sergei. She wanted to pretend she hadn't noticed but couldn't help saying, "Don't talk nonsense. These people didn't persecute Sergei. They haven't done anything wrong; they have simply come to express the usual official condolences. Nobody persecuted Sergei."

"Yes they did," said Alexandra Prokofievna and went out of the kitchen.

Olga sat down on a stool and for a minute was motionless—her heart was beating very hard. Sergei had not been persecuted. The harm done to him had not been intentional; it had simply happened because certain people had been pursuing their own ends. That was a different matter. She heard Alexandra Prokofievna go into her room and lock the door.

Olga felt awkward in front of these strangers. Still, let them come—it meant nothing. She stood up, went into the living room carrying something in a little bowl. The two from the trade-union committee were sitting at the table, frozen in attitudes of profound dejection. The woman was just perceptibly nodding her head and staring at the floor. Probably she imagined that this pose and the faint nodding expressed sincere sympathy. "What a fool she is," thought Olga. Bezyazichny immediately leaped to his feet and began to say that they had come literally only for a minute, she shouldn't have gone to the trouble of making tea for them. He had short legs, a rosy complexion, a robust, young-looking face, gray hair in a short crew cut. It was impossible to tell his exact age; he was perhaps around fifty. He wore a black suit, the jacket crumpled, with disproportionately broad, padded shoulders. "He put it on specially to visit a widow," she thought with indifference. "Black. Out of mothballs."

"Here are a few articles that belonged to Sergei Afanasievich." He took out of his briefcase a tin box that had once held Czech cigarettes and in which something rattled; a ruler; a folding hunter's knife that had obviously been used for opening cans and pulling corks during the parties that took place fairly frequently in Sergei's department; three tattered books; a comb with a long handle; a soccer calendar for 1969; a copy of *Foreign Literature*; and an old notebook full of telephone numbers with dogeared pages. He took out each object and placed it on the table with as much care as if it had been made of glass.

With a fixed stare, Olga gazed at this trivial, random collection of junk which for some reason they had brought to her, and thought: "Don't they realize that it must be painful to have to look at my dead husband's possessions? Why are they doing it?" She wanted to pick it all up and throw it away. Instead she gathered up the things and carried them over to the windowsill.

Bezyazichny said something and handed her an envelope.

She thanked him and began to pour out the tea. Some money from the committee, no doubt. Drinking his tea in noiseless sips, Bezyazichny told her how everyone in the department grieved for Sergei and how much they missed him, because many people there had liked him. This remark stung Olga and brought her to life. Why did he say *"many people"* had liked him? According to the rules of this game he should have said "everybody liked him," or "people liked him at the institute," or at least "he was liked." But he had said *"many people liked him,"* which implied that there had been—and still were, now that he was dead—*a few people* who hadn't liked him and still didn't. Of course there were such people. Olga had no doubts about the existence of those *few people,* but it was rather strange to hint about them to his widow in the very first minutes of this visit.

She looked hard at Bezyazichny, trying once again to recall what Sergei had said about him, but nothing came to mind.

"You talk as though Sergei Afanasievich had been working in peace and concord with everyone right up to the very last day. As though he hadn't submitted his request to resign," said Olga. "He practically regarded himself as already dismissed."

"But that's not so. You are profoundly mistaken." Bezyazichny clasped a hand to his chest. "I know about his request. But first, the matter remained undecided up to, so to speak, the tragic day. . . . The director was on vacation. And Gennadii Vitalevich Klimuk most definitely didn't want to make the decision."

"Gennadii Vitalevich didn't want to? Don't talk to me about Gennadii Vitalevich. More than any of the others he wanted to get rid of Sergei—but only if someone else would actually do it."

"I assure you—you're mistaken."

"No, I am not mistaken."

This man had had an ulterior motive in saying "many people liked him." He had shown his hand. It was now clear that he was one of Sergei's enemies, or perhaps sympathized with his enemies. Had they really sunk so low as to send this person on a visit that required such tact?

"Sergei Afanasievich was working in the same field we do," said the woman in a quavering voice. Taking off her spectacles and pressing her fleshy chin into her chest, she began to polish the spectacles with a handkerchief. Her face took on a lachrymose expression and her voice was scarcely audible. "The revolution and the civil war . . . He and I worked together for six years. He was a fine man, extremely kind and responsive . . . a good man."

The fleshy chin quivered. Olga gave the woman a cold look. "It would be interesting to know how both of you voted at the hearing of Sergei's notorious 'case,'" she said.

The woman started; her eyes widened and described a momentary revolving movement. Olga had, of course, put the question rudely and no doubt placed her visitors in an awkward situation, but then they were making things just as awkward for her by simply sitting there, drinking tea and talking about Sergei.

"I didn't vote at all, because I was out of Moscow at the time. I was in Poland, on official business," said Bezyazichny with a contemptuous wave of the hand. "In any case, you know . . ." His gesture and tone of voice implied, "Is it really worth resurrecting all that nonsense?"

Sorokina said, "I, as it happens, voted for the whole thing to be brought out into the open." She blushed. "In the circumstances it was the only proper way . . ."

At that moment Irinka entered—or rather burst in unceremoniously, as she always did—and asked for a ruble and a half before the store closed. Having fired off this request, she noticed the visitors and said, "Oh, hello!"

Olga introduced her daughter, who smiled a very charming, welcoming smile, in the way she always did whenever she needed to wheedle money out of somebody.

Olga fumbled in her purse, looking for silver and copper.

"Oh, look!" Irinka shrieked with delight, rushing over to the windowsill. "I've been looking for it everywhere. How did it get here?"

She seized the long-handled comb.

"They brought it from your father's office. There's a ruble fifty for you."

"Oh . . ." Hesitating, Irinka put the comb back on the windowsill, then asked, "Mother, can I have it, please? You did buy it for me, remember?"

"Take it," said Olga.

Irinka ran out. Someone was obviously waiting for her in the hall; there was whispering, and then the door slammed. There was no more to talk about. It seemed the right moment for them to get up and go, but Bezyazichny started talking about Sergei's unfinished dissertation. The academic council, it seemed, was of the opinion—no decision had been taken yet, but the word was going around—that the institute should undertake the job of completing the dissertation and then publish a monograph. They would assign some special people to it. It would be incorporated into the official schedule, so the whole department would be involved. They would have to process a certain amount of unused source material and find what was still left in Sergei's papers in his desk. They were all counting on Olga Vasilievna's help. She felt irritation beginning to boil up inside her.

"I'll do it when I have the time and the energy," she said. "Right now I don't intend to go looking for anything."

"Of course, of course," mumbled Sorokina. "Only when Olga Vasilievna feels she is able to . . ."

"It will be entirely in Olga Vasilievna's own interest," said Bezyazichny.

Out in the foyer Bezyazichny said unexpectedly to Sorokina as he was helping her into her coat, "Excuse me, Paulina Ivanovna, but I won't be able to see you out. There is a little matter I have to discuss with Olga Vasilievna . . ."

They went back into the living room. Olga did not want to carry on the conversation in the hall, right outside her mother-in-law's door. She sensed that something unpleasant was impending. Bezyazichny said that he found it embarrassing to mention this, but he had no alternative because it was an official matter. He was chairman of the institute's staff credit union. Sergei Afanasievich had borrowed a hundred and sixty rubles with an undertaking to repay it within six months, but almost two years had passed, the money had not been paid back, and now a complication had arisen: the fund was empty, several requests for small loans were outstanding and they could not be met. The board of management had come to a unanimous decision . . . they felt . . . they were worried . . . the situation was . . .

Olga listened, stunned. The words reached her through a dense fog.

"I don't have that much money," she said.

"The fact of the matter is . . . You see, we haven't the right . . . If there were a general meeting of all the union's shareholders . . . but on the other hand if you were to make a voluntary . . ." Bezyazichny mumbled on, his heavy red face twitching as though he were sneezing, which no doubt indicated his extreme state of embarrassment. "Believe me, I find it very distasteful. But I am only carrying out . . ."

Olga said that there were a hundred rubles in Sergei's savings account, but it would be some time before she could get that money—not until the court had granted probate, in fact. As for the hundred and sixty rubles borrowed from the credit union, this was the first she had ever heard of it.

"When did he borrow this money?"

Bezyazichny produced a notebook from his pocket, leafed through it, and found the entry: the money had been advanced on March 5, 1971.

Where on earth had it all gone? Why had he needed so much? "A woman." This was the first thought that came into her head, and it made her temperature climb. Nevertheless she replied very calmly, "This is really the first I have heard of it. He usually told me everything about his expenses, his debts." This was not the complete truth, but it was true enough in broad terms.

"In that case it makes it even more embarrassing for me. I am sorry."

After a pause he said, "I'll do everything I can to persuade the members of the board of management, in view of the circumstances . . . You might perhaps care to write a statement. I'll do what I can." He clasped his hands to his chest and bowed his head. "Most of his colleagues were on good terms with him, so I hope . . . I'll have a preliminary word with one or two people . . ."

He went on muttering in this vein, pressing his hands to his chest and bowing, while he moved out of the room and into the hall. Everything had apparently been said. It was over for the time being. Why had they given her money in that envelope he gave her if they then demanded it back from her? It was all so confusing. Olga stared at this short, stocky, grizzled little man in his crumpled, old-fashioned black suit dating from the fifties and made some mechanical, meaningless remark.

As he was leaving he said, "So they'll phone you about the monograph. Do have a look around and collect whatever material you can find. The folder I mentioned is the one tied with pink ribbon."

In the past, whenever sudden troubles had arisen and she hadn't known what to do, she had always asked Sergei's advice—usually at night, before they went to sleep, when Irinka was already asleep and her mother-in-law had shut herself in her room. Although he was never very successful in solving his own problems, he always gave her sensible advice. He was good at soothing her when something had upset her. But now—who was there? Her mother-in-law mustn't know, because she would feel nothing but malicious satisfaction. She would regard it as confirmation of her belief that Olga and Sergei had never been really close and that he had led a separate life.

Olga was oppressed by a feeling that was not jealousy but something else, an emotion of a different quality—the burned-out remains of jealousy. It was as if she had been handed an urn containing these strange ashes, the ashes of a jealousy that was dead but whose remains she was holding in her hands, clutching them to her heart.

She was convinced that a woman was mixed up in this somewhere. Ashes, ashes, nothing but ashes. Yet her hands were trembling. In her own savings account she had two hundred and eighty rubles, which she and Sergei had put aside for a specific purpose—to buy a television set. To take money out of that account to pay off some questionable debt would be stupid.

Sergei used to say, "Don't fuss, old lady."

It was his favorite catch phrase, which he repeated ten times a day, in and out of season. Really, what a way to behave: to ask a widow to settle an unpaid debt with her husband not a month dead. But one thing she knew for certain: she and Sergei had been truly close. No other person was closer to him. So her mother-in-law could shut up. In recent years he had stopped sharing his thoughts with his mother, and had concealed all kinds of problems from her. "There are things I can't explain to her," he used to say.

There was a great deal that his mother had been incapable of understanding, and her lack of comprehension infuriated him. But no such gap in understanding had existed between him and Olga. She had fully understood everything that worried him, recognizing the significance of his slightest sigh. And even if he had been seeing another woman, it meant nothing.

With these thoughts she tried to persuade herself there was no cause for worry, trying to remain calm and imperturbable, but in reality she felt no calm. And there was no one to help her. It was no good telling Faïna, because although she was her best friend she would interpret it in her own way, and wrongly. No doubt she would also secretly rejoice, because the situation tended to favor her own admitted objective, which was to pull Olga out of her comatose state. This required the casting of mild aspersions on Sergei; but Olga didn't believe, refused to believe that Sergei might have been at fault. There was some kind of mystery about this business, and thinking about it was giving her a splitting headache. Olga put on her coat, took up her purse, and went out.

There was a slight but steady drizzle of rain. The last customers were hurrying into the delicatessen; it was twenty minutes to closing time. Olga went in to buy butter, yogurt and something for Irinka to have with her tea. The cleaning woman was swishing her mop, muttering with bad-tempered irritation as she made the customers step back from the counter. Olga stood in a short line at the cashier's desk, then went over to the dairy counter, thinking of how many people she knew: she had plenty of acquaintances, several women she counted as her friends, but there was no one to whom she was truly close—and that meant there was no one to whom she could turn. The worst thing that lay in store for her was loneliness. Death and grief were a mere prelude to the worst. How was she to go on living when there was no one to give her advice, no one to whom she could tell everything? The other people standing in line had vacant, abstracted looks, as if they were there by mistake—late evening customers, their thoughts far away. Indeed, most of them were late getting home; at this hour they were usually sitting in front of the TV wearing their slippers, or washing their underclothes in the bathroom, or ironing a school uniform in the kitchen, having spread on the table an old flannel blanket marked with yellow scorch marks from the iron. All this still remained to be done; yet they did not hurry. The salesgirls moved slowly about their work, the tiredness of the day lying on their faces like a thick coating of makeup.

Olga heard a familiar voice behind her and looked around—it was Irinka! Her daughter was standing beside one of the tall tables at which people drank coffee and ate cakes, but now it was too late for coffee and cakes. The snack bar was closed; she was standing there with two of her girl friends, and all three were talking and chewing something. Irinka's long, thin legs in dark stockings, the skimpy little overcoat that she had grown out of (she ought to have a new one—every time she looked at that pathetic little coat Olga felt an inward twinge, a momentary stab of guilt; but she never brought up the subject of buying a new one, and Irinka tactfully refrained from mentioning it too: it would somehow last through the autumn, and for the winter there was a quite presentable fur coat)—her daughter's round-shouldered, lanky figure with her fashionably long, straggly hair produced in Olga a convulsive upsurge of tenderness. It was so strong that she almost ran over to her. "My poor little orphan," she thought, almost in tears. "She doesn't understand yet what that means. But I know!"

Olga took a few steps toward the girls, conscious that the tallest of the three, the most poorly dressed, the prettiest and the nicest one—her daughter—was the one person close to her. She could talk to her about anything. No one was closer to her now than this young girl. As she approached the table, one of the girls—Irinka's best friend Dasha, a pretty little oriental girl, always extremely pale, with long eyes rimmed with eyeliner—noticed Olga, stopped twittering and smiling, and looked frightened.

"So this is where you fritter your life away," said Olga. "I wonder what you were talking about?"

"We were talking about tomorrow's sociology class, Olga Vasilievna, when there'll be a very interesting discussion on the individual and society. We were wondering about the best way to prepare for it." The look of fright on Dasha's pretty little face gave way to an expression of triumphant sarcasm.

The other little girl burst into giggles. Irinka gave Dasha a sullen, warning look that was mixed with a gleam of delight; the sullen glance referred to the appearance of her mother, while the delight, of course, was for Dasha's benefit. Olga didn't like Dasha, whom she regarded as insincere, affected, and, worst of all, precociously grown-up. From certain careless remarks dropped by Irinka she gathered that Dasha had a somewhat complicated private life, and that somewhere in it was a much older man whom she called her "friend." No one seemed to know quite how far that friendship went. Olga had made some cautious attempts to find out, but Irinka refused to be drawn into it. One could hope it was nothing serious—after all, the girls were not yet seventeen and Olga herself at that age had had nothing on her mind but her studies. The tenth grade—a lot of responsibility!

"By the way, I gave you that money for things you needed at the department store, not to spend here," said Olga. Dasha's impertinence irritated her. The stupid little creature would not take her eyes off her. "But I see you just squander it on cakes and cigarettes. Now, girls, why do you smoke?"

They mumbled in chorus something completely and purposely unintelligible but which to them was funny and sarcastic. Olga knew her presence was making them uncomfortable. Irinka, stupidly embarrassed, was not even looking at her mother; yet she was hanging on her friends' every word and laughing unnaturally loudly. The third of the trio, Lena Kukshina, was a limp, anemic, fat girl from a very well-off family; she was wearing a suede overcoat, and on one small puffy finger was a ring set with a stone. (Disgraceful! In Olga's day no schoolgirl would have dared wear a ring.) An extremely elegant folding Japanese umbrella lay on the table beside her; one of Olga's friends had a similar one, so she knew how expensive they were. The Kukshina girl exuded an aroma of prosperity and wealth, in the same way that men who have just been to the barber reek of cheap scent. It was an aroma that Olga found hard to tolerate. Irinka, however, always insisted that Kukshina was a nice girl, even though she didn't like the way Kukshina groveled for Dasha's favor. This Dasha, in fact, was the absolute uncrowned queen among them; she wielded enormous authority despite her diminutive size.

Olga said sternly, "Come on, Irinka, let's go home. It's dinner time," and took her arm above the elbow. Not because she intended to pull her away from the table, but simply because she wanted to touch her. "It's time, dear, let's go."

"Mama, I'll come home when I want to," Irinka snapped with sudden hostility.

"What do you mean—when you want to?"

"I mean what I say: I'll come when I want to."

"No, you're coming with me now."

"No, I won't."

Olga felt a kind of helpless fury welling up inside her. "How could you . . . treat me . . . at a time like this . . . ," she stuttered, breathless.

"And how could *you*? I have my problems too. I need to talk to my friends."

"*You* have problems!" Olga shouted. "You little . . ."

She turned around and walked out of the store. One of the girls ran after her and seized her arm from behind.

"Olga Vasilievna! Stop!"

It was Dasha. Again the look of fear in those gorgeous dark-brown eyes.

"It's true, Irinka's been having problems with a boy—you know, Boris—and we really do need to talk a bit more, about another ten minutes. They'll chase us out anyway, because it's closing time. We'll just walk a little way up the boulevard."

"She's just a little piece of trash," said Olga.

As the elevator in the apartment building was going up to the eighth floor, she thought: "*This* is the truth. Alone in a closed steel box. You can read the graffiti, scratched on the walls with nails. But there's no one to tell how much your heart aches. No one will hear. In solitude we creep higher and higher up the shaft or lower and lower downward—the direction is immaterial, it merely depends on which you regard as the top and which the bottom."

"No one can hear!" she said aloud.

"Hullo! What's that? Speak louder!" a hollow, terrifying voice barked out just above her ear. She jumped: it was the elevator watchman, answering her through the loudspeaker of the emergency call system. Normally, when you really needed him you could never get through to him, but this time he had heard. It was a sign: it meant that one must speak, one must shout, even if there are only bare walls all around. Somebody *will* hear.

It was not ten minutes but an hour later that Irinka came home. Olga had already forgiven her, and when she opened the door and saw her, head bowed and sniffling—naturally she was frozen after walking for a whole hour up and down the boulevard in that thin little coat—she also saw the childishly guilty look on her face and was again overcome by a wave of warmth and sympathy. "How could I? Why did I bark at her?" she said to herself, her mind suffused with pity. "The wretched child is an orphan, she has no father, no one to protect her. If I don't, who will . . . ?"

Without a word she stroked her daughter's hair. The girl suddenly darted forward, embraced her mother, pushed her wet-nosed, puppyish little face into Olga's cheek, into her ear, whispering something in a miserable voice. And Olga whispered too. Neither heard what the other was saying. It all happened in two seconds, and suddenly both softened in each other's embrace; barely holding back their tears, they went into the kitchen to be alone together for a little while, just the two of them, without Grandma, because no person was closer to either of them than the other. No one on earth was closer. They sat there for a long time, drinking tea, while Irinka told about Boris. Secretive by nature, she rarely shared her troubles and fought her life's little battles in silence. This meant, though, that when she reached the limit of her strength, as she had now, she really needed help. Boris had stopped calling her, and in school he wouldn't come near her any more. She guessed it was because of a girl he had met on his vacation in the South. Dasha had promised to find out. Boris was a boy from a parallel class. He was even rather ugly—Irinka had never been particularly taken by his looks—but the wretched girl appeared to be in a state of genuine distress.

Olga whispered some soothing nonsense. Irinka calmed down and went to the bathroom to wash her hair. Olga began to clear away the table and put the dirty dishes into the sink; at that late hour the hot water was unreliable and tonight it wasn't hot enough, and she did not want to heat water in the kettle. She decided to leave it all until tomorrow: she would get up at seven o'clock. At that moment the phone rang. It was the woman who had come with Bezyazichny.

"Excuse me for calling you so late. It takes me so long to get out to Kuzminki, where I live, and then there are so many things to do. . . . Let me tell you why I'm calling, Olga Vasilievna. I imagine that Bezyazichny tried to frighten you with the business of your husband's debt to the credit union, didn't he? Well, you've no cause to worry—the debt will be written off. The decision, in fact, has already been made. Do you see? And please—don't hand over a single folder or a single sheet of notes. I shouldn't be telling you all of this, of course, but it's simply because I greatly liked and respected Sergei Afanasievich. Please excuse me, dear Olga Vasilievna, for bothering you at this late hour. Good luck!"

This strange conversation, that "Good luck!" perplexed Olga, but not sufficiently to divert the flow of her thoughts. At night she could only think of the past, never of the future.

She should have done something about it long ago but had lacked the strength. All his folders, notepads, notebooks thick and thin, newspaper clippings clumsily glued into scrapbooks, pages ripped out of journals, heaps of scribbled-over paper, were scattered all over the apartment—some things were in the drawers of his desk, others on the lower shelves of bookcases, some folders lay gathering dust on top shelves of closets, just below the ceiling, where no duster had reached for months; whenever she had a cleanup Olga angrily demanded that Sergei remove all his "junk" and put it somewhere else, preferably into the trash can. She called it "junk" on the ground that if it had been of any value he wouldn't have kept it lying around, covered with dust, on the tops of wardrobes and closets. Some of his papers had even found their way out onto the stair landing during the last spring cleaning. But the papers were still, as it were, his flesh; his smell, the emanation of his physical being was still upon them, and she could not bring herself to touch them. She knew that sooner or later this feeling would pass, but so far she could not do it. She was equally unable to look at or touch his clothes in the wardrobe. Faïna told her she should sell them; she said all widows did that, to remove one of the sources of pain and grief, and she promised to find a buyer for them. Louisa, Fedya Praskukhin's wife, who had been widowed eight years ago, said that she sold Fedya's clothes right after his death, all at one time, but Olga lacked such resolve.

In any case, there was no time to spare for such things. Louisa didn't have a job at the time (lately, though, she had started to work as an insurance agent) and had nothing to do but sit at home with the children. What's more, she had someone to help with the children, and her mother lived with her. If Olga had stayed at home, she would have gone out of her mind.

There was something else that was unbearable: photographs. Hanging on the wall was one particularly good snapshot of Sergei, taken when he was younger; he was smiling gently and pensively, a blade of grass in the corner of his mouth. Olga loved that photograph. She had hung it there long ago, in Sergei's lifetime, and had grown accustomed to it. Now, though, whenever Olga came into the room she tried not to look at it, or at the most only fleetingly, for a second. As for their family album, she had hidden it as far away as possible. Every contact with the past meant pain. Yet life is made up of such contacts, for the threads to the past are a thousandfold and each one must be wrenched out of the living flesh, out of the wound. At first she had thought that repose would come when all those threads, down to the tiniest and thinnest, were broken. It now appeared, however, that this would never be, because the number of threads was countless. Every object, every familiar person, every thought, every word—every single thing in the world was linked by some thread to him. Would it last all her life? Yesterday her work had taken her to Novo-Basmannaya Street; she had got out of the subway at Lermontovskaya station, and immediately she had felt a stab at her heart as she remembered how last winter, in bitter cold, they had run from this station down Sadovaya Street to visit some friends. Seven months, and it wasn't getting any easier to bear. People said that five years had to pass, but Louisa had said this was untrue, and she ought to know, having been widowed for longer than that.

She had chanced recently to meet Louisa on the street. They had both been delighted to see each other; there was so much they wanted to say, so much to ask: How are you? How do you feel? What's happening to you? Is it getting . . . even just a tiny bit?

Louisa looked at her with gray, desolate eyes: "I don't know how to measure it. There's no such instrument . . ."

Olga also wanted to ask her, "Have you found someone else?" but she did not dare. In this battle, each one fought alone. Louisa looked well in her old fur coat, although cleaning had lightened its brown color and given it a rather vulgar pinkish tinge.

Olga asked, "How are the children?"

"Just fine," Louisa replied. She answered "Just fine" to every question.

Eight years ago, early one morning in September—so early that Irinka had not yet left for school—the doorbell had rung long and loud. When she opened the door, Olga was amazed to see Gennadii Klimuk—then still known familiarly as "Gena," their old friend—who at that hour should have been doing his morning gymnastics before breakfast on the pebbly beach at Koktebel. Klimuk's face was covered with purple blotches. Without even saying good morning he asked, "Where's Sergei?" Then he stepped into the foyer and collapsed sideways against the wall. Sergei came out of the bathroom, his face lathered with shaving soap.

"Sergei, you must tell her . . . I can't . . . I don't have the strength. . . ." This huge boy, with his round, prematurely old-looking face, swayed, and his legs crumpled as he gently slid down the wall to the floor. He did not quite fall, but somehow ended up sitting on his haunches, where he stayed for two or three seconds, breathing heavily.

Two days earlier, Klimuk and Fedya Praskukhin had driven south together for a week's vacation. Fedya had just bought a new Moskvich. They sometimes organized bachelor outings— or, as Klimuk liked to say with conscious archaism "sorties"— to which they tried to entice Sergei, but Olga did everything in her power to dissuade him from joining these excursions. It might have been that she was jealous of this male friendship, or that she was worried about his morals in the company of old friends, who had still not lost the freewheeling habits of their student days (whenever the three of them got together, these usually dormant habits were somehow galvanized back into life: they would start to play the fool, to brag, and to egg each other on to God knows what lunacy); or maybe she was worried about his health, because wherever Klimuk was, there was hard drinking. The plain fact was that she didn't like it when Sergei disappeared out of her sight. He should always be alongside, nearby, best of all in the same room with her. This was, no doubt, the greatest failing in her character, but she could not change herself and indeed had never even tried to.

She always did everything possible to counteract the wiles of Klimuk or Fedya or anyone else who attempted to take Sergei away from her. Sometimes she would skillfully find genuine reasons, sometimes invent plausible excuses—pleading, for instance, some ailment of hers that demanded his uninterrupted presence—and sometimes she would appeal flagrantly and directly to his conscience or his innate kindness. It was, in effect, the clash of two brands of egotism. He loved these stag outings, which were a change from everyday tedium, from work, from home, and he specially enjoyed the "sorties" to see Fyodorov, his old friend from the museum, or going anywhere with Fedya Praskukhin in his car, even just to the Sevan bar; she knew he liked it, and that for a number of reasons he needed it, but she couldn't help herself: whenever he disappeared, she almost got sick. Sometimes she even started to develop a nervous rash. Sergei, however, was relentless in his struggle for independence and rarely gave in to her. That rare occasion was in September. The institute was being redecorated, work had stopped, everyone was loafing around at home; Fedya and Klimuk took it into their heads to go South for a week's fresh air and tried to persuade Sergei to come too. There was such chaos at the institute that no one would notice they had gone. In any case, who was there to notice? As academic secretary, Fedya Praskukhin himself was the boss.

Sergei very much wanted to go, but some instinct prompted Olga not to let him go on any account. Hell, no, it wasn't instinct at all; she was simply annoyed at the thought of his leaving her behind while he went South, where he would have fun, horse around, and, of course, drink. She pointed out that they were broke, that none of his projects were getting anywhere—his dissertation, the book he was supposed to be getting published with the help of that fraud Ilya Vladimirovich—and how it was all right for Fedya Praskukhin and Gena Klimuk to fritter away their time and energy—they had tenured jobs—but he couldn't afford to behave like that.

"The thirty rubles that I can give you for the trip won't go far; you'll just be sponging off the others. Doesn't that worry you?"

No, he said, it did not. The three of them, he said, had a healthy male attitude about these things, not like the miserable female habit of counting every kopeck they spent between them. He even went so far as to say, "It's something you'll never understand."

Poor man, how wrong he was. Olga said that if he went with them, she would divorce him. Someone called up, it might have been Louisa or it might have been the stupid

Mara Klimuk, prompted by the men, to try to persuade her to relent and let Sergei go. But she was adamant. If he went— it was divorce. Sure, go if you like, no one's stopping you, but when you come back I won't be here, that's all—I'm going back to mother. Can it have been that she was prompted by a voice of prescience from those unearthly regions into which Sergei was later to descend and where his own destruction awaited him? Sergei was furious and refused to speak to her for several days, but he did not dare go. At dawn, on the Simferopol road south of Kharkov, a deaf old man who couldn't hear their horn had started to cross the road in front of them; Fedya could not slow down in time; he swerved to the left and was hit by an oncoming truck. Fedya had died in the local hospital without regaining consciousness, while Klimuk had escaped with nothing more than bruises. He had somehow managed to brace himself with his arms against the sides of the car—he had strong arms—and although the car turned over twice, he had survived intact.

Now, his lips white, he could barely whisper, "Fedya's body is being brought back by bus. . . . I paid a hundred and twenty rubles. . . ."

He begged Sergei to go to Louisa and break the news to her. Sergei went. He knew how to be a friend. That was why "many people liked him," flew to him whenever things were going badly—and undoubtedly they exploited this quality of his.

That night she could not restrain herself—she should never have said it, but the words just broke through—and said quietly into his ear, "Sergei, I saved your life. See what a good prophet I was?"

Without saying a word he pushed her away and turned over toward the wall.

She immediately realized that she had said the wrong thing, but the inner pressures prompting her to speak had been very strong indeed: terror, pity for Fedya, of whom she had been fond; and some strange, irrepressible inward feeling of secret self-satisfaction. No doubt, she thought, people experienced the same feeling in war when their comrades were killed beside them while they themselves somehow stayed alive and unharmed. She should not have said it. In the very instant that the thought was given utterance it inexorably turned false.

After a silence he said, "I was hoping that you might bite your tongue off rather than say it. But no, you had to . . ."

Of course she shouldn't have said it, but he shouldn't have been so angry with her, either. Because it was true: she *had* saved his life. He talked about Fedya, about how he was the best friend he would ever have in his life. True, they had been friends; all three—Sergei, Fedya, and Gena Klimuk— had been university classmates. But so what? She was always amazed at this childish attachment to friends from school or university days. Sergei always managed to overlook their failings, never saw what was ridiculous or unpleasant about them. For him the labels "schoolmate" and "classmate" were the highest possible forms of recommendation and a guarantee of all the virtues. It was friendship not by choice but by force of circumstance: if someone happened to share a school desk with me, I am therefore his friend. All men, what's more, shared this peculiarity: they couldn't live without their old pals. Yet Olga managed very well without female friends, and when Sergei was alive she could go for months without seeing Faïna or anyone else. She needed no one but him. Well, she saw Louisa and Mara now and again, but only because their husbands loved doing things "all together": "Let's go, all together!" or, "Why haven't we all been together for such a long time?"

Now they were linked by their common interest in the institute and everything that went on there. Gena Klimuk used to joke, saying with a wink, "Let's set up our own little group, our own clique, our own cosy little gang."

Fedya, however, did not just chatter; he got things done. He was really helpful: he bent over backward to get Sergei into the institute, helped his progress in every possible way, got him a higher salary, persuaded Ivan Demchenko, the popeyed director of the institute, to change his mind and accept an alteration in the topic of Sergei's dissertation, and pacified Sergei's supervisor, Professor Vyatkin, who was by no means pleased with the change of topic. None of this was easy, but Fedya did it. If Fedya had not been killed in the car wreck and had remained academic secretary, he, of course, would never have countenanced the disgraceful way Sergei had been treated, which was the fault of his old friend Klimuk and his "little gang."

Gena took over the post of academic secretary so quickly and with such readiness that one might have thought he had arranged the accident on purpose, like the diabolical Woland in Bulgakov's *The Master and Margarita*.

It was after Klimuk's appointment to the job that things imperceptibly began to deteriorate. For a long time Olga did not notice anything. Whenever Gena called up, he was as cheerfully friendly with her as ever; sometimes Mara called, to give Olga the latest tips on knitwear and cosmetics (she had a very enviable job, in an exclusive store on the Petrovka near the Arcade), but several months went by before it occurred to Olga that she wasn't actually seeing either Gena or Mara any longer and that their contact was limited to phone calls. It was a long time since Gena's joyous catch phrase "Let's go, all together!" had rung out. Once aware of the situation, Olga put it down to Fedya's death. It was, after all, most often at Fedya's place that they had all met. Apart from the three couples, there were other friends of Fedya's—a physicist, Shchupakov, with a Bulgarian wife named Krasina, a couple by the name of Luzhsky who were both doctors, she a radiologist, he a psychiatrist; in fact, it was because of the Luzhskys that Olga had first started visiting Fedya and Louisa because she was very much interested in medicine and loved talking with doctors.

But after Fedya's death Louisa stopped inviting friends; they had forgathered only after Fedya's funeral and then once again on the sixth anniversary of his death. Even in the old days Gena Klimuk had never been very hospitable; he was always remodeling, redecorating, repairing, or changing apartments, inexorably enlarging his living space and moving into ever more fashionable districts. Now, it appeared, he had made it to the New Arbat, in the skyscraper above the Melodia record store.

At some point Sergei had said with a chuckle, "Our Gena has really become a big wheel. He makes it rather obvious, too. When Fedya had that job, I somehow never noticed . . ."

She asked what characteristics of big-wheeldom were showing in Gena. Sergei grinned and said nothing. She knew, however, that he would be unable to keep it to himself for long,
and he did tell her a few days later. The committee of the
institute's staff association had been given a number of travel
vouchers for a trip to France of eleven days, six in Paris and
five in Marseilles, Nice, and so on—the dream of a lifetime,
and costing a tidy sum. Since there were only four of these
vouchers, the staff association decided not to advertise them
but to distribute them, as the saying goes, on the sly. Sergei
learned about this quite by chance, and not from his friend
Gena but from the director's secretary, who had a soft spot
for Sergei. Many people wanted to go on the trip. At first the
committee intended to draw lots, but then Klimuk showed
caution, saying that drawing lots would introduce an im-
proper element of chance and a dangerous lack of control by
giving the vouchers to people who had no *need* to go to
France at all, while passing over others for whom it was a
genuine *necessity*. In fact, this argument was perfectly reason-
able and logical, as was every position that Klimuk adopted.
But the catch was: Who would decide who needed to go and
who didn't? At one point Sergei told Klimuk to his face that
he needed to go to Paris not for sightseeing or amusement—
there was a touch of hypocrisy in this, of course—but to look
for research material that was essential for his work. Everyone knew—and naturally Klimuk was well aware of this too—
that in studying the czarist secret police the historian would
inevitably be led to France, to the Russian political émigrés
who had gone there and the police agents whose job was to
spy on them. The point was quite easy to explain by rational
discussion, because Sergei was right and had an entirely lawful
ground for claiming one of the vouchers, but Klimuk merely
gave a sort of grunt, cross-questioned him, demanded specific
evidence—although what was there to grunt about when the
claim was absolutely justified?—and Sergei, losing patience,
said something rude and personal, something like: "Stop being such a bore!" or, "Lay off the bullshit, Gena!"

Klimuk shrugged and replied coldly, "Submit your claim in
writing. The three-man committee will decide. Do try to
understand—the matter isn't as simple as it looks."

"**Do** try to understand" was the only human, friendly remark he made during the whole conversation.

Sergei became very depressed as he told the story.

Olga decided that Sergei might be exaggerating, that he was too easily offended by trifles, especially the main trifle: the fact that Klimuk had talked to him like a boss. But what could one do? One had to come to terms with it. He *is* the boss, you *are* the subordinate. It's something you have to live with. Without telling him, when Sergei was out of the house, she called up Mara simply as one friend to another—why haven't you called, what's become of you, how are things with you, and so on. She realized that she had to act. Sergei was already despondent, even though nothing was decided yet; what would he be like if he really didn't get the trip? She wanted him to go. A little "escape" to Paris might give him new strength and become a turning point. When one failure after another hits a man, or doesn't even hit him but simply settles on him softly and habitually like birds settling on a tree, he starts to grow wooden, loses all feeling and gradually turns into a tree himself. The trip would cost a great deal of money, and they didn't have any, so they devised a plan. He would raise half of it by selling his eight-volume collected works of Stefan Zweig to an acquaintance who was a secondhand book dealer; published by Vremya, it was a magnificent edition in very choice bindings with red leather spines, for which he had originally paid fifteen hundred old rubles; Olga would ask her mother to lend them the other half.

So she called up Mara and chattered to her in a voice of phony, cheerful friendliness, not knowing exactly where the conversation might lead. The aim was to sound her out, but Olga's probing revealed nothing; Mara prattled on in her affected, would-be amiable voice, passed on bits of silly gossip, laughed out of place—in other words she was unbearable, but there was nothing new in that, so Olga, feeling slightly relieved, decided that all was normal and Sergei was getting into a panic over nothing. Mara, however, was too dense and lacked the subtlety to react to indirect suggestion; to find out anything useful meant talking to Klimuk himself, so to her own surprise Olga invited Mara and Gena to visit them at the *dacha,* out in the country at Vasilkovo. It was early summer, a lovely time of year; they could swim, sunbathe, wander through the woods . . . how about it, then? Why don't we all get together soon, without planning too far ahead, on Saturday, or even Friday—whenever you like. Mara said she herself would love to come, but she would have to check with Gena. He was working terribly hard; they never went anywhere nowadays and had grown quite unsociable. Gena was in the next room. He asked Mara to say hello for him and promised they would come as soon as they could make it.

Sergei grumbled, "It looks a bit weird: I see him practically every day and don't invite him, while you never see him—and you invite him."

On balance, though, Sergei was pleased. There is nothing so touchy as a friendship that is cracking up.

Every evening she would ask him, "Did you see Klimuk? Are they going to come?"

"I saw him, but I didn't ask . . . I didn't want to push it. . . ."

What had once been easy and natural to do had turned into a problem. His tongue wouldn't form the words needed to ask the simple question: "When are you coming to see us, Gena?" One day, however, he came back from the institute in some excitement and announced that Klimuk had himself come into Sergei's room and said that if the invitation to Vasilkovo still held good, then they would like to come for a short while on Saturday.

"For a short while?" asked Olga.

"Well, I don't know. That's what he said."

On Friday they bought food, two bottles of vodka, two bottles of white wine, a few bottles of beer, and took a taxi out to Vasilkovo. Irinka and Sergei's mother had been there all that week, with Aunty Pasha, the old peasant woman from whom they rented the *dacha*. Getting out to the *dacha* on weekdays was always rather a struggle: it was a long way from the station, it meant getting away from work early, and the train ride lasted nearly an hour. Even so, whenever she did manage to get away early enough and stepped out onto the platform, however exhausted she was by the long ride, the pushing and shoving and standing in line in the stores, however heavy her cartload of packages, paper bags, loaves of bread, cans, and books, stuffed into string bags and baskets, she felt immediately refreshed by the cool forest air. She would take deep, deep breaths, of the kind one never once took in a whole day in the city, and she was pleasurably aware of the tiredness slowly ebbing away as her whole being was filled with new strength. It was so lovely! Where did that strength come from, after an exhausting, grinding, relentless day? From the sky? From the woods? From the fact that Sergei was walking beside her and carrying the bags, humming to himself, or bringing her up to date on the news from the village as he puffed at a cigarette? Aunty Pasha had bought some sour cream from the village store. . . . Ginger, the dog, had been chasing the neighbors' chickens again. . . .

There were fixed days on which he had to attend the institute, but on other days—sometimes three or four in a row—he could work out at the *dacha*. He would meet her on the platform and pick up the bags for her. At first they followed the same road as the crowd of other weekenders; past a green hedge, they would turn off through a little oak wood where the other people usually dispersed, group by group, to their cottages; then, leaving the wood behind them, they crossed a field, after which they were on the road leading into Vasilkovo village, and by now they were generally alone. The weekenders tended to live near the station, while the people who lived in Vasilkovo did not take the trains from Moscow. The field they had to cross was enormous and rose to a knoll at the far end. The village lay beyond it, at the bottom of a steep slope, as though it had fallen over the edge of the field and tumbled down into the valley below. There the scattered cottage roofs peeped up, with their long protruding television antennas; willow trees clustered like piles of tarnished silver along the banks of an invisible river; a boy in a red shirt rode a bicycle along the path that cut across the field; and the silence was disturbed only by the puttering of a distant tractor. The clear sky was so bright that it made you want to look up. In the city no one ever noticed the sky or felt the urge to look upward.

It was a two-mile walk to the village. Back in town Olga

would think longingly: just let me go the distance, hauling the bags, then have a quick bite to eat, drink a cup of tea—and sit down exhausted in Aunt Pasha's big living room, which smelled of fresh hay and thyme, bunches of which were stuffed into crannies of the woodwork to stop drafts and scent the air. Yet every time what happened was quite different: after tea they would go walking in the woods with Irinka; at ten they would put her to bed and afterward Olga and Sergei would take another long walk by themselves. If Alexandra Prokofievna joined them they would go only a short distance and soon return, but the old lady didn't often do this; even she realized that husband and wife needed to be alone together. Or else they would bathe in the deep water at a bend in the creek, where they would sit on the bank and gossip with neighbors, all the while absorbing new strength from some mysterious source and not feeling tired at all.

There were, of course, days when it was wet and cold, when the path across the field turned into an impassable quagmire—and then came the onset of the Great Boredom of country life. Alexandra Prokofievna wrote interminable letters, Irinka whined and complained first of earache, then of tummyache, sending Sergei running through the rain to fetch Agnia, the local nurse.

Klimuk arrived in his old Pobeda, bringing with him another visitor—Kislovsky, the deputy director of the institute. No one had expected Kislovsky. Olga noticed that as Kislovsky stepped out of the car Sergei cringed for a second and his face took on the expression she knew so well, which meant: "Oh, hell!" With Klimuk was Mara, wearing a stunning dark-green pants suit—it was when pants suits were just becoming fashionable and were being imported—white sandals, white purse, and white earrings: a dazzlingly chic figure, her hair transformed by henna into a deep auburn. Everything about Mara was new and unrecognizable and took Olga's breath away. It was not exactly a pleasant surprise: you're sitting at home with an apron over your drab workaday clothes and suddenly the woman you thought of as a friend turns up in all this gorgeous plumage. . . . But it wasn't Mara who struck the jarring note. She couldn't help the fact that she simply oozed stupidity; poor thing, if only she had the good sense to sit in silence and smile thoughtfully as she held a cigarette in her thin fingers, she would be irresistible, but she would insist on butting into every conversation. She even tried to argue with Olga about biology. No, Mara was hopeless but harmless; it wasn't she who spoiled the atmosphere for Olga.

The trouble lay elsewhere: the woman who had come with Kislovsky. Although she had long since forgotten her name, Olga disliked this young creature on sight—a dark, loose-jointed Gypsyish creature, thin and affected. She was adorned with masses of jangling silver bracelets and beads; her jewelry was, in fact, beautiful and expensive, but it was absurd to festoon oneself like that for a day in the country, and it showed her lack of taste.

As soon as possible, seizing a convenient moment, Olga whispered to Mara, "What does Kislovsky's wife do?" To which Mara, as Olga had guessed she might, replied, "If she's his wife, then I'm your grandmother."

In other words, it was one of Klimuk's usual bits of effrontery. Once he had produced some dubious-looking girls who, he claimed, worked in TV; what's more, he had brought them, without asking or phoning, to their apartment in Moscow. Sergei, always ready to bend over backward to humor a friend, was just about to offer them cookies and the last vestiges of some French brandy when Olga came home from work; rapidly sizing up the situation, she firmly put a stop to it all and escorted the uninvited guests off the premises. Klimuk was furious. Now, however, he felt he was the boss—and the invitation had been so pressing. Besides, this time Mara was with him.

"We've only come for a moment . . . we're on the way to the reservoir. Just thought we'd drop in for a second or two," they said as though apologizing for descending like this and bringing these strangers with them; at the same time their remarks implied more than a touch of condescension, because they made it clear that the visit was a quick one, a mere drop-in and therefore did not count as a real visit.

Olga rushed about trying to cope with the extra numbers, but Irinka helped, and Aunty Pasha lent a hand by clambering down to the cellar for sauerkraut, dill pickles, and pickled mushrooms, and sending her son Kolka off to the village for bread—he roared away on his motorbike, in joyful anticipation of the drinking to come—and only Alexandra Prokofievna stayed out of the kitchen, touched not a piece of crockery, and instead retired behind a screen on the verandah to continue her endless letter writing. She answered readers' letters for some newspaper, which ran a column entitled "Consult Our Lawyer." Long ago she had been a defense attorney in the courts. Olga could not believe that her mother-in-law had ever been a good or successful trial lawyer; but although she felt convinced of this, she never discussed it with Sergei.

They had lunch in the garden behind the house. The day was hot, the air under the apple trees sultry. Most of all they drank ice-cold well water, which Kolka brought by the bucketful. The water in Vasilkovo was truly delicious; Olga had never drunk water that was so sweet and so cool. It was even better than the water in Yerevan, which the Armenians boasted was quite special. . . . But what good was nostalgia? Something was depressing her; she was irritated by the girl who had come with Kislovsky, annoyed by the way she was giving Sergei the eye and flirting with him under the pretext of asking questions, to which he reacted by putting on a stupid frown and mumbling in embarrassment. She was irritated, too, by Mara's brainless chatter, worried that there wasn't enough food and wine to go around, that Sergei wouldn't find an opportunity to talk to Klimuk about the trip to France, and perplexed over how to treat Kislovsky, a smarmy, rubbery man who had the look of a double-jointed acrobat in a circus. Yet despite it all there was such a feeling in the air of something genuine, young, summery, unique— well, of what?—well, of happiness, she supposed. . . . Yes, for a little while they were happy in that country backyard, where it smelled of a mixture of earth and manure and sweet, lush June greenery. From behind them came a grunting sound and much scrabbling and stomping as Matilda, the sow, pushed the creaking gate open and lumbered into her sty, while Aunty Pasha, slightly drunk, fiercely shook her little brown fist: "Now she's in paradise, God bless her, the lazy brute." By now the visitors' "second" had long since flown, the whole day had flown and evening had come, and they were all still sitting there, drinking, laughing and chattering; the bottles were almost empty, and Kolka had roared off again on his motorbike to get some moonshine vodka from an old woman at the other end of the village.

Olga was just going into the bedroom when she saw Kislovsky clasping his girl friend around the waist, trying to push her onto the big double bed. Her silver ajangle, the girl was resisting.

Olga went out into the backyard and sidled up to Sergei, who was talking to Klimuk about something trivial and unessential, and whispered into his ear that she had just seen some rather tasteless goings-on in their bedroom.

"Suppose it's love?" he asked, giving her a glazed look. He was not, in fact, as drunk as he made out. His expression was one of submission to fate.

"Well, there are special places for that sort of love," said Olga, "and not Aunty Pasha's cottage."

Aunty Pasha, not understanding what they were talking about but hearing her name, bristled aggressively: "What's that about Aunty Pasha? You leave Aunty Pasha alone! I'll give you 'Aunty Pasha'! I'll show you all up." And she wagged her finger. "I'll unravel all your secrets. You tell 'em, Kolka. . . ."

Kolka was an auxiliary policeman, which he bragged about a great deal, telling it to everyone as a great secret. His real job was being a carpenter on a state farm. Short, thin, with a consumptive pallor on a soft, girlish face, he wore his hair as long as a seminarian at Zagorsk, played the guitar rather badly and was, it seemed, besieged by girls every evening. Aunty Pasha was annoyed with him for not getting married and for "just frittering his strength away." Kolka had been rejected by the army as physically unfit because of a weak heart, and he was forbidden to drink—at any rate forbidden to drink more than one glass of vodka a day, as he said, quoting the doctor; this annoyed him, but at the same time he told it with a certain pride, as proving the special peculiarity of his organism. Needless to say, the prohibition was violated almost daily.

Alexandra Prokofievna kept a sharp eye on Kolka's health;

she always scolded him when she saw him drunk, and she was, it must be said, the only person to whom he paid any attention. This was typical of the strange effect the old woman had on people: her relatives completely ignored her—and with reason, for they knew her character only too well—yet outsiders respected her and were even slightly awed by her. Evidently this was the result of her compulsive need to domineer, to which simple souls of limited intellect naturally submitted, while thinking people instinctively resisted it.

That same evening, when they all went for a walk in the woods after their greatly extended lunch—Kislovsky could be enticed out of the bedroom only with difficulty—Alexandra Prokofievna started up a carping, tactless conversation (more like a courtroom cross-examination) with Klimuk, whom she always treated with scant respect. She remembered him when he used to come to visit as a very young student, dirty, thin and hungry, from the student hostel ("Whenever he came he was always hungry; he would eat whatever was put in front of him and more—five, eight, twelve large meatballs, fantastic quantities"). Sergei would invite him to stay over for the night. They would play chess till midnight, smoke endless cigarettes, bone up for exams together, quarrel and make up. She called him Gesha and thought he was a nice kid but not too bright. Sergei had to coach him for his exams in Russian and dialectical materialism—and now he had shot so far ahead that he was Sergei's boss. She noticed how her son's relationship with Gennadii Klimuk had changed, unnoticed by anybody, even by Olga; Alexandra Prokofievna, however, had been a witness of that relationship from its very beginning, when they were boys in lumber jackets drinking tea in the kitchen, spreading apple jam on enormous hunks of bread; and there had been a third boy who talked in a deep bass voice, who acquired a wife and son well ahead of the others— the unfortunate Fedya, of whom she had been very fond. Nowadays, she noticed, her son behaved toward this stupid Gesha with a sort of stiff embarrassment and even a certain shyness, in the way that a subordinate is supposed to act in the presence of a superior; she found this intolerable, and felt offended on Sergei's behalf. If Klimuk's head had swollen and he had turned into one of those self-important Soviet bureaucrats she had derided as long ago as the twenties, then Sergei had no business to play up to this style of behavior; instead, this lanky young upstart should be taken down a peg or two and taught sense. So Alexandra Prokofievna made a point of patronizing Klimuk whenever she talked to him, called him Gesha as she did in the old days, and did everything she could to deflate his ego.

"I seem to have forgotten; my memory has started to play tricks on me," she said. "It's strange, because I always prided myself on my memory when I was a schoolgirl. . . . What year was it, Gesha, when your brother came from Kremenchug? He stayed with us and I found him a lawyer. He was in some sort of trouble, something to do with embezzlement . . ."

"Alexandra Prokofievna, what's the point in digging up ancient history?" Olga put in, sensing that Klimuk was irritated and starting to sulk, which was not going to make the forthcoming conversation any easier.

"No, I well remember I called up Elizaveta Markovna at the city College of Advocates, and if it was Elizaveta Markovna that means it was embezzlement. She liked those cases— or rather she didn't particularly like them, but she knew how to handle them because she had studied accounting. After all, what is important in such cases? The precise amount that was embezzled. It must be established, down to the last kopeck."

The old woman's force of character was such that the drunken guests quieted down and sobered up slightly as they listened to the story. Her complaints about her memory were completely unfounded: she remembered it all perfectly. Klimuk scowled in an effort of self-control, then suddenly burst into laughter:

"But this is the theater of the absurd! Pure Grand Guignol! My God, what on earth is the point of bringing all this up; what use is it to me, to you, to anybody? There's such a thing as historical expediency, you know. Do you know who my brother is now?"

Laughing and bragging, he told a story about his brother, at which for some reason everyone else started to laugh. And so, shrieking with pointless laughter, they all walked down to the bend in the river where there was a sandy beach, the bathing place. By day it was seething with children, the weekenders lay sunbathing, the village boys would be diving in off the iron jetty, but now it was deserted, scraps of newspaper glowed white in the twilight on the gray sand. The water was cold and smelled of mud. The men went swimming; the women sat down on the grassy slope and talked, but sitting on the grass and chatting was too feminine and too petty bourgeois an occupation for Alexandra Prokofievna; she announced that she would bathe, away from the men and farther still from the women, and asked them all not to go past the alder tree. About twenty minutes later a cry of help came from beyond the alder tree: Alexandra Prokofievna could not climb out of the water up the slippery clay slope and asked Sergei to give her a hand.

Imperceptive though she was, Mara had grasped a certain amount of what was going on and whispered to Olga: "You have my sympathy."

That evening was memorable, however, for something else. Sergei latched on to Klimuk's words about historical expediency. It was obviously a sore point with him. They started off with a friendly slanging-match in the water as they fooled around and splashed each other like boys; then the dispute got really serious and on the way back to the village they were arguing hammer and tongs. After their dip in cold water all their drunkenness had vanished and the remarks started to get personal and Kislovsky joined in. It was something to do with Sergei's work and someone else's work, and with a view of history in general.

It may be that it was on that drunken evening in Vasilkovo—in fact it was probably earlier, but that evening impressed itself on Olga's mind as the beginning—that there began the long feud between Sergei, Klimuk and all the rest, which caused him such pain and ended so tragically.

By the time they arrived back at the cottage and sat down on the verandah to drink tea, Sergei and Klimuk were shouting at each other in real animosity. Olga had no idea that Klimuk was capable of being so angry.

She knew, of course, that when Sergei got into an argument

he was gripped by a kind of frenzy: he forgot about the rules of propriety and lost all sense of fairness and generosity. He wanted one thing only—to prove his point.

"In Aunty Pasha's bedroom there's an antique clock in a wooden case. Where did it come from, Aunty Pasha?" shouted Klimuk, thrusting out his right hand as though speaking from a rostrum.

"How do I know? Father brought it from somewhere. He exchanged it for food, he told me, during the famine in twenty-one."

"He exchanged it, he brought it—it's all the same now. Whichever it was, it doesn't *matter* now. What does matter is that the clock keeps good time and plays Strauss every half hour. Am I right, Aunty Pasha?"

Aunt Pasha pursed her lips primly: "Right or not, young man, I did not give you permission to call me Aunty Pasha."

"Well said. Nothing matters and nothing has any meaning except historical expediency—remember that Aunty Pasha, and pour me some more tea, please. My mother, by the way, is another Aunty Pasha just like you, except she's called Aunty Paulina and she lives near Shebekinsk, Belgorod province . . ."

"This historical expediency that you keep talking about," said Sergei, "is something vague and treacherous, like a swamp . . ."

"It's the only solid thing that's worth hanging on to."

"I wonder who decides what's expedient and what isn't? The academic council—by a majority vote?"

Sergei was now so carried away that he had forgotten that Kislovsky was chairman of the academic council. Olga hoped that people who had spent the whole day drinking and talking nonsense would forget who had said what, but it turned out later that they remembered Sergei's outbursts only too well. It is not the meaning of what is said that offends people but the intonation, because the intonation reveals another meaning—the hidden real meaning.

When Sergei had asked jokingly, "The academic council—by a majority vote?"—and grinned sarcastically, his sarcasm had been more offensive than his words. And Kislovsky, if no one else, was unlikely to forget it. Sergei was talkative, indiscreet, and careless, and he had made enemies—a host of them, thanks to his jokes, his arguments, his venomous remarks, his inability to stop himself in time and think twice. A typical example was the nickname he had made up for Klimuk at the time when they were not yet out-and-out enemies but were moving toward it: he took Klimuk's name and patronymic, which were Gennadii Vitalich, and ran them together to make the hilarious but somewhat indecent combination of "Genitalich." People in the institute seized on it with delight. But why did Sergei have to do it? Why be so offensive?

It was late, but none of them showed any signs of going. The men were still arguing at the tops of their voices, smoking, drinking the last of the liquor—Kolka had again been dispatched for another consignment of moonshine—while the women were nodding off and Irinka had long since been sent to bed. Olga was yawning and visibly exhausted, and from high in a midnight-blue sky the moon gazed down through the open windows.

And still they refused to go. The visitors, too, were yawning, stretching, giving every indication that they were dead tired and wanted to lay down their heads and curl up for the night. Then a conversation took place between Sergei and Klimuk while the men made their way to the outdoor privy at the end of the yard, and when they returned the visitors immediately started to depart. Olga realized that something had happened between the two of them: after the evening's second round of drinking both had relapsed into gloomy sobriety. Kislovsky was heaved into the car in a state of lethargy. Mara took the wheel, having purposely refrained from drinking so that the men could let themselves go. It was strange: Olga found herself thinking that the feather-brained Mara was in fact the only normal human being among the four of them. As she gave Olga a farewell kiss on the cheek, she whispered, gratified: "Sergei was right not to let those two stay here. Really. And to think who they are."

Kolka blew his police whistle, waved his arms in front of the car's headlights and shouted: "Hey, what's all this—driving after drinking? Who's responsible? Out you get: this car's not going anywhere."

Later, Sergei told Olga that Klimuk had asked if Kislovsky and his girl friend could stay for the night. This was, in fact, the reason why they had come. Sergei lost his temper at this and refused. Klimuk tried by every possible means to persuade him to change his mind:

"You invited Mara and me to spend the night here, so I have a claim to sleeping room for two in your *dacha*. Well, I'm merely giving up those places to my friends." Then he switched to threats: "You're acting very stupidly, old man. You'll have only yourself to blame for any consequences." Finally, almost with tears in his voice he begged: "Do it for my sake, old man. I promised him. On your word. How am I going to look if I let him down?"

Sergei told Klimuk that he felt a sudden and insurmountable aversion to the whole thing. Describing this, he said: "I suddenly realized that the man I work under was a cheap little wheeler-dealer. Our *dacha* was a consignment of goods in some deal he was fixing. He had promised this to Kislovsky, who had promised him something else in return, and now, thanks to me, the deal was off. He threw a fit of hysterics. He positively hissed and boiled with rage. 'You're no friend; no one can rely on you. You simply hate other people.' And all this quite genuine fury was not because he sympathized with his friend Kislovsky but because someone was taking something away from *him*. I had robbed him, you see."

Why, though, couldn't the couple have been allowed to stay over for the night? Granted that the Gypsy-like girl was fairly loathsome, but since Kislovsky was such an important figure and Klimuk had asked. . . . They could have given them the bedroom, and Olga and Sergei could have slept out on the verandah. Even in serious matters that could affect his career, Sergei's attitude to everything, however, was based on a peculiar criterion of taste. He did what pleased him and he didn't do what displeased him. Herein, incidentally, lay a fundamental cause of the constant trouble in which he found himself.

"I suddenly felt that I was a cheap little fixer too, and I was taking part in some squalid and protracted trade-off. I felt nauseated, and I refused, using you as an excuse: I said you had very strict moral standards. . . . Anyway, to hell with him."

God, it was obvious now what a chain of absurdities and pathetic subterfuges it had been. She shouldn't have invited them to the *dacha* in the first place. Once having invited them, he shouldn't have argued in such a pigheaded way and offended them. And both shouldn't have been so desperate about that trip to la belle France. At Vasilkovo, of course, Sergei had not said a word to Klimuk about the trip (and he was right not to have done so), but in that case, what was the point of all that frenetic hospitality?

Two days passed, and Sergei went to the institute. Returning that evening to the Moscow apartment, he described with joyful excitement how Gena had been unusually affable and friendly, how he had made kind inquiries about Olga, her mother-in-law, Irinka, Aunty Pasha and Kolka and hoped that the guests hadn't done anything stupid while they were drunk. In the same half-joking tone Sergei had said, "Did Kislovsky say anything? About the shortage of beds in the hotel?"

No, he hadn't said anything, because he had been in no fit state to talk: he hadn't made a sound all the way back to Moscow. Only as they reached the city did he utter his first words in a hoarse voice. For some reason he had asked: "Have they brought it?" They never did find out what he meant.

Standing in the corridor as they talked, Sergei and Klimuk had laughed and parted. And what about France? So far, vagueness, although Klimuk had promised to say a word in the right quarter.

"Don't fuss, old lady! Gena will fix it, no problem."

At that moment he seemed sincerely to believe it.

The problem was to find the money. As a first move, Olga had secretly spoken to her mother, who often used to help her out by lending or giving her small amounts, but this time her mother hesitated: she was shocked by the amount Olga asked for. She simply didn't have that sort of money; Georgii Maximovich gave her money every month but it was only enough for housekeeping expenses.

"Is this trip really so necessary?" Olga's mother tried feebly to resist. "There's so much that needs doing to your apartment. You need a fur coat; Irinka has grown out of everything. And then—if you were both going it would be different."

Olga explained that it was quite impossible for them to go together; in any case, such a suggestion had never been made. In every sense, it was Sergei who would benefit from the trip. Olga's mother could not quite understand what was meant by "in every sense"; this was difficult to explain, because it was a matter of certain rather vague, intangible factors—such as intellectual stimulus, self-affirmation—but she believed Olga. In the end her mother always believed her. She promised to talk to Georgii Maximovich. Next day she called up to say that Georgii Maximovich had asked Sergei to go and see him.

They were certain that "go and see him" simply meant to go and collect the money. All three of them went together on Saturday. For the past three years Olga's mother and Georgii Maximovich had been living in a new apartment, not far from the old one on Sushchevskaya, where Georgii Maximovich still kept his studio. His affairs were now prospering; he had some appointed position, was in charge of something or other, did some teaching and no longer worked so hard. His doctors had forbidden him to work too much, but he still liked going to the studio every morning, and even if he wasn't drawing or painting he would quietly busy himself with his pictures, knock nails into frames with a little hammer, sort out his prints, and touch up a painting without straining his eyes; or he would invite a friend from the second or third floor and they would make tea on the stove, discuss their work and reminisce about the past while they inspected Georgii Maximovich's enormous collection of reproductions that he kept in huge portfolios.

Sergei got on rather well with Georgii Maximovich; he regarded him as a decent, honest man and felt something like gratitude toward him—not because of his creations on canvas or paper, but because he was such a good stepfather to Olga. One day, though, he said to Olga:

"There is a certain kind of picture they make for children: look at them through a piece of pink cellophane and you see one picture; look at them through a strip of blue cellophane and you see quite a different picture. Forgive me, but your stepfather reminds me of one of those pictures: now I see him as an artist, a real artist, who has sacrificed everything for art—and then I see him simply as a businessman, grubbing around for commissions."

Olga did not like this; it degraded her mother, who could never have loved a businessman. The man she had fallen in love with was an unfortunate, unrecognized, hungry, poor but honest artist. And what sort of people prospered in the conditions of wartime evacuation? If he had really had a business sense, he would have prospered. He was incapable of working simply to make money; he couldn't do anything, in fact, except slap a brush on paper. One morning he had tied string around his only pair of boots—large black boots with square, squashed toe-caps (Olga remembered them well)—because the soles were coming away. It was later, years, decades later, that his fortunes improved and he started to earn good money for his work.

Olga's mother had once whispered to her that Georgii Maximovich had quite a lot of money in his savings account. Olga was glad, of course: she was assured that her mother would be taken care of, and it meant that she herself had somewhere to turn if she ever needed to be helped over a rough patch.

But that Saturday, Sergei did not want to go to see his father-in-law; it was as if he had a foreboding of something unpleasant.

"You go by yourself," he begged Olga. "Please . . ."

"No, I'd feel too embarrassed. You're the one who's asking for the money for your trip. If you don't come, they'll think it incredibly rude of you. You hardly ever go and see them, anyway."

"Tell them I'm sick. I really don't feel too good."

"No, if you don't go, I'm not going either. Then he'll withdraw his offer."

His unwillingness to see his relatives struck Olga as extremely hurtful. They had made a noble gesture: who else would lend them such a large sum of money? Their friends? Like hell they would! And in return for this generosity Sergei was merely being asked to show the absolute minimum of courtesy—to sit and drink a cup of tea, to talk to the old folks for a while. And, of course, to say "thank you" or "I'm most grateful," just a word or two as a token of his gratitude. Surely that wasn't so difficult, was it? No, it wasn't difficult; he even enjoyed chatting with Georgii Maximovich, who had such a vast fund of experience and who had actually lived in Paris himself, on the rue de Mouftard, but . . .

"Hell, what's the use of talking? If it isn't immediately obvious to you why I don't want to go, then there's no point in trying to explain. Having to ask people for things is sickening, unbearable, and that is what turns all the tea and talk and visits to relatives into something strained and awkward. Now, once again, I'm in the intolerable position of being a supplicant, and that's why I asked you, if possible, to save me from this ordeal. But if you can't, then by all means let's go. . . ."

She should have understood his feelings, but she didn't, because she was preoccupied with thoughts of her mother, who had also been placed in an awkward, perhaps, too, an intolerable position; but she had managed to overcome her distaste and had *asked* Georgii Maximovich.

"There are times when we have to do something unpleasant." Olga was adamant. "I know you don't like it. Now make up your mind: Do we go or do we stay at home?"

They took the trip in silence. Olga now had another cause to feel angry: Just why did he think he had the right to be resentful? What, in any case, was there to resent? The fact that he was going to France while she stayed behind? Irinka was silent too. She was very sensitive to arguments and tiffs between her parents, and she reacted in her own way. Unlike the role so often assigned to children in novels and movies, she did not try to distract them, cheer them up or make peace between them; she behaved in just the same way as her parents: if they sat in gloomy silence, so did she; if they were snappish and irritable, then she would adopt exactly the same irritable, querulous tone—little old woman.

So the bus ride to Sushchevskaya was spent in silence. They walked past the old house, then plunged into a maze of back alleys, where thanks to demolition and rebuilding nothing was any longer recognizable. Strange riddle: Why was Olga in such a glum mood as she approached her mother's house? And why was he? After all, they were both young, healthy, and working at jobs of their choice; he was about to go abroad, while she was planning to use that time to rearrange their apartment and was also counting on his bringing a few nice things back from Paris (she had already told him exactly what she wanted). And they were all three together . . . together! It was *their life*.

Yet they were gloomy as they went in the front door, gloomy as they got into the elevator. The only remark that Olga made was a stern command to her daughter: "Don't lean against that dirty wall!"

Her parents' apartment was small and comfortable. The hallway was decorated with some beautiful Hungarian wallpaper, carmine in color, while the wallpaper in the living room was a wood-grain pattern. Here Georgii Maximovich had tastefully arranged the remnants of his antique furniture; he had fixed up some shelves, placed bookcases here and there, and everything that in the old house had seemed like junk here acquired a special, expensive look of old-world distinction. In addition there was, of course, a multitude of pictures, engravings and drawings on the walls, not only by Georgii Maximovich but by other artists too; among these trifles were two little studies by Levitan and Korovin, some drawings by other notables, and—the pride of Georgii Maximovich's collection—a wavy pencil sketch by Modigliani, depicting something vaguely erotic. On all the shelves, bookshelves and the big bookcase stood candles: thin candles and fat candles, ornamental candles, candles of unusual shapes and shades that burned with a perfumed aroma, candles bought abroad by friends of Georgii Maximovich—on doctors' orders he himself no longer traveled abroad—and now all these were smoking, flickering, burning and giving off a sweet, delicious smell.

"The illuminations are in your honor, mesdames et monsieur!" With a flourish, Georgii Maximovich invited them into the living room. The words in French were spoken intentionally, and this obviously displeased Sergei: Olga noticed his lips pouting slightly in a familiar grimace. Although the act of generosity—making a loan to his wife's relatives—was being carried out at home, it was being done with ceremony. Georgii Maximovich himself had a ceremonious look: he was dressed in a black velvet artist's jacket (recently made for him in the tailoring workshops of the Moscow Society of Artists), a snow-white shirt, a violet silk foulard at his neck, and pants in the fashionable shade of charcoal gray, although the effect was a little spoiled by the fact that he was wearing his worn old carpet-slippers.

They began by sitting down to tea and cake. Irinka described her life at school, to which Olga listened with great interest, because at home Irinka never said a word about school; yet as soon as she was in the company of her grandparents or of other people who were not too close to her but also not absolute strangers, she revealed a genuine talent for descriptive storytelling and delighted in showing it off. Then Olga's mother took Olga and Irinka off to her bedroom and left the men together for a talk.

Georgii Maximovich began by describing his life in Paris, on the rue de Mouftard, which the Russian expatriates in Paris, his friends of those days, called the "Mouftarka." Two were from Odessa, one from Elizavetgrad and one from Vitebsk—the one who later became world famous. About the others, though, he now knew very little: one of them, he thought, had gone to America, others had died in obscurity, and one had been killed by the Germans when they occupied Paris. It had all happened so incredibly long ago. It was in the youth of the century, the youth of the epoch, the youth of airplanes, movies, soccer, modern art—everything that the world was crazy about now—and—coincidence!—it was Georgii Maximovich's own youth, too. So there were a lot of girls in his memories—their little jokes, their gestures, the way they took their clothes off and closed their eyes and what they said while they did so; he remembered being hungry; he recalled the cafés; he recollected working furiously, joyously, all through the night on some painting that no one had commissioned and was never going to earn any money. In recounting his memories Georgii Maximovich grew more and more animated, his large, fleshy, big-nosed face grew red; he took a violet silk handkerchief out of his jacket pocket to mop his bald head and his cheeks.

Olga imagined all this very vividly, because Sergei later retold the conversation in much colorful detail, just like an actor, imitating Georgii Maximovich's voice and movements.

"Actually I lived in Paris twice. . . . The first time was when I was just a boy, before the first war, but I understood nothing in those days. The second time was in the twenties, I was sent there officially, and then I understood a bit more. How shall I explain it? The second time we lived on the rue Vaugirard. It's the longest street in Paris. . . ."

Sergei thought: "The prologue is taking a very long time. When will he come to the point?" Georgii Maximovich talked for a little longer with fading enthusiasm, sweating and mopping himself with his handkerchief, telling something about his first wife, with whom he had lived on the rue Vaugirard and who had worked as a typist in the Soviet embassy. He had made sketches for a big picture of the Paris Commune—a picture which somehow never got finished.

"Now what can I tell you about Paris?" Georgii Maximovich mumbled in an unexpectedly weary voice. "Paris, of course, is beautiful. But it's no more beautiful than Odessa or Kiev. It doesn't have the Black Sea or the Dnieper, and the Seine, to be honest, is a rather dull and dirty river. In summer it's so hot and humid, you can hardly breathe.—"

Sergei asked whether Georgii Maximovich was implying that there was no point in going to Paris.

Georgii Maximovich shook his head and smiled a sly, meaningful smile. Oh no! Not at all. As an old, experienced gentleman who had seen a lot in his time, Georgii Maximovich was saying that in the past people had gone to Paris for two reasons. Firstly when they were very poor, hoping to cheat fate and make their pile there, and secondly when they were very rich, seeking to buy themselves some pleasure and squander their money. And as for modern tourism, Georgii Maximovich had no idea what it was like and didn't propose to venture an opinion. Sergei laughed. "I get you. I don't belong either to the first or the second category, and anyway . . ."

"Heavens, my dear boy, I'm not trying to dissuade you from going. In fact, at your mother-in-law's request I've taken out a certain amount of *argent* so that you can.—"

A wad of ten-ruble bills appeared from a pocket of the velvet jacket.

"There you are," said Georgii Maximovich, showing all his plastic teeth as he beamed with pleasure and kindness and handed the wad to Sergei.

"Thank you," said Sergei. But he did not take the packet of money. As he said later, in that second he felt a strange shift of perception: it was just as if everything suddenly started moving backward.

Georgii Maximovich put the money on the table alongside Sergei. They went on with their conversation. Georgii Maximovich asked him about his work and how his dissertation was progressing.

His dissertation was going badly. Sergei didn't like talking about it. His answers started to get spasmodic and offhand, and to one of Georgii Maximovich's questions he gave no reply at all, but simply switched off, hummed a tune, and looked out of the window, obviously thinking about something else.

"Couldn't I help you in any way?" asked Georgii Maximovich.

Sergei thanked him and said that no one could help him. What could anyone do to help? He wasn't painting a fence or digging the garden. He gradually became more heated. Georgii Maximovich was showing him sympathy, and sympathy being something he particularly detested, it was then that he finally decided not to take the money.

"Do you know what I used to do whenever my work wasn't going right?" mused the old man, failing to sense that at this moment the tactful thing to do was to say nothing. "I found the strength in me to scrap what I'd done and start all over again . . ."

"Yes, yes, I understand." Sergei nodded, smiling.

"You're up a blind alley—isn't that so?" The old man outlined a shape with a vague gesture. "You need to step back a few paces and start looking—am I right?—for some new way, a different approach. One must always be flexible, and then . . ."

"You're absolutely right, *cher maître*. And your work is a

perfect example . . ." (Olga came into the room at that moment and as she heard these words she groaned inwardly, realizing that Sergei was in the last stage of irritation and was about to resort to sarcasm) ". . . but please don't worry, Georgii Maximovich. Everything will work out all right, I promise you." Seeing Olga, he said hastily, "Come on, we've already stayed too long. Time to go home."

Georgii Maximovich exclaimed, "Wait, you've forgotten something! Take it!" He waved the bundle of money over his head like a flag.

The word "something" produced a new burst of sarcasm from Sergei:

"Not 'something' but a certain sum of money, which you, Georgii Maximovich, have very kindly . . . and so on. I am extremely grateful to you, but I can manage without it, thank you. Thank you very much."

Out on the street, after a long silence, he told Olga that she shouldn't talk to her parents or to anyone else about his problems with the dissertation—or about any of his affairs for that matter. The presence of Irinka restrained him somewhat, but Olga could see that he was seething. He hissed a series of short, cryptic remarks whose meaning Irinka could not understand, but she could see that her parents were quarreling and that it was her father who was on the attack, so she took Olga protectively by the arm and stared angrily at Sergei. She was eleven years old at the time, and already quite able to join in grown-up conversations. He was saying that he found any sort of sympathetic inquiries, advice, and recommendations drawn from other people's experience not merely useless but—oh, they could all go to hell! For a long time Olga kept herself in check as she could see that he was abnormally wound up, but when he said something that was an obvious slander— "I've warned you more than once not to tell anyone about my affairs, but you just can't help shooting your mouth off about them, can you?"—she could restrain herself no longer and retorted that this was a lie: she never indulged in indiscreet chatter, and there was no need to take out his bad temper on her.

"Then how does Georgii Maximovich know about them in such detail?"

"You told him yourself!"

"Anyway, why can't you write a dissertation?" shouted Irinka.

"You keep out of this." He slapped his daughter on the top of her head. "Shut up!"

Irinka ran ahead of them, shouting and leaping up and down in time to her words:

"You're no good! You're no good! Can't write a dissertation! Can't write a dissertation!"

Irinka's silly outburst had an unexpected effect on Sergei: he laughed aloud, then fell silent and did not utter another word until they were home.

But what was happening to him? She could not understand it. This was not that she was too preoccupied with her own work at the laboratory or with the complex relationships that existed as much in her professional world as everywhere else— she had, in fact, a talent for getting on well with people and was not afraid of the complexities—but because his subject, history, seemed to her such a baffling fusion of simplicity and mystery. What could be simpler, one might think, than describing *what had already happened*? All the exact sciences were concerned with advance, with moving forward, with constructing something new, creating what had never existed before, and only Sergei's discipline, history, was devoted to restructuring what was old, recreating the past. Olga had a mental image of history as a vast, endless sequence in which epochs, nations, great men, kings, generals, and revolutionaries stood in line one behind the other; to her, the historian's job was rather like that of the policeman who was stationed outside the entrance of the local movie theater to keep order whenever a film was being premiered: to ensure, in other words, that the epochs and the nations didn't get mixed up or change places, that the great men didn't try pushing ahead in the line, didn't quarrel, and didn't try to get a ticket to immortality out of turn.

This simple policemanlike activity, however, caused Sergei a great deal of frustration and distress—and herein lay the mystery that her mind could not grasp. Why couldn't he just sit diligently in the archives for a month, or two months, or five months, or however long was necessary, and extract from that gigantic lineup everything that concerned the czarist secret police in Moscow in the period immediately before the February Revolution, and then carefully work up all that material into presentable form? After all, the historian didn't have to create something totally new. He didn't have the problems that faced her and her colleague Andrei Ivanovich in their work on BSCC—biological stimulation of cell compatibility; they were trying to create something that had never before existed—not in America, not in Japan, nor in Ancient Greece, nor in Egypt, nowhere in the world. Sergei sat in the archives from morning till night. He had filled thirty-six notebooks with transcribed material. Thirty-six! She had recently counted them. And yet he still felt that something was missing, some final bit of information, some ultimate insight; or perhaps the missing factor was his own lack of dedication, of will power.

Being, in fact, prone to a sudden fading of interest, or to be more exact, to the development of an interest in something else, he had decided against the trip to France. He suddenly announced that he had lost all desire to go: "I can't spare the time right now." They called him up from the committee to tell him that the size of the party had been reduced and that he, unfortunately, would not be going. He listened with indifference and in a languid voice—as though out of mere politeness—he murmured a few words in response: "Oh, really? What a pity. . . ." The committee members no doubt thought he was exhibiting amazing self-control while actually being overcome with disappointment. But Olga saw that his indifference was genuine: he had simply lost interest.

He said to her, "What's the point of going to France? Everything that I need can be found here."

At first he needed a very great deal of material. Not being fully aware of the nature and scope of the work he had planned to do, she felt with increasing frequency that he had taken on something that was too big, even perhaps boundless. She cited as an example Andrei Ivanovich's dissertation—a doctoral, not a master's dissertation—on biological stimulators, written with amazing terseness and economy, without a single superfluous detail. The whole thing worked, as it were, by springs; it was as simple and dynamic as a Yale lock, of which the spring was the central idea—Andrei Ivanovich's single insight of genius into the diffusional structure of stimulators. It was this that made Olga ask Sergei: "And what is *your* idea? Do you have in your mind some all-embracing concept that will weld all your notebooks, transcripts, facts and quotations into one integral whole?"

It was not said as a reproach, but from a desire to help. Sergei, however, never talked seriously to her about his work— or rather he never finished saying what was on his mind. She felt he always left some thoughts stored in the cellar, like some emergency reserve. But suppose . . . suppose it turned out that there was no reserve there at all, and all his evasions had just been a bluff, or more precisely that he had been *bluffing himself?* Gena Klimuk had hinted at this when he came to see Olga one day—still at the beginning of his career as an academic administrator—for a confidential talk about Sergei.

She had found it difficult to understand what Klimuk had wanted; it had not been clear then and was now even less so, since the details had been forgotten. He had suddenly appeared on a day when Sergei was in Leningrad; he was carrying a bunch of mimosa, wearing a red shirt and red socks just as if he were a student again. He embraced Olga and even gave her one of his pecks on her cheek. She said, "Genitalich!" Threatening him with her finger, she added: "You're only supposed to kiss your friends' wives when their husbands are there."

He told her not to use that idiotic nickname, because ladies were frightened by it.

For a moment a look of cunning flickered across his aging little boy's features, and Olga felt—in her heart, as usual when it was something to do with Sergei—that the cunning was only a mask for feelings of bitter animosity. What did he want? He droned tediously on about a "false position," about some "obligations," about the institute's having accepted Sergei on certain conditions but that Sergei had managed—with Fedya's help—to get the topic of his dissertation changed and this was, for some reason, a bad thing. She couldn't understand why it was bad; apparently it spoiled the institute's plans or something of the sort.

"We met him halfway," he said in a tone of increasing

severity. "We agreed to his request to our own detriment."

He was not talking like a friend but like an official. This startled her. For the first few minutes her attitude toward him was familiar and very slightly scornful, because she was aware that from having been a friend he was now changing for the worse, and she wanted to teach him a lesson, but after a while his language and the tone of his voice so stunned her that quite involuntarily and out of sheer perplexity she began responding to him as though she were a subordinate.

"All right," she said, "I'll tell him. I'll give him the message."

One thing was clear: The institute officials could, if they wanted to, prevent the submission of his dissertation.

The whole diatribe was dressed up in the guise of concern for Sergei—how he was destroying himself, how he had taken the wrong direction and was rummaging around amid the debris of history and had lost the guiding thread.

"Sergei is horribly obstinate, you know that"—he suddenly interrupted his pompous speech with this one human remark—"and if he's not stopped in time, he'll ruin himself."

She couldn't decide whether to tell Sergei or to keep it from him for a while. He came back from Leningrad tired and angry: everything there had been terrible—the weather, the hotel; his colleagues had been disrespectful and failed to show him sufficient attention, and worst of all, he had failed to find what he had been looking for in the archives. But she told him all the same. To her amazement, he took the news calmly and was even able to dismiss it with a condescending laugh:

"Poor fools, they're terrified that I'll defend Brosov . . ." Tolya Brosov was a researcher whom Klimuk was trying to hound out of the institute.

That was not, however, the real matter at issue: Brosov, it transpired, had nothing to do with the case, and two years later, when Sergei's own "case" was being investigated, Brosov and Klimuk joined forces to mount a concerted attack on Sergei. They objected to the method that he insisted on using and that he called half-jokingly, half-seriously "grave-robbery." The letters "GR" were written on the covers of many of his notebooks, the metaphor describing his quest for the threads that link the recent past with the distant past and with the future.

From remarks that he made at various times she managed to piece together his guiding principle, which was that the individual is the thread stretching through time, the super-sensitive nerve of history that can be teased out and separated—and from which one can then learn a great deal. Man, he used to say, is never reconciled with death, because implanted in him is a sense that the thread of which he forms a part is endless. It is not God who rewards man with immortality, nor is the concept of immortality instilled into him by religion, but by that innate, genetically coded awareness of being a link in an infinite chain. She used to smile when she listened to him holding forth in this vein at dinner or in bed, at moments when he would suddenly feel the urge to smoke and philosophize. Did he expect her, a biologist and a materialist, to put forward a refutation of these theories of his? If only she could refashion her cast of mind, even if only for a moment, but unfortunately it was not within her power. The only thing she knew firmly was that everything began and ended with chemistry: in all the universe, and beyond its bounds, there was nothing that could not be expressed in chemical formulae. Several times he had asked her quite seriously:

"You don't really think, do you, that we disappear from the world without a trace? That I will disappear?"

And she had replied with genuine amazement: "Do *you* really think that we won't?"

To this his answer was that no matter how he might rack his brains or strain his imagination, he could not conceive . . .

And now he had disappeared. He was nowhere; he had merged with the infinite, which he had once discussed so lightly while smoking a cigarette. My God, though, if everything begins and ends with chemistry, why was there such pain? Because that sort of pain wasn't chemistry, was it? And *their life,* which had suddenly been extinguished like a burned-out light bulb—had that simply been a combination of formulae? A person departs from the world, his departure is accompanied by an emanation in the form of pain; then the pain will fade and at some point—when those who feel the pain themselves leave the world—it will vanish completely. Completely, completely. Nothing but chemistry . . . Chemistry and pain—that is all that death and life consist of.

For Sergei, what he called "grave-robbery" (but was more precisely his way of trying to make contact with that endless thread) began with his own family, with the thread of which he himself was a particle. He started with his father, for whose faint memory he felt a great love. He thought of his father as a great man, which was no doubt an exaggeration and, in a certain sense, arrogance. It derived in large measure from his mother, who had worshiped her husband and had placed him in a private hierarchy of the great, the sequence of which ran approximately thus: Gorky; Lunacharsky, the first People's Commissar for Education; Nadezhda Krupskaya, Lenin's wife; and her husband, Afanasy Dementievich Troitsky. After the civil war, Afanasy Dementievich had held some post in the field of education. In 1917, after the February Revolution, while still a student at Moscow University, he had worked in the commission investigating the archives of the czarist gendarmerie. The commission had revealed the names of the secret informers who had worked for the police. When Sergei discovered this fact—his father's participation in the work of this commission—he had begun burrowing in the archives and became fascinated with the whole story. From there—in an attempt to find out why his father had undertaken this work and what were his origins—he began studying his father's family, then his grandfather's family as far back as his great-grandfather, for which purpose he traveled to Penza.

Olga guessed that he had somehow ventured too far and too deeply into this research. It was all very interesting, entertaining even, but—what was it for? It was like the occasion when someone had given them an address at which, if they wanted to, they could meet the grandson of a famous poet, and he had seized on the idea with enthusiasm.

"Yes, we must go!"

The invitation came from a woman who worked with Olga. The poet's grandson, she said, would not have much time to spare; he would drink a cup of tea, stay for perhaps a half-hour and then leave not later than five o'clock. The meeting took place in one of the high, slablike apartment houses in the new suburb of Cheryomushki. Everything in that totally anonymous, standardized little room seemed to consist of fragments salvaged from the wreckage of the past. Around the table, covered with a plain tablecloth—the hostess pulled back a corner of it and showed them the carefully polished inlaid antique tabletop—alongside the usual hideous mass-produced chairs stood two simple, elegant chairs of the early nineteenth century with gilded sphinx-heads on their high backs, while the party drank tea out of antique cups that were made in the Kuznetsov and Gardner factories and were, of course, also fragments of long-scattered tea services.

The poet's grandson was middle-aged, ash-blond, with a wrinkled face and fashionably close-cropped hair. He wore a blue jacket adorned with several little medallions and badges. He clinked his teaspoon against the side of his cup, drummed his fingers on the table and monopolized the conversation with a long, breathless, wordy yet incoherent story about his attempt to exchange apartments. Now and again he repeated the phrase "with regard to." Olga stared wide-eyed at the grandson and felt shy at first, not knowing what to say to him; Sergei, too, said nothing and sat looking sulky, but then Olga began discussing the business of changing apartments and gave the grandson some advice, as she and Sergei themselves had recently completed a satisfactory exchange of apartments.

"With regard to the fact," muttered the grandson, "that we are approaching the centenary of Lenin's birth . . . With regard to that I have composed a letter . . . Academician Veleglasov has promised to sign it, and Sanin, the actor, has already signed it. . . ."

The old ladies talked to each other in French. Soon the grandson hastily took his leave, pecked one of the old ladies on the cheek, kissed the hands of the others and said, as he wrapped a sandwich in a table napkin: "There's nowhere to get anything to eat there; it's an awful place with regard to that."

One of the old ladies asked: "Where are you going today, Alexis?"

"Oh, a long way away, *ma tante*."

The grandson made a sibilant, whistling noise when he talked. "But transportation for getting there is excellent: by metro to Sokolniki and then a five-minute bus ride. . . ."

When he had gone the old ladies explained that on Sunday afternoons he refereed soccer matches. What else could he do? He was an engineer, his salary was low, and he had a sick wife and two children. . . .

Olga and Sergei walked along the dark boulevard. He was gloomy. "It would have been better not to have come. . . . One of two things: either there is some untapped mystery hidden inside that blockhead or the famous poet had something wrong 'with regard to' his head."

Sergei thought that the thread of human continuity should function as a channel through which certain indestructible elements were transmitted between the generations. The concept had more to do with biology than with history. Now that he was engaged in a detailed study of the Moscow secret police on the eve of the February Revolution and was using documents to compile lists of secret informers together with their professional "achievements" and their "services to their country" (a tedious job, which took no less than two years of painstaking work, although it was only one part of his dissertation), what interested him as much as anything was the same thing that had driven him to meet the poet's grandson: the search for those elusive threads. It seemed to Sergei that something extremely important was concealed behind all this. At times he worked with furious enthusiasm. He would come home from the library or the archives with a face the color of putty, he could hardly stand and could not sit down to dinner straightaway: he would have to lie down for several minutes to rest his heart. For the last two years before his death he had become so weakened that he even stopped drinking. If they were invited out, he refused. His work absorbed him so much that he put into it much more than he should have, more than it could absorb.

One day he came home looking as if he had been drinking. He had an odd smile on his face. She was frightened, because if he had been drinking it meant that something terrible had happened.

"Have you been drinking?" she asked.

"No. Just one on the way home."

He kept smiling that strange smile. She could see that there was some reason for it.

His mother sensed something, too, and hovered around the kitchen, where Olga was cooking dinner. She knew that he was not always prepared to speak frankly in front of his mother, so Olga refrained from asking Sergei any questions as long as his mother was in the kitchen. Meanwhile Sergei sat with his legs crossed, like a stranger who didn't belong there, wagging the toe of his shoe and staring out of the window. As soon as her mother-in-law had left the room, Olga said quietly:

"Tell me about it . . . I can see something's happened."

He nodded and said nothing. When his omelet was ready, he prodded it with his fork and left it uneaten. His mother came back into the kitchen, ears cocked to catch every word, so Olga purposely started telling him some trivial piece of gossip that she had heard at work. Then he drank some strong tea, after which his pallor left him and he looked visibly better. They went to their bedroom (now, since exchanging their apartment, Irinka had her own room, Alexandra Prokofievna had hers, and Olga and Sergei had a shared room in which *their life* took place), he shut the door firmly, took Olga by the hand and said:

"Well, they've really given me a bashing this time. My supervisory committee discussed my dissertation in front of the academic council and they shot so many holes in it that I'll have to do two more years' work on it, if not longer, before I can submit it. Only don't tell Mother!"

He said it all in a voice of utter gloom, but his final remark—"Only don't tell Mother!"—was spoken with a nervous intensity that betrayed something like real fear. At all costs his mother mustn't know. Olga couldn't decide whether his motivation in this was genuine concern for his mother's peace of mind or—which, if true, was appalling—his perpetual dependence on the old woman's opinion and moods, his compulsion to explain and justify himself to her.

The news, of course, was bad. She knew what it meant when a dissertation failed at the preliminary discussion; she had been anxiously waiting for this to happen, but he had concealed the fact that the discussion was being held today. What extraordinary people he and his mother both were. They were always having to stress that they were loners, that they could manage on their own, that they would somehow always cope. He had gone to the discussion without telling anyone, just as eight years ago his mother went to hospital for a dangerous operation without letting them know. "Grandma went out this morning and said she would be late getting home," Irinka had said. The old lady had called up that evening to announce that she was in hospital and that it was all over—but *what* was all over, for God's sake?!—and she would be coming home next day.

Olga was overwhelmed by Sergei's news. She was also annoyed by the remark, made with real fear in his voice: "Only don't tell mother!" She said it was a stupid thing to say and this wasn't the moment to be worrying about his mother's feelings. He asked, "Well, what should I be worrying about?"

"Worry about the real problem—how to get out of trouble— and not about domestic trivia."

Of course she shouldn't have let her irritation show. Was he anxious about his reputation as a model son? She knew, of course, that he wasn't a model son at all, and therefore it annoyed her even more when he suddenly insisted on acting as if he were. She had to bite her tongue until it hurt, in order to prevent herself from shouting it out; because he really was in trouble and you don't hit a man when he's down. Yet a demon egged her on, and in a half whisper (afraid that her mother-in-law might knock or even walk in without knocking), with unusual venom in her voice she said: "Instead of worrying so much about your dear mama, you should have shown the same amount of concern for your dissertation."

Looking exhausted and resigned, like a man prepared to accept anything, he asked, "What do you mean?"

"You should have prepared the ground. Talked to people. Talked to everybody whose influence counts. But you with your usual sloppiness just let everything take its course. It's your own fault. That's not the way things are done."

He shrugged. "But I thought they would . . ."

"Why did you think that? Why should they? What are you to them?" and more advice in the same shrill, schoolmarmish vein. Sergei said nothing, looking at her with a glazed stare;

he had the same look whenever he was suddenly plunged into thought.

Then he asked, "Do you seriously mean it?"

As she continued her lecture, irritation brought her basest feelings boiling to the surface. He gestured defensively and went out, to return a minute later with a suitcase. At first she didn't realize that he was intending to go away, but when he said he was going to spend a few days in the country at Aunt Pasha's cottage (which was absurd: no one had invited him to Vasilkovo; there was no room for him to stay there, because now that the summer was over Pasha's relatives had all moved back into the cottage from their summertime shacks), she lost her temper and her self-control, shouting at him that he was running away like a coward and that if he went to the country now she would wash her hands of all responsibility for his health and well-being, and furthermore, she would give him no money. She yelled incoherently, shamefully, in the way people yell only in the grip of furious anger. The shouting brought her mother-in-law and Irinka running in from their rooms. And Sergei immediately told his mother about the discussion, about the savage criticism of his dissertation and the news that its submission was postponed by at least two more years. Olga found it incomprehensible: at one moment he was ordering her not to tell his mother—and at the next he himself was explaining it to her in detail.

It was, of course, a blow to his mother, but not such a blow as it was to Olga. The old woman always assumed an air of dignified authority at difficult moments, whenever she felt that a display of wisdom and sang-froid was called for. At such times she liked to think of herself as indispensable.

"Keep calm, comrades, there's no need to panic. Whatever we do, let's not panic," she declared in the tones of a commissar encouraging the troops. "What, precisely, has happened? You've been given a reprimand? Good. The more criticism you get, the better, because then the quality of your finished work will be higher. I really don't see why you're being so weak-kneed about it, Sergei . . ."

"No one's being weak-kneed. It's just that I don't like the whole disgusting business."

"You're not meant to like it. How could anyone like it? But

you can't just . . . When your father . . . If it had been your father . . ." As she tried to calm him down, her tone gradually changed from commissar to kind old granny; she finally even patted him on the cheek. This gesture struck Olga as false. She talked to him as if he were a ten-year-old boy, and he played up to it. Olga said that there was, in fact, no panic; what Sergei had to do was to think it all over calmly, to take note of the adverse comments, to revise whatever was necessary and whatever, in his own view, was genuinely in need of revision—in other words, to roll up his sleeves and get down to the job but *not* to give way to weakness. Sergei wanted to go to the country, which was wrong: that was simply running away from the problem.

Essentially right though it might have been, Olga's view was mistimed at that particular moment. She should not have used the word "weakness." Sergei listened to her gloomily and went on tossing things into the suitcase.

"No, you're wrong, Olga," said Alexandra Prokofievna, switching back from her grandmotherly tone to one of metallic, commissarlike firmness. "You're profoundly mistaken. If he feels he ought to go to Vasilkovo, then let him go. He can take his books and his notebooks and work in peace."

"But he *won't* work! He'll drink vodka with Kolka. And at night he'll feel bad."

"Papa, Mama doesn't want you to go, so don't go!" said Irinka as she went up to the suitcase and started throwing her father's clothes out of it.

He slapped her and she ran away, clutching some of his underwear and his electric razor. The argument about whether he should go lasted until ten o'clock that night, without any decision being reached. By then it was too late to go. Alexandra Prokofievna continued to act out her self-chosen role of family arbiter, full of nobility and justice:

"I don't understand why you both look so miserable. The submission is postponed, so Sergei's raise in pay is postponed too—is that what's worrying you? Forget it. You'll survive. At your age we never thought about money at all. Who bothered about money? Private traders, grasping peasants, and people who had lost their property at the revolution. But we had no time for that sort of thing. We were too absorbed in life, work, friends, events. Yes, events! Don't smile, Irinka. At your age I was up to date on all the political news, I knew what was happening at the front, I cut clippings from the papers, but all you can think about is movies and ice cream. In the twenties, Sergei's father had a very modest salary, the furniture in our apartment was supplied by the government. We needed nothing except books—and even books Afanasy Dementievich borrowed from libraries. He never owned a suit, he never wore a tie. Don't worry, Sergei, if necessary I'll help you out if money gets really tight. You've got to work without worrying about anything."

Two days later he went to Vasilkovo.

What hurt Olga was the fact that whenever things were going badly for him his instinct was to go away somewhere, and not with her but alone. This implied that she was no support to him. His mother thought this, which was unfair and dishonest—as dishonest as her suggestion to him that the only reason why Olga was worried about the failure of his dissertation was that they would lose the extra money that would accrue when he got his master's degree. She didn't think about money! The thought of money never entered her head. In fact, apart from Irinka, who saved money in a piggy bank to buy a new record or perhaps a three-ruble necklace, no one in their family thought about money. There was no need to be so self-righteous about being "above" such considerations. What really hurt Olga—and was the reason why she had exploded and shouted at him so disgracefully—was that his instant reaction was *to go away from her*. As though she were the cause of all the trouble, as though without her he would be saved. After a while, though, when she had calmed down a little, she became reconciled to the idea, and Sergei, also having cooled down and thinking things over, decided not to go to Vasilkovo. But the arrival of Klimuk upset everything again.

Klimuk came on the day after the discussion. He and Sergei went out for a walk. It lasted a long time—so long, in fact, that Olga started to worry. Sergei returned at half-past eleven.

"That's it!" he said. *"Finita la commedia!* After a row like that, Gennadii and I are through. He's hopeless."

There was no regret in his voice. The inevitable had happened. She only asked, "What was the reason?"

"Huh!" He gestured dismissively. "Everything . . ."

His expression was distracted, as though he didn't want to tell her what had happened and it wasn't worth the trouble. But soon afterward he told her everything. They made love. Somehow she had a particularly vivid memory of their lovemaking that night, when he first told her about Kislovsky. Usually he fell asleep immediately afterward; making love affected him like a sleeping pill, whereas Olga, on the contrary, stayed awake for a long time, and the more intense their lovemaking the longer it took her to go to sleep. That night, however, he was keyed up and wanted to talk; he told her that Klimuk had tried to persuade him to hand some research material over to Kislovsky, who needed it for his doctoral dissertation. He had refused, saying that he didn't want to lose such valuable material, which was not to be found even in the archives and of which he possessed the only copy. Klimuk said it was better to lose the material than to lose one's dissertation. This really started the swearing match. The question of this material was, it seems, a long-standing bone of contention between them. Klimuk called Sergei an idiot, and he said to Klimuk: "You're a shit!"

What was this material? She could only remember that when Sergei acquired it—which happened unexpectedly, by sheer chance—he had been excited beyond all measure. It was the lists of names of the secret informers working for the Moscow division of the czarist police during the period from 1910 right up to the February Revolution of 1917. The material was, of course, priceless, because all the records of the czarist secret police had been destroyed. Somehow or other he had managed to acquire these lists. He had found a man, who may have been an alcoholic or a crook, or maybe just a seedy old tramp (Olga never saw him; he had an odd name—Selifon or Selivan, or something of the sort) who sold the lists to Sergei for thirty rubles. Apparently his grandfather had been a minor official in the czarist police and had kept the lists in order to extract money from people by blackmail. For a time

Sergei had been very interested in this man's story, which was quite fantastic. Some of the people at the institute didn't believe Sergei and said that Selifon had fooled him, that the lists were forgeries, that someone had fabricated them, if not recently then in the twenties, though they might well have used them for blackmail. In particular there was a certain Professor Vyatkin at the institute who hotly contested the authenticity of the lists. It was during his dispute with Vyatkin that Sergei had conceived the idea of going to Gorodets. And of course it was these lists—in the folder tied with pink ribbon—that Bezyazichny and now Klimuk were so keen to have Olga hand over.

Why should she? Kislovsky wasn't in the institute any longer. She would never give them up; she could see no reason why she should help Klimuk in any way.

When Sergei went away alone to Vasilkovo—by then it was the last week in September—her sufferings began. A day, another day, a third passed. At first she fought against her feelings. She tried to conquer the nagging unease, the awareness of missing him, worrying about him—which was nothing other than *deadly, humiliating dependence on him,* and she adjured herself not to think, not to remember him, to load herself with work. He didn't want her to go and join him. He needed to be alone—and she understood that need, she truly understood it. But disquiet, or longing, or God knows what else it was—a sort of merciless, corrosive anxiety—grew inexorably within her, and she knew that sooner or later she would go to him; it was only a question of finding a pretext. And at that very moment along came a letter bearing the official seal of the institute, containing the formal notification and results of the assessment of Sergei's dissertation: the discussion had taken place, such-and-such modifications had been suggested (here followed a long list), and the date of submission for the completed dissertation was postponed until such-and-such a month of the following year. Without even waiting until the weekend, Olga took a day off from work on Friday and went, armed with the letter.

Vasilkovo had been part of *their life* for a long time. Irinka was about four or five; their tenancy of a *dacha* on the Klyazma River had ended, and they were in a hurry to find a new one. They were advised to try the countryside to the north of Moscow, and one day they just took the train, without any address, and got off after a fifty-minute ride—they simply liked the deserted platform, the clumps of trees, the expanse of meadows—and walked toward the little village on the horizon.

Aunt Pasha's cottage was distinguished by a wooden plaque on which hung an ax. It was this that made them stop. Why a hatchet? What was the reason for it? As they stood discussing it with Irinka, Pasha came out into the yard and they asked her about it ". . . because our little girl is curious to know." Aunt Pasha explained that when there was a fire in the village, a hatchet was always needed. Other cottages had plaques with other implements—one had a bucket, another a grappling hook. So they stayed, and arranged to rent the house from Aunt Pasha, the "house with the hatchet." Years later, after they had spent several hot, or cloudy, or damp, or sunny summers with Aunt Pasha (her husband Vanya, or Ivan Panteleimonovich, to give him his full name, was a quiet, insignificant little man, a carpenter who traveled the countryside with his cooperative team of carpenters, so that he was never at home in summer and no one regarded him as the head of the household: that was unmistakably Pasha and only Pasha, a tall, powerfully built, hard-working, loud-mouthed but kindhearted woman) and Sergei had come to know her and her family thoroughly well, he would often revert in conversation to their first discovery of the house, to the hatchet. He was particularly fond of talking about it when he was a little drunk: "The house with the hatchet! There's a hidden meaning in it. It's a symbol . . . full of significance. . . ."

Sometimes he would seem to philosophize on it quite seriously, and at other times, when neighboring weekenders dropped in for a cup of tea or to borrow some pickled mushrooms—such as Lev Semyonovich, a physicist, or the charming old Goryansky, a retired vaudeville actor—he would gabble endless nonsense about the hatchet, fooling around and assuming a high-falutin', old-regime style of language: "Are you aware, gentlemen, of the name of this dwelling in which you are drinking your vodka? It is the house with the hatchet.

So you must be careful . . ." It seemed now as if he had played the fool once too often and brought disaster on himself as a result.

The day was crisp and clear, but already there was a chill in the air; the sky was cloudless; the path through the woods smelled of fallen leaves, a favorite smell of Olga's, like the smell of soured wine—and she hastened onward, noticing nothing around her, breathing in that smell and growing intoxicated by it. She was hurrying to see him as if they had not seen each other for years. Yet only four days had passed. He was sitting on the porch with a book and when he saw her he said: "Oh, it's you . . ."

He didn't smile, didn't jump from his chair, didn't kiss her and didn't even relieve her of the weight of the heavy bags she was carrying, full of food in cans and packages, and two bottles of Egri Bikaver, the red Hungarian wine (their shared fondness for dry red wine, which began countless years ago, still persisted, although nowadays it was more of a tradition, an echo of better times; Olga, in particular, especially cherished the memory of red wine, and the fact that she had carried two bottles of it all the way from the city meant a great deal in their language); he only sketched a limp movement with one hand which might have been either a halfhearted greeting or a gesture meaning "It's no good; I'm all washed up," and went indoors. Despite this lukewarm welcome, she had decided to forgive him for everything. She picked up the book he had been reading: Pushkin. It was somewhat tattered and dirty, and no doubt it came from Kolka's bookshelf.

Olga sat down on the porch, not knowing where he had gone and why. She put her bags down on the floor.

After a short while he came back, and asked with an angry look, "Why did you come?"

She should have said that she simply couldn't bear life without him, that she hadn't the strength for such an ordeal; it was absurd, because they were not having a quarrel; they had parted on good terms, and she understood that he needed to spend some time alone. But what could she do if she hadn't the strength? Instead, she waved the letter from the institute at him, speaking some banal-sounding nonsense. He shouted, "Why did you come?" And shook his two fists in front of his face.

Afraid that he was about to burst into tears and fall down, she ran indoors, calling for Aunty Pasha. The house was empty. She scooped up a mug of water from the bucket and ran back out to the porch. Sergei was lying on a folding cot, facing the window. She sat down beside him, stroked his hair and said in a low voice that she had been worried about him because he had left home in such a bad mood. They were all worried—his mother and Irinka too. The mention of his mother and daughter should have had a calming effect on him, but instead he shouted: "Don't lie! Don't try and drag Irinka and Mother into this."

She tried to explain, but he refused to listen.

"Don't lie! Don't lie, I tell you," he repeated. "You came of your own will, and of course only because you are imagining the most idiotic suspicions . . ."

"Nothing of the sort! What nonsense!"

Her denial was sincere, because she never admitted to herself the suspicions that did, in fact, plague her. It seemed to her that what upset her was something else. Therefore her suspicions did not, as it were, exist, so she could deny the accusation with an honest expression of anger on her face. But, God, how relieved she had suddenly felt when she saw him sitting alone on the porch and reading a book.

"What are you talking about? What suspicions? Forget it, my dear; we're past it at our age. You've missed that boat by now, and so have I for that matter. . . ."

She was thirty-nine at the time. And he was forty. But she never lost an opportunity to remind him that his days of philandering were over. It always amused her whenever he sat down in the metro and began staring at some girl sitting opposite. She would sometimes tease him on this subject and he would get angry. . . . She started talking again about the letter from the institute, which she was still holding in her hand. He snatched the letter away from her, crumpled it and threw it into the bushes.

"I don't want to read it, I know it all already . . . to hell with it," he muttered. "Brilliant, aren't you? There's only one

way to treat that crap: Forget it! But you, as if on purpose
. . . I need that letter like I need a hole in the head!"

She wanted to help him, but she didn't know how to. Pasha
and her husband, Ivan Panteleimonovich, came back from
digging potatoes in some distant field. They were delighted
when they saw her:

"Lord! It's you, Olga Vasilievna! Your man has been quite
down in the mouth without you."

Everything was confused, because these people didn't understand what was happening between her and Sergei. She felt
extremely sorry for him and wanted to help. What had driven
him out here, to this age-blackened frame house and its old-
fashioned country porch, with strings of onions hanging from
the rafters, with a jumble of cans and sacks piled on the floor?
Aunty Pasha's hands, as she cooked supper, smelled of earth.
Ivan Panteleimonovich twiddled the knobs on his transistor
radio and talked to Sergei about the American president and
the Suez Canal, while Pasha with warm interest inquired
about Irinka and Alexandra Prokofievna, also about Olga's
mother and Georgii Maximovich, who made occasional visits
to Vasilkovo. Georgii Maximovich used to say that Pasha had
"an interesting face" and induced her to pose for him. Then
Pasha and Ivan Panteleimonovich complained that the potatoes this year were small and the crop poor, that it was almost too late to try digging them now; there was no hope of
borrowing a horse and cart, it was a long way to carry sacks
of potatoes on your back, and the potato field was now "on
the poles": that is, it lay across the path of a new high-voltage
power line; a trench had been dug right across the middle of
it and planted with poles. As Olga listened, looking at Aunty
Pasha and Ivan Panteleimonovich she thought to herself:
"They're old, Pasha is over sixty and he is nearly seventy, but
they still toil away with all their strength, dig the soil, carry
sacks of potatoes and do countless other sorts of hard work
day in and day out; yet they don't think their life is particularly hard." Suddenly she said on impulse, for a joke:

"Sergei, you sit here reading a book while these old folk
break their backs digging potatoes. You should get up and help
them . . ."

Pasha turned on her, while Ivan Panteleimonovich simply

waved the suggestion aside: "Why should he? The very idea. Let him rest. And let's not hear another word about it."

From outside came the roar of a motorcycle: Kolka had arrived. Both he and his father were short and thin, with pale, finely molded features, blue-eyed, fair-haired (although the old man's hair was mostly gray); both had a trick of twisting their lips into a look of cunning whenever they smiled, while in conversation Kolka still lowered his eyes bashfully, like a girl. Only after a few drinks did he become bold and talkative.

As he spooned up his cabbage soup, with which he ate first a slice of brown bread and then a sausage—he had brought home a huge sackful of sausages, from which Pasha immediately took a dozen and fried them; she was very pleased with Kolka's booty. He told how the lumber store at Istomino (the same village at which he had been so lucky with the sausages) had gotten in a stock of fence rails, laths and squared beams, just what they needed to repair the gate, and how he had tried to make a deal, but for some reason the old man in charge of the store had refused to agree with his offer. As he said all this, Kolka seemed strangely embarrassed and would not look at Olga. She had long ago noticed that the young man was shy in her presence. One day she could not help mentioning this to Sergei:

"You know, I think Kolka . . ."

"Well, what?"

"I think he rather fancies me."

He looked at her in amazement: "Why do you tell me that?"

He purposely assumed a façade of coldness and indifference whenever there was the hint of a cause for him to feel jealous. What causes could there be? There were none. Sometimes she would invent something just to tease him, to provoke him into showing some interest, but he grew used to her tricks; and when he knew she was making it up he paid no attention. With Kolka, however, it was something like the truth. She sensed it; perhaps Sergei sensed it too, but just didn't care. His mind was preoccupied. Gradually he became reconciled to her arrival, and toward the end of the day—after they had taken a walk down to the creek—he even admitted that he was glad she had come. That night was good together.

They did not sleep until early morning. He told her absolutely everything about his work, down to the smallest detail. He asked her advice: What should he do? The chief problem was that he had irrevocably ruined his relationships with the people at the institute. He had been rude to Klimuk and made an enemy of him; he had said the most offensive things to him in front of other people, for which Klimuk would never forgive him. But he and Klimuk had been heading for a breakup anyway; there was a certain inevitability about their clash; but did Sergei have to be offensive to Professor Vyatkin, an influential man? That was *not* very clever, was it? And what about Kislovsky? What about that cunning, rubbery, devious creature, whom Olga imagined to be a dangerous, ruthless man? To hell with those damn lists, for which Sergei had paid thirty rubles; he should have handed them over to Kislovsky and the whole business would have been finished and forgotten. Unfortunately, in saving thirty rubles, the chances for his dissertation were ruined.

It was now obvious to Olga that the whole of Sergei's strange family had something in common which doomed them to failure in life: his father had once been an outstandingly able man; yet he had never made it to the top; his mother was a nonpracticing lawyer with principles and high standards— and Sergei was similar in nature to both of them. His sister, too, was cast in the same mold. She had died an old maid, whose misfortunes, unhappiness and depression had all contributed to her final illness; it was said that a man had loved her very much and might have made her happy, but she had spent her whole life in love with another, wretched, insignificant man whom she had known since their schooldays. Some kind of emotional ineptitude and a compulsion to do only what pleased them had destroyed this family.

That night he suddenly said: "Do you know why everything I do seems to go so wrong?" Barely audibly, he whispered: "Because the threads which stretch out from the past . . . don't you see? They are fraught . . . They are fraught. Do you see what I mean?"

"Fraught . . . with what?"

"But it's obvious." He laughed. She felt a sudden sickening

awareness that he was going out of his mind. "Nothing, you see, breaks off without leaving a trace of some kind. There is no such thing as a total break with the past. Don't you understand? There has to be continuity, there must be. It's so obvious. . . ."

She looked at him and turned cold with horror.

Madness! She had always been afraid of it, knowing how highly strung and unstable he could be. She embraced him with her bare arm, pressed his head to her breast and stroked his hair. He gave a little snort of laughter, which made her shudder.

"I expect you think I've gone off my head, don't you? Nonsense, I'm perfectly all right. But you know my theory about the unbroken thread running from generation to generation. . . . If one can dig deeper and deeper, and farther backward, then it must be equally possible to trace the thread leading forward. . . ."

It was not madness—or rather, up to a point it might have been madness, and to some degree a joke, but to a greater degree he was quite serious. Mad and serious—it was all one. Olga burst into tears as she listened to his incoherent babbling. She had the feeling that he was finally cracking up. He rambled on with some confused story about his own ancestors, runaway serfs and religious dissenters whose branch of the family tree eventually led to an unfrocked priest at Penza, from him to some political deportees who had lived in a commune at Saratov, thence to a teacher in the depths of the Turan swamp land, who was in turn the father of a future St. Petersburg student who thirsted for justice and social change: common to all of them was a seething, bubbling urge to dissent. There was some trait in them that had never been eradicated by the sword, by the lash, or by time, something innate in the genetic stem. . . . Suddenly the impression of nonsensical raving stopped, and what he was saying seemed rational and coherent, maybe even highly intelligent; yet even so Olga was nagged by the fear that he really was going out of his mind. Whatever connection could there possibly be between an unfrocked priest in Penza a hundred and twenty years ago and the problems that Sergei was having with his dissertation? He said there was a connection. It was that night that he made up his mind to go to Gorodets.

Professor Vyatkin had doubted the authenticity of the lists, which Sergei had acquired by not entirely orthodox means. Quite recently she had dug out the folder tied with pink ribbon, buried under a pile of other folders on the bottom shelf of the big bookcase; the folder was made of the shiny, marbled, yellow cardboard that was much in vogue in the years before the revolution. She read the contents, although without fully understanding them; the letters danced around in front of her eyes, because reading these lists made her realize bitterly how much of life is made up of irreparable gaps. What an enormous part of Sergei's nature had remained unknown to her. She had thought she knew quite enough, indeed more than enough about him; yet she found all the material in this folder totally uninteresting. It was hopeless. She turned over the brittle, thin, musty-smelling sheets of paper and tried desperately to force her brain to make sense of them, only to realize with despair that their meaning eluded her: empty and lifeless, they refused to yield up their secret.

To her they were just a series of names, dates, villages, counties, towns, code names, occupations, addresses. Many of them had several code names. What could anyone do with it all? She did not understand. Anguish gripped her heart. Before putting the sheets back into the folder, tying the ribbon in a bow and shoving the folder under a heap of other, thicker and heavier folders, she noticed in one list the name of Yevgenii Alexeyevich Koshelkov, peasant, born 1891 in the village of Gorodets, Moscow Province, by trade a tailor, employed at the Jacques menswear store on Petrovka Street, Moscow.

The name Koshelkov was linked with one distinct memory: a misty September morning, the silence of a deserted pathway, already a touch of overnight frost on the ground, the yellow rustling leaves of the birch trees, the smell of mushrooms. As she and Sergei walked along the path through the woods, they were not hurrying but not dawdling either, because they had a long way to go. Sergei was in a wonderful, cheerful mood; he joked, played the fool and held her hand, making their arms swing as if they were a couple of teenagers in love. He even said words backward. He had suddenly become what he had once been long ago, and Olga thought: "Is this, I wonder, what's called happiness? A bright morning, a path through the woods in the fall?" No, Irinka was missing. Once they had gone to Vasilkovo in March, during the winter break between Irinka's school semesters, and went skiing in the woods. Sergei was far ahead; Irinka could hardly keep going. Evening was coming on, the light through the tree trunks was reddish-yellow, and the late afternoon glare from the snow was blinding. Irinka asked: "Mama, happiness—what is it?" She was ten years old, and one had to give serious answers to all her questions; Olga thought how to answer briefly and comprehensibly but could think of nothing really suitable, so she just said, "An evening like this in the forest, the three of us on skis—that's happiness. Do you see? That's what it is." Irinka, of course, didn't understand. And in fact Olga herself, having said it, didn't really understand either. *Their life* had yet to come to an end.

When they set out from Vasilkovo to the station that September morning, she was afraid of getting sore feet. Her new shoes were not suitable for long walks, and they felt tight. But in the end all was well. They were going to the village of Gorodets in the hope of finding some trace of Yevgenii Koshelkov, once an informer for the czarist secret police under the code names of "Tamara" and "Phil." Sergei said that of course there would be no surviving relatives or offspring after so many years and so many changes and upheavals, but at least some trace must have survived, some fragments of the thread, a few sparks that could be struck in someone's memory. If only one scrap of evidence could be found—such as an entry recording birth and baptism in the parish register of the local church—it would mean that the list was genuine. They had chosen Gorodets because it was the point nearest to Vasilkovo—a distance of twenty-eight kilometers.

First they took the train, then a bus. The village had grown into a town. Around the old garment factory, built by a French industrialist in the nineteenth century, had grown up an ugly clutter of four-story, slablike apartment houses with clusters of TV antennas sprouting from the roofs; when they crossed the bridge over the slimy, weed-choked little river called the Voprya, to the left rose a steep hillside dotted with old black rotting shacks and squalid little frame houses. It was not clear whether they were still inhabited or whether they had been preserved as a historic relic of prerevolutionary poverty and social inequality. In front of a single-story building—the sign said "Grocery and Produce"—stood a few men whose expressions had that look of slackness and lethargy which was the unmistakable sign of enforced idleness and the lack of something they all needed at that moment. Sergei walked over to them to make inquiries. A quarter of an hour later he was still leaning up against the brick wall of the building with a group of three of them, drinking vodka out of paper cups and eating tomatoes. By now Olga was feeling nervous and uncomfortable. The men were joking; Sergei seemed very relaxed and cheerful. It was a gorgeous blue-gold day. They wandered around the little town, which in places still seemed just a village, went in to several houses, talked over fences where it smelled of apples. Toward the end of the day they found an old man, very rosy-cheeked and fit-looking, but who could walk only with slow, short, little steps on legs clad in black felt boots: he had had a stroke the year before and had thought he was going to die, but recovered. Smiling with his handsome mouthful of white teeth the old man said:

"The Indian summer has finally come."

It was none other than Yevgenii Alexeyevich Koshelkov.

When Olga returned home from a trip to Leningrad in March (she flew back by plane, because she missed Irinka so badly) the first sounds to meet her ears were complaints from both her daughter and her mother-in-law. Irinka said that Grandma had kept her under martial law, had refused to give her any money, wouldn't allow her to go anywhere and had behaved horribly to Irinka's friends who came to visit. She had thrown them out of the house, when it wasn't late at all— well, eleven-thirty at the latest. The girls went, and Irinka went too, to see them home, and came back an hour later to find Grandma in hysterics, having called up each of the girl's homes in succession—Dasha, Tamara and Bella. Everyone had gone to bed by then, so she had awoken them. She had gone completely insane.

"After that, I didn't talk to her for three days."

"But perhaps you weren't entirely in the right."

"What did I do wrong?"

"Well, why did you spend so long seeing your friends off? You stayed out far too late in my opinion. She was worried about you."

"But why did she have to be rude to them? There was no need for that at all."

The conversation had started immediately on her return, before she had had a chance to change clothes or unpack her suitcase, in which lay the few modest presents she had bought in Leningrad. Her mood had not yet had time to turn sour. As she listened to her daughter and mildly reproached her, she stroked Irinka along her bony spine: her shoulder blades protruded, and her blue, short-sleeved blouse was noticeably too small for her and wouldn't last the summer.

A quarter of an hour later Olga, having changed into a bathrobe, went into the bathroom, turned on the hot water and started to scrub the tub furiously with scouring powder and an old loofah. Soon she was humming a tune half-aloud—something she hadn't done for a long time, perhaps six months. She seemed to have lost the habit; now she was doing it unconsciously, and if she had suddenly realized she was humming, she would no doubt have stopped it at once. When the door of the bathroom creaked she heard Alexandra Prokofievna's voice:

"Don't leave Irinka in my charge again. I can't cope with her any more; she's a big girl now and she can do what she likes, but don't expect me to control her."

"All right, let's talk about it later," said Olga.

"Or else you can try staying at home a bit more often and put up with the boredom for a change. I have my own work and I must get it done."

The old woman was very proud of her pathetic "work"—

running the legal advice column on a newspaper—which she had managed to get on a nonretainer basis after many letters and phone-calls: they gave her the job only because they felt sorry for her as a pensioned-off veteran of the law courts. In everyday life, however, after long experience of the cut and thrust of the courtroom, she had an undoubted ability to guess her opponent's sensitive spot and to probe it. So it was now: the words "put up with the boredom for a change" touched a sore spot, but Olga was still in no mood for a quarrel and answered peaceably:

"Very well, Alexandra Prokofievna, let me take a shower first. We can talk about it later."

It turned out that Irinka had gotten wildly out of hand, that she refused to do a single thing that she was asked to do: she wouldn't go out to the store, or to the laundry, wouldn't even sweep the floor; she answered impertinently and did nothing but make demands, demands, demands all the time. Irinka, who had sidled up to the kitchen door and was listening to her grandmother's accusations with a mocking air, asked:

"What did I ever 'demand'?" Her tone of voice most certainly was cheeky and rude.

"I do not wish to talk to you. I am telling your mother about your behavior; how she deals with you is her problem."

"Oh, so you don't wish to, do you? I never 'demanded' anything from you."

"Irinka, don't speak to your grandmother in that tone of voice. Go to your room and leave us alone."

"Oh, so I have to go away while she tells lies about me . . ."

"Did you hear that? 'She' . . . 'tells lies' . . ."

"Irinka, do as you're told."

"All right, I'll go, but please don't believe what she says. The only thing I asked for was enough money to go and see *A Taste of Honey* at the Sovremennik Theater. She wouldn't give it to me, so I borrowed three rubles from Dasha. She promised me a pair of winter shoes, but I knew all the time she wouldn't buy them. Situation normal, in fact."

"I believe I explained to you why I couldn't give money either for the theater or for the shoes," said Alexandra Prokofievna. "I have never patronized the sort of black-market dealers from whom you wanted me to buy those shoes, and I am not going to start now. I will not support illegal trading. When you see a nice pair of shoes in a store, then tell me and we'll go and buy them. I have told you that many times. After this display of misbehavior, however, you can forget about them."

Olga could feel the pain beginning to bore into her head just above her eyebrows. Irinka went out, while her grandmother continued to recite a catalogue of her sins: she was naughty, malicious, stupid, badly brought up—all of which, of course, was her mother's fault. As this accusation was twisted into an ever-tighter knot, from whose bonds there was absolutely no escape except her oncoming migraine, for which there was no remedy, its effect was to make Olga plunge further and further into a pointless and bad-tempered argument in defense of her daughter:

"You never see any good in her. And she needs kindness and affection—after all, she has lost her father . . ."

"How dare you remind me of that!"

Tears started in the old woman's narrow little eyes, her face turned pale, her lips slackened and began to tremble. This sudden change in Alexandra Prokofievna's features somehow spurred Olga on, and she stood up. Pressing one hand against her forehead as though trying to hold back a pain that was thrusting itself outward and waving the other hand in front of her—self-control had left her—she said loudly and incoherently: "Because there's no kindness in you. You're an evil woman! But I won't allow you to . . . I won't let you . . . Because she has no father, you think there's no one to stick up for her, don't you? I . . . I won't let you!" A spasm gripped her throat. "Why didn't you give her those miserable three rubles? Were you afraid I wouldn't pay them back? The girl has to beg from others, like a pauper. She's not a beggar. As long as she has a mother, she's not a beggar—do you hear? Why did you lie and tempt her with those damned shoes?"

With a look of scorn and disgust, the old woman shook her head and retreated to the door. Her face had turned to stone. Olga could no longer hear her own voice. Suddenly she heard a cry: "Mama! Stop it!"

She saw her daughter's face distorted with fright. Irinka embraced her and led her off to her room. Then Irinka disappeared. Olga lay in semidarkness, the curtains drawn, and thought: "My daughter's grown up. She'll defend me. I can't manage without her. I must tell the old woman once and for all: Don't dare . . ."

It was dark when she got up and had supper alone in the kitchen—Irinka had gone out to the movies. Her mother-in-law took something out of the refrigerator and silently put it on the stove. Why had Irinka sneaked off to the movies, knowing that her mother was so upset, knowing that there was a row in progress? What a strange character she had. There was a streak in it of excessive pliancy, of instability, of inconsiderate thoughtlessness—just like her father, in fact. She had the same tendency to disappear and run away from problems. At one moment she could show genuine compassion, revealing a capacity for pity and sympathy, showing—briefly—that she possessed a mind that was perceptive and mature, and then at the next moment she would confound them with some juvenile prank, some childish caprice or some act of such calculated selfishness that it took one's breath away. It was true, of course, that she had been subjected to conflicting influences: her grandmother had said one thing, her father another. For Olga, the most important thing was to teach Irinka to be independent of others. Nothing was more pathetic than a wretched person psychologically dependent on other people. Olga had been like that all her life. That life was now over, and she found herself the victim of another kind of scourge: she was independent—but empty.

For Irinka, despite her spoiled-child behavior, her outbursts of selfishness and rudeness, had a weakness: she was highly vulnerable to the will of others. The business at the theater in January during the holidays was typical. In the past, getting theater tickets had always been Sergei's responsibility. He still had some friends from his student days who were in the theater world: one had become an actor at the Mossoviet Theater, another had become a highly placed theatrical manager who wielded a lot of influence. But the problem was to get Sergei to call them up. How he hated asking favors. Olga and Irinka both had to nag him for a whole week. If he managed to get three tickets, they would all three go together; if he could only get two, then Sergei stepped down in favor of his daughter. Irinka loved being taken by her father: he was more generous at the buffet during the intermissions. Now she was going to the theater for the first time since her father's death. Dasha had got the tickets, and as it happened they were for a play at the theater to which Irinka had been most often with her father—the Mossoviet. Olga was worried that the place might have too many upsetting memories for the girl; she herself would not have gone to that theater again at any price. Olga spent the whole evening in a state of gnawing unease, and called up Dasha's mother to inquire whether any arrangements had been made to collect the girls from the theater and bring them home. Dasha's mother seemed amazingly unconcerned. Irinka came home around eleven, looking miserable. She refused supper and ran straight to her room, saying only that she had a headache. A quarter of an hour later Olga looked in, and Irinka was crying. Overcome by a surge of pity, she hugged her daughter, stroked her hair, consoled her and could hardly keep herself from bursting into tears too. When she had calmed down, Irinka told a story that was somewhat unexpected: Dasha, it seems, had invited another girl to the theater as well and had spent the whole evening talking to her and not to Irinka. During the intermission they had strolled around together arm in arm, treating Irinka as if she were a stranger and whispering secrets to each other. This annoyed Irinka so much that after the theater she ran off home without saying goodbye. Olga was astonished. Irinka had loved her father so much; yet the thing that really upset her was the childish behavior of a silly little girl. And she very quickly made it up with Dasha; soon afterward, she said happily to Olga: "Dasha says that Maya is stupid! She's not worth talking to—she doesn't like Fellini. . . ."

Loud noises, the slamming of doors and footsteps pounding in the hall announced Irinka's return from the movies at eleven o'clock. Before she had taken her coat off, standing in the middle of the room and unwinding her long woolen scarf, she announced the latest news: tomorrow she wanted to go out of town for a couple of days, to stay with Dasha and some friends at her family's *dacha*. She realized, of course, that this would be a blow to her mother, who had been missing Irinka badly and was looking forward to spending the weekend with her. A look of furtive mischief lurked in Irinka's eyes. Olga tried not to show her annoyance and disappointment.

"First take your coat off."

Irinka took off her coat and sat down at the table. She could have sat down on the divan alongside her mother, but chose to sit at a distance, which meant that she was preparing to put up a resistance. At that moment Alexandra Prokofievna came in to say that tea was ready. Olga asked Irinka who else was going on this outing to the *dacha*.

There followed a recital of about eight names, several of them unknown to Olga. It was good for her health to get out of town and breathe a little fresh air, wasn't it?

"And does that mean you'll miss school?"

"Well, so what?" She dismissed it with a wave of the hand. "We only have one class on Saturday anyway. Everyone's sick; there's an absolute epidemic of colds in Moscow at the moment."

"Which class?"

"Physics."

"No," said Olga. "I don't like you to miss classes."

"Oh Mama, why?"

"I don't like it when you miss a class."

"But why, why? Why does it matter so much? It's only one class, for heaven's sake."

"If you don't understand why, I'm not going to explain. I don't like it, that's all."

It was not only missing school that Olga didn't like; she probably disliked much more the fact that her daughter was so ready to rush off and leave her, having barely seen her again after a ten-day absence. How, for God's sake, could she be so obtuse, so unaware of her mother's feelings? She inherited it from her father; there had been many times when he had been totally insensitive. Her grandmother was standing nearby and listening in silence. She could not, of course, approve of Irinka's adventure, but to say a couple of words in support of Olga was more than she could bring herself to do.

"There are plenty of things you don't like. Maybe there

are a few things I don't like, too." Irinka was sitting bolt up-right at the table, her legs crossed, glaring at the tablecloth with a disdainful expression, swinging her right foot up and down. She was, in fact, the very image of that independent personality that Olga so much wanted her to have.

"What don't you like?"

"This and that."

"For example?"

"Lots of things. For instance, the fact that you go away so often. First you go to Chelyabinsk, then to Leningrad . . ."

"I go, my dear, on official trips that are essential for my work. I am sent, like it or not. ("God, why do I have to justify myself to her?") Do you imagine I go from choice?"

"I know you go because of your work, but you also enjoy getting away from home, having a bit of fun, don't you?"

"What do you mean—fun? What stupid nonsense you talk."

But it wasn't all nonsense. The blood rushed to Olga's face. Alexandra Prokofievna continued to stand there in silence.

"Whoever gave you the idea that I want to go away 'for fun'? Who's been telling you that?" Olga was not looking at her mother-in-law, but she felt her presence with all her being. She had the impression that the old woman was smiling.

"Of course we all find it hard without father," the girl mut-tered, "only Grandma and I can never go away anywhere. But you . . ."

"What about me?"

"Well, you can take a breather every now and again. Maybe I get fed up staying at home all the time and I want a bit of fun for a change. Just for a couple of days."

"You're such a little fool," said Olga in a weak voice, wip-ing her eyes with the palm of her hand. "I never enjoy these trips; I'm always so longing to get home. I call you up every evening. I count the days until I can see you again, you heart-less girl. And you say I go away for fun. . . . You're an un-grateful little monster. Go away, I don't want to see you!"

Irinka ran out of the room.

Alexandra Prokofievna announced into empty space: "She should not, of course, be allowed to go out of town."

"Why didn't you say that to her face?" asked Olga. "Or were you trying to be nice?"

After that, Olga washed clothes until midnight. Irinka, idle
little devil, had done none of her own laundry. But Olga
would have had to wash it all again anyway, because all Irinka
ever did was shift the dirt around. Next day, before she left
for school, seizing a moment when her grandmother was out
of the kitchen, Irinka asked forgiveness. As usual, she gabbled
her apology in a perfunctory whine: "Mother, I'm sorry, forgive me please, I won't go if you don't want me to." Olga,
however, felt that this was a significant act of contrition. She
forgave her, saying that she would call up Dasha's mother
and between them they would come to a decision. But the
real reason was that she was once again overcome and reduced
to weakness by pity. She glanced sidelong at Irinka and her
heart was wrung: an orphan, always alone, alone in her room,
no father, her mother always away out of town . . . how
could she refuse to let her go? And she let her go.

The little old man in black felt boots padded noiselessly
around the yard without even making the dead leaves rustle,
smiling all the time:

"Yes, the Indian summer has come through. . . ."

Olga did not like the old man. She thought uneasily: "My
God, but why 'come through'?" There was something unsettling in the glorious weather, in the remote overgrown
garden, in the old man's lack of memory; she sensed it plainly,
yet could not quite pin down where the feeling came from
and why. The whole of this search was an unnecessary amusement. Sergei had finally tracked down this mossy old relic,
who had once worked in the Jacques menswear store on
Petrovka; he had pulled him out of oblivion, like pulling an
ace out of a deck of cards—so what next? The old man remembered nothing, wanted nothing, knew nothing, because
after his days at Jacques, life had come crashing down on him
like a heap of rocks and everything that might have remained
alive in his memory was buried and crushed.

"Do you know what Monsieur Jacques was like? Oho! Not
like a Frenchman at all."

"Do you remember the last days of February 1917?"

There was nothing, absolutely nothing to be coaxed, prized or squeezed out of the cavernous depths of old Koshelkov's memory. It was full of wars, hard times, distant lands, icy cold, death and destruction, whereas the peace and quiet of Gorodets with this little garden had only recently come to him, like a patch of bright sky in the evening of his days. And the Lord be praised for small mercies. Sergei took out a notebook and pencil, but he never managed to take any useful notes. The old man's daughter, a stocky, glum-faced peasant woman, invited them out onto the verandah for dinner. Also there was her daughter-in-law, who was a nurse, and her two children. Soon they were joined by the nurse's husband, the old man's grandson, who was called Pantyusha—a name they were to remember.

Pantyusha was round-shouldered and stooping, a head shorter than Sergei, dark, with bushy eyebrows, beneath which two sharp, malevolent little eyes, like rats' eyes, gleamed out from deep eye-sockets. Either he was drunk, or sick, or he was simply endowed by nature with a surfeit of seething malice which threatened to overwhelm him, just as some people suffer from high blood pressure. At first he said nothing and passed the time staring at Sergei's pants, his shoes, his watch, and his sweater, then with equal intentness inspected Olga's shoes and her suede jacket, which in those days was still new, unstained and very beautiful. He spent a particularly long time looking at the jacket, until it began to make Olga feel uncomfortable. Sergei did not notice Pantyusha's surly, hostile attentions (just as he seldom noticed people's appearance, looks or facial expressions; what interested him were their words) and continued obstinately in his efforts to wring out of the old man some details about his work for the secret police in prerevolutionary Moscow. Suddenly Pantyusha touched the sleeves of Olga's suede jacket and asked, "Where do jackets like this come from?"

"It comes from Hungary," Olga answered.

"Oh, so it's not made here? Say, it's just like velvet."

"It's suede, that's all," said the nurse. "Can't you see?"

"I can see. Sure I can see."

"Well, sit down and shut up. Don't touch it. I'll bet you

haven't washed your hands, and the slightest bit of dirt or grease will stick to suede. Oh, dear—I do believe you've stained it already."

She seized a handkerchief and hastened to wipe the mark off the sleeve of the suede jacket. The children leaped up and clustered around, itching with a desire to touch the exotic garment. Pantyusha ground his teeth. The old man, who had seemed to be absorbed in his conversation with Sergei (and appeared to have great difficulty in hearing him), suddenly interrupted the conversation about the jacket with an entirely pertinent remark:

"What d'you mean—it's not made here? You used to be able to get it at Schultz Brothers' store on Kamerger Street. *'Gemsleder'* it's called. Gloves, vests . . ."

Pantyusha brushed aside his grandfather's interruption with an impatient gesture.

Boiled potatoes were served in a cast-iron pot. The weather turned suddenly overcast and dark, so they switched on the porch lights. Sergei was still trying to make notes, to extract from old Koshelkov some information about a fire that occurred in February 1917: who started the fire, who put it out, who was giving the orders. The old man had been an utter little nobody at the time, a speck of dust in a tornado—yet fifty-three years had gone by and by some strange quirk of fortune that little speck had survived, was still dancing in a ray of sunlight, while all else around him had been obliterated, swept away. And Olga understood why Sergei was listening with such avidity to the old man's semicoherent mumbling. The chief question, which puzzled and tantalized them, was: How did he survive? Hadn't the authorities ever . . . picked him up?

"Picked me up? Of course," said the old man with a smile. "They tried to take me off to the war; then they put me in prison. I was lucky, though: being a tailor's a good job, keeps you out of harm's way. . . . We made uniforms for the officers, so we always had a crust of bread. . . . They tried to order us to be moved to another prison, but our warden, comrade Gravdin, wouldn't let us go. So they even quarreled over us. . . ." And the old man winked gleefully.

Pantyusha, who had gone out somewhere, appeared again at the table. "Why are you bothering the old man?"

"Your grandfather has had a very long and interesting life," said Sergei. "We were talking about his life."

"And who are you writing it down for?"

"I'm a historian. It's important for the history I'm writing."

"What history?"

"The history of the February Revolution in 1917. The February Revolution and everything connected with it. It is a complicated period that hasn't yet been fully studied, and every new firsthand witness is valuable. Forgive us for boring you—we're going soon."

Sergei spoke calmly and patiently, but Pantyusha was in a mood to make trouble. Suddenly he shouted, "You won't get a thing out of him! That's enough! That's what I think of you historians." And he thrust a gnarled finger in front of Sergei's face. "I won't allow it."

Pantyusha's mother and wife tried to calm him down, but timidly and ineffectually. It was time to go, but Sergei never could leave at the right moment; he always felt that something was still to be finished—the drinking or eating, the explanations, the hurling of the last insult. Now, his neck turning purple, seething with fury, he set about trying to explain to a drunken fool what history was and why it was needed. Pantyusha listened with a sarcastic, hostile sneer, and accompanied his objections with a furiously wagging finger:

"We learned all about history in school. We know it all. Why are you trying to muddle me? History, history . . . forget it. There's only one history, and we don't need any more."

"Listen, Pantyusha, what's your job? What do you do for a living?"

Whenever Sergei talked to uneducated people, especially when he started to argue with them, for some reason he invariably adopted an unpleasant, condescending tone of voice, which was clearly involuntary, but which irritated them. Pantyusha answered rudely: "Where I work's no business of yours. Maybe I dig graves at the cemetery for three kopecks a time. Say, are you one of those snoopers from the police or the social security?" This was spoken in a threatening voice, and he no longer shook just a finger but a clenched fist under Sergei's nose. Olga tried to drag Sergei away from the table, but he remained obstinately seated and plunged headlong into the increasingly tense dispute.

"No, listen, I haven't said anything to offend you. I'm simply interested to know why you pitched into me like that."

"I don't give a damn about your history. Just stop bothering the old man."

"History isn't *mine*—it belongs to you, too, and to your grandfather. It belongs to everybody. Did you know, for instance, that Gorodets is a very ancient town . . ."

The nurse whispered to Olga that she shouldn't be offended by her husband, he was a bit weak in the head, and whenever he had a drink he always acted crazy and pestered people. Because of this he was often getting beaten up, but he had a good job as a mechanic at the grain elevator and was really a decent man at heart.

Old Koshelkov, once an informer for the Moscow section of the czarist secret police—but so long ago that nothing perceptible remained of it except burnt-out ashes—was dozing peacefully, his nodding head crowned with its little circlet of pale hair. Sergei was telling some story about the feudal lords of Gorodets in the middle ages and about the Tartars. The children were listening to him. Pantyusha frowned with a glare of manic distrust.

"Suppose I punched you on the back of the neck?" He ground his teeth. "That would be the end of you and your history."

It was a long walk to the bus stop and it was in the dark. Olga was shivering, either with fear or with cold. The golden day had changed into an icy fall evening. She tried to make Sergei hurry, but he could barely walk straight, his legs weakened with vodka and euphoria as he babbled delightedly about his success with the old man. To Olga this was nonsense; what good was it all? Some dogs started barking, and a few particularly fierce ones ran out into the road and chased them; Sergei waved his arms at the dogs and threw stones, which only made them more furious.

"Stop it!" she begged.

Sergei, however, seemed to enjoy his skirmish with the dogs. At any moment men with sticks or pitchforks might emerge from the darkened yards. God, how angry she was with him! It had all been such a stupid, childish escapade—the trip to Gorodets, sitting there till late at night, talking to a senile old man.

"Arrf! Arrf!" he teased the dogs, laughing as they barked at him.

"My God," she thought, "and this man is almost middle-aged, almost a professional historian, almost a scholar. . . . No, he'll never make it." This sudden insight, which came to Olga that evening on a pitch-dark country road, was mingled with fear as her husband fought off the dogs. They were now surrounded by them, ranging from sizable farmyard curs to yapping little mutts that bounced around them like fleas. Suddenly came salvation—the roar of a motorbike engine that scattered the dogs, dazzling them with its headlight, as it drove up before them and stopped.

"Hop on, Mr. History!" rasped Pantyusha. His white motor-biking helmet and white gauntlets shone in the darkness like a police patrolman. "I'll run you to the railroad station at Voronov. It's only seven kilometers, we'll be there in no time!"

Olga hesitated—the man, after all, was crazy, and drunk as well—but Sergei was already pushing her into the sidecar, while he climbed astride the pillion, grasped his recent adversary around the waist as if he were his best friend (men were amazing: alcohol could so easily reconcile and unite them, so quickly enable them to forgive each other), gave a wild whistle, as he had not whistled for years, and—off they went. The journey was short, lasting probably no more than a quarter of an hour, but it was unforgettable. Olga wondered whether they would ever come out of this mad adventure alive. She was thrown around, flung from side to side and bumped so hard that her teeth rattled; she wanted to cry out but could not open her mouth or take a deep enough breath. Worst of all was her fear for Sergei, who insisted on standing up, flinging his arm into the air and shouting in a thunderous, parade-ground voice: "Hurrah for the glorious workers of Gorodets!" or "Hurrah for the heroic collective farmers of Baranovka!" Pantyusha clearly approved of these slogans, because he joined in with shouting "Hurrah!" The road was winding, houses would suddenly rush toward them in the glare of the headlight; signposts flickered by, lit for a moment; vague shadows loomed in the ditch beside the road. "Hurrah for a lone walker!" roared Sergei, waving his cap at one of the shadows. Although Olga was terrified, at the same time she was laughing so hard that she cried, or perhaps crying from the violence and utter confusion of her emotions. She was both angry with him and full of love for him. That noisy, irrepressible, arrested adolescent had not much time left on earth to shout and misbehave.

Klimuk suddenly demanded that Sergei corroborate the fact that Kislovsky had asked him, Sergei, to give him some documents for his dissertation; in return, Klimuk promised his support when Sergei came to submit *his* dissertation. What Klimuk said of Kislovsky was no doubt true, but Sergei had only heard about it from Klimuk himself, who had acted as go-between, and who now for some reason had made a 180-degree turn and was trying to set a trap to catch Kislovsky. Sergei was incapable of intrigue; it angered and disgusted him, and out of spite he responded to Klimuk by doing the stupidest things. Lord, if only he had allied himself with Klimuk at that moment. How Klimuk begged him. Everything might have turned out differently. He would have stayed alive. He would have lived on in good health, he would have gone on working, telling jokes and skiing; he would have climbed up the career ladder and lived to a ripe old age. But nobody knows why people die. Unexpectedly, something dries up, runs out: *the grace of life,* as Tolstoy put it. The "grace" of his life endured for a while longer: he still drove himself on, still looked for something, still strove to get somewhere.

He could still meet new people and acquire, as he thought, new friends. Suddenly Darya Mamedovna appeared. It was painful to recall her, but it was equally impossible to avoid thinking about her. This was the woman who for the first time gave Olga a real fright, because it suddenly became a distinct possibility that Sergei was drifting away and might disappear. Later, in fact, he did disappear altogether, for which Darya Mamedovna was distantly responsible, in so far as she was the ill-omened starting point from which was unwound the whole skein of disaster—like the blizzard in Pushkin's *The Captain's Daughter* which develops out of an almost invisible little cloud. During the course of a lifetime, people surround us in clusters, like incrustations: these formations suddenly crystallize around us and then just as suddenly they fall away, in obedience to some obscure laws. Once there had been the friends of their youth, student companions like Vlad—they had vanished without trace; these had been followed by neighbors at the Sushchevskaya studios—artists, old men, drunkards, Valerii Vasin and Zika—they too had sunk beneath the waters of time; then there were friends from the museum, and others, like Ilya Vladimirovich—gone, as if they had never been. Later came colleagues at the institute, neighbors at Vasilkovo—they too had disappeared into oblivion. And now there was Darya Mamedovna.

The first time Olga saw this woman with her tawny-olive complexion, a hint of blue in the whites of her eyes, her smooth black hair without a curl or a wave hugging her snakelike head as though poured over it like water, she sensed with her heart: Trouble! A bit over forty, but with the figure of a twenty-year-old girl. It was not her figure, however, or her dark complexion, or her shapely legs that worried Olga, but her widespread reputation, inflated by sycophants, flatterers and various brands of charlatan, which claimed that she was quite unusually intelligent. What nonsense. Pure invention. Olga had seen her several times, at parties, at the theater and at the Luzhskys', once even in her own home, and had talked to her on all kinds of subjects, from Darya's favorite, parapsychology, to modern poetry, and she quickly realized that the empress had no clothes. Everything was approximate, superficial, purely for show, but she also had a diabolical self-confidence and a firm, categorical way of expressing herself as though delivering a judgment that was not subject to appeal. A most unpleasant creature. But a lot of fools were taken in by her. Imagine—she had a master's degree, almost a doctorate; it was ridiculous, but people talked of her in a phrase that she herself had probably coined: she was "five-minutes-to-a-doctor." Well, in philosophy or psychology or something, she had devoured a mass of books and she had the gift of gab, but that wasn't everything. You can stuff yourself full of information, but that doesn't make you any more intelligent.

It was the sixth anniversary of Fedya's death, and Louisa his widow had invited a few friends—Boris and Vera Luzhsky, Shchupakov and his wife Krasina, some other people from the institute, and Gena Klimuk and Mara. By now, Sergei and Klimuk were almost outright enemies. Louisa was nervous about this, and she called up Olga to ask her advice. It was impossible not to invite Klimuk. The change in him had come about after Fedya's death; in Fedya's lifetime Klimuk had behaved tolerably well, and Louisa knew him as a decent man, an old friend. Sergei said, "To hell with him. Of course let her invite him. I won't touch him."

Louisa was very fond of Sergei and he was her favorite guest—because Fedya had been so fond of him too—but Klimuk had also been Fedya's friend, his companion on his last journey and, apart from that, had organized some financial help from the institute. He had arranged a once-only, non-repayable, *ex gratia* payment (and as Olga was to discover later, the sum was not a small one—twice as big, in fact, as the amount she received), and every summer he sent Fedya's children to the summer camp run by the institute. There were strong reasons, therefore, why she was bound to invite Klimuk.

"I know that many people don't like him and think he's strange, but he's always been kind to me," she explained to Olga. "Every New Year he sends a card, and he calls with good wishes on Fedya's birthday, even brings me flowers. And Sergei forgets . . ."

Sergei did indeed forget. There were times when he forgot even Olga's birthday, and he constantly got the day wrong— he would wish her "Happy birthday" on the third instead of the fourth of June. Klimuk never got anything wrong. For some reason he felt a need to be kind to Louisa. Apparently Louisa was hoping that Klimuk would not want to sit down at the same table with Sergei and drink vodka with him and might therefore make some excuse not to come. But he came.

Mara wanted to show off in front of her erstwhile friends, to talk about her new apartment, about the blue-tiled Dutch stove, the simulated-oak wallpaper, the amazing intelligence of her spaniel Rudi, and, of course, about her impressions of their trips abroad—so much had happened since they had last seen one another.

It was indeed a long time since their last meeting. In one way or another, all of them had lost some of their luster, had somehow withered. Shchupakov's wife, Krasina, a beautiful Bulgarian woman, had acquired a yellow tinge to her complexion. Boris Luzhsky, the psychiatrist, with whom Olga so much enjoyed talking, had turned into a wizened, middle-aged little man who wore heavy American spectacles that made him look older than he was. Vera, Boris's wife, had a liver complaint and couldn't eat anything. But the most noticeable change had occurred in Louisa; she had grown much thinner, she had a pronounced stoop and the dress she wore was so appallingly tasteless and cheap that Olga was horrified: the woman had so obviously stopped caring. She felt very sorry for her. Louisa had, of course, made a colossal effort to invite all these people and feed them properly; the table was richly spread, but from the greedy looks of the children and from the way in which they sneaked pieces of ham or cheese from the plates it was obvious that they didn't often eat in such abundance. There were two bottles of vodka. In the old days they would have drained them in a moment and somebody would have gone out for more, but now they barely managed to empty one bottle, and even then without much enthusiasm: one person had hypertension, another had a paper to write that night, Klimuk and Boris Luzhsky were driving. Sergei, of course, did not refuse, but the person who punished the vodka most heavily was Mara. She was, it seemed, the only one who had blossomed during those six years: she had filled out, put on weight and turned into a sleek, well-upholstered lady; reddened with an alcoholic flush, her little round face positively gleamed, expressing complete satisfaction with life. Irritated, Olga felt no wish to talk to her, still less to listen to her tactless bragging.

As soon as Mara started talking about her spaniel, who

understood a hundred and forty words, or about her trips abroad: "Imagine, horrors, there we were in Nice walking down the boulevard . . ." Olga purposely interrupted her in a loud voice, asking her to pass a dish, or switch on the television—anything. Of course it was rude to interrupt, but Olga couldn't help herself: listening to the self-satisfied Mara was intolerable. Both she and Klimuk had apparently managed to forget that Sergei had tried for a long time to get a trip to France, which he needed for his work, but had somehow failed to make it; yet this squawking little parakeet, this nonentity, who did no work of any kind, had already been to Nice, to Paris, to Rome, and to God knows where else. All right, so you were clever enough to play the game and wangle yourself all those goodies, but at least show a little tact and don't shout about it from the rooftops, least of all in front of Sergei.

In fact Sergei appeared not to be listening to Mara's twittering about her experiences abroad and was preoccupied with his own thoughts, but it made Olga good and mad. People who acquire an ever-thicker skin in proportion to their increasing success and affluence are obnoxious, and she always tried to keep her distance from them. In the past she had treated Mara tolerantly, even amiably. Olga regarded her as a cheerful little birdbrain, remote from the machinations and intrigues to which her husband devoted himself. Now, however, it turned out that she had an insatiable appetite for the fruits of those machinations and intrigues.

"Louisa, darling, everything is so delicious," said Mara in condescending approval as she ate her way through the contents of the fruit bowl. "Why don't we get together more often, as we used to do?"

The children watched longingly while one after another of the juicy pears, as if on a conveyor belt, disappeared into the toothy maw of the fat, rosy-cheeked lady in the blue wig.

Klimuk, on the other hand, seemed in a somber mood, or he was, perhaps, overconscious of his own importance: he was not his usual talkative self, he didn't tell any jokes, and when Louisa produced a guitar—the famous guitar that had belonged to Fedya, on which he played so wonderfully—and asked him to sing Fedya's favorite song, Klimuk said that he hadn't time for such amusements any more and politely refused, with the excuse that his voice had quite gone.

He was too great a man nowadays to accompany himself on the guitar and sing a risqué little song, like a student in a railroad car. Of course, if the song had been something like "My Beloved City, My Golden Moscow," that would have been different. At home, after the party, Sergei sneered as he recalled Klimuk and the changing moods of the evening, which had ended in quarreling and abuse. It was awful that they had been unable to control themselves and had caused an embarrassing scene on such an occasion. And it was just as much Sergei's fault as Klimuk's. At first all was quiet and peaceful; they were seated at opposite ends of the table and did not talk to each other. Their relationship was not yet one of deadly enmity, as it became later, but their feelings for each other were openly contemptuous: Sergei despised him for his blatant careerism, while Klimuk despised Sergei for his alleged enviousness; he was convinced that Sergei couldn't bear the fact of his, Klimuk's, great success.

Everything might have ended with decorum, especially since the Klimuks had planned to leave early, had it not been for a stout lady from the institute, her black hair streaked with gray (Olga had since forgotten her name), who suddenly began with great fervor to praise Fedya's unselfishness and unworldliness.

"There simply aren't such people any more!" she exclaimed. "In that respect Fyodor Alexandrovich was absolutely unique. He never used his position to get anything for himself, not even *that* much."

The lady's voice quavered with emotion. She was, of course, exaggerating; Fedya had been a good man, but by no means such a plaster saint as she was making him out to have been. Someone else spoke up in similar terms, and then everyone began recalling Fedya's kindness, his love of helping others, and at the same time (with a touch of pathos) his improvidence and impracticality, which were indeed his outstanding characteristics. Suddenly Louisa burst into tears and began a litany of complaint: how Fedya had never taken them anywhere except to the Crimea; how he never possessed a decent winter overcoat; how he had never managed to exchange their apartment for a better one, although everyone else seemed able to do it. . . . Now there was no hope left for her.

"He always thought last of all about himself, always about other people, always," Louisa whispered, bowing her head, now noticeably streaked with gray.

Nobody had wanted these tears, these embarrassing complaints. The atmosphere of restraint was broken; everyone began talking at once, seized by a wave of affection for Fedya— so pure, so unlike the common run of humanity (God, it was all so exaggerated, but at that particular moment it felt as if they had perceived the ultimate truth!)—moved by this woman's grief, by the sight of her pathetic little apartment with its shabby old furniture, and, no doubt, aggravated by Mara's insensitive prattle about Klimuk's prosperity. . . . And Olga wondered how her own apartment would look in six years' time.

The praise of Fedya had the unintended result of seeming, by contrast, to condemn Klimuk. Although he, too, added some laudatory remarks about Fedya, he was visibly strained and his voice betrayed his tenseness. The situation was building up to an explosion. The bearded Shchupakov, a friend of Fedya's since their schooldays, and unconnected with the institute, inquired naïvely: "Does the academic secretary have any special opportunities for feathering his nest?"

The question, in fact, was probably not quite as naïve as Shchupakov tried to make it sound; he just happened to be the first to strike an overt blow. The black-and-gray lady immediately responded: "What do you think?"

"I don't know. That's why I asked the question."

"Quite a few opportunities. There's Gennadii Vitalevich sitting opposite you: he will confirm that, I think."

Klimuk opened his eyes wide in a look of guileless honesty, shook his head and confessed that, with the best will in the world, he could not think what these "opportunities" were: "I really can't imagine what you mean."

"Oh come, come, Gennadii Vitalevich! It's all in your hands!" exclaimed the lady in sincere amazement.

"Exactly *what* is in my hands?" Klimuk laughed. "I wish I knew."

"Everything. Absolutely everything."

The lady laughed too, this time with a hint of flattery in her voice. Klimuk shrugged his shoulders. It might have all dissolved in jokes and inconsequential chatter had not Sergei suddenly remarked in quite a different tone—hard and contemptuous—that Fedya's talented dissertation had never been published, whereas Klimuk's extremely mediocre piece of work had been published in two editions—in a symposium and as a separate book.

Klimuk pretended not to hear. He did not even look in Sergei's direction. There followed a few irrelevant remarks from other people, after which Klimuk said with a sigh: "I feel sorry for you, Sergei. How painful it must be for you, always having to be a witness to other people's successes."

It was said without malice, in a voice of apparent sympathy. Sergei exploded: "What successes, for God's sake? You make me sick! That's not success—it's crap!—" And more of such comments, spat out in fury. Louisa turned pale. Olga signaled furiously to Sergei to shut up; she was terrified of what he might do next. Squeaking indignantly, Mara rushed to her husband's defense. Several of the institute people—and none more heatedly than the stout lady—rounded on Sergei. Klimuk smiled vengefully. The stout lady exclaimed: "Unparliamentary language! You have used unparliamentary language!"

Klimuk and Mara left, and soon afterward the other guests from the institute left too. Their faces, as they said goodbye to Sergei, expressed disapproval. The stout lady—who was, it transpired, an important functionary, and a member of an influential committee—whispered anxiously: "Sergei Afanasievich, I hate to tell you, but that is what is known as a *casus belli.*"

Sergei laughed unconcernedly: "Ah, hell . . . who cares?"

His mood had turned cheerful. He became talkative and noisy, he told stories and gave a hilarious description—as only he could—of the trip to Gorodets and the meeting with old Koshelkov. Louisa calmed down, everyone else gradually relaxed, while Shchupakov and Krasina, of course, had always been on Sergei's side. The unpleasantness and the shouting were somehow smoothed over and gave way to a happier atmosphere (the episode could not be forgotten, but they all did their best to forget it), and it was then that the name of Darya Mamedovna came up for the first time. Sergei was saying that his list of czarist police informers included three important people, known only by their code names, whose real names were still undisclosed. The arrests that took place in 1916 were probably connected with these three, or with one of them. He was constantly preoccupied with this topic. Olga even used to make jokes about it:

"What are you—a historian or a private detective?"

A few minutes earlier, Krasina, who was a sweet and kind woman but not too bright, told a story about a peasant woman from a mountain village in southern Bulgaria who had the gift of second sight and other parapsychological talents, which were so amazing that people came to see her from abroad, and a woman of Krasina's acquaintance had been given an exact answer to her question about a friend who had died in mysterious circumstances. Someone then said jokingly that Sergei should find a clairvoyant like that, ask her about the anonymous informers, and perhaps the secret would be revealed. And then, roaring with laughter at the idea, someone else suggested that they ought to hold a spiritualist seance and summon up the spirit of Colonel Martinov—the chief of the Moscow secret police in 1916—who would surely know all the answers. At this point Boris Luzhsky told them about Darya Mamedovna Nigmatova. He described how she was engaged in serious research into parapsychology and was also interested in all sorts of occultism, oriental magi, psychic mediums and other obscure matters. She was also a highly educated woman who spoke four languages and gave lectures. Her father came from the Caucasus (hence her unusual patronymic "Mamedovna"); he had been a homeopathic doctor, very rich, who had died during the war, and Darya's mother was of aristocratic descent.

The fact that Vera referred to Darya Mamedovna somewhat coldly as "that woman" put Olga even more on her guard. Obviously Vera, too, sensed danger here, and Vera was not a person to be alarmed without reason; she was a rational, intelligent woman. Olga asked her: "Vera, do you know this Darya Mamedovna?"

"I saw her once. On that same occasion, at the Kostins'."

"Well, what did you think?—An oriental beauty?"

"No, not exactly . . ." Vera answered hesitantly. "That is, not unless you like that type. But our Boris definitely *does* like that type. In my opinion, she bowled him over at first sight."

"Boris—you must introduce me to her at once," cried Sergei. "Call yourself a friend? Aren't you ashamed of keeping her away from me?"

"Forget it—you'd never make it with her."

"I wouldn't make it? And who would—you, I suppose?"

"I am questionable—but still, there is a chance. Because I'm a psychiatrist, which is close to her interests. But you, old boy, with your history of the February Revolution, you haven't a hope . . ."

As they continued to banter in this vein, Olga felt her heart gripped by an evil premonition. Gradually more details about Darya Mamedovna came to light: she was forty or so but still looked marvelous; she was very athletic and swam a lot. She was once married, but her husband had died. A year ago the magazine *Science and Life* had published an article of hers on parapsychology, entitled something like "The Mysterious World Around Us," and now that issue of the magazine was unobtainable: in libraries, people stood in line to borrow a copy. Boris wagged a warning finger at Olga. "Olga, this husband of yours is really out to score. You should keep an eye on him."

Everyone laughed, and Olga made a great effort to smile and reply in the same frivolous tone.

Three months passed, in which nothing more was heard of Darya Mamedovna. Then Olga discovered that Sergei had met her: he mentioned it casually, in passing, as something quite insignificant. Perhaps he really thought it was, or perhaps he was pretending. Describing his visit to an exhibit by an artist called Presnin, he let slip the remark: "By the way, I met that woman Nigmatova when I was there."

"Nigmatova? Who's she?"

"You know—Darya Mamedovna. Don't you remember? Boris was talking about her at Louisa's.—"

How could she forget! Olga went cold. Presnin, it turned out, had been a friend of this woman's husband, the artist. Had this meeting been arranged in advance? Nothing of the sort—it was pure chance. There was nothing of the *femme fatale* about her. She was rather skinny, sun-tanned, rather like a Gypsy to look at. She had said that she was being heavily attacked for her writings, even persecuted. Presnin had arranged a little buffet supper for his close friends after the private viewing, and some people from the Sushchevskaya studios had been there. One of them had told him that Georgii Maximovich was sick. . . .

Olga interpreted the reference to her stepfather as a smoke screen and did not pursue the subject. She knew from her mother (with whom she talked almost daily by phone) that Georgii Maximovich had had some tests done and the results were disturbing, that he was weakening and complained of pain, and would probably have to be hospitalized. All this was by now common knowledge; Olga felt very sorry for Georgii Maximovich and was worried about her mother. But right now she was amazed to learn that Sergei had been to some buffet supper—without her!—where he had met and talked to this creature. At the mention of her name Olga experienced a strange sort of asthmatic irritation, as though she were slightly short of breath. What exactly was Sergei up to? In this state of irritation, gasping for breath a little, she began to scold him for taking unfair advantage of the fact that while she worked to strict hours he had no fixed timetable and so was free to go roaming around on his own—visiting friends, going to art exhibits, making new acquaintances. Just as if he were a bachelor. . . .

It was unfair of her to have such thoughts, and even worse to utter them. As soon as she had spoken, she was ashamed of herself. But it was like a disease, an allergic reaction that made her gasp for breath, unable to control herself.

That winter Aunty Pasha arrived from Vasilkovo in tears: Kolka was under arrest; he was due to appear in court and might get a heavy sentence. The Vasilkovo people had gotten into a fight in the club with a bunch from the nearby village of Semkovo, and Kolka, as an auxiliary policeman, had tried to separate them and had knocked one of the Semkovo men to the ground. The man had almost died, and was still in hospital, where the doctors had just managed to save his life. Kolka had never seen the man from Semkovo before in his life, and now—this terrible accident. What had Kolka hit him with? An ax. Of course, as a police reservist he had only been trying to separate them, and they, drunken fools, had turned on him and he had lashed out. Alexandra Prokofievna remarked that an ax was an odd sort of weapon for a police reservist.

"Have you forgotten?" said Sergei. "The house with the hatchet—remember?"

Weeping, Aunty Pasha begged them to help her in hiring a lawyer—it didn't matter how much it cost, she would raise the money somehow. She would sell the cow, sell the motorbike. Although she regarded the case as hopeless, Alexandra Prokofievna went into action. She went out to Vasilkovo and to Ryabtsevo, the district center, where Kolka was detained under arrest. There she talked to the state's attorney and the local police chief. When she made the first trip it was in the late fall, toward the end of November. The weather was horrible, cold and sleety, and everyone tried to persuade her not to go. Sergei shouted at her: "I forbid you! Don't you dare go. You're an old woman and you should behave like an old woman." He was seldom as rude as this, and it was a sign that he was really alarmed. She replied: "I will never behave like an old woman. I made a promise, Pasha is expecting me, so therefore I must go."

He shouted some more, threatened her and went off to the institute convinced that his mother was not yet totally out of her mind and would stay at home. Olga went to work, Irinka went to school—and the old woman put on her 1920s hiking rig, took her umbrella, pulled on her rubber boots and set off for the station. When she returned that evening, worn out and soaked to the skin, looking like a weird, pathetic scarecrow, she announced that the facts of the case were not at all as Pasha had told them. They were both worse and better. Sergei was furious with his mother, refused to listen and demonstratively left the table. Since Olga was never the most sympathetic of listeners when the old woman was holding forth, Alexandra Prokofievna started telling the whole story to Irinka. Strangely enough, her voice sounded firm and confident.

She had found out that Kolka, of course, had been as drunk as the rest of them and that the fight had not just been the usual drunken brawl. The cause of all the trouble was a girl called Raisa. The Semkovo boys had been pestering her; they were out for revenge because she had dropped one of them in favor of Kolka. It emerged that Kolka—the apparently shy, sickly and unprepossessing Kolka—was in the habit of sleeping around with lots of girls and was looked upon, for some reason, as a most eligible catch. Raisa claimed she was already pregnant by Kolka, but Pasha insisted that she was lying and that Kolka had no intention of marrying her.

"I persuaded her that they must base Kolka's defense on exactly the opposite standpoint, do you see?" Alexandra Prokofievna explained to Irinka. "That is our only hope. Kolka must claim that he acted in a fit of jealousy to defend the honor of the mother of his unborn child. . . ."

She talked to Irinka as though she were grown up; yet the girl was only fourteen at the time. Olga didn't like it, but to express her disapproval was out of the question: her mother-in-law would have instantly taken offense, resulting in yet another row. Olga patiently endured all the endless discussions, phone calls, telegrams and fuss about Kolka. Alexandra Prokofievna took the case very seriously and did indeed find a lawyer, a tough old war horse named Lupovzorov. Gradually Olga was more and more amazed: whence all this zeal, why all these exertions in the defense of people who were, after all, outsiders? What were Kolka and Aunty Pasha to her— to all of them, for that matter? Merely the landlords of the *dacha* they happened to rent—and landlords who charged, what's more, a shamelessly high rent every summer. Otherwise they had nothing whatsoever in common with them, and Alexandra Prokofievna, as a rule, hardly ever spoke to them at all, except to give them an occasional scolding. Of course, she felt sorry for Kolka. . . .

These events happened to coincide with a very difficult time for Olga's mother (caused by the serious illness of Georgii Maximovich) and with the looming shadow of Darya Mamedovna. Everyone in the family got on Olga's nerves. She was irritated by her mother's inability to cope, by her daughter's selfishness, by her husband's muddled and aimless life—what *was* he doing all day while she was at work?—and now by her stupid mother-in-law and her preoccupation with the affairs of people who were virtual strangers, instead of trying to help by doing some housework or going to the parents' meetings at school, as all grandmothers and grandfathers did when the child's parents were working. It was no use expecting Sergei to be any help, and Olga was run ragged. If only the old woman would go to the post office and pay the utility bills during the daytime, when it wasn't crowded—was that really so difficult? Everything was too difficult. Much more difficult than taking the train out of town in bad weather, sloshing along muddy country roads, sitting for hours in court on behalf of people she hardly knew. Much of it was an act, a show of martyrdom. As always with that woman.

One day, in a state of extreme irritation induced by all this—not so much irritation as a wave of such total exhaustion that one's brain ceases to function and one gives way to all the subliminal irritants at once—she told Sergei that Kolka's fate interested her far less than Georgii Maximovich's illness. And would Alexandra Prokofievna with her showoff philanthropy kindly leave her—Olga—alone. It was an unfair thing to say. Alexandra Prokofievna actually bothered her least of all, but Olga couldn't help hearing the ceaseless legal consultations over the phone, the detailed bulletins over the dinner table, on top of which Sergei would later repeat more news that he had heard from his mother. Besides, Olga had just come back from seeing her mother, who was fluttering around aimlessly, distracted with grief as she watched her beloved husband die. Georgii Maximovich had already been in hospital for two weeks, and he was getting steadily worse. Three days ago he had been operated on by Professor Rodin, a famous specialist; the hospital was excellent (they had difficulty in getting him admitted; it was eventually arranged with the help of string-pulling by Vlad, whom they had successfully tracked down), and everything humanly possible was being done for him. Yet even so, Olga's mother reproached herself: she was convinced that she should have given Professor Rodin two hundred rubles before the operation. Someone had given her this idiotic idea, but she hadn't done anything because she had heard about it too late. Now she was tortured by the thought that perhaps because of this the operation might not be effective. Professor Rodin had spoken to her in what she felt was a rather cold, off-hand way, saying: "Unfortunately I can't give you much hope, although I can't say that it's the end either."

Olga's mother was utterly crushed by that remark.

"I think it's insulting to talk like that to the relatives!" she said indignantly through her tears. "Who gave him the right? He spoke to me like some bureaucrat . . ."

Then she immediately started blaming herself and cursing herself for being so cowardly that she had failed to offer money to Professor Rodin. For although her friend had suggested this to her when it was already too late, she had, in fact, thought of it herself earlier but had been unable to make up her mind to do it. Now, after the operation, she had somehow to get hold of a rare Swiss drug, erythrin. The only way was to find someone who might be able to help. As she was now exhausted, and obliged to lie down with an attack of tachycardia, Olga spent two hours at the telephone. A few people promised to try to find out or to ask others who might know, but most said that they themselves were trying to find scarce drugs and couldn't get any. Olga returned home at about nine o'clock in the evening, drank some tea and then decided to call her mother up, because she had left her in such low spirits, simply to find out how she was feeling and whether the tachycardia had subsided. But it was impossible to get to the phone.

Alexandra Prokofievna was talking to Lupovzorov, Kolka's lawyer; their conversation had already lasted exactly forty minutes. Finally Olga went right up to the old woman and whispered that she urgently needed to make a phone call. Her mother-in-law nodded irritably, spoke for another minute, then hung up the receiver.

"Lupovzorov was telling me about the trial. It's very important to me," she said sternly.

Olga replied with equal firmness: "And I have to call my mother. She's not well."

No, Alexandra Prokofievna did not ask what was the matter with Galina Yevgenievna, whether she needed help or perhaps some medicine that she might be able to get at the polyclinic on Kirovskaya Street. She was hardly likely to be able to get erythrin, but she might at least have asked. She was not hostile to Olga's mother, and had never quarreled with her; if there had been restrained arguments between them, it had been long ago, when Olga's mother had been looking after Irinka and Alexandra Prokofievna had preached at her. In those days their common delight and love for the baby had occasionally given rise to tiny outbursts of disagreement, but it was all long forgotten. Now had come the time of placid indifference to each other. Any stranger needing Alexandra Prokofievna's "professional" help was closer to her than her daughter-in-law's mother.

It was after that tiny little spat by the phone, ending in a draw for both sides, that Olga made the remark about "show-off philanthropy." Sergei immediately flared up, like a watchful sentry reaching for his rifle: "Kolka got three years instead of seven. You call that 'showing off'? No, my dear, that's the real thing, something *you* are incapable of comprehending."

She muttered something in reply, taken aback by the alacrity with which he leaped to his mother's defense. Well, maybe she had been wrong; in fact, she certainly had been wrong: there were times when her mother-in-law did help people partly out of pure altruism (although there was little merit in it for she did it mostly out of habit, instilled into her by her professional training)—but she should also be able to understand what a state Olga was in when she came back from seeing her mother. And now Sergei decided to take offense. She was suddenly aware that he was walking into the room dressed in cap and overcoat, with that expression of stony gloom, jaws clenched, which he put on at moments when he felt mortally offended. He circled the room, looking for something.

"Where are you going?"

"To Fyodorov."

Having found what he was looking for—his briefcase—he threw a few papers into it.

Fyodorov, Sergei's friend from his museum days, was, to Olga, a complete nonentity, one of those idle gasbags to whom Sergei was strangely attracted and who dragged him down to their level. Nowadays they met less often, thank God, because Fyodorov had moved to some place on the distant outskirts of Moscow, beyond Kuzminki. She asked, "What's the hurry?"

"No hurry, I simply promised to go and see him." After a pause he added: "Darya Mamedovna will be there."

It turned out that Fyodorov knew her well. She would be coming later, after she had given a lecture. This news produced on Olga the same effect as if a bolt of lightning had struck the next room, flooding the room they were in with light and making an audible crackle.

In a weak voice—she thought it was all over and he was going away forever—she asked how he imagined he was coming back. It was half-past ten o'clock. He said he would stay over there for the night. He spoke calmly, even slightly querulously, as if she were pestering him with trivialities, and she lacked the strength to protest and shout: What the hell game are you playing? What makes you think you can just walk out of the house and spend the night God knows where?

He acted like a man who was doing something completely natural, but of course to go visiting somewhere beyond Kuzminki at half-past ten at night meant staying over there. What was so odd about staying overnight with a friend now and then? There was nothing odd about it, for God's sake! It was simply something that wasn't a part of *their life*. It had never happened before; yet here was Sergei exploiting a sense of grievance in order quite callously and calmly to introduce this novel form of behavior. Olga said no more, dumbfounded by it all—and in particular by Darya Mamedovna. Sergei said "Goodbye" and left.

In the past when they had quarreled, they had sworn at

each other furiously, and he had stomped out or she had fled to her mother, but this was different—quietly, without any door-slamming, just to pick up his briefcase and say "Goodbye." They were like strangers parting—for an hour or for a lifetime: it made no difference.

At the funeral of Georgii Maximovich Olga wept uncontrollably, until she almost fainted—it was a cold spring day, jackdaws were screaming in the air over the crematorium—and she had to be held to prevent her from falling. Indeed she wanted to fall, into oblivion if possible; to go on living seemed pointless, because on the previous day Sergei had said "Perhaps" and then had gone out again until late at night. He had demanded that she *stop tormenting him*. It was impossible to make the most innocent remark: he would instantly flare up and walk out. She had simply asked him: "I suppose you're having an affair with this Darya?"

Sometimes he would go to Fyodorov, sometimes elsewhere. He said that he was seriously interested in parapsychology, and in fact he was reading a lot of old books, trash like Madam Blavatskaya's *Voices of Silence,* journals such as *Rebus* and *The Afterlife Herald*—who gave them to him?—as well as new American and English magazines, from which he would transcribe passages, dictionary in hand. He even made jokes at himself, but to Olga it was no joking matter. As a biologist, she knew quite well the true worthlessness of all that junk. And he was being led astray by a woman who wanted to gain power over him.

"Why do you need all this?"

"I don't. I simply want to understand something that has occupied people for thousands of years. Besides, my Colonel Martinov was a spiritualist and a member of a secret society. Because of it, he actually got into trouble with his superiors in 1916. . . ."

When Sergei jokingly announced that he had been to a spiritualist seance at Fyodorov's place and they had summoned up the spirit of Pobedonostsev, the mentor of Czar Alexander III, who had uttered the obscure remark: "Not thus have we conquered," Olga and Sergei argued furiously for two hours about what it might mean, until his mother could restrain herself no longer and created a scene. She shouted that Sergei's father would have died of shame if anything of this sort had happened while he was alive. The son of Afanasy Troitsky—a spiritualist! The son of a revolutionary, a comrade-in-arms of the great Lunacharsky! If his father were to rise from the grave . . . Sergei observed maliciously: "Aha, so you do allow the possibility that someone can rise from the grave?"

In all this, of course, there was a large element of Sergei's incorrigible love of buffoonery and teasing, but it was also in part a form of escapism, an evasion of the failures that plagued him incessantly. And there was the worst part of all, of which Alexandra Prokofievna knew nothing: Darya Mamedovna. At first when he went miles out to the distant suburbs to Fyodorov's place for the seances he invited Olga to go with him, but she had no desire to go so far to listen to nonsense, and she refused, laughing and sneering at him. All to no purpose. Once Olga spent a whole evening reading *The Spiritualist* magazine for 1906 and several tattered brochures in paper covers that were lying around on Sergei's desk—they were simply appalling in their pathetic intellectual poverty. Sometimes they made her laugh, sometimes angry, but above all she was amazed that so much unbelievable drivel—all these mediums, planchettes, lower spirits, higher spirits, voices from beyond the grave—had actually persisted into the present day. Having read the magazine, she came to two conclusions, both of which frightened her. The first was that the most fervent enthusiasts for all this garbage were women. Somewhere in all this was some hidden enticement for the female mind: the famous Blavatskaya, the authors of *The Spiritualist,* Bykova, Speranskaya, Shchegolkova, a particularly active woman named Kapkanshchikova. "Was it because they were rich, with nothing to do? They should have tried running from store to store, standing in line for shoes. . . ." The second conclusion was even worse: the empty futility of the whole business of conjuring up spirits and meddling with an imaginary "other world" was so obvious that if he continued spending time on this nonsense it meant that there were *other reasons.* That was why, when he answered her question by saying "Perhaps" and went out, her heart sank just because she had been expecting exactly that reply. And no one had wept more bitterly than Olga at Georgii Maximovich's funeral in the Donskoi Monastery.

Sergei supported her on one side, Vlad on the other. She could feel Sergei's granitelike calm. At one point he said, "You must pull yourself together!"

Then Vlad solicitously led her aside—it was at the moment when the music started to play—to a seat by the wall, took a bottle of medicine and a small glass from his pocket and gave her a dose to drink.

As she looked into his aging, pockmarked face she said, "Georgii Maximovich loved you, Vladik."

Vlad nodded mournfully but with a hint of restrained superiority in his demeanor. A black official car was waiting for him on the driveway in front of the crematorium. Olga realized that everything would have been different if Vlad hadn't brought Sergei on that vacation, and she would not be suffering now. How quickly life passed. Without looking around, Sergei was standing very straight and now supporting Olga's mother. The music smothered everything. Afterward they went to the studio on Sushchevskaya, where kind neighbors had arranged everything. In charge of it all was Henrietta Osipovna, an energetic and efficient lady from the Moscow Society of Artists, whom they did not know but who was exactly the right sort of person for the occasion—she called Olga's mother "my dear." The artists had very soon drunk too much and started arguing at the tops of their voices, talking about Georgii Maximovich in such absurdly exaggerated terms that they sounded hypocritical and insincere. All the objects in the studio—pictures, frames, plaster models, jars, brushes—seemed orphaned, unneeded and displaced. Uncle Petya, who had turned into a scrawny, white-haired old man, coughed noisily all evening and kept shouting "Oh, stop it!" at someone.

Amid this crowded hubbub Olga's mother seemed lost, with the air of someone who happened to be there by chance. Olga was terrified when she thought about her mother: How was she going to live now? Olga stayed to spend the night with her mother, while Sergei, Irinka and Alexandra Prokofievna went home.

Georgii Maximovich's first wife was also at the crematorium and came on to Sushchevskaya afterward but did not come to the gathering in the studio, although she was invited. Instead, in a tasteless and unnecessary gesture, she arranged her own funeral party—on the same floor, in rooms belonging to a woman artist. Some of the guests moved back and forth from one party to the other. Once Uncle Petya flung open the door and shouted menacingly into the empty corridor: "I'll come over there in a moment—and I'll smash all the crockery. The idea—having two funeral parties at once!"

From the other party something was said in reply, but it was inaudible. Olga sat on a couch beside a bearded old artist called Likhnevich, who would not go home but repeatedly filled his glass first with tea, then with liqueur, and wept as he described their life together in Paris a hundred years ago, when he and Georgii Maximovich, young and brash, thought they would conquer Paris. Marc Chagall had been with them in those days, too—and how had it all ended? A funeral party on Sushchevskaya. He advised Olga to sell two drawings—a church in Montmartre and a self-portrait with a wry expression on the face—and to give all the rest away to anyone who would take them, because Georgii Maximovich had personally burned all his best work in the thirties; it was a foolish thing to do—a moment of weakness, and a whole life was smashed to fragments, like that piece of fallen plaster: it could never be picked up, never put together again. All his later work was just trash, despite his official rehabilitation, despite the committees he sat on, despite the commissions he received ("Don't think I envied him, Olga; I pitied him, poor Georges"). But Olga, having already cried for her stepfather and worrying about her mother, unable to imagine the future, was wondering why Sergei hadn't stayed with her—Irinka could have gone home with her grandmother. He should have stayed with her, but he had not wanted to. "Well, we're off," he had said. "I'm taking Irinka home. It's time she went to bed."

Sergei lived a separate life. His work had ceased to interest him; his dissertation was getting nowhere. Instead, he told endless stories about the funny answers and amazing prophecies that were produced at the seances he attended. She still refused to believe in "that nonsense"—well, how could anyone seriously believe they had made contact with a Franciscan monk named Brother Arnulf, who had lived in Switzerland in the sixteenth century, and that now Sergei was holding regular conversations with him. She became more and more firmly convinced that Darya Mamedovna had bewitched him.

Olga saw her once, quite by chance, in the theater. They had gone to a première at the Sovremennik and were walking in the upstairs foyer during the intermission when suddenly Sergei squeezed her arm very hard—she had a huge bruise afterward to prove how painful it had been—in a purely reflex gesture that felt like a nip from a pair of pincers, and he whispered, "That's Darya Mamedovna over in the corner!"

Before looking toward the corner, she looked at him. He had gone red in the face. Darya Mamedovna was dark and thin, with streaks of silver in her black hair. When Sergei and Olga approached her, she looked at him with an unsmiling, even unwelcoming expression. Beside her sat an unshaven young man in a dirty white polo-necked sweater. Sergei said hello and introduced Olga. The young man was at least twenty years younger than Darya Mamedovna. She did not introduce him. No conversation took place, although Sergei shuffled from foot to foot for two or three awkward, unnecessary moments, in which Olga felt painfully embarrassed, before they moved away.

"I pity you," said Olga.

"Why do you pity me? What nonsense. I don't know what you mean," he blustered. Having decided to take offense, he didn't talk to Olga again for the rest of the intermission.

The play was funny, but they did not laugh. It was then that she suddenly felt—like a wave of coldness—a premonition of disaster.

Another meeting took place in a house on one of the embankments, a house with caryatids and little rooms that recalled the partitioned room they had long ago occupied on Shabolovka. It was the home of one of Fyodorov's friends, a highway engineer, who was a spiritualist and a collector of books on magic and occultism. He showed them an old book called *Sorcery.*

Once again Sergei invited her to come to a seance and see what happened, but she desperately did not want to: she felt that his invitation was insincere, that he didn't mean it when he said, "Come on, let's go together. . . . We'll have a good laugh."

In reality, though, she knew *he did not want her to go.* Therefore she had to overcome her aversion, so this time she said yes. "Their life" was falling apart, turning into something fragmented, a mosaic, as in a dream; a dream is always fragmentary, whereas waking reality is a unified whole.

Olga arrived at the seance with a headache. In the lobby of the apartment there hung a poster that read: "Silence—thou art best of all I have yet heard." The air was full of a sweetish smell, as in a church, of candle smoke and hot wax. Everyone spoke in barely audible whispers and flung their coats in a heap on some chests in the hall. Olga noticed that the parquet floor had not been scraped for a long time and was gray with dirt.

She was filled with a blind determination, of the kind that one feels only in dreams: to talk with *that woman.* Darya Mamedovna, however, was not there when Olga and Sergei arrived; she came two hours later, when the seance was over. The people who had seated themselves around the table shared a look of tenseness and covert unease. No one joked or smiled; they tried not to look at each other, gazing instead at the middle of the table, where a small glass stood in the center of a sheet of paper on which the letters of the alphabet were written out in a circle. There were five women and four men. Sergei had said they wer mostly engineers or technicians, and one of the women, it later transpired, was a cashier in a theater box office. Fyodorov was present, unnaturally silent and grim-looking. In charge of the proceedings was a highway engineer, a pale man with a red spade beard, who spoke in rapid, abrupt sentences. Every remark that he made sounded slightly like a command, which was unpleasant. The man himself, affectedly dressed in a thick-knit red woolen vest, a bootlace instead of a tie, struck Olga as altogether disagreeable. He had long fingers tinged with white around the nails. Throughout the evening he never once looked at Olga, although she felt that he was keeping her under ceaseless scrutiny with all his senses. Someone said they should open a window, others objected, and this gave rise to an argument. The two women who wanted the window open argued with extraordinary heat and fury, and even threatened that if their demand was not met they would leave the meeting, which would then—so it was implied—lose all meaning. It was clear that the real matter in dispute was not fresh air but something of sublime, universal significance. The host, after hesitating for a while, found a solution by compromise: he opened the door into an adjoining room and flung open a window in there.

Sergei was sitting opposite her. His expression was impenetrable. What was he thinking about? Olga's heart ached with worry and with pity for him: he was as unhappy as she was. Back at home things were waiting to be done: housework, shopping, clothes to be taken to the laundry (it was open until nine o'clock in the evening, but every day tiredness or other chores prevented Olga from getting there on time) and she had to write a report, while his notebooks, folders and books awaited Sergei, all the material for his dissertation that was bogged down halfway along—and instead of tackling it . . . The man in the red vest commanded them:

"Place your left hand on the right arm of your neighbor . . . Foot against foot . . . Form a chain . . ."

The little glass really did seem to come to life beneath the touch of nine hands; at first it jerked around indecisively, then darted briskly and convulsively across the paper from letter to letter, and after an initial spell of confused gibberish, sentences began to form. Father Paisios said, "Be not chary of doing good, it shall repay thee an hundredfold, thou fool." The word "fool" caused some perplexity. Why should he speak contemptuously of someone who was doing good? One of the ladies explained that evidently the spirit of Father Paisios was being ironic at the expense of earthly morality, since by our cynical present-day standards the doers of good deeds were regarded as fools. The spirit of Torquemada held a long and muddled conversation, but to the general disappointment his remarks were for some reason couched in banal journalistic clichés.

Then followed an experiment in psychography: one of the women held a pencil poised over a sheet of paper while the others sat around the table as before and tried to summon up the spirit of Alexander Herzen. At first the great man obstinately refused to appear. Someone suggested they should leave him alone, others did not agree, until the host in an angry whisper demanded that they cease arguing and get on with the task in hand. The lights were put out, the tension rose until amid total silence they could all finally hear the squeak of pencil on paper. The woman, sitting at a separate table, was actually writing! No one doubted that her pencil was being guided by the hand of Herzen himself. When the light was switched on, the woman was leaning back in her chair exhausted, her face streaming with sweat and terribly pale; she was immediately given a dose of valerian. Then they rushed to look at the paper, which was entirely covered with huge, sprawling letters.

Seizing the sheet of paper, the host read out in a voice hoarse with excitement: "'My . . . rifuge . . . the river . . .'"

Olga heard Sergei giggle. She could not have been mistaken, because she knew that malicious snigger of his only too well, but when she looked at him, his face was as inscrutable as before. Voices were heard saying:

"What else? Isn't there any more?"

"Nothing more, only those four words," replied the host, still in the grip of excitement.

The paper was examined, the scrawled writing was carefully studied, and again an argument broke out. What did "the river" mean? And why "rifuge"? They agreed that "the river" was probably a symbol for time—the river of time—and the spirit of Herzen was no doubt expressing a conviction that time would vindicate him. The word "rifuge," however, put them in a dilemma. Could the spirit of Herzen make such a crass error in spelling? The writer was sternly asked whether she was sure she knew how to spell the word "refuge." The woman—it was the theater cashier, who was distinguished by her mediumistic sensitivity—indignantly rejected the suggestion that she could make such an elementary mistake.

"What do you think I am—illiterate?" she said, on the verge of tears.

Sergei remarked that in that case, they would have to admit that Herzen was the one who was illiterate. This started another argument, with everyone talking at once, until the host cleared up the problem: spelling mistakes were of no significance; the important part of the message was its content, not its form. He explained that when the writing on the wall had appeared at Belshazzar's feast—*mene, tekel, phares*—it had never occurred to anyone to discuss whether the words were correctly spelled: everyone who saw it was just seized with horror. Incidentally, in the Book of Daniel the words were given as: *mene, mene, tekel, upharsin*—a normal example of tautology and transposition of letters that occurs in psychography. . . . Feeling that her headache was getting worse, Olga could no longer bear sitting there and went into the next room to lie down on the divan. It was cold. Someone came in behind her and shut the window.

It was one of her very worst attacks of migraine, accompanied by nausea. Sergei brought a glass of hot tea and a tablet and covered her with some kind of throw. She wanted him to stay and sit beside her—just to be alone together for a while. She held him by the hand and asked: "You do realize that all this is nonsense, don't you?"

He said that he did. Through the terrible pain that was boring into her temples, another pain thrust itself in like a needle: "If he realizes it, then why does he come?" But she did not ask that question; she felt too weak.

"It's all auto-suggestion. . . . It's third-year psychology stuff," she whispered.

About twenty minutes or a half-hour later someone came into the room and switched on the table lamp.

"How are you feeling?" a woman's voice asked, and Olga saw that it was Darya Mamedovna.

With a great effort she raised herself and sat up. Sergei was not in the room. As before, her head was splitting.

"Better," she said.

She looked at the woman's dark, sharp-chinned face with amazement. Why had she come? More than once Olga had imagined this: she would talk to this woman alone, choosing words of venomous hatred; yet now all those words had suddenly vanished, her malice dissipated as though by a draft of air, and the only thing Olga felt was a faint asthmatic shortness of breath.

"I wish Sergei wouldn't spend his time on all this trash," she said, gasping slightly.

The woman held out a glass. "Drink this."

Obediently, Olga drank it down.

Darya Mamedovna sat down beside her on the divan and said in a calm voice that she, too, thought Sergei was wasting his time on nonsense. Although, in fact, it wasn't so much nonsense as an amusement, a game. A Saturday entertainment for tired, overworked people. Some gambled at poker, some played mahjongg, others were chess fanatics. . . . And more such banalities. But the effrontery of the woman: *she* was against it too! No one in the world beside Olga had the right to be against anything that Sergei chose to do. "Stupid woman!" Olga thought. "And everyone says she's so intelligent." This insight calmed her greatly and even made her head ache a little less.

Darya Mamedovna said, "I've been wanting to talk to you for a long time . . ."

"Why can that be?" Olga wondered, quite without alarm. Aloud she said, "Do you want to talk now?"

"If you feel well enough." Darya Mamedovna produced cigarettes and a lighter from her purse, and without asking Olga's permission—a charming and characteristic trait—lit a cigarette. "Sergei once told me that you were working on problems of cell compatibility. . . ."

Ah, so that was it! Was that all she wanted to talk about? Darya Mamedovna went on to say that some of her research was concerned with questions of incompatibility. So she was interested in it from the opposite angle. Olga told her a little about her work. Darya Mamedovna inquired about Olga's colleague Andrei Ivanovich, whom she had known at university. Then she began talking about her own work on extrasensory perception, about all the different kinds of tests, trials, and research projects, about the thousands of experiments that had been done abroad and how Soviet research had fallen behind and needed to catch up. "You, as a biologist," she said, "studying problems of communication and biological incompatibility, must constantly come up against this. What about bats and their locator mechanisms? And what about fish? You must agree there are no *a priori* grounds to deny the existence of special, extrasensory means of communication in the structure."

Olga didn't want to argue with her, but even so, gasping for breath a little and in a weak voice she said: "There is too much fraud involved in parapsychology. In no other science— if you can call it a science—are there so many swindlers. Why do you think that is so?"

"Because, Olga Vasilievna, people remain in a permanent state of self-deception: they think everything is known already."

Olga said, "Talking of incompatibility . . . One of the great riddles is still the problem of allergy. Do you know that there are people who exhibit a morbid reaction to a particular person: they start coughing, suffer from shortness of breath . . ."

"Oh yes. Of course. The question is, What is the mechanism that produces this effect?"

As Olga replied, looking at the other woman's dark Caucasian forehead, she thought: "They want to dig down into everything, to reveal the structure, find the means of communication that transmit hatred, jealousy, fear. And love. Then if they find the means of communication—will they then want to control them?" Someone opened the door, wanting to come in. Darya Mamedovna said sternly, "Shut the door!"—and it was shut.

"Darya Mamedovna, I want to talk to you . . . about a certain thing—" Olga suddenly said in a miserable, quavering voice. "If only Sergei wouldn't get wrapped up in all this, interesting though it is . . . You see, he's no longer exactly a young man, his health isn't too good, he has his own work, he has responsibilities."

Darya Mamedovna widened her dark, blue-rimmed eyes in a strange fashion, and bent her head over toward her right shoulder. "What do you mean? I don't understand."

"I mean, Darya Mamedovna, that he is destroying himself.

Everything has stopped, his dissertation is not getting written . . ."

"But my dear, what can anyone do about it? His dissertation's not getting written?" She suddenly laughed. "And a good thing, too! Please don't be offended, Olga Vasilievna. The fact is, I don't like—no, that's not true, it isn't that I don't like—I pity people working in the humanities, all these literary scholars and historians, all the scribbling brotherhood who are forced to do nothing but talk, talk, talk, nothing but talk—and it's all so much hot air. I pity them, poor creatures. Really, to think of devoting one's entire life to such trash—and it really is trash—as finding out about all the informers who used to work for the czarist secret police in Moscow. Who needs it? I laughed when he talked so enthusiastically about those, you know, discoveries he had made in that tiny little microcosm . . ."

A burst of laughter was heard in the next room, someone thumped on the wall with his fist and shouted, "Nigmatova, come here!"

". . . and this at a time when the fate of the world is in the balance—when people are literally faced with Shakespeare's question: 'To be or not to be . . .'"

Then quite suddenly she started to tell Olga how she became interested in parapsychology. Several years ago her husband Nigmatov, an artist, had died in an air crash. That night in a dream she saw his face, distorted with terror.

She described it quite dispassionately, simply as one of the facts of extrasensory telepathic communication. Olga felt no pity for Darya Mamedovna. She thought: "If Sergei is in love with this woman, then he is profoundly unhappy."

It was late. Irinka, for whom she had promised she would do something that day, was waiting for them at home; so as soon as Sergei came into the room she said they must go home, and she got up. He gave them both a rapid, penetrating look; he was evidently satisfied, because he said calmly:

"Good, let's go."

Usually he had to be dragged home with a tractor.

Out on the street, he said that everyone had been intrigued to know what she and Darya Mamedovna had been talking about for so long. "It's not like her. She's not a great talker. That means she must like you."

"Yes. She liked me," said Olga. "We were talking about you. She pities you."

"Me? She pities me? Let her pity me; there's plenty to pity me for."

"She thinks your work is so much trash."

"Oh, come on!" He laughed and gave a sly wink, like someone who can't be fooled.

Even so, she felt relieved.

Yet after a few days it all started again—he would go out, he disappeared, lived a separate, unknown life, and Olga suffered torments.

In Irinka's early childhood, when she was about seven or eight, strange things had happened to her. She used to get up at night and go sleepwalking, bumping into things, and once at the apartment on Shabolovka she had frightened her parents' guests by appearing in the doorway like a little ghost, in a white nightdress. She had walked up to the table—looking asleep, eyes closed—and said as she stretched out an empty hand: "Would you like my Gypsy?" She meant her favorite doll, a Gypsy girl. After that it occurred less and less frequently, and by the time Irinka was ten it stopped altogether.

Sergei remembered about these strange incidents in Irinka's childhood, and he decided that they might mean she was one of those "psychic" persons that he was seeking in order to pursue his hobby. He was becoming seriously interested in parapsychological experiments. He exasperated everyone at home with his attempts to guess what they were thinking about or what they intended to do, and by his efforts to project his will on to them. To begin with, of course, his will only involved something trivial, like picking up a box of matches or switching off the light in the hallway. Once he joyfully exclaimed, "Bravo! At last! For half an hour I've been willing you to shut the window."

Sometimes, equally unexpectedly, he would show irritation and annoyance, even sounding resentful: "No, really, you are so thick-skinned, it's impossible to get through to you. I've been sending out waves of suggestion and you don't even . . ."

All this was simple boyish fun, reminiscent of the games

played by inquisitive schoolboys in the "Psychology for Fun" club, and Olga might have treated it as such, half jokingly and half approvingly, because it actually seemed to enliven Sergei; it made him more cheerful, the tone of his life visibly improved and his cheeks looked pink, which showed that his new enthusiasm was doing him some good. Like everything else it was good if taken in moderation, but this game was turning into something bigger. Olga was alarmed to catch hints that all this was simply a series of preliminaries, a search for a method, and that when he had freed himself of some of his commitments he was going to take up the full-time study of psychology and parapsychology. She said this sounded somewhat naïve; it was like saying one intended studying physics and metaphysics.

"Aren't you afraid of turning into a Jack-of-all-trades and master of none?"

He looked at her vacantly. "Be more careful in choosing your jokes. Right now it is the only thing in life that interests me."

After a remark like that, what was there left to do? She stopped joking and waited to see what would happen. At any rate, it seemed to her that his infatuation was over.

God, what a mistake that was! She shouldn't have waited. She shouldn't have stopped fighting, shouldn't have surrendered him to the absolute power of Darya and her bunch of table tappers. What a naïve fool she was: it was, after all, obvious that he was moving away, casting off, like a ship slipping its moorings from the quayside, having hoisted all sail and flags—and she kept waiting for something, hoping for something. She didn't realize that he was going through the midlife crisis. Her chief torment was her failure to understand him. One day she decided to act positively, as though nothing had happened, as though his damned hobby had not come between them like a wall; without telling him she bought tickets to a movie that the whole of Moscow was fighting to see, so that the tickets were like gold dust. He said he was sorry, but at ten o'clock that evening he was busy. Busy? What with? Was he going out? No, he would be at home. But from ten o'clock onward he was busy.

She felt extremely hurt, but she did not try to make him

change his mind; swallowing her pride, she went alone. In the movie theater she could not hold out for longer than a quarter-hour, and she ran home. Surely on top of it all he hadn't started lying to her? She felt powerless: if he were cheating, it was only because he had finally gotten himself so hopelessly entangled and disorientated—he had never cheated on her before—that he was beyond her help. There is no greater agony than incomprehension and a total inability to help. But when she came rushing home she saw that he had been telling the truth—he really was busy.

He was shut in their room, a look of grim concentration on his face as he laid out his deck of Sehner cards, special cards with squares and stars for parapsychology tests. It appeared that he and Darya Mamedovna had arranged to have a seance at ten o'clock that evening: acting as the "percipient," the person who has to guess the cards, she was sitting in Bolshevo, at the Film-Makers Club.

He had driven Irinka nearly crazy with these cards. At first he had told her that she was very gifted, that her percentage of correct answers was significantly higher than the median of probability.

"You could become world famous. I'm not joking. You'll be invited to go abroad, and Mama and I will go with you."

Fairy tales of this nature were meant to keep up her interest and encourage her, because soon, of course, the business began to bore her. Gradually her success rate got worse and worse. Sergei became nervous and bad-tempered. She never again achieved such high scores after the first few days.

"Think! Concentrate!" he would say irritably. "What's the matter with you?"

In the past, too, he had lacked patience when he tried to help Irinka with her homework, and his efforts always ended in a quarrel. Now it was just the same. One day Irinka burst into tears. Sergei's mother thumped the table. "That's enough! I can't bear to watch you crippling this child's mind. You may send yourself crazy with all this obscurantist nonsense if you like; you're a grown man and can answer for yourself—but leave Irinka alone."

They began to argue. As always, their arguments were conducted without shouting and without rudeness but with extreme venom and, probably, with a mutual infliction of pain. Alexandra Prokofievna was also inspired, no doubt, by memories of the celebrated disputes over metaphysics that took place in the 1920s between Lunacharsky and Archbishop Vvedensky.

"If you admit even for one second the existence of life after death and a higher power, namely God . . ."

"I didn't say that. You're not in court now, so don't try your old lawyer's trick of misrepresenting me."

"What is it, then, if not agnosticism?"

"In your view, I suppose, the train has reached the last station and stopped, has it? And the track leads no further forward?"

"Your track, Sergei, is not leading forward but backward to the Dark Ages. But I can't understand why you lead a double life. Take your beliefs to their logical conclusion: put on the black habit, shave the top of your head, take your vows and go and live in a cave or in an abandoned stone-quarry on the road to Paveletsk, sit there and contemplate your navel, like a Tibetan lama. Live on locusts and wild honey. Your wife can bring you locusts from the pet store.—" There were times when the old woman could turn out a brilliant line in sarcastic wit. At the same time she could never admit that the disgraceful state of affairs was Sergei's fault alone, so she had to drag Olga into it. "But that wouldn't suit you, would it? You'd have to leave the institute, which pays you a salary."

"I might leave it. By the way, that's not a bad idea of yours. If they do set up a laboratory for the study of extrasensory perception in one of the research institutes, as has been promised, I would gladly go there."

At this stage, all this was said in the heat of argument and with the aim of annoying his mother. Again he assured her that he was interested in science and science alone. But in this universe of ours there were still too many mysteries—antimatter, quasars, mysterious particles that had neither fixed mass nor electrical charge—so why could one not predicate the existence of suprasensory means of communication as yet unknown to science?

"Sergei, I am horrified to see that after forty years your head has filled itself with the most incredible jumble . . ."

"Whereas over the same period you, Mother dear, have remained totally undisturbed by a single new idea. I suppose that in itself is an achievement of a sort."

"And I'm proud of it. I don't think about death, as other old women do. I know that when I breathe my last, I shall vanish from this world without a trace—and so will everyone else. There's nothing to discuss."

"Yes, yes, there's nothing to discuss," Sergei mumbled, nodding. "How wonderful to see it with such clarity. And what about the death of those you love, your family? Will they too disappear without a trace?"

"I hope those of my family that fate has so far spared will not go before I do. But if—God forbid—such an injustice were to happen, then as far as I'm concerned the people who are dear to me—I repeat, as far as I'm concerned—would not depart absolutely without trace. For me, they would still be here." And she slapped the spot in the middle of her chest where, at times when she felt a touch of heart trouble, a mustard plaster was applied.

Olga could not bear listening to conversations of this kind. She only knew one thing: she could not help. And this reduced her to despair. When she came back into the room a little later, she saw that Sergei was alone.

He was standing in an attitude of indecision, half turned toward the window—it was not clear whether he was about to walk away from the window or step toward it—and looking down into the yard. It was as if he were reflecting on something with enormous concentration. Olga saw his bent back, his stooping shoulders and the gray among his thinning hair. It suddenly seemed as if an old man were standing there.

"My old man," she said quietly, walking up to him and putting her arms around him.

He did not turn, did not respond, but remained standing and looking down into the yard. The summer was over. It had been an unhappy one for Olga: her mother was slowly expiring with loneliness in the apartment on Sushchevskaya; it was the first summer in which they hadn't rented a *dacha*—a foretaste of homelessness to come. Faina's eyes had opened wide and shone with voluptuous curiosity; she pitied Olga, pitied her with all her heart, she even groaned with pity: "I'll go to the Scientific Workers' Union. I'll teach that Darya to keep her hands off married men." Her voice shook with anger. Nothing is sweeter than compassion for one's best friend. She didn't go to the Union, thank God. But she told Mara. And it all started to move and to grow, like a magic tree that a fakir conjures up out of nothing before one's eyes. She did not learn the details until the day when they went out to the woods on a mushroom-picking excursion. She knew only one thing: that he had handed in his resignation.

It had suddenly seemed the best thing for him to do.

That fall, on a day in October when it was still warm and the leaves were still on the trees—everything was over, except the warm weather, except the mushrooms and the forest—they left the institute by bus at four in the morning. Almost everyone from Olga's laboratory came on the trip. Sergei was sitting beside her, his head on her shoulder, asleep. It was such a pleasure to feel the weight of his head. She wanted everyone to be quiet so that he could sleep, wanted it with all the force of her will power. Gray, misty, the countryside around Moscow flowed past the window; first there were mounds of dirt churned up on construction sites, chalky-gray slabs of new apartment houses, fields of watery green, birch trees, aspens, then fir trees. The road dipped downhill, more new houses rose up among the fir trees, a shower of rain flattened itself in a watery layer on the window and then suddenly disappeared. By the time they got out of the bus fifty-two kilometers outside Moscow, beyond Pakhra, the rain had stopped. The forest was wet, smelling of tired, sodden grass. Under the trees, where no grass grew, the layer of brown pine-needles covering the ground looked dark and swollen with moisture. There were not many mushrooms to be found. All the others on the outing had scattered in different directions.

Sergei said that if he had publicly admitted himself to have been at fault in having attended those idiotic seances, if he had stung himself with his own tail like a scorpion, the institute officials would still not have left him alone. Klimuk was now deputy director of the institute, having successfully levered Kislovsky out of the job, and a young man called Sharipov occupied Klimuk's old post as academic secretary. This Sharipov, twenty-eight years old, was a real go-getter, with a master's degree and several books to his credit. He had conducted the "case" against Sergei with an unwavering hand. There was no reason, indeed, why he should have found it difficult. He had never shared meat or drink with Sergei; they had met for the first time on the staircase, when he had stopped for a moment and inquired briefly and amiably: "Excuse me, Sergei Afanasievich, is it true that you go to spiritualistic seances?" Sergei had replied equally casually: "Yes, I used to go last winter out of sheer curiosity. I've also been looking for people who are receptive to extrasensory stimuli, because I'm fascinated by parapsychological experiments. It's very interesting. Parapsychology is undoubtedly the science of the future." Sharipov listened, smiling sympathetically. Hustlers like him have a gift for asking sudden pointed questions, smiling sympathetically, and running rapidly upstairs. Klimuk kept himself clear of the affair. He signed no statements on behalf of the institute, although he could have—the director was away in Bulgaria—and he invited Sergei into his office, where he made a show of trying to persuade him to withdraw his resignation and even mumbled a few absurd, patently insincere remarks, such as: "How is Olga? . . . You must call us up sometime . . . ," at which Sergei simply laughed and said, "Are you joking?" Nothing terrible actually happened, no positive action was taken against him, but he was nevertheless glad that the episode had taken place, because the moment had come to start another life. Hell, there was so little time left for another life; but he must, finally, take the plunge and start. Start what? Start doing what truly excited him. Everybody had something that truly excited him, but you have to struggle and claw your way up to get there.

It amazes us that we don't understand one another. Why don't other people understand us? This lack in our lives seems to be the source of all evil. Oh, if only we were understood. There would be no more quarrels, no more wars. . . . Parapsychology is a visionary attempt to get inside another person's mind, to surrender oneself to another person, to heal oneself through understanding; it is an age-old desire that shows no sign of abating. . . . But then why do we, wretched creatures that we are, strive to understand others when we cannot understand ourselves? We should try understanding *ourselves,* my God, for a start. But no; we lack the strength, we lack the time, or perhaps we lack sufficient intelligence or courage. There is Olga, for instance, a biochemist, in charge of a laboratory; she is in good standing, she wins prizes and earns bonuses, but is this her real vocation? She herself has said, "How I wish I had gone into applied art. I so love making things with my hands, modeling, carving." And did not Sergei used to say that history was a major mirror in which one might foretell the future, that he was prepared to spend his whole life studying it, staring into it? Yes, he did say that, he did! He felt it, he thought it. Yet perhaps in thinking it, there was a quite different, concealed, unadmitted motivation at work: to study in order to foretell. Because he now felt that all those minuscule details of details, those crumbs from the tables of banquets long past were of no use to anyone except perhaps five or six people in the whole world. If one thought only of oneself, to whom these few details were of most value, then perhaps there was some point in continuing one's work, but it was so boring to think always of oneself. And one day the boredom became quite intolerable. Suddenly, like a faint gleam, like the feeble light of dawn through the tree trunks, came the idea: another life . . .

Olga felt her heart contract with fear. Where, for God's sake, was a new life to be found? What could possibly bring it about? Moving from one house to another? Buying a new briefcase? Going to this office every morning instead of to that one? Basically, things were the same everywhere. Sergei objected:

"Oh no! To talk like that is like saying that all women are the same. But how awful to spend one's life with a woman one doesn't love. Which, of course, is the way most people live."

He said this calmly, as though discussing something extraneous that had nothing to do with Olga and himself, but even so it was terrifying. As they were talking, they had wandered deep into the forest, completely forgetting that they had come to pick mushrooms. In any case, there were few mushrooms. They met a woman with a bucket half full of white milk-cap mushrooms. They asked her whether that kind was edible. The woman explained how you had to boil them down, pour away the liquid, and then marinate them in diluted vinegar. Having told them this, the woman disappeared, and they forgot to ask her the way back to the road. The aspens and birch thinned out, giving way to a dense fir plantation, heavily sodden with the damp. Here there was absolutely nothing to be found; they pushed their way through the thicket of conifers, because somewhere ahead there was a glimmer of brighter light, a glimpse or two of a glade or a clearing. That was where another life would begin.

They sat down on a tree stump; Sergei was tired, his face was gray and he was breathing heavily. Then they moved on again. The humidity in the pine forest was oppressive, the smell of rotting wood drifted up from the dead branches underfoot, from the depths of gullies and ravines. Here and there they found themselves on black, swampy ground as they walked on and on, talking, enticed by the brightness ahead. The cloudy, overcast weather cleared up a little, but still no pathway, no clearing opened out beyond the trees. She already realized that they were lost. Suddenly Irinka appeared beside them, and Olga tightly clasped her cold little hand. Irinka was now only twelve. Olga had to ask Sergei something painful that concerned only the two of them, and Irinka's presence was embarrassing. But later Irinka went away, and Olga asked about Darya Mamedovna. Was it true? One thing alone worried her: Was it true? Sergei laughed and said that it wasn't. Then she asked him: "And what about the money that you borrowed from the credit union? After your death they came and demanded the money back. What did you spend it on? Please tell me truthfully—no one can hear us, we're in the forest." He said, "I didn't spend it on anything; I just lent it to various people and they never gave it back."

How absurd—and how like him. He mentioned some names, all of them unknown to her. Even so, she believed him, instantly and totally. She wondered how she was going to live in this forest alone. They really should run, or they would be late; the bus was waiting on the road, but they had no idea where the road was or which way to run. So they just ran—straight ahead, jumping over gullies, plunging through the dead, mildewed fir-branches that covered the ground or scratched their faces and hands. Finally they came to a fence. It was high and solid, painted dark green and they only saw it when it suddenly loomed up close in front of them. What was behind the fence? Nothing could be heard or seen, except that the same fir trees appeared to be growing on the other side.

They walked beside the fence along a not very clear path—obviously few people ever came here—and the farther they went, the less hope there seemed of finding the right way. Four men and a woman were sitting on a bench alongside a gateway in the fence. One of the men was huge and pudgy; he had a large prominent forehead, little piglike eyes, and a face with that expression, obtuse but good-natured, typical of people suffering from Down's syndrome. The others were an old man who continually nodded his head, and two of middle age, one bearded, who stared grimly from two eyes like glowing coals, the other short, with a flat, unhappy face, whose little legs dangled from the bench without touching the ground. All four men sat silent and inactive, while the woman, in a gray hospital robe, was reading a newspaper. Olga asked the way to the road. The men did not know. The large man with Down's syndrome said there was no road in these parts. Sergei started to get angry and insisted that there was a road: they had come here by bus, and the bus was waiting on the road. No, they said, no bus comes out this way and there is no road. Sergei grew even more heated. "Don't argue with them," said the woman, laying aside her newspaper. "They don't know. Come on, I'll show you the way." When they had gone some distance away from the men, who remained sitting on the bench, the woman said, "They're patients. They don't know where the road is."

The woman led them through the thick of the forest, where there was no path. No doubt it was a shortcut. Olga squeezed Irinka's hand. "Please forgive us for putting you to this trouble," she said to the woman. "We're late, and the bus is waiting for us on the road."

"I understand," the woman replied. "That's why I'm taking you by the shortcut."

Twilight set in and it began to grow dark. Almost imperceptibly, the daylight was fading away. They had to clamber down between fir trees growing on a steep slope, then plunged once more into the dense undergrowth. "We'll soon be there," said the woman. They were very tired and barely had the strength to go on. Suddenly the woman said, "Here we are."

They were standing in front of a small woodland swamp. "What's this?" Olga asked.

"This is the road," said the woman. "There's your bus—over there." She stretched out her arm, pointing to a clump of sedge growing on the far side of the swamp. Olga felt herself turning numb and very cold, gripped by a sudden icy lassitude that struck like a flash of lightning. Just then a noise cut through her consciousness. A moment later the news arrived from the other world: Time to get up. . . .

The alarm clock rang at seven, wrenching her out of clinging, enervating oblivion. So it continued for many days, each one like the other, although at times it was sunny, at times it rained or snowed. One day, though, she woke up before the alarm. She walked barefoot over to the window, pulled back the draperies and looked out toward the park: there, above the treetops, above the jagged dark horizon of roofs and chimneys, the red globe of the sun was sliding up into the faintly glowing sky. She opened the little casement at the top of the window. The wind blowing from across the park caressed her tired skin, and her breasts tautened with the cold. Through her bare feet she felt the floor quiver from some vague, subterranean rumble.

Whenever they had two or three hours of free time, they would ride out to Spasskoye-Lykovo and take a walk there: by trolley-bus to the last stop, then a short walk and a half-hour trip on the riverboat. The village was perched on top of some high hills, thickly grown with pinewoods. Moscow had long since sent out its tentacles on all sides of this ancient semirural, semiresidential township, had flowed around it, surging westward, but had somehow not quite swallowed it up: the pine trees still stood unfelled, the water-meadow shimmered in its lush green, and high on a hilltop over the river and above the pines floated the bell tower of the old Spasskoye-Lykovo church, visible from far away on every side. After stepping down from the wooden jetty onto the path that wound along the bank, they would walk on and on, talking, breathing the river air, walking around the anglers and looking disapprovingly at the little cars that somehow or other managed to drive here, blocking the path at the very water's edge, even though there was no proper road leading to the riverside. This was their refuge, their riverbank, their grass. Anyone else who found the way here was an interloper, an alien.

Moscow was no place for them. Too many people knew them both, and none of these people, friends and acquaintances, would understand. Olga, too, could not understand it; she could only marvel and feel ashamed that another life had begun so suddenly and so quickly. Once they had dreamed of another life, searched and striven to attain it. But it is not something to be attained; it comes, if at all, by itself. He had weak lungs, easily caught cold and always suffered badly; a little chill would last a long time because he had an unusual constitution and could not tolerate antibiotics. He lived as though in the nineteenth century, treating himself with raspberry juice and herbal tea. Olga worried about him, because she could not be near him when he was sick. She felt that the people around him could not give him the kind of care he needed. As they climbed a slippery path up the hillside, she told him news of her job, about experiments; she told him about Irinka, who was planning to marry soon, telling him without embarrassment her innermost thoughts about Irinka. He, too, told her about all his concerns, about difficulties at work, about the people who worked under him, and asked her advice; but he did not care to talk about his home. And she understood him.

One day they climbed up the bell tower of Spasskoye-

Lykovo church. It was an exhausting climb, he stopped to rest twice on the stone staircase, and when they came out at the top, under the bell, his heart was thumping very hard and they each took a sedative. But their reward was to see Moscow stretching away in the twilight. The towers shone for a moment, then faded, the light faded, everything turned blue and blurred, like a memory; but if they strained their eyes Olga could just make out the slablike skyscraper of the Hydroproject building near her house, and he could discern the faint spire of the skyscraper on Vosstanie Square, next to the building where he lived. It was windy up there, and suddenly it hit them with a violent gust. She stretched out toward him to screen him and save him from the cold, and he took her in his arms. There was nothing wrong in what she was doing, she thought. There was nothing wrong, because another life was already around her, as inexhaustible as that cold, windy expanse, vast as that boundless city fading from sight with the coming of evening.

The House
on the Embankment

Not one of those boys is alive today. Some were killed in the war, some died from sickness, some disappeared without a trace, while others, though still alive, have turned into different people; and if by some magic means those different people were to meet their past selves—in their cotton twill shirts and canvas sneakers—they would no longer know what to say to them. I fear, in fact, that they would not even guess they were meeting themselves. Well, to hell with them, if they're so imperceptive. They have no time to spare, anyway; they have to hurry on, to swim with the current, paddling with their hands, farther and farther, faster and faster, day after day, year after year: the shores change, the hills recede, the forests thin out and vanish, the sky darkens, the cold sets in, they have to hurry, hurry—and they no longer have the strength to look back at what is behind them and fading away like a cloud on the edge of the horizon.

On one of the intoleraby hot August days of 1972—Moscow that summer was suffocating in the sultry heat and smoky haze, and it was Glebov's bad luck to have to spend time in town because they were expecting to move into a new apartment— Glebov drove out to a furniture store in a new district, somewhere near the Koptevsky market, and there a funny thing happened. He met an old friend from way back—and he forgot the man's name. Glebov had come here to get a table. He had been given a tip about the table: the people who tipped him off didn't know exactly where it was at the moment—that was a secret, but they described it—antique, with inlaid medallions, a perfect match for the mahogany chairs that Marina

189

had bought a year ago for the new apartment. They said there was someone called Yefim who worked in the furniture store near the Koptevsky market and who knew where the table was. Glebov drove there after lunch in the grilling heat, parked his car in the shade and walked over to the store. On the sidewalk in front of the entrance, among heaps of trash and torn wrapping paper, were stacks of furniture that had just been delivered or were waiting to be picked up—wardrobes, sofas, all kinds of shiny plastic-finished junk—surrounded by a milling crowd of customers, taxi drivers and scruffy-looking loafers who would do anything for a three-ruble tip. Glebov asked where Yefim was to be found. The answer was: in back, in the yard. Glebov walked through the store, where the stuffiness and the reek of spirit-based varnish made it almost impossible to breathe, and went out through a narrow door into the backyard. A workman was dozing in a spot of shade by the wall, squatting on his haunches. Glebov said to him, "You're not Yefim, are you?"

The workman raised a bleary eye, frowned and just managed to purse his lips until a contemptuous dimple formed on his chin, which was supposed to mean "No." From that dimple and from something else indefinable Glebov suddenly realized that this wretched, heat-dazed and drink-sodden furniture porter had once been a friend of his. It was not his eyes that told him this, but an inner sensation that felt like a slight thump. But the terrible thing was that although he knew this man perfectly well, he had completely forgotten his name. As he stood there in silence, swaying slightly back and forth in his squeaky sandals, he stared at the workman and racked his brains to remember, bringing a whole era of his life suddenly flooding back. But what *was* his name? It was something unusual and funny, and at the same time childish, a unique name. His nameless friend was settling down to doze again; he pulled his cap down over his nose, and his mouth fell open as he tipped his head back.

Disturbed, Glebov walked away and peered around here and there looking for Yefim, then went back into the store, where he asked several people if they knew where he might be. No one did and Glebov was advised to wait, but he could not. Mentally cursing these unhelpful people, he went out again

couch, thinking how today—provided all was well and she actually returned alive—he must talk to his daughter about Tolmachev and make her see what a nonentity this young man was. At twelve-thirty came the pop-popping of a motorbike, followed by the sound of voices downstairs; Glebov was relieved to recognize his daughter's high-pitched, twittering voice. At once all his anxiety evaporated, the desire to give his daughter a talking-to disappeared and he began to make up a bed for himself on the couch, knowing that his wife would now stay up into the small hours chattering with Margot.

The two women, however, burst noisily and unceremoniously into his study. The light was still on and Glebov was wearing only his white underpants, with one foot on the carpet and the other on the couch as he snipped at his toenails with a little pair of scissors.

All the blood seemed to have gone from his wife's face and she said plaintively: "Do you realize she's going to marry Tolmachev?"

"What?" Glebov looked shocked, but he was not really shocked; it was just that Marina looked so extremely unhappy. "When?"

"In twelve days' time, when he comes back from a business trip," Margot gabbled breathlessly, the speed of her diction stressing the categorical and irrevocable nature of the impending event. She smiled as she spoke, while the slightly puffy cheeks, the little nose, the spectacles and her mother's black boot-button eyes that made up her immature face shone and glistened, blind with happiness. Margot flung herself at her father and kissed him. Glebov caught the smell of liquor. He hastily slid under the sheet. He didn't like his grown-up daughter seeing him in his underpants; what was worse, she was not in the least embarrassed by it and even seemed not to notice her father's appearance. In fact, at this particular moment she was not seeing anything at all; her whole behavior was completely infantile. And this little fool was intending to launch out into an independent life with some man. Or rather, with some no-good punk. Glebov asked her:

"What business trip? You don't mean to tell me Tolmachev has a job?"

"Of course he has. He's a sales clerk in a bookstore."

"In a bookstore? A sales clerk?" Glebov was so astonished that he flung his arms out from under the sheet. This was news to him, no doubt some underhand trick. "Why haven't I heard about this before? You told me he was an artist. You even showed me some of his pictures . . . still lifes, candlesticks and an iron . . ."

"No, she did tell you where he works. Yes, she did," Marina said, anxious to be fair. "But that's not the point . . ."

"Oh, Mother, how I love you both!" Margot burst out, kissing her mother and laughing. "Daddy, you look so pale. How are you feeling?"

"And where is your fiancé at this moment?"

"Dad—please—you're not to worry about *anything*."

"Margot, answer me. Where are you proposing to live?"

Sales clerk in a bookstore. It could hardly be worse. It was a long time since he had seen a look of such sublime happiness, heard such inane laughter. Giggling, Margot said, "Is that really so important?"

"But your father and I want to know."

"Oh, you want to know, do you? Are you devoured by curiosity?" More laughter. "Well, suppose we say . . . here. Is that bad? Will you let us?"

"You mean you'll take the bus into Moscow? Get up at five o'clock every morning?"

"Mom, none of that matters."

Suddenly, both women were gone. Minutes later, Glebov listened as the female voices came floating up from below, joined by the muted burbling of his father-in-law and mother-in-law. Glebov's heart ached with premonitions of change, and he decided to take a sleeping tablet. Suddenly he had a happy thought: "Maybe it won't be so bad after all. Let things take their course. As they always do. Those two will probably separate after a year anyway, and that'll be that." And he started to think about something else.

At about one o'clock in the morning the phone rang. Half asleep, Glebov could feel his anger rising, his heartbeat getting faster, and then, nimble as a young man, he jumped up from the couch and almost flung himself at the telephone on his desk: he must reach it before Margot picked up the down-stairs phone. He'd give that cheeky young slob an earful. He was sure it was Tolmachev calling.

The voice, however, was unknown. It sounded slurred, coarse and insolent: "Hullo, Dunya, happy new year . . . Don't recognize me, eh?" croaked the offensive voice. "One moment you recognize me, next you don't. What an asshole . . . What's the time? Just after one . . . hell, that's nothing. We intellectuals aren't in bed yet, are we? We're still up, solving problems. I'm sitting here with some guy . . . Hey, d'you remember the sheath knives I used to have?"

"Yes, I do," said Glebov. And he did remember: there were five of them, all of different sizes. The smallest was no bigger than a cigarette. Lev used to bring them to school and show off with them; he also had had a gleaming nickel-plated revolver with a bone handle, just like a real one.

Marina came into the study and flashed him a frightened, inquiring look: "Who is it?" Glebov winked at her and signaled that it was nothing important. But for some odd reason he was glad Shulepnikov had called up.

"All right, that's it then. Sleep well, Comrade. Sorry I disturbed you. It took me three hours to find your phone number through Information. . . . Are you listening? When you saw me today I didn't want you to know I recognized you. 'What the fuck use are you to me,' I thought. I really used to dislike you. . . . Hey, did you hear that, Vadim, for Christ's sake? I mean what I say: I really disliked you."

"But why?" asked Glebov, yawning.

"God knows. You never did me any harm, really. I guess you must be a doctor or a professor or some kind of big wheel now, the cherry on top of a cake of shit. I couldn't care less, though. Doesn't bother me. I'm not in that ball game. . . . But when I got home I started thinking: 'Why did I give old Vadim Glebov the elbow, huh? Maybe he wanted some piece of junk, and I could've helped him. Then when he comes next time I may not be there.' They're sending me you-know-where for three years . . ."

"Oh God," thought Glebov. "In his condition, he'll be dead by then . . ."

"Lev, please, call me tomorrow."

"No, I won't call you tomorrow. Only today. What are you, a minister? Call me tomorrow, indeed! Who the hell d'you think you are? You must be out of your mind to talk to me like that. I've just spent three hours tracking down your phone number, this guy and I. . . . He's a foreign diplomat, great guy. . . . He got your number through Information at the Ministry of Foreign Affairs. Say, Vadim, d'you remember my mother?"

Glebov said he did remember her and was about to add that he also remembered Lev's father—no, his stepfather—or rather, his two stepfathers. But there was a click in the earpiece, followed by the buzz of the dial tone.

Marina was still looking frightened.

"Just some idiot . . . Actually it was the guy I saw at the furniture store this afternoon." Glebov was standing barefoot beside his desk and staring thoughtfully at the telephone. "What a schmuck, though . . . What the hell did he want to call me up for?"

Almost a quarter of a century ago, when Vadim Alexandrovich Glebov was not yet balding and fat, with breasts like a woman's, flabby thighs, a big paunch and sloping shoulders, which obliged him to have his suits tailor-made instead of buying them off the rack (while his jacket size was fifty-two he could barely squeeze into pants of size fifty-six, and sometimes had to get a pair of fifty-eights); when he did not yet have bridgework in both his upper and lower jaws; when the doctors had not yet noted the irregularities in his EKG that indicated cardiac insufficiency and stenosis of the coronary arteries; when he was not yet a martyr to morning heartburn, dizzy spells and general listlessness; when his liver was still working normally and he could eat fatty foods and greasy meat, drink as much wine and vodka as he liked without fear of the consequences; when he did not yet know that pain in the small of his back which was caused by stress, extreme cold or God knows what else; when he was not afraid to swim across the Moscow River at its widest point; when he could play volleyball for four hours without a rest; when he was thin and bony and fast on his feet, with long hair and round spectacles that made him look like a young nineteenth-century revolutionary; when he was often broke and worked as a loader at the freight depot or chopped firewood in suburban backyards; when near-starvation had brought with it the possible onset of tuberculosis, luckily averted by being sent to the Crimea; when his father, his Aunt Paula and his grandmother were still alive and they all lived together in one room on the second floor of that little house on the embankment, in which six other families also lived and shared eight tables in the kitchen; when he loved singing songs with girls; when he wasn't called Vadim Alexandrovich but Glebych or Daddy-Long-Legs; when tortured by insomnia and the wretched inadequacy of youth, he dreamed of all the things that later came to him—but which brought him no joy because achieving them used up so much of his strength and so much of that irreplaceable something that is called life: in those days, almost a quarter of a century ago, there had been Professor Ganchuk, there had been Sonya, Anton, and Lev Shulepnikov, all of them Vadim's neighbors. There had also been other people who gradually disappeared; and there had been himself, totally unlike his present self, which was large but as unprepossessing as a slug. And Marina was as yet nowhere in sight.

Now Marina was sitting on the verandah in the shade of the birch trees, carefully writing in her childish hand on the little white paper drumheads stretched tight over the tops of glass jars and fastened by thread around the necks of the jars: "Gooseberry 72," "Strawberry 72." Anton had died long ago and Sonya, too, was gone. No one knew what had become of Professor Ganchuk; most likely he was dead too, and even if he were alive, he might as well be dead. Lev Shulepnikov was squatting in a patch of shade in the backyard of a furniture store, propping up the wall, with a cigarette between his teeth, dozing and dreaming: always the same dreams—dreams of spacious rooms with high ceilings and the huge orange-colored lampshades of the thirties . . .

It was like a play: first act, second act, third act, eighteenth act. In each act the characters are slightly changed. But years,

decades pass between the acts. Act Two began when Shulepnikov turned up at graduate school (emerging out of nowhere
in that natural way that is possible only in the first half of
one's life, when everything seems to happen with ease and by
design) in Glebov's third year. The business with Ganchuk
and all the rest took up the fourth year and part of the fifth.
From the very first Shulepnikov stood out among the other
students—explicable, no doubt, by the offstage presence of his
stepfather, who wielded enormous influence. Few of the students knew this, though of course it was well known to Glebov
and Sonya to whom Lev Shulepnikov was simply good old
Shulepa. The others saw him as a smartass, very knowing and
hell-bent on making a rapid and successful career: he was on
this committee and that committee, had a finger in every pie
and took his pick of all the best-looking girls. In reality he was
nothing but a bullshit artist pure and simple, but it took them
some time to find this out, and at first he annoyed a lot of people. Once, a big hefty Ukrainian from Kharkov called Smyga
came up to Vadim in the corridor and said:

"Say, Glebov, weren't you in school with this Shitupnikov
character?"

Glebov said, "Yes, I was, but there's no need to make tasteless jokes by mangling people's names."

"All right, we'll leave his name alone, and we'll mangle his
face instead," promised Smyga. "Tell Mr. Shitface to keep his
sweaty hands off the girls in our class. Or else we'll give him
the treatment."

A few days later Smyga appeared in the lecture hall with a
swollen face, as though he had a dental abscess. With genuine
astonishment Lev explained what had happened: "This elephant attacked me in the men's room and started shouting
that he'd warned me but I hadn't paid any attention. He went
on yelling at me, so I used some unarmed combat techniques
and knocked him down. He smashed one of the toilets with
his thick head."

At first Glebov did not believe him, knowing that Lev was a
confirmed liar, but he later discovered that the toilet really
had been broken, after which he not only believed that Smyga
had indeed been cruelly humiliated but he also believed all the

other fantastic tales that Shulepnikov told about his life. There was, for instance, the story of how during the war he had been through some special, top-secret training school where they were taught to shoot, to throw knives, to kill with their bare hands and to speak foreign languages; they were then sent on mysterious missions far behind the German lines, but Lev had been demobilized early when he developed a stomach ulcer. There were reasons to doubt the truth of this story, because Shulepnikov spoke very bad German, was not much good at knife throwing, was generally loud-mouthed and indiscreet and lied about trivial things—none of which fitted in with the image he tried to create. Glebov finally decided that Lev probably had, in fact, been sent to this top-secret school (his stepfather had no doubt fixed it) and had aimed to become a sort of Lawrence of Arabia, but for some reason he had not made the grade. Smyga, who had so hated Lev, became his most devoted henchman and sycophant; this took place a year later, when his stepfather gave Lev a captured German Volkswagen as a present, and Lev would roll up to classes in this cherry-red beetle, which made all the poor students so envious that it deprived them of the power of speech. Smyga followed Lev wherever he went, ran errands for him and introduced him to all the girls that had once belonged in his preserve.

In those days—the zenith of Lev's checkered and devious career—one's attitude to Lev Shulepnikov could only be expressed in two ways: servile devotion or spiteful envy. Glebov, Lev's oldest friend, was never his slave, even in grade school, where some boys are so apt to toady and fawn on others who are strong and rich; in graduate school, too, he had preferred not to be one of Lev's clique of flatterers, although the temptation to do so had been there. A cloud of hangers-on had revolved around Shulepnikov, who had led a special sort of life—houses in the country, cars, theater people, sports. It was the time when ice hockey (then known as "Canadian hockey," or simply "Canada") was just being popularized in the Soviet Union. It was fashionable—and still fairly exclusive—to be an ice-hockey fan; the stadium seats always contained a liberal sprinkling of women in Persian lamb coats and men in overcoats with beaver collars. Shulepnikov used to be seen around act. In each act the characters are slightly changed. But years, with some of the star players in the Air Force team. Although Glebov was intermittently attracted to this sophisticated life-style, he also saw it as phony and ultimately boring, and while Lev always remained generously well disposed toward him for old times' sake, Glebov kept his distance. This came not only from a slightly touchy unwillingness to be the tenth spoke in someone else's wheel, but also from his innate caution, which he sometimes utilized without the slightest apparent reason, by pure instinct. In an expansive moment Lev would say, "Glebych, you're in demand!" This meant that one of Lev's girls had noticed Glebov, had heard something about him or wanted to meet him (there was nothing odd in this; in those days quite a few girls were attracted to Glebov). Lev, of course, might have been exaggerating and the girl might not have asked to meet Glebov at all; it was just Lev offering him a taste of the joys of life. Lev was by nature a sociable creature. Glebov, however, always invented reasons to decline the offer: he was expecting Sonya, he had a date with Sonya, Sonya was ill. In reality this was his secret mechanism of self-preservation at work, which was amazing, because no one in those days could have guessed at the disasters that lay ahead.

But there was also something else, a feeling that Glebov could never quite throw off, that tortured him throughout those years, starting from a very early age—an aching, deeply rooted sense of resentment. His efforts to combat it or to rise above it always failed. It was like a chronic disease: at times severe, at times imperceptible, at other times so intense as to be unbearable. Why was it, for instance, that the good things in life simply fell into some people's laps, as though ordained by some higher being, whereas he, Glebov, always had to struggle for everything, could attain his desires only by the sweat of his brow, by straining every muscle and sinew, only to find that, having gained whatever it was, his nerves were in shreds and his muscles stiff as dried leather? This pain—perhaps the best name for it was "agony from the unfairness of things"—had begun long ago, probably in the fifth or sixth grade, when Shulepa moved into the big apartment house— the house on the embankment. Glebov, by contrast, lived in the same two-story house in which he had been born.

Alongside the huge gray apartment house with its thousand windows giving it the look of a whole town, among the backyards, behind a church surrounded by stone ruins sticking to it like fungus to a tree stump, there nestled a slightly lopsided house with a roof that sagged in places, with four pilasters along its facade, known to the inhabitants of the surrounding streets as the "Deryugin house"; Deryugin Street was also the name of the alley in which stood this beautiful house that was slightly askew. The vast gray pile next door towered over the street and kept the sun off it in the morning, while in the evening radio voices and phonograph music floated down from above. Up there in those lofty stories, it seemed, a life went on that was utterly different from life in the small house below, painted yellow in keeping with centuries-old tradition. There was *unfairness* for you! Some people were never aware of it, some were indifferent to it, while others regarded it as right and proper, but for Glebov it was a source of burning resentment from his childhood onward—perhaps a kind of envy, perhaps something else. His father had worked as a foreman-chemist in an old candy factory, while his mother had done countless jobs without ever having a real occupation: she had been a seamstress, had worked in various offices, and had sold tickets in a movie theater. Her job in that movie theater, a shabby little place in a back street across the Moscow River, was the source of no little pride to Glebov, because it endowed him with one enormous advantage: he could see any film without having to pay, and occasionally, during the daytime when the auditorium was almost empty, he was even allowed to bring a friend or two with him—always provided, of course, that his mother was in a good mood.

This privilege was the foundation of Glebov's influence in his school class, and he used it sparingly and cleverly: he would invite boys whose friendship he wanted to cultivate or from whom he expected something in return; some he would tantalize with promises for a long time before inviting them, while there were some villains whom he would deprive of his bounty altogether. On this basis Glebov's power—well, if not power, then authority—lasted unchallenged until Lev Shulepa appeared on the scene. Lev moved into the big apartment house from somewhere in the suburbs, or maybe even from another city. He made an instant impression because he wore leather pants. From the first he had an arrogant air; he would gaze at everyone with a lazy, contemptuous look in his blue eyes, he never started a conversation and he shared a bench with a girl. His leather pants squeaked unbearably during class. Some of the other boys decided to teach him a lesson, or rather to take him down a peg. Or more precisely still—to humiliate him. There was a form of initiation known as "ohoho": the victim would be lured to the backyard, where a gang of boys would fling themselves on him with cries of "Ohoho!" and pull off his pants. It promised to be great fun: they would yank off his amazingly squeaky leather pants, and while he struggled and shouted the girls, who had been told in advance, would be watching it all from a window. Glebov egged the others on to deal with Shulepa, whom he did not like—in general he disliked anyone who lived in the big house—but at the last moment he decided not to take part. Perhaps he felt slightly ashamed. He looked on from a doorway that opened on to the back staircase.

After class, Lev was enticed into the backyard. There were five of them—a boy whose nickname was "The Bear," Syava, Manyunya and two others—who surrounded Lev and started an argument; suddenly The Bear, the strongest boy in the class, grabbed Lev around the neck and flung him prone in a single jerk, while the rest threw themselves on him with cries of "Ohoho!" Lev fought back, lashing out with his feet, but they inevitably overcame him, rolled him over onto his back, and someone sat on his chest. Suddenly there was a loud bang, as though a car tire had burst. At once all five leaped aside, and Lev got to his feet. Still wearing his leather pants, he was holding a pistol. He fired another shot into the air. There was a smell of powder smoke. It was a moment of horror. Glebov felt his legs sagging underneath him. The Bear raced toward him with eyes staring, pushed him aside and ran upstairs, leaping several steps at a time.

It later turned out that Shulepnikov had a toy pistol, a beautiful foreign model that fired special caps and made a noise like the shot from a real pistol. Shulepnikov emerged from the incident with great prestige, while his attackers were disgraced and subsequently made every possible effort to make peace and become friends with the owner of the remarkable cap pistol. Anyone possessing such a weapon could rule the roost in all the backyards along the embankment. It was easier for Glebov to make up to Shulepa than for the others; he had not, after all, taken part in the attack. Shulepnikov showed no vindictiveness and seemed satisfied that the boys now tried to ingratiate themselves with him and were prepared to pay dearly for the chance to fire a shot from his pistol. But the matter didn't end as simply as that. Suddenly the principal appeared together with the director of studies and a policeman, and he shouted that these young "gangsters" must be punished. The principal was unrecognizable: he was shouting—that had never happened before—he was pale, his cheeks shook and he was in a vengeful mood. The director of studies said that what had happened was obviously an act of premeditated terror. The policeman stood there in silence, but his mere presence made everyone feel uncomfortable.

The principal demanded to know the names of the attackers. Shulepnikov refused to name them; he said he had not been able to see who they were: they had pounced suddenly and then run away with equal speed. The principal called two more such meetings but without the policeman. The principal's name was Bagsunder, and people thought that this strange name derived from the fact that he had bags under his eyes. He had a long white face and puffy white half-moons under his lower eyelids. He fidgeted nervously and never sat quietly on his chair like the other teachers but paced back and forth in front of the blackboard like a clockwork toy. No one liked the class teacher, a thin woman nicknamed "The Tube," but they all felt sorry for the principal because he looked so harried.

"My friends, I beg you to show courage. Courage lies not in keeping silent but in speaking out." His white face and stammering voice spoke of anything but courage. For all their sympathy for this worried old man, however, the class kept silent, as did Shulepa. He later told the others that his father had punished him by locking him for a whole evening in the bathroom, which was dark and alive with cockroaches. And he had demanded names. But Lev refused to divulge a single name.

Thus from having been marked down for public humiliation, Shulepa was transformed into a hero. It was probably after this episode—the leather pants, the cap pistol and Lev's heroic behavior (one girl even wrote a poem in his honor)—that Glebov first began to feel that leaden, sickening resentment in his innermost soul. Because, he dimly felt, one person shouldn't have *everything* handed to him on a platter. This feeling was, if you like, a protest by nature herself—or nemesis. Later, Lev Shulepnikov was to feel that same nemesis, to feel the teeth of the dragon on his own wretched skin; but in those days, in the half-dream of childhood, no one could have imagined that one day everything would be turned upside down. Only Glebov sensed something—impossible now to say exactly what it was—something disturbing, like the muffled voices of the waking world heard in sleep. No, envy is far from being the petty, squalid emotion that it is made out to be: envy is a part of nature's protest, a signal that perceptive souls should be able to pick up. But none are so unfortunate as those stricken with envy; and there was no more crushing misfortune than that which overcame Glebov at the moment that should have been his triumph.

In the little movie theater where his mother worked they were showing an old picture called *The Blue Express,* full of bloody adventures, shooting and murder. All the kids were longing to see it, but for some reason children were not allowed in. Glebov of course was admitted by his mother. The picture was incredibly exciting: for an hour and a half Glebov sat on his tip-up seat shivering as though from a chill. He naturally had to see the movie several more times, and so began the period of his ascendancy and undisputed dominion, because except through him there was no way his classmates could hope to see this marvelous film. The plot centered around an attack on a Red train by the Whites, who massacred the women, old men and children but were in the end beaten by the Reds. The shooting and hand-to-hand fighting took place on the open platforms at each end of the passenger cars, on the roofs and underneath the cars as the train raced along at full speed. Few grown-ups seemed to want to see this movie, so the little auditorium was practically empty during the daytime.

Glebov would choose one or two of the more worthy applicants, making his selection with great care; he would announce his decision after class, and then they would race headlong over the bridge in order to get to the theater in time for the start of the afternoon showing. His mother could let in four or five at a time, but Glebov did not throw his favors around too generously: there was no hurry. He hoped that Shulepa, too, would ask him, would beg like the others, but Lev showed no interest in the movie. One day he said off-handedly: "I've seen it a hundred times already!"

This was, of course, a lie. During class Glebov would enjoy himself considering the various petitioners: one had offered him a whole set of French colonials with a stamp album thrown in for good measure; Manyunya had promised that his father would take them both to the races. There were other offers—and there were even threats. One girl had written him a note promising to kiss him if he took her to the movie. This note greatly excited Glebov. He had never received notes from girls before and he had never been kissed. The girl's name was Dina Kalmykova, nicknamed "Lampshade." She was rather fat, with very red cheeks, dark brown eyes and black eyebrows; as she was not particularly pretty, Glebov had never paid her any attention before, but from then on he was to remember her all his life.

When he received her note, Glebov felt a momentary stab of hot fear. He was afraid to move, and even more afraid to turn around and look—Dina sat two rows behind him. His first action was to tear the note into tiny pieces. Then he began feverishly to consider what to do. He could, of course, have said to her: "I'll take you to the movie, but you don't have to kiss me." But that would perhaps have sounded rude. She was really very plump, a regular fatty in fact, although she was very light on her feet. In phys. ed. classes she ran faster than any of the other girls, and she was good at walking along the beam and at rope climbing. She wore a pair of voluminous raspberry-colored shorts with frills around the bottom of the legs; someone said they looked like a couple of lampshades, and that was how she got her nickname.

If the note had been sent by Svetlana Kirillova or Sonya Ganchuk, Glebov would have been much more excited. Glebov thought Svetlana was beautiful; she held herself proudly, she was slim and lithe, with dark-red braids, and she always looked as if she was keeping an important secret that no one else knew. Sonya Ganchuk, on the other hand, did not attract him with beauty but with something else. Perhaps it was the fact that her father, Professor Ganchuk, was a hero of the Civil War, and on the walls of his study, where Sonya had once secretly taken Glebov, hung daggers, guns and a Turkish scimitar. If only Svetlana or Sonya had promised to kiss him. But Dina Lampshade put him in a dilemma.

Even so, choosing a minute during break when Dina was alone—she was standing with her back to the window, smiling and gazing up at the ceiling—he went up to her and muttered, "We can go today if you like. Walrus and Chemist are coming too. . . ." He paused, then added: "That is, of course, if you want to."

"Yes, I want to," said Dina, continuing to smile and stare at the ceiling.

"Only don't delay, or we'll be late. It's at two-thirty. Put your things on right away after class and we'll run. All right?" He spoke briskly, with no hint of sentiment.

The best part of *The Blue Express*, with all the shooting, was still to come, when Dina whispered in Glebov's ear, "I'm going home. I have a stomach ache." She got up and left the auditorium. After a moment's thought—he was enjoying the film even though it was the tenth time—Glebov went out after her. He wasn't quite sure why he had followed her; they both felt embarrassed and neither of them spoke. Dina walked fast, almost at a run, and Glebov kept pace alongside her. In silence they crossed the street and emerged onto the Kanava Embankment. The water under the bridge was black and smoking with wisps of vapor. Here and there ice floes were still floating down the river. It was April and impossible to tell exactly whether it was warm or cold, but Glebov's teeth were chattering slightly and he was somehow shivering all over. He was now longing for Dina to kiss him, but he could not imagine how to remind her about it. After all, he hadn't missed half the movie and followed her out for nothing. In fact, it had worked out very well, because Walrus and Chemist had stayed in the theater; otherwise the four of them would have had to go home together. That would have been awkward.

Glancing sideways at Dina Lampshade, he saw her crimson cheek, her snub nose, her black hair curling out from under her woolen ski cap. He noticed that she seemed to be puffing from walking so fast. Her thick lips were parted, and the sight gave him pleasure—because he felt that Dina Lampshade, fat and not very pretty though she might be, was at that moment in his power. And she herself had agreed to it. His heart was thumping. He clenched his fists. Suddenly Dina slowed down, and Glebov, too, slackened his pace. They were passing an old four-story house, but it was not her home: she lived on the Polyanka. Dina opened the heavy front door, went inside without looking around, and Glebov went in after her. She ran up the stairs to the second floor, onward up to the third and fourth, with Glebov close behind. From the fourth floor a small narrow staircase led higher, and Dina climbed up it. Glebov followed her. At the top was a low, dark, smelly little landing in front of a small door leading to the attic.

Breathing hard, Dina turned to him and said, "All right."

"What?" he asked, panting.

"You may kiss me."

"Why do *I* have to kiss *you*? You promised . . ."

"You fool!" said Dina.

They stood in silence, growing a little calmer as they got their breath back. She refused to go away and said softly, "Oh, you're such a fool."

He had firmly decided to wait until she kept her promise. About three minutes passed in complete silence and immobility, and then an ear-splitting cat's screech came from behind the door leading to the attic and something furry shot past them in headlong flight. They burst out laughing, and suddenly Dina brought her hot, fat face close to his and he felt the touch—lasting for one second—of something damp around his lips, and that was the first kiss of his life. He felt no particular pleasure, merely relief. They ran back down the stairs and parted at the front door: she had to go to the right and around the corner to the Polyanka, while he ran home across the bridge.

A day or two later, at the height of Glebov's supremacy, came his downfall. Shulepnikov invited several of his classmates to his home after class. Glebov had been in the big house before: he had occasionally visited Walrus on the tenth floor, where the windows looked out over the Crimean Bridge and the trees of Gorky Park; in summer you could see the park's huge Ferris wheel turning around. At other times he had visited Chemist, who lived on the floor below and had fixed up a signaling system with Walrus consisting of flags on a piece of string between their balconies; he had also been to see Sonya Ganchuk and Anton's little apartment on the first floor, where he lived with his mother, Anna Georgievna. Of all the inhabitants of the big house, Anton Ovchinnikov was the one whom Glebov really liked. He regarded Anton as quite simply a genius—as indeed did many others. Anton was a musician, an admirer of Verdi; he could sing the whole of *Aïda* from beginning to end. Apart from that, he was the best artist in the school, with a remarkable gift for painting water colors of historic buildings and drawing profiles in India ink. He also wrote fantastic science-fiction novels concerned with the study of caves and archeological remains, while he was also interested in paleontology, oceanography, geography and mineralogy. Glebov was attracted to Anton not only because of his abilities, but because he was modest; he never bragged, he wasn't a know-it-all—unlike the other inhabitants Glebov knew of the big house, every one of whom showed, in however small a degree, a certain arrogance that he found obnoxious. Anton, by contrast, lived unpretentiously in a one-room apartment, furnished with plain government-issue furniture; he owned no German shoes, no Finnish woolen sweaters, no flashy knives in leather sheaths and he never, as some did, brought to school carefully wrapped ham or cheese sandwiches whose aroma wafted around the whole classroom.

Glebov never particularly liked going to visit kids who lived in the big house—or to be more exact, he didn't dislike going there, but he also felt slightly wary because the elevator operators would always look at him suspiciously and ask whom he was going to see. You had to give the name and the apartment number, and sometimes the elevator man would call up the apartment and check whether So-and-So was expected. It was unpleasant to have to stand and wait while being checked out. As he talked on the house phone, the elevator operator would watch him with a penetrating stare, as though afraid that Glebov might slip into the elevator and go up without permission, and this made Glebov feel almost like a criminal caught red-handed. And one never knew what the people up in the apartment might say in reply: in Walrus's home there was a deaf maid who could never understand or explain anything properly, while in Chemist's apartment the phone was often picked up by his grandmother, a nasty old woman who kept an ever-vigilant eye on her grandson and all his doings. One day she said to the elevator man that he was not to let young Glebov come up, because Chemist hadn't finished his homework. It was only when Glebov visited Anton that he was spared the agony of being interrogated and cross-questioned, because Anton's apartment was on the first floor and the most that the elevator operator could do was to watch with stern attention as Glebov rang the bell and the door was opened to let him in. Glebov noticed, too, that even the kids who lived there were scared of the elevator men and tried to sneak past them.

Lev Shulepnikov, however, although he had only recently come to live there, behaved differently. The elevator operator, a gloomy, bespectacled man with pendulous cheeks, would first greet Shulepa with a nod and make a little movement as if to stand up behind his large desk, while Shulepa would walk past without paying him any attention. The elevator would hold only five people, and even then the doors were barely able to shut. Once the elevator man tried to stop Lev and his friends but timidly, trying to make a joke of it: "Hey, you won't get stuck between floors, will you?" Boldly, Lev answered "Who cares? Shall we risk it?" And everyone, of course, shouted in chorus: "Let's risk it! An experiment! Let's check the lifting capacity." And as the elevator rose, the bespectacled man's face froze in a look of fear.

In the apartment, whose gigantic dimensions always amazed Glebov—the passages and rooms reminded him of a museum—the mood of tomfoolery had continued. They took off their shoes and slid in their socks over the highly polished parquet floors, falling over, bumping into each other, and roaring with laughter. Suddenly from out of a white door with purple frosted-glass panels there appeared an old woman with a cigarette in her mouth who said: "What is all this hooliganism? Stop it at once! Put your shoes on and go straight to the nursery." Lev obeyed, grumbling, and the others followed asking him, "Who's that? Is she your mother?" He said it was Agnes, a woman who taught French to his aunt and told tales on him to his mother. "One day I'll poison her with arsenic. Or I'll rape her."

Everyone burst out laughing, although at the same time they were shocked and amazed: the things Lev said! None of them would have dared to say the word "rape" aloud; they all knew what it meant, and although they often uttered much more indecent words without a twinge of conscience, the startling thing was the casual, free-and-easy way that Lev used the word in relation to himself and the old hag with the cigarette in her mouth. And the more clearly Glebov perceived the special qualities that distinguished Lev Shulepnikov, the heavier grew that "agony from the unfairness of things" in Glebov's heart until it eventually turned to lead. Ever since those crazy years Shulepnikov had gotten such a habit of using that word absolutely pointlessly, simply as an empty threat or a cheap joke, that he went on repeating it in later life, when he was already grown up and a graduate student: "If she doesn't give me at least a 'B,' I'll *rape* her."

Back then in the nursery, furnished with strange bamboo furniture, with carpets on the floor, with bicycle wheels and boxing gloves hanging on the wall, with an enormous glass globe that revolved when the lamp inside it was switched on, and with an old-fashioned telescope on the window ledge, firmly fitted on a tripod for ease of observation—Lev said it was fun to pass the time in the evenings looking into the windows on the other side of the courtyard—it was in that room that Glebov's fragile power was destroyed. Lev brought out a movie projector, hung a sheet on the wall and showed a film. It was *The Blue Express*. The projector rattled, the film kept breaking, the titles flickered past illegibly; even so, everyone was thrilled, and Glebov suddenly felt deeply hurt and offended.

He thought: "Why the hell should one person have everything, absolutely everything? Even the one thing that someone else has, which he can be a little proud of and make use of, is taken away from him and given to another who already has everything." In time, he came to terms with it. People who can't change things come to terms with them.

Glebov got used to the big house, which kept his street in the shade in the morning; he got used to its hallways, to its elevator men, to the fact that he was invited to drink tea and that Alina Fyodorovna, Lev's mother, could prod a slice of cake with a fork and push it away, saying, "This cake is stale"— and the cake was removed. When this happened for the first time, Glebov was secretly amazed. How could a cake be stale? It struck him as an absolutely stupid idea. Cake was a rarity at home; it appeared only on somebody's birthday, it was quickly eaten, and it never occurred to anyone to say whether it was fresh or stale, because it was always fresh, deliciously fresh, especially the gorgeous kind decorated with roses made of pink frosting.

Glebov also came to terms with his own apartment. After a visit to the big house he at first used to feel somehow depressed whenever he suddenly saw, as if he were a stranger, his little lopsided house with its yellowish-brown coating of stucco; whenever he climbed the dark staircase, where you had to go carefully because the steps were broken in places; whenever he approached the front door, dotted with nameplates, inscriptions and bells like an old patched blanket; whenever he plunged into the many-layered, kerosene-smelling atmosphere of the building, where something was always bubbling in a saucepan and someone was always boiling cabbage; whenever he washed his hands in the bathroom, where movement was difficult because of all the planks that covered the bathtub, in which no one ever took a bath or washed laundry, but which was covered with the bowls and washbasins belonging to the various tenants of the apartment; whenever he saw, felt and noticed much else besides on returning from Lev Shulepnikov's or someone else's in the big house: but gradually it all subsided, softened, and ceased to upset him.

One day, after a visit to Lev, he was excitedly describing the chandelier in the dining room of the Shulepnikovs' apartment, the hallway that was so long you could ride a bike in it, the candies that were served at tea—it wasn't the candies that amazed him but the size of the box they were in—and his mother and grandmother were questioning him with great curiosity about this, that and the other in Lev's home, when his father suddenly winked at Glebov and said:

"Just listen to them—sounds to me as if they'd like to live in that house. Would you?"

"Well, why not?" said his mother. "I'd like to have my own hallway too."

"And I'd like to live somewhere where people don't rattle crockery," said Nila, Glebov's grandmother. Their next-door neighbor used to come home from work late and at midnight would start shuffling back and forth between her room and the communal kitchen, always for some reason carrying crockery that rattled. Old Nila slept on top of a large trunk by the door, and the neighbor's rattling crockery used to wake her up. Father looked pityingly at mother and grandmother.

"What am I to do with you? You're like a couple of old hens clucking away in a barnyard. . . ."

He was always making harmless little jokes like that—his pet name for his wife was "my speckled hen." The women would pretend to be indignant and would go for him, waving their arms, but mother never really lost her temper with anybody, and father would nudge Glebov and wink.

"Did you ever see such silly hens?" he said now. "Don't you two realize that if you don't have a hallway in your apartment there's all the more space for the other rooms? And as for rattling crockery—why, it's music. I wouldn't move into the big house if you gave me two thousand rubles. . . ."

Although his father almost always seemed to be half-joking and flippant and constantly teased mother, grandmother and mother's sister, Aunt Paula, with practical jokes that would give them a fright (at times it was hard to tell whether he was really acting in fun), in reality—it was not until Glebov was almost grown up that he realized this—he was not at all flippant by nature and not really a cheerful person either. It was all an act, put on for the family. Deep inside his father's personality, like a hidden core around which all the rest of him was wound, was a significant quality—caution. The phrase that he often spoke, laughingly—"Now my children, obey the sign in the streetcars: Don't stick your head out!"—was not just a bit of fun. It was a wise maxim, which, diffidently and as though unintentionally he was always trying to instill in the family. But *why* shouldn't one stick one's head out? He apparently regarded this rule as so important, the sense of it so self-evident, that it needed no explanation. He seemed to feel suffocated, as though by some ancient traumatic fear. He was much older than his wife; with his curly gray hair he looked like an old man, although he was only fifty, but those had been fifty years of struggle, adversity and hard knocks. He had come from the very poor family of a clerk, who had worked at the Dux factory. His father's brother, Uncle Nikolai, had been an aviator, one of the first Russian pilots to be shot down and killed in the war against Germany. The family was very proud of him. They had nothing else to be proud of. The portrait of Uncle Nikolai in his high school student's cap hung in a prominent place. Even Glebov's friendship with Lev Shulepnikov—for some incomprehensible reason Lev liked Glebov; he often invited him home and gave him books (he seemed indifferent about books in general, and Glebov harbored the suspicion that he pinched them from his father's library, because some of them bore a blue stamp showing a man with a hammer, the rays of the sun and the inscription "Ex libris A.V.S.")—even in this childish friendship Glebov's father perceived some danger and advised him "not to stick his head out." He suggested that Glebov go less often to the big house and not to be flattered by Lev's friendship because "the Shulepnikovs have their place in life, you have yours, and you shouldn't try and mix them."

For some reason his father always seemed to think Glebov would soon start to bore Lev Shulepnikov, or worse still, Lev's parents, and that this might cause unpleasantness. Deep inside, Glebov himself sensed this, too; somehow he didn't really *want* to spend time in the big house; yet he went there whenever he was invited, and sometimes even without an invitation. The place was tempting because it was so unusual—the things he and Anton talked about, the books Sonya Ganchuk showed him from her father's library, the marvels that Shulepa used to brag about. At home, on the other hand, everything was deadeningly familiar, everything was dull and tedious.

His father rarely said anything directly—it was usually implied in hints and little jokes. Glebov, though, insisted on making him spell out his feelings about Lev. "Why do you talk like that about him? Why do you think Lev isn't good for me?"

His father never fathomed the real reason why Lev wasn't "good" for Glebov, or rather the thing that provoked that horrible, leaden, sinking feeling inside him. His father had other considerations in mind; but he always avoided explaining what they were, or he would say something absurd, such as: "In principle I have nothing against Lev, or Shulepka, as you call him. . . . By the way, I'd advise you not to use that nickname. Just call him Lev. . . . The fact is that he is badly brought up. For instance, he never says 'thank you' when he gets up from the tea table."

This was, of course, nonsense; his father was just being evasive. He disliked Lev for some other, some more significant reason. Yet whenever Lev came to visit, his father always welcomed him, even treated him kindly and courteously as though he were a grown-up; he would make a point of calling him "Lev," which Glebov thought very funny. Apart from that, in Lev's presence his father always became unusually talkative and discussed all sorts of things with him, and became—to Glebov's embarrassment—prone to boast and exaggerate.

One day, when talking about Uncle Nikolai, he announced that his brother had been the first Russian pilot to shoot down three enemy airplanes in one dogfight, including the plane flown by the famous German air ace Count von Schwerin. The count's plane had crashed, but by a miracle the count himself survived and was soon flying again, having announced that his one ambition was to meet that Russian again in a dogfight and have his revenge. The story had been published in all the newspapers.

Glebov listened, squirming with embarrassment. His father said to him, "Even you don't know about this. I've never told you before."

Lev Shulepnikov said, "Last time you told me about it, you said he had shot down two airplanes."

"I did? Impossible. I couldn't have said it was two, because that wouldn't have been a record. Two wasn't a record. The whole point was that he shot down *three* enemy planes in one dogfight."

, Another time his father had described how, during the Civil War, he himself had served in the Caucasus under the command of comrade Kirov (it was true that he had indeed served sometime in the Caucasus) and how he had even been with a cavalry detachment in Persia, where he had seen fire worshipers. Lev Shulepnikov immediately topped this with an invented story about his father, who, he claimed, had personally shot a fakir in Tiflis. Glebov's father then said that in northern India he had seen a fakir who had made a magic tree grow to full size before his very eyes. (His father had never been in northern India—that Glebov knew for sure.) Not to be outdone, Lev said that his father had once captured a gang of fakirs, imprisoned them in a cellar, and was going to shoot them as British spies, but that when he went into the cellar the next morning, there was no one there—only five frogs. And there had been five fakirs.

"He should have shot the frogs," said Glebov's father.

"He did," said Lev. "But have you any idea how hard it is to shoot frogs? Especially in a cellar!"

Glebov's father laughed, wagging his finger in a mock threat that also expressed approval.

"I see, Lev, that you have a lively imagination. That's good, I like that. But joking aside, I really have seen live fakirs. Firstly in northern India, as I've said, and secondly here in Moscow, on Strastnoi Boulevard. . . ."

There was a certain similarity to the senior Glebov and Lev Shulepnikov—that was why conversation between them flowed so smoothly and enjoyably. This annoyed Glebov. He was irritated by made-up stories that were passed off as truth, though not because his father exaggerated but because he said one thing behind Lev's back and something else to his face. He said to his father:

"But you said you didn't like Lev. So why do you act like

that? You smile and tell him funny stories—just as if he were your boss. . . ."

At this his father lost his temper. He hardly ever got angry or shouted, but now he began shouting at Glebov: "At your age! You dare to lecture me, you cheeky young puppy!" ("Cheeky young puppy" was one of his favorite expressions.) "I smile and tell stories because I was taught good manners. All you young hooligans can ever do is bellow: 'Hey, Lev! Hey you! Wanna fight?' What incredible cheek, to lecture your own father on how to behave."

He got so steamed up that he complained to Glebov's mother and grandma, and they joined in the scolding. That evening, however, Glebov overheard his mother and father whispering behind the screen: "Why do you have to talk such nonsense in front of that brat from the big house? It upsets Vadim."

"He's too cheeky. Trying to teach his father."

"Well, you shouldn't show his friend such deference."

"You're all fools! You don't understand."

A day or two later, when he had finally cooled off, Glebov's father calmly had it out with him: "By the way, about the remark you made to me the other day . . . when you implied that I treated your young Lev as though he were an important person. It was quite sharp of you to notice. He really is—well, if not Lev, let's say his parents are *personages* of some importance, although you must never say I said so, because everything around us is all mixed up, tied together with invisible links. . . ."

It was not long before this was confirmed: one thing really was tied up with another. Suddenly one day Uncle Volodya, Aunt Paula's husband, was in some sort of trouble. The family began wondering whether they might not be able to help him through Shulepnikov, Lev's father. Uncle Volodya and Aunt Paula lived nearby on the Yakimanka, but they used to pop in and out practically every day, especially Aunt Paula. Glebov's mother and grandmother were very fond of her. She was regarded as the most beautiful, the most successful member of the family, with a very good job as a designer and modeler in a toy factory. And Uncle Volodya was a typesetter in a printing shop. Some unpleasantness blew up around him, and he was practically accused of sabotage. Aunt Paula wept: "God, how could Volodya ever be a saboteur? What harm has he ever done anyone? The only person he has ever harmed is himself." He did himself a great deal of harm, in fact, because he was a heavy drinker. Glebov's father constantly reproached him. Mother and Grandmother alternately pitied Aunt Paula and scolded her:

"It's your own fault for letting him get in such a state. Why do you buy drink for him?"

"Well, I'd rather he got drunk at home," was Aunt Paula's excuse, "than the street with his cronies."

Grandma Nila and Glebov's mother insisted that Uncle Volodya's trouble was all due to drink, but Aunt Paula would not agree: "It's other people who have done him in. He's just that kind of person."

It was true that Uncle Volodya was a very good, guileless and kind man, but even at his young age Glebov had come to realize that it was exactly such softhearted and guileless people who spelled trouble for everyone around them. Aunt Paula was crying, Grandma Nila was suffering in sympathy, Glebov's mother could think about nothing else, and his father swore. That spring they had planned to buy Glebov a bicycle, but now his mother said, "There's no money to spare right now. We have to help Paula."

And suddenly the thought came to them: Ask Lev's father to help. At first they rejected the idea with much finger wagging. "Keep away from him, don't get mixed up with people like that." Now, suddenly, it was proposed to appeal to him through Lev. The reason for this was that everyone was so impressed by the business with the Bychkovs.

The Bychkovs were a noisy, cheerful family who lived in the Glebovs' building and behaved like lords. Everyone was afraid of them; they were rude and did exactly as they pleased. They would lock the kitchen in the evening and let no one else in until they were finished; even if the neighbors called in the police, it had no effect. Old man Bychkov, Semyon Gerasievich by name, worked in a tannery, where his job was to soak leather in vats of stinking liquid. He also made boots at home, the most expensive, fashionable sorts of boots, most of which he did not actually stitch himself but gave out to others to make while he procured the leather and drummed up customers.

God, the shouting that went on because the Bychkovs locked the kitchen! The neighbor who lived across the hallway and who came home late made more fuss than anyone else. Glebov's mother also got very indignant. Firstly—there was the smell; secondly—the obnoxious behavior.

Sometimes Mother would leap out into the hallway, shouting, "I'll get you for this! How dare you!"

Old Semyon Gerasievich would answer back, burbling away in his deep voice. Father joined unwillingly in the fray. At once the whole Bychkov clan would pour out of the "hall"— a large room in which all six of them lived, which for some reason they had named the "hall"—and the hum of voices became a roar, which sounded like a thunderstorm rumbling and crashing down. The chief villains were Taranka and Minka. Taranka was ten and was in third grade; Minka was fifteen and didn't go to school anywhere, because he had twice been kept back in fifth grade, then expelled, after which he went somewhere as an apprentice but dropped out. He was mixed up in some shady dealings, ended up in a pool hall in the park and probably, some thought, the gang he belonged to were pickpockets. He was the uncrowned junior king of Deryugin Street and its environs. And he was an evil king. People were afraid of meeting him in the street because everyone knew that he always carried a knife. Once he ran into the school after class and started demanding: "Who hustled Taranka yesterday? Who made a grab at him on the staircase? Was it you, you bastard?"

He already knew who it was, because Taranka had already complained to him—or had made up the story. Most people took care not to touch the scrofulous Taranka, but there were some, of course, who didn't know the score and hadn't heard about Minka, so when Taranka behaved in his usual impudent way, these unfortunates would box his ears or flick the side of his head with their fingers, without guessing at the appalling consequences. In front of the brick wall in the schoolyard, to which he led his victims by the ear, Minka would set up a brief, cruel kangaroo court:

"How dare you hurt my brother? What's the matter with you—bored with life?"

He publicly humiliated and crushed Yura the Bear, a strong boy who was not afraid of even tenth-graders. Minka twisted his arm behind his back until he yelled with pain. Minka only twisted harder until the Bear fell to his knees, at which Minka ordered him:

"Say 'Forgive me, Taras Alexeyevich, for offending you. And I'll never do it again.' "

All the while Taranka, a skinny little brat with ginger eyelashes, just stood watching and laughing. Yura stuck it out to the limit of his endurance, groaned, ground his teeth and shook his head—he didn't want to give in—but in the end Bychkov won out. Taranka came up to him and shoved his foot in Yura's face, and Minka twisted his arm harder and harder:

"Come on, punk—give! Or you'll lose your arm."

Then Yura whispered, barely audibly: "Forgive me, Taras Alexeyevich . . ." and all the rest. No one came to Yura's rescue: there were no big boys in the yard, and the smaller ones could do nothing. Glebov was also afraid of Minka Bychkov, but not in the way the others were. Minka was, after all, a neighbor. Now and again he would ask Glebov to do him a favor, and at other times he would give him something in return. Sometimes Glebov secretly felt proud that everyone else was afraid to go down Deryugin Street because of Minka Bychkov and his gang, but he was never afraid. He would even walk along the street late in the evening or at night and no one touched him. Glebov was keenly conscious of his superiority in this respect, and he even felt—with a certain secret shame, never admitting it to himself—that if he was ever attacked Taranka and Minka would stand up for him and hit back in his behalf.

Glebov, however, never squealed to Minka about anyone, and in general he never made use of the possible sinister advantages of being under Minka's neighborly protection, because beneath his smug sense of security, deep down there lurked another feeling—fear, which turned his heart to ice, a fear such as no one else had experienced, because no one else knew those Bychkovs quite so well, the Bychkovs whose mere voices made his mother turn pale and his grandmother cross herself.

His mother had said to him, "For God's sake, never have anything to do with either Minka or Taranka." But how could he help it, when they forced themselves on him? How could he keep away from them? They had a sister called Vera, a girl of sixteen, who worked in a factory. She looked absolutely like a grown-up woman—at least, so it seemed to Glebov. She was all fleshy curves, with big jutting breasts and squeaky shoes, and she always reeked of eau-de-cologne.

Taranka once enticed Glebov out in the hallway and said urgently, "Want to see Vera naked? Gimme twenty kopecks."

Glebov, of course, had no such desire. He was completely uninterested in looking at Vera in the nude; the mere thought of it gave him an unpleasant feeling. And where was he to get twenty kopecks? Pinch them from his mother or beg them from his grandmother? But Taranka was fiercely insistent and threatened him with the dog: the Bychkovs had a large black dog called Abdul, which was regarded as Minka's property. Glebov knew Abdul well, but even so, once they set the dog on him, you never knew how it might end.

They went into the bathroom, took a washbasin off the planks across the bathtub, put a stool on the planks, and Glebov climbed up on it. Up above, just below the ceiling, was a small internal window that looked into the "hall," covered by a little curtain on the bathroom side. Taranka pulled the curtain aside and Glebov watched Vera washing herself all over in a tin tub in the middle of the room. Vera saw what was going on but for some reason was not embarrassed. Glebov saw everything.

Then Taranka sank his teeth into Glebov like a tick: "Gimme twenty kopecks right away!" The whole family was like that—give, give, hand it over now. It happened more than once that Glebov's mother came in so flustered that she was almost in a state of panic: "Alevtina wants to borrow my sewing machine again. What shall I say to her?"

Alevtina was the wife of the oldest Bychkov son and mother of Minka, Taranka and Vera. Mother hated lending her sewing machine to this woman. She tried her best to weasel out of it now, but Alevtina always got what she wanted. It was impossible to escape the clutches of the Bychkovs.

Their rule came to an end in the following way. One day Lev and Anton were walking down Deryugin Street, although they were not coming to see Glebov; they were simply using the street as a shortcut that led through several backyards to the Kanava Embankment. The Bychkovs intercepted them, Taranka first taunting them with stupid remarks: "Hey, kid, wanna ess in the kay?" which meant "Want a sock in the kisser?" and was in effect a challenge to a fight. Naturally they paid no attention to Taranka and simply brushed him aside. This was the signal for Minka's gang to pour out of a doorway—this was their standard scenario—and start a rumble. One of them let Abdul off the leash, and although he didn't actually bite anyone, he gave the victims a bad fright and tore their clothes. This didn't bother Lev too much, but to Anton every scrap of clothing was precious. The next day a man in a long leather overcoat came to Glebov's house and straightaway knocked on the door of the "hall." Abdul barked loudly.

Old man Bychkov, Alevtina and Taranka were at home. There was a noise, voices; Alevtina shouted and the dog barked and whined. Glebov was not allowed to go out into the hallway and the whole Glebov family sat and listened intently. Then came the sound of three revolver shots. . . . Abdul, it was said later, had crawled under the divan and refused to come out.

Glebov was disappointed: he had thought the dog was brave and fierce, but he had behaved like a coward. He felt rather sorry for the Bychkovs, especially Alevtina and Taranka, although everyone else in the building rejoiced. After the destruction of Abdul, the whole Bychkov clan seemed to fall apart. Minka was arrested for complicity in a robbery, old Semyon Gerasievich fell down in the yard and was taken to the hospital, and soon all the other Bychkovs vanished, no one knew where, as though they had been blown away by the wind. The "hall" was partitioned into two rooms and decorated with new wallpaper. The new tenants, by the name of Pomrachinsky—husband, wife and daughter Lyuba—were as quiet and unobtrusive as mice and always talked to one another in whispers.

I still remember all those trifles of childhood, the losses and the finds; how he made me suffer when he wouldn't wait for me and went to school with someone else; how the building where the pharmacy was was moved—complete—to another site; how the air in the backyards was always damp, smelling of the river, and how the smell of the river penetrated into our rooms, especially my father's big room, and how when a streetcar crossed the bridge the metallic clatter and squeak of its wheels could be heard from far away. I remember running in one breath all the way up the huge flight of stone steps at the side of the bridge; in the evening, running into the Deryugin Street gang under the archway as they came tumbling out of the movie theater like a pack of coyotes—and walking toward them, fists clenched, petrified with fear.

The whole of our childhood was enveloped in a crimson cloud of vanity.

Oh, those exertions, that striving, that thirst for a moment of glory! The world was small, made up of five or six others—Anton, Chemist, Walrus, perhaps Sonya and Lev too, and of course Yarik, the class clown—and our little universe seethed with a longing to do one thing: prove ourselves. Tender, juicy, scarlet flesh of childhood. Everything was unique, incomparable: the first time I ran out onto the embankment during breaktime, onto the sun-soaked asphalt; the first time I realized that spring simply meant a cold wind that made your teeth chatter. A thin, stooping man in a short overcoat, wearing a large brick-red woman's beret on his head, was walking rapidly along the sidewalk and talking to himself. Some insane preoccupation devoured his sunken cheeks and deep-set eyes. Reading the name of our school as he passed by, he suddenly stopped and shouted, "It can't be! It doesn't exist in nature. Do you hear?" He was not shouting at us, a frightened bunch of kids huddling beside the parapet of the embankment, but to some invisible person who had inflamed his hatred.

" 'B.O.S.O.M. High School.' What bosom? What is this crap? My God, do they know what they're doing?"

Eyes flashing, he uttered a few more angry imprecations, then suddenly leaped up onto the narrow granite coping of the parapet and walked several paces along it with as much ease and unconcern as if he had been walking along the sidewalk. The boys froze; the girls shrieked in horror. The man in the beret seemed to notice them for the first time; he stopped, stared down at them from above and said, "Unfortunate children!"

After which, he ran for several yards along the parapet with a lunatic gait, jumped down and hurried away in the direction of the Moskvoretsky Bridge. It was my first encounter with a madman. This man stunned us all. When he was a safe distance away, we began laughing crazily. Chemist went up to the parapet and climbed onto it, hauling himself up with his hands. We could see that he was afraid and could hardly bring himself to straighten up; yet he was the first to stand up on the parapet. Then he pulled an agonized face, waved his arms and shouted, "Unfortunate children!"—and collapsed onto the sidewalk like an old sack. We laughed—until Anton Ovchinnikov, pale as death, lips pressed tightly together, strode up to the parapet and also climbed onto it, straightened up and put out his arms like a tightrope walker. We knew that Anton had flat feet, that he was nearsighted and subject to epileptic fits, but no one stopped him. We were all overcome by a sort of madness. It appeared that to walk, even to run along the parapet was incredibly easy. After Anton, the ponderous fat boy known as Walrus climbed up and shuffled along the granite coping-stone without lifting the soles of his shoes and crouched like a monkey, but when he jumped down onto the sidewalk, his legs gave way under him and he fell to his knees. Then I climbed up, then Yarik.

It wasn't all that difficult; the trick was not to think about anything but to keep looking at the granite pathway under your feet. A fearful shriek from one of the teachers wrenched us out of our strange trance. It was probably that shriek that saved Yarik, who was the clumsiest and most helpless of all of us; he couldn't run, couldn't wrestle, couldn't hold his own in the school backyard, the scene of fistfights in which the first to draw blood was the winner. Yarik was red-haired, white-faced and somehow totally soft, like a rubber toy. He reminded one of a bird that couldn't fly. He was bullied by kids from other classes who were always on the lookout for someone to beat up. He was a tempting prey: so big and so boneless. Once even a third-grader beat him up. The whole trouble was that Yarik was simply incapable of hitting anyone: his fingers would not clench into a fist, and so he never resisted when anyone went for him, even little kids. We always defended Yarik, and sometimes pitched battles would develop from our attempts to save him; he was, after all, the property of our class, and anyone who raised a hand against him was insulting us all. Suddenly there would come a shout: "Yarik's in trouble!"—and we would gallop headlong up to the second or third floor, to the gymnasium or into the yard, wherever the villains were giving our Yarik a hard time: they would crowd him into a corner and punch him up or make him give some big fat lout a piggy-back ride. But that time on the embankment, as he approached the parapet and with a desperate look bent his long, stilt-like legs to jump up, we all stared at Yarik with delighted interest, expecting an entertaining spectacle. In fact, if that teacher hadn't shrieked, he would almost certainly have fallen into the water and drowned.

That was how it all began—testing our nerve. After we had learned not only to walk but to run along the top of the parapet—almost all of our gang, except Yarik and a kid who had one crippled leg (he was permanently excused from phys. ed.)—Anton dreamed up another ordeal: walking down Deryugin Street at night. The nastiest district on the island, and probably in the whole of left-bank Moscow, it was a haunt of the shadiest characters: muggers and robbers to whom nothing was sacred; bandits who attacked merchants' wagons, privateers and pirate crews like those led by the one-legged Long John Silver. Any kid who ventured into the street was unscrupulously robbed: one would lose a ten-kopeck piece, another fifteen kopecks, while others were relieved of a penknife or fountain pen. Parents forbade their children to go there.

But did we ever get our own back if any of them were rash enough to stray into *our* yards?

Anton practiced jujitsu. As an exercise—at break, in class, at home, reading a book or listening to music on the radio—from morning till night he would hit the outer edge of his right hand against some hard object. This was supposed to make the hand as hard as iron. He called it "armoring" his hand, and as in everything that Anton did, thanks to his almost inhuman persistence and self-discipline, the "armoring" technique proved successful. After about two months, his hand had become embellished with a thick, hard callus. None of us others would have had the patience to achieve this. So when the Deryugin Street gang jumped out of a doorway and barred our way and Minka Bychkov—big and tough and already sprouting a mustache—asked, "What are you doing here? Are you coming to see Vadim Glebov?" Anton answered, "No!" Anton and Lev did sometimes go visit Glebov; they thought he was OK and not too much of a crap-eater. Most of the kids in our class were, of course, crap-eaters. But on this occasion Anton firmly said, "No!" although if he had said they were going to Vadim's, the gang wouldn't have touched us. If we had shouted, "Hey! Baton!" (Vadim Glebov's nickname was "Baton") and Vadim had looked out of the window, there might have been no fight.

Anton, however, had set up the whole escapade to test our nerve, and we were not supposed to lighten the ordeal in any way. Lev Shulepnikov had purposely left his blank-cartridge pistol at home. Poor Anton Ovchinnikov certainly didn't look like a hero or an athlete—later, after the fight, legends about him sprang up around all the neighboring backyards—but he was short and stocky, one of the shortest kids in the class; he always wore short pants right into the coldest part of the winter as a way of physically hardening himself, and this made him look excessively young and childish. People who didn't know him never took him seriously. To top it all, he wore glasses whenever he went to the movies or traveled out of town. He was, it seems, wearing his glasses then, in Deryugin Street. So when the gang lazily closed in on us—one of us was tripped up, another was jostled, somebody tried to snatch Anton's glasses off his nose—suddenly something happened that was like a bomb exploding: Anton hit his attacker in the pit of the stomach with the edge of his hand, and the guy collapsed. He hit another, who also fell down; then he lashed out at a third. . . . They fell instantly, without shouting, without struggling, as though of their own volition, like well-trained clowns falling onto a mat in the circus ring. Those were fabulous moments. Then they beat us up horribly, and there was that dog. . . . Anton was in bed at home for a month with a bandaged head, but somehow we rejoiced immeasurably at the whole affair. Yet what did we have to be pleased about? It seems so strange and inexplicable now. We visited Anton in his rather dark little apartment on the first floor, where the sun never penetrated, where beside the portraits of composers there hung his water colors, in shades of yellow and blue, where a young, clean-shaven man with officer's insignia looked at us from a photograph in a heavy wooden frame on the piano—Anton's father had died in Central Asia, killed by the *basmachi* rebels; where the radio was always on; where in a secret drawer of his desk lay a stack of thick fifty-five-kopeck school notebooks, every page covered with tiny handwriting; where cockroaches rustled over sheets of newspaper in the bathroom (there were cockroaches in all the bathrooms in that section of the building), where we all sat in the kitchen and ate cold potatoes, sprinkling them with salt, in between bites at big slices of delicious black bread; where we laughed, fantasized, reminisced, dreamed and rejoiced—God knows why—like fools.

A gain the talk turned to Uncle Volodya: could he be helped through Lev Shulepnikov's father? It now appeared that the latter was a powerful man. It was Glebov's mother who raised the subject. His father hesitated. "You shouldn't bother people," he said, obviously extremely nervous. "It's a trivial matter to a man like Shulepnikov; it's embarrassing to ask." Mother said, "You never liked Volodya. But he's my brother. And I feel sorry for Paula and the children. No, I shall definitely ask Lev to speak to his father."

"I forbid you to do that!" shouted Glebov's father.

Glebov's mother rarely argued with his father, but she usually did what she wanted anyway. One evening Lev Shulep-nikov came to visit—Glebov was helping him with his algebra, and in any case he just liked to drop in and chat—and they were sitting down to tea and bagels; Lev liked drinking tea with the Glebovs, complaining that they never had bagels at home. Suddenly Glebov's mother again raised the subject of Uncle Volodya, asking whether someone could find out about it and help, because there had obviously been a misunder-standing. Lev agreed casually: "All right, I'll tell my dad." Mother handed him a piece of paper with Uncle Volodya's full name, which she had written out in advance. Glebov could almost physically feel his father go tense and contract his muscles; he was stirring the sugar in his tea glass at that mo-ment and suddenly the movement of his hand and the tinkling of the spoon stopped, and he froze, motionless, without lifting his head. But Glebov's mother was smiling, her eyes glistening, and when she drew close to him Glebov realized that her breath smelled of liquor. He wasn't very pleased with his mother's initiative either, because Shulepa was after all *his* friend and if he had to be asked about something then he, Glebov, should have done it.

When Lev had gone, Glebov's father bombarded his mother with reproaches: "Aren't you ashamed of yourself? You're drunk! You talk to our guest in a state of intoxication." Mother, of course, denied that she was drunk and told him not to talk nonsense. In fact she was not drunk; she had simply taken a nip or two for Dutch courage. Glebov's father flew into a temper, shouting that he wouldn't answer for his actions, that he declined all responsibility: the exact nature of his threat was not very clear. He was generally rather fond of uttering obscure threats. Glebov had rarely seen his father so upset. He even banged his fist on the table and shouted in confused anger: "I do everything for you! Every step! And you—what the hell do you do? Chicken-brains!" Only later did Glebov realize that his father was frightened to death. He also had another characteristic: he only got angry about things that he refused to talk about aloud. One had to guess what the real reason was; this was difficult to do, at times impos-sible. But when he caught Mother with a glass of liquor, which she was surreptitiously drinking in a little bar on the Polyanka, the reason for his anger was clear: the conversation about Uncle Volodya. He had categorically forbidden it, and Glebov's mother had disobeyed him.

Only when he had finally finished blowing his top and had shouted himself hoarse, did he say, apparently casually: "And as for that stupid business about Volodya . . . How could you bring yourself to say it?" Glebov's mother burst into tears and his father angrily stomped out of the room, slamming the door. But his grandmother said calmly to Glebov, "Dima, you must remind your friend Lev about it. Don't mind all the fuss. We've got to help him."

Grandma Nila had a gift of always quietly saying something simple and sensible when everyone else around was losing his head and shouting nonsense. Glebov loved this bent little old lady with her gray hair still faintly streaked with pale blond, a neat bun on the back of her head, and a tiny little yellowish face. She was forever pattering about the house, doing chores and scurrying here and there. In fact, she bore the whole household on her back, and was on her feet from early morning till late at night. And she alone, it seemed to Glebov, *sometimes* understood him.

One frosty day Glebov was sitting in Lev's room playing chess when Lev's father suddenly came in. It was their third game, and they were playing "best of three." Glebov hardly ever saw Shulepnikov senior—perhaps three or four times in his whole life. Lev used to say that his father worked around the clock; he was hardly ever at home and even slept at work. Lev called him "dad," although in fact he was Lev's stepfather; his real father, who had a strange double-barreled surname, had died or disappeared in some mysterious fashion from Lev's life. Prokhorov-Pluhnge. That was Lev's father's name, and twenty years later Lev himself reverted to his real name: Prokhorov, but without the Pluhnge. But that was in quite a different life. Besides Shulepnikov and the vanished Prokhorov-Pluhnge, there was a third father, whose name was Fiveisky or Flavitsky. It was easy to get confused between Lev's fathers, but his mother always remained one and the same. She was a remarkable woman; Lev used to say that she came from a noble family and that through her he was a descendant of the princes Baryatinsky.

Alina Fyodorovna, Lev's mother, was a dark, olive-complexioned woman with a stern voice and a proud bearing. Glebov had the impression that she was the real head of the family and Lev was more afraid of her than of his stepfather. She was something in between Boyarina Morozova in Surikov's picture and the old countess in Pushkin's *The Queen of Spades*. Shulepnikov himself, Lev's stepfather, was a short, unprepossessing man with slightly protuberant eyes, who spoke in a quiet voice; his face astonished Glebov by its almost absolute bloodlessness. Glebov had never seen such pallid, immobile features in any other human being. Lev's stepfather wore a gray military tunic belted in by a thin, silver-buckled Caucasion strap, gray breeches and boots. He came into the room, watched the chess game for a short while and asked:

"Vadim Glebov—that's you, isn't it?"

Glebov nodded.

"Come with me for a minute."

Glebov hesitated. He didn't want to abandon the game in a winning situation, when he was two knights ahead of Lev.

"That's it! A draw!" shouted Lev, and swept the pieces off the board. Dispirited, thinking how lowdown and unfair Shulepa was, Glebov followed Lev's stepfather into his study. He had no inkling of what he was about to hear.

"Sit down."

Glebov sat down in a dark-cherry-red leather armchair, which was so soft that it was like falling down a hole, and he felt slightly alarmed, but quickly recovered his composure and found a comfortable, relaxed position. Lev's stepfather said: "Lev has given me a note from your mother about . . ." He put on his spectacles and read out: ". . . Vladimir Grigorievich Burmistrov. He's a relation of yours, isn't he? Very well, I'll try and find out some information about his case, if that's possible. If not, please don't blame me. But I have a favor to ask you, too, Vadim."

Sitting behind a vast desk, Shulepnikov senior looked so small and downcast, his shoulders slumped with exhaustion, doodling on a sheet of paper.

"Tell me, Vadim, who was the ringleader of that gangster-like attack on my son Lev in the schoolyard?"

Glebov was stupefied. He never expected to be asked any such question. He thought that affair was long since forgotten—after all, it had happened several months ago. He too had been one of the ringleaders, although he had ducked out at the last moment. But it was always possible that someone had told this about him. All this instantly passed through Glebov's mind and he began to get cold feet. Seeing that Glebov was reduced to embarrassed silence, Shulepnikov said sternly, "Attacking my son is not a trivial matter. It was done by a group, but there must have been ringleaders who organized it. Who were they?"

Glebov mumbled that he didn't know. He felt extremely uncomfortable—so much so that he began to feel a gnawing pain in the pit of his stomach. Lev's stepfather didn't seem to be a man given to anger; he didn't shout or swear, but in his low voice and the look in his bright, slightly bulging eyes there was something that made it uncomfortable to sit opposite him in a soft armchair. Glebov was convinced that there was no way out of this situation and he would have to own up. Perhaps the fate of Uncle Volodya depended on this. He began by trying to mislead, by talking about Minka and Taranka, but Lev's stepfather brusquely cut him short, saying that business was over and no longer of any interest. Who was the ringleader of the attack in the schoolyard? So far these boys had not been discovered and had not been punished. Agonized, Glebov hesitated, lacking the courage to open his mouth, and they sat like this in silence for some time until the unforeseen happened: a loud and very obvious rumbling came from his stomach. It was so unexpected and so shameful that Glebov shrank, pulled his head down between his shoulders and froze into horrified immobility. The rumbling would not stop, but Lev's stepfather paid no attention to it. He said:

"You see, Lev has a great failing—he is obstinate. He has dug his heels in and refuses to testify out of a false sense of comradeship. You know, I expect, that he is not my own son—he is Alina Fyodorovna's son—and that complicates the matter, because I am unable to, shall we say, exert any pressure on him. What am I to do? You must help me, Vadim. You're twelve years old, you're a big boy now and you know how serious this is. It is very, very serious." And he raised a warning finger.

The rumbling in his stomach had stopped, but Glebov was afraid that it would start up again at any moment. Prompted by this fear, he told his tale: he named the boy called Yura the Bear, who really had been the chief instigator and whom Glebov disliked because he sometimes used to take advantage of his strength to give someone an unprovoked rabbit punch, and he named Manyunya, who was notoriously grasping and selfish. He told himself this was quite fair, because those who would be punished were bad. Yet even though he had done no more than tell the plain truth about two bad boys, he had an uncomfortable feeling of having betrayed them—and that feeling stayed with Glebov for a long time, probably for several days.

Later, Lev came to see Glebov to say that his father had been unable to find out anything about Uncle Volodya. No one was particularly annoyed or disappointed, because they had already guessed that nothing would come of it. Uncle Volodya was already in a prison camp in the north and had written a letter home. Nor did anything very terrible happen to the Bear or Manyunya either. The Bear's parents changed jobs and left Moscow, taking their son with them, and Manyunya got such bad grades that he was expelled from school; he was sent to a reformatory, from which he ran away, got mixed up with a bunch of crooks and spent the war years in a prison camp. There was one more incident: that spring, soon after Manyunya's expulsion from school he came to the courtyard of the big house, lay in wait for Lev and roughed him up. The rumor went around that this was because of some girl, but Glebov knew what it was really about.

It is all so long ago now, it has all become so blurred and distorted, fallen apart like a piece of old, rotten fabric that it is hard to remember what really happened. Why did this happen, why that? Why did he act like that and no differently? Only trivia survive, fixed in the memory: they are imperishable, immortal. The rumbling in his stomach, for instance. And what was it that stuck in his memory several years afterward, when fate again brought him together with Lev Shulepnikov in graduate school and when Sonya and her father Professor Ganchuk crossed his path once more? Again, trivia: the sight of Professor Ganchuk greedily eating a napoleon in a café on Gorky Street after the meeting at which he was destroyed. Glebov had happened to pass by and had seen him through the window.

In the fall of 1947, when Glebov caught sight of Lev Shulepnikov in the courtyard of the institute and recognized him, despite the fact that in the intervening seven years Lev had become a different person—tall, with a prominent forehead and the beginnings of premature baldness, wearing a little dark red Caucasian-style mustache, which was not merely a fashion of the time but indicated character, life-style and even ideological outlook—apart from amazement and curiosity, in that very first second Glebov felt a stab of that forgotten, *leaden* feeling that was forever linked with Shulepnikov. They roared with laughter, punched and pulled at each other, bellowing cheerfully: "Who's that?" "Who's that character over there?" "What's that guy doing here?"—yet at the same time Glebov felt the familiar depression weighing on him. In his out-at-elbow jacket, his lumberjack and patched pants he was once more, if not the poor relation then the impecunious friend of this darling of the fates. Shulepnikov was wearing a magnificent brown leather American combat-type jacket, adorned with numerous zip-fasteners. Jackets of this kind could sometimes be found in secondhand clothes stores, but very rarely, and they cost a heap of money. Glebov could not even dream of buying one, although he constantly pined for one. In those days he was often at Sonya Ganchuk's home, where a fairly select crowd tended to gather and where he didn't yet feel sufficiently self-assured, even though he was an old friend of Sonya's, and he longed passionately for just such a jacket. It had everything: masculinity, elegance, the last word in fashion, practicality. God knows what he would have given for one. As he talked to Lev he could not take his eyes off its soft leather folds. Lev was telling him something about Germany, about a failed marriage, about his father, about the house where he now lived: across Gorky Street from the Central Telegraph Office, over a cocktail bar. Glebov, too, brought him up to date on his life. They talked in tough-sounding voices about tough times. The war had knocked all the boyish illusions out of them, or at least so they thought.

In fact, they were both still boys.

Glebov said, "That's a really great jacket you're wearing. Where can one get them?"

"No problem."

"No, honestly—where can I get one?"

"I'll ask the old man; he'll say the word to an operator he knows. . . ."

Two hours later they were sitting on high stools in the cocktail bar—it was the first time Glebov had been there, and he thought the stools were stupid and uncomfortable, more like perches for birds and as they swung their legs, chain-smoked and gradually got drunk on very strong cobblers, they told each other about their stormy adventures of the past seven years. And there was plenty to tell. Glebov had been evacuated to Glazov, where his mother had collapsed and died in the street from a heart attack. When it happened, Glebov had been in the forest, working in a lumber camp, and he knew nothing about it. Lev had flown to Stamboul on some diplomatic mission, and from there he had been sent to Vienna with a false passport. Glebov came back from the forest after his mother's funeral; he then almost died himself, from inflammation of the lungs, and was nursed back to health by his grandmother. Then his father returned from the front, having been wounded in the head, unable to do any work that demanded the slightest mental effort. He got a job as a stamp-press operator in a small workshop. Walrus had died in the fighting around Leningrad. The Bear and Chemist had vanished without a trace. Virtually everyone from the big house had been scattered to the four winds. Sonya Ganchuk was the only exception. Shulepa's wife had been an Italian woman,

Maria, a creature of rare beauty. In Glazov, people had died of starvation; Glebov had had to learn to eat soup made of grass and to drink acorn tea. Maria had been seven years older than Lev Shulepa. At one time he had preferred older women, but then he began to find them boring; they tended to develop complexes. No, Glebov's women had all been younger—all of them, except one. She was absolutely unique . . . well, some other time, maybe; it was a long story. And when did Anton die? Apparently in the fall of forty-two. It was incredible that he was mobilized at all: he was chronically sick, nearsighted and prone to epileptic fits. And he had very bad hearing. What? Anton had very bad hearing? Of course—you remember how in class he always asked for questions to be repeated and he sat in the front row. But he was amazingly musical—he knew the whole of *Aïda* from memory. Well, so what? Wasn't Beethoven deaf? Yes, it was really sad about Anton. He was a genius. Of course, he was a genius—and in the Leonardo da Vinci mold, a "renaissance man." An absolute genius, say what you like. Ought to go visit his mother. Apparently they had a very hard time in evacuation. But his mother still lives in the same first-floor apartment, on the central courtyard. The one with the cockroaches. Lev had shot a quartermaster of the Allied forces, was court-martialed and threatened with the firing squad, but later it turned out that this quartermaster was a dubious character who had had links with the German *Abwehr,* and there was talk of giving Lev a medal, but he didn't get it. Obviously this was a pack of lies, but at the time Glebov believed every word of it and was so thrilled to have met Shulepa again that he was prepared to shell out the last of his cash for another cobbler, but this was unnecessary—Lev paid. And still Glebov longed for one of those leather jackets.

They then loafed around the Telegraph Office, insulted passers-by, tried to pick up women, and Lev bragged as a policeman watched them complacently without interfering: "They all know me around here. They're only hoping that I won't touch them. . . ."

He frowned and shook a threatening finger at the policeman. Then they went up to his apartment on the fourth floor,

where they had some more drinks. Lev's mother, Alina Fyodorovna, had remained absolutely unchanged since prewar
days. It was astonishing: everything around her had changed,
Lev had grown into a hefty young man and was already going
bald; Glebov's mother had died, he himself had almost died,
at first in Glazov from inflammation of the lungs, then on several occasions when the Germans bombed the airfield; countless other people had died and disappeared—yet Lev's mother
was utterly unchanged, with her dark, sunken cheeks, her endless cigarettes, and her strange frowning sideways stare.

"Do forgive such a trite question, Vadim, but are you married yet? You're not? Well done—you were always sensible.
You're not offended if I call you by your first name, are you?"

The voice was unchanged, too: husky, lazy, with a very
slight aristocratic burring of the letter "R." Although she was
a remarkable and highly intelligent woman (Lev used to say:
"I admire my mother, she is very gifted in her way—but she
has a character like Ivan the Terrible"), he felt she could have
treated him more like a grown-up. Glebov wanted to behave
with dignity. His answers were brief, his smile restrained, and
he carefully did not stare at the carpets, the pictures and the
knick-knacks that were scattered everywhere, as though he did
not notice them at all. Later, having taken a look around, he
discovered that the furnishings of the rooms were noticeably
different from those in the apartment in the big house: the
luxury was even more splendid, there were more antiques and
a great deal of things connected with the sea. There were
models of sailing ships on top of the bookcase, here a framed
seascape, there a picture of a sea battle that might well have
been by Aivazovsky (it later turned out that it really was by
Aivazovsky), and a pattern of gilded anchors on the walls. He
said: "I don't see any of your old furniture, Alina Fyodorovna.
Everything appears to be different."

If he had not been half drunk at that moment he wouldn't
have allowed himself to make such an impertinent remark
and in such a familiar tone, but something inside egged him
to speak out. After all, people during the war had sold their
last possessions in order not to starve to death—Nila, Glebov's
grandmother, had sold her silver spoons, a silver glass-holder,

a rug and several shawls, everything of the slightest value that they had brought with them from Moscow, even the little cross that she wore around her neck, because Glebov was dying and a liter of milk in the market cost approximately the value of a silver spoon—yet here was a newly acquired collection of valuables including an Aivazovsky. To be able to acquire an Aivazovsky was no joke. Glebov purposely went over to the wall and began to inspect the picture intently, leaning close to it like a connoisseur. Lev laughed.

"Look how observant he is. No, Mother, you may say he's drunk, but he has a sharp pair of eyes."

Alina Fyodorovna said, "The ancients used to say: No man should step twice into the same stream. That's right, isn't it? I'm not mistaken, am I, young man? You, Vadim, stepped into our stream"—she linked her son and herself with a gesture— "in roughly what year was it? It must have been when we moved into that awful house, in thirty-something-or-other. . . ."

"Well, the exact date doesn't matter. It was about ten years ago," said Glebov. "But I remember your apartment very well. In the dining room, I remember, there was a huge mahogany sideboard, with an upper part that was supported on thin, spiral columns. And on the doors of the lower part there were some little oval majolica plaques, with pictures of shepherd-esses and sheep, cows and things. Am I right?"

"Yes, we did have a sideboard like that," said Alina Fyo-dorovna. "I had forgotten about it, but you remember."

"Well done!" Lev slapped Glebov on the shoulder. "Hell-ishly observant, fabulous memory. You can get a job with tal-ent like that. I'll give you an introduction. . . ."

When they were alone in the room, Lev explained that Alina now had another husband. Shulepnikov had died, and this apartment with all its costly junk belonged to Fiveisky, Alina Fyodorovna's new husband. He too was a big wheel. He had, in fact, investigated the case of Shulepnikov's death: the latter had died in strange circumstances—he was found dead in his car inside a locked garage. It might have been murder by carbon monoxide, or he might have simply had a heart attack. He had, after all, constantly worked around the clock for years. Fiveisky had investigated the case, and so had come to know Lev's mother. Glebov almost asked why they hadn't brought the furniture from the old place over to Fiveisky's apartment. Things were slightly vague on this point. In Lev's life there were many things that were vague. Better not to ask. Lev said that his new "dad" was all right—former navy man, fond of drinking and chasing ballerinas. He had once invited Lev to an actors' party, which had been very nice, but everyone there was a bit on the old side. Fiveisky was sixty, but incredibly fit. Glebov asked: "What about your mother? How does she take his interest in ballerinas?" Lev shrugged his shoulders: "How is she to know about it? It's a purely male matter."

Glebov heard this with some amazement, then he brushed it aside: the hell with them, let them live how they like. But something nagged at him, irritated him, as though an old scab had begun to itch intolerably. Later he saw this Fiveisky person three or four times at the apartment on Gorky Street and once at the Dynamo Stadium. Fiveisky was a rabid soccer fan and acted as "godfather" to some special team, to which (thanks to his connections) he attracted the best players from other clubs. For a while Lev, too, was badly bitten by this nonsense. His new "dad" was a man of huge stature who talked in a deafening voice and shook hands with a grip like a vise; he also had a head as bald as a peeled peanut, drooping Ukrainian-Cossack mustaches, and with all that he wore goldrimmed spectacles; in a word—a character.

The big house on the embankment, which played such a significant part in Glebov's earlier life—it had oppressed him, thrilled him, caused him agonies, yet had irresistibly attracted him like a magnet—had now, since the war, relapsed into the shadows. There was no one there now to visit except Sonya Ganchuk. At first, however, he did not go to see Sonya (for a long time Sonya belonged, as it were, to his childhood, which had gently faded away in his memory along with everything else that had become surplus mental baggage and had been forgotten under the weight of the years) but visited her father, the professor. This was a pure coincidence, which Glebov had discovered casually and with mild interest. It was not until he had been studying at the institute for about eighteen months that he made up his mind to say to the professor: "You and I, Nikolai Vasilievich, are old acquaintances in a way. I used to come to your home when I was a boy." Leafing through a book, the professor drawled indifferently: "You don't say?" And that, on this occasion, was that. The professor had either not understood him or had pretended not to understand.

Glebov was not particularly embarrassed, and decided to remind him more firmly—he was not very interested in Sonya, but Professor Ganchuk himself was an important figure. He, Glebov guessed, could be extremely valuable to him in his early days in graduate school—and one day after class he seized a suitable moment and sent his regards to Sonya.

"How do you know Sonya?" Ganchuk said with astonishment.

"But I told you, Nikolai Vasilievich . . ."

"Really? Did you? Oh yes, of course. That's right, I remember, there were always lots of youngsters in our home."

"And that row of little white busts of the great philosophers—is it still in your study?"

"Well now—you even remember those busts." The professor smiled with pleasure. . . .

Life was getting back to normal. There were still ration cards, but gradually more of life's little pleasures were returning. Yes, the busts were still there. They had survived the war, evacuation, hardships, the destruction of people and ideas—that's because they were, after all, philosophers. For some reason Ganchuk was especially delighted and grew quite enthusiastic when Glebov recalled those little plaster busts—in fact he was much more delighted than when Glebov mentioned his childhood friendship with Sonya. He at once invited Glebov to visit: "Come up for tea sometime; Sonya will be so pleased. . . ."

Later, Sonya too sent her regards, followed by an invitation. Ganchuk was often ill, and people frequently went to his apartment for consultations or to hand in their term papers.

Sonya had grown into a tall, pale, rather thin girl, with pale, full lips and big pale-blue eyes that radiated kindness and concern. She was studying at the Institute of Foreign Languages.

"Vadim, what happened to you? What does this mean?"

were her first words after six years of separation. "Why did you disappear so completely?" She said it as though, on parting, they had promised each other to be friends forever. Then and now, however, their relationship was purely and hopelessly one of comradeship, as flat and unemotional as a brick wall. Sonya was just one more element of that bright, variegated, multifaceted, vanished world known as childhood. And if Professor Ganchuk had not reappeared on the scene, no doubt Sonya would have disappeared forever down the memory drain.

Glebov sat in the professor's study on a little chaise-longue with its hard, curved mahogany back—in those days little settees like this could be had for a song in secondhand stores, though nowadays you can't buy them for love or money—engaged in a pleasurable discussion of the innumerable literary cliques and factions of the 1920s—the fellow travelers, the formalists, the RAPPists, the "Proletcult" movement—and many other topics in which Glebov was deeply interested. The professor was a mine of information and fascinating detail. He had a particularly clear memory for all the twists and turns of the literary skirmishes and pitched battles of the 'twenties and 'thirties. He spoke crisply and decisively: "At this point we dealt a heavy blow to the Bespalov group . . . They were backsliders, and had to be hit hard . . . We fought them head-on . . ." Yes, in those days there really were *fights*, not arguments. True understanding was thrashed out in the cut and thrust of polemics. Glebov listened respectfully, imagining the clash of battle, the smashing of idols, the books flung overboard into the raging sea—and this solid, plump, little old man seemed like some heroic, legendary warrior which was, in some way, not far from reality. Glebov greatly enjoyed those tea-drinking sessions in the professor's study with their intimate recollections: "By the way, we disarmed him, and do you know how? As a scholar he was a complete nonentity, but he kept his job thanks to a certain female person. . . ." Glebov loved the smell of the carpets and old books, the circle of light thrown on the ceiling by the huge lampshade of the table lamp, he loved the walls lined with books from floor to ceiling and on the very top shelf the little plaster busts lined up in a row like soldiers. Which of them was Plato, which Aristotle? It was impossible to distinguish them from below, because the ceilings in that house were very high, not like the ones they build nowadays, probably at least twelve feet in height. Glebov had the feeling that these indistinguishable little white statuettes—this schoolroom adornment—had been acquired in Germany during the inflation of the mid-1920s, when the eager young Ganchuk, the recent Red Army soldier, committed poet and orator at army political meetings, had plunged into higher learning with the undimmed keenness of a bright boy in high school—these toy sages also took part in the battles, struck blows, lashed out, exposed their opponents and ordered them to lay down their arms.

Gradually and in a new and different way Glebov crept back into the aura of the big house on the embankment. There were no longer any elevator men in the entrance hallways, and the tenants were somehow not the same as before; they looked shabbier and simpler and they talked differently. As before, however, the elevator shafts were full of unusual smells: shish-kebab, something fishy and tomato-ish, sometimes expensive cigarettes, sometimes dogs. Glebov had grown unaccustomed to dogs over the war years; dogs had somehow been left behind in his childhood, along with ice cream in round wafers, swimming off a sand-spit in the river, and all sorts of other trivia. In the elevator on the Ganchuk's entrance, Glebov saw a dog for the first time in years and he examined it carefully. It was a huge German shepherd, yellowish with black streaks, sitting with calm dignity against the back wall of the elevator, under the mirror, and it studied Glebov with equal intentness. Alongside the dog, holding it on a leash, stood a despondent-looking old woman in a head scarf. Glebov was amazed by the enormous dog's quietness and well-mannered behavior, yet at the same time he seemed to detect in its unblinking, nut-brown eyes an awareness of calm superiority: the dog, after all, lived in this house and Glebov was only a visitor. He felt an involuntary urge, a naïve movement prompted by childhood memories, to stroke the dog. He stretched out his hand, but the dog growled, shook its muzzle and bared its teeth. "Hands off! Stand at attention!"—was written on the arrogant black muzzle: "Just because you are allowed into this house and are riding this elevator does not mean that you belong here." Glebov got out at the ninth floor landing in a bad mood.

"It smells of dog in your elevator," he said to Sonya. There were moments when he wanted to needle her.

His life in those days was hard, hungry and fun, as it was for many others; when one thinks back, it was a time of true poverty. There was never an extra pair of shoes, never a spare shirt or tie. And one was perpetually hungry. Everywhere Glebov went—to the institute, visiting friends—he wore his old army tunic, not only because he had nothing else suitable (he had grown out of all his prewar clothes and could buy nothing new), but also to remind people that he had been *in the war*. He had been drafted in the last year of the war and had served in the Air Force as ground crew. After the death of his mother, life at home became even drearier than before. His father took to drink. Old Nila, his grandmother, slaved away to the limit of her strength to keep the household going. Looking back, he could not understand how on earth she had managed it. Once a week Nila would take her string bag and ride the streetcars to the Danilovsky market for greens, dried mushrooms, sorrel and rose-hips. God, the gallons of rose-hip tea they drank! Nowadays he couldn't stand the stuff at any price, but in those days Nila even offered him cold rose-hip tea as a cure for hangovers: "Drink some rose-hip, dear, it'll do you good. . . ." Do him good! And yet in a way it must have done him some good, as did everything about that life on their dark, perpetually twilit little street, in their one long, low-ceilinged room that was more like an underground vault—because they kept going, they survived. Grandmother grew more and more bent, walked ever more slowly and began to go faster downhill. Father started working overtime, for which he earned at the rate of time-and-a-half. It was then that his affliction started to get worse. Yet nobody seemed to notice it—he was just always in a hurry to get out and join some friends, to spend his last money on Saturday evenings in some cheap restaurant or in the bar on the Serpukhovka.

Whenever Glebov visited the Ganchuks, he acted the serious, dedicated academic. At first it was done gropingly, as though feeling his way. Sonya actually hindered him, as she was always wanting to drag him away from her father to talk to her friends, and other irrelevancies.

He also began to get slightly alarmed. Surely, he thought, poor Sonya couldn't be making a play for him? He had no thoughts of anything more intimate than to be praised by the professor, and then entirely within the framework of his program of study. Yet at an early stage he had formed an image of himself as a figure dangerously attractive to the female heart. It had begun with a forty-year-old woman during the evacuation. At first he had thought that for her it was just as transient an affair as it was for him, but then passions rose and there were stupid threats. Lord, what a fright that gave him! It taught him to be on his guard: games of that sort could end in tears. He sensed in himself—not without a certain self-satisfaction—a sort of radioactive charge, to which women were prone to fall victim, although not just any women but those of a certain kind. He had a particularly devastating effect on intellectual women who were older than he was, as well as on younger, serious-minded ones who tended to be not very pretty and wore spectacles; when he began teaching, it was usually his best female students who fell under his spell.

It was for this reason that he became slightly nervous whenever he noticed a certain gleam in Sonya's kindly, pale-blue eyes and a slight smile on her full, pale lips. Sonya loved to invite guests home. Among them were her girl friends from the Institute of Foreign Languages, brilliant, brightly dressed girls who twittered and giggled, showing off their fashions; some of them aroused instant and painful longings in Glebov, but he restrained himself, knowing that his brand of radioactivity never worked on such women.

When Glebov became secretary of Ganchuk's seminar, he started visiting them almost every week. The professor was classically absent-minded and, to be honest, hopelessly muddled. They would occasionally have the most absurd and irritating conversation, when the professor would open the door wearing his pajamas and with eyes round with astonishment would say: "But my dear fellow, I asked you to come on Monday!"

"No, Nikolai Vasilievich, you said Saturday."

"How could I have said Saturday, when I . . ."

"But I remember it quite distinctly."

All this took place in the doorway. The stupidity of it made Glebov feel increasingly nervous, until Sonya suddenly swooped into view: "Father, you ought to be ashamed of yourself, making people stand in the doorway like this. Have you gone mad?" In actual fact, Ganchuk was always glad to see Glebov and would immediately find him something useful to do. He became particularly well disposed toward Glebov after the latter brought him a complete bibliography on a topic that was important for Ganchuk's own work, and that he had compiled remarkably quickly. Ganchuk was touched by this devotion. Glebov did not tell him that he had worked on it for several nights in a row. He was by no means obliged to exert himself so hard—indeed, he wasn't obliged to compile the bibliography at all—but as it turned out, this feat proved to be amazingly useful.

One evening, Sonya gave a party for a collection of girls and young men of various sorts who turned up, God knows where from, as was usual in those hungry days, to take advantage of the professor's food and drink. Some of the girls brought their friends, who in turn brought theirs. Fortunately, the professor's living room was big enough to accommodate fifty people; nowadays rooms of that size are unheard of, except perhaps in condominium apartments in privately financed housing projects. Among the guests were some musicians, a chess champion, and a poet who had been deafening people at student parties with his crashingly metallic verses—in those days, for some reason, they were regarded as highly musical—and there was the usual gaggle of colorless, loud, shy or insolent students. The poet hit the party like a bolt from the blue: no one knew him, apart from one man who had a fleeting acquaintance with one of the girls and who had never been to Sonya's home before. Hardly had the poet entered the room than he asked in a loud voice, copying the example of certain more famous poets: "Where's the john?" This produced a rustle of excited half-whispers: "He's a poet . . . doing it for effect . . . thoroughly unconventional. . . ." No one remembered any of the poems that he recited all evening in a loud, tinny voice, but the remark about the john . . . Nowadays, thirty years later, the poet is still grinding out his brassy verse, but no one any longer thinks it musical—just tinny. One of the students, after vamping a few chords, started singing in a piercing, hysterical shriek:

> *The Moor of Venice, one Othello,*
> *Called upon his love one day . . .*

Everyone roared in cheerful chorus:

> *Shakespeare, an observant fellow,*
> *Saw him there and wrote a play . . .*

People in those days loved this kind of nonsense. They roared until they were hoarse, until tears came into their eyes:

> *Desdemona was his lady's name,*
> *Most beautiful of all by far . . .*
> *Admiring of Othello's fame,*
> *Bedazzled by his general's stars . . .*

What on earth was there in this junk that was so exciting, that set your heart beating faster, gave you such pleasure that you wanted to share it with others?

There were, however, other parties at the Ganchuks' when different songs were sung around the pale, gently smiling, silent figure of Sonya: her father would come and join the young people in tossing back his glass of lemon-flavored vodka, Sonya's mother, Yulia Mikhailovna, would sit down with them, and to the beat of the old man conducting with a fork they would all sing "Through the valleys, over mountains, the division marched ahead . . ." or "Far away, across the river . . ."

Sonya could sit in silence for hours, listening to other people with her mouth half open, a habit caused by her adenoids, which had not been removed. Once it occurred to Glebov that she would make someone an excellent wife, the best wife in the world. She had so many superlative qualities, up to and including the ability to listen to others in silence with her mouth half open. He thought about this in an absentminded and disinterested spirit, without making the slightest connection with himself; he might say to himself, for instance: "Now Sonya would be an excellent wife for Lev." There actually was a time when he played with this idea, imagining that Sonya might exert a good influence on that blockhead Lev, and that the latter might have a calming effect on the bright-blue gleam of Sonya's eyes, which so alarmed Glebov. Lev couldn't possibly, after all, find any objection if he were to put the idea to him. Glebov himself never felt the slightest desire for a grope with Sonya in a dark corner, as happened with other girls, even with some of those who came to Sonya's parties—for instance with one of her girl friends from the I.F.L., a dark-eyed, plump little creature—what was her name? He'd forgotten her name, but he had a vivid memory of the touch of her well-covered shoulders, a second's furtive caress in the darkness of a check-room, hung all around with soft fur coats. . . .

The fact was that with some women he got cold feet and retreated primly into stony reserve, while with others he would suddenly and incomprehensibly behave aggressively and boldly, quite unlike his usual self. He had picked out that plump girl at once; she too lived in a little alleyway like Deryugin Street. Sonya, however, was completely out of it as far as he was concerned; with her he didn't have to make any effort to let himself go, because she had never excited him at all. Later, there came a time when he wanted this to happen; later still, Sonya began to arouse him, but probably two years went by before he reached that stage.

At the party with the poet—it was then that he started to feel the first little glimmerings of interest in Sonya—there was too much liquor around and people got drunk, to the point where the host and hostess began to worry. Some of the men went out to the hallway to smoke. There was one kid there (Glebov had forgotten his name, of course; he never appeared on scene again anyway), a clumsy, curly-haired lout in spectacles and a necktie. He seemed extremely fit; in fact, there was something of the weight lifter about him, and in a surprisingly thin, high-pitched voice he suddenly said in the group of men smoking in the hallway: "I don't quite get it, you guys. Who's humping our hostess, this chick Sonya?" The kid just wanted to know whether the post was vacant, but his tone was rude and out of place and grated on everyone else's ears. People shrugged their shoulders. Then one of the students nodded toward Glebov. "Could be comrade Vadim here . . ."

"Me?" said Glebov in amazement. "That's news to me."

It was a nasty moment: other people had noticed something of which he himself wasn't aware, something which in any case had never crossed his mind. Or had it? He found himself telling them that he and Sonya had been classmates at school. The kid who had started the conversation said: "Who wants to, anyway. She might as well be a nun in a convent." He nodded toward the open door into the apartment. "Too much like hard work . . . Still, there's something about her . . . you know, like one of Turgenev's women."

"Shut up, slob," said someone.

The weight lifter took offense, threw away his cigarette butt and went back into the apartment. Nobody liked him.

"Who brought that thug here?"

"God knows. I think he's from the Literary Institute."

"Shall we give him a hard time?"

They agreed. One of them went inside to get him to come out in the hallway again. He was gone for some while, and when he did return he said the body builder had guessed they wanted to beat him up and refused to come. All right, they decided; they'd give him the treatment later. He wouldn't get away from them. The chess champion was particularly fierce. They had all had a lot to drink. Something unusual, however, happened to Glebov: he suddenly and oddly became completely sober. He was sobered up by the thought that that kid had expressed in such a crude way. "He's not a fool," thought Glebov. "*We* are the fools." This made him feel an even stronger urge to rough the guy up—well, maybe not rough him up but just throw him out. "He slithers in here where he doesn't belong . . . Sneaky bastard!"

Glebov strode angrily into the living room. They never did get to rough up the kid in glasses, for the simple reason that within a half-hour he was dead drunk. At twelve-thirty the guests said goodbye, hoping to catch the last metro. They all left except the bespectacled weight lifter, who could not even be pulled off the divan, much less put on his feet; he lay sprawled in a revolting attitude, showing all the patches on his threadbare student's pants, with his sweater rucked up and a gap between belt and sweater revealing his navel amid an expanse of bare stomach. He had thrown his arms behind his head, which was hanging over the bolster at the end of the divan, and he was snoring horribly. It turned out that the guy who had brought him had long since left with his girl friend, a classmate of Sonya's. No one even knew what his name was. The Ganchuks were in a quandary. Vasyona, the maid, advised sending for the police. With her solid German common sense that had survived thirty years of living in Russia, Yulia Mikhailovna suggested putting a glass of water and an aspirin tablet alongside the sleeping youth. Vasyona snorted with indignation: "Aspirin tablet indeed . . . As soon as he wakes up he'll start looking for the way out and he'll smash the glass in the bookcases in the middle of the night . . ." Old Ganchuk himself was all for using the old army method—dragging him out by the ears. Sonya, however, came to the defense of the drunken lout and forbade them to touch him.

"Don't you feel sorry for him? Look at his nice little face and that sweet bulldog's jaw."

Glebov suggested firmly that he should stay for the night, just in case; he would sleep here in the living room on a folding cot, and that character could stay on the divan—only we ought to take his shoes off.

So Glebov spent the night in Sonya's apartment; for a long time he could not sleep, because he had started to think about Sonya in a quite new and different way. He just lay there unable to sleep, and thinking. Now and again he dozed off, dreamed short, muddled dreams, woke up again and once more started thinking. Little happened; Sonya slept in her own room behind a firmly shut door and the drunkard did not stir; what did happen happened to Glebov that night, for he got up a different person the next morning. He realized that he could fall in love with Sonya. The feeling as such had not yet manifested itself, but it was somewhere on the way, getting nearer, like a mass of warm air billowing in from the south. People with vascular trouble can feel the onset of a change in the weather before it comes. At dawn, around six o'clock in the morning, the lout turned over, fell on the floor and began, as Vasyona had predicted, to blunder around the room, muttering and hiccuping. Glebov dragged him out into the hallway, jammed his cap on his head and tried to shove him out of the front door. The unwanted guest refused to go; and they swore at each other in whispers:

"Where are you pushing me, you monster? I don't have anywhere to go, don't you see?"

"Go back where you came from."

"Where I came from? Can't you understand what Dostoyevsky wrote . . . ? When a person has nowhere to go . . ."

In those days there were quite a few such semidestitute students who practically lived on the streets. They were constantly shunted along as they tried to cadge a night's sleep from friends, sneaked from one student dormitory to another, slept in railroad stations. Now this student clung longingly to this haven from which he was being thrown out. Glebov spent a good half-hour persuading him to go, and finally pushed him out, after which he returned to the living room and lay down on the cot. An hour later Sonya walked past in her bathrobe. He saw her pale thin legs and slender ankles. Later she looked in again and asked: "What happened to him?"

"I gave him the heave-ho." Glebov made a movement with his knee depicting a push in the posterior. He felt himself a hero, a protector of the weak, but to his surprise Sonya was angry.

"Who asked you to do that? He didn't want to go, did he?"

"No, he didn't. I spent an hour in the lobby trying to get rid of him."

"And you threw him out? How horrible of you, Vadim. You ought to be ashamed of yourself. Kicking out a hungry man. Maybe he didn't have anywhere to go . . ."

"He didn't have. Because he's a bum."

"I don't know what that is."

"But I know. I live among them. Deryugin Street is full of bums."

Sonya only shook her head, giving him a new, distrustful look, and went back to her room, obviously displeased. Glebov did not know what to do. Should he go? Sonya's annoyance surprised him. Later, when he came to know her better, he realized that the chief trait in her character was an almost morbid, unselective proneness to pity others—anybody, no matter who or what they were. At times he found this characteristic tedious, even painful, but later he got used to it and stopped paying it any attention. Her first reaction to any real-life confrontation with people was to pity them. He would tease her about it: "Oh, I feel so sorry for that poor mugger who beat up three people at a streetcar stop. . . . Just imagine the agony in his soul . . ." Sonya herself was aware of the absurdity of this side of her nature and it pained her.

When they sat down to breakfast, just the two of them, at a little round table by a window, she was embarrassed and tried to make excuses for her earlier bad-tempered outburst: "If only you had given him a cup of tea."

"Don't worry," said Glebov. "He'll survive anyway. His kind always does."

He looked down at the gigantic curve of the bridge, with cars and streetcars rolling across it, at the far bank of the river with the Kremlin wall, palaces, fir trees, gilded domes—it was all astonishingly picturesque and somehow looked unusually fresh and clear from this height—and it occurred to him that clearly a new phase in his life was beginning.

To have a bird's-eye view of all those palaces every morning at breakfast! And to pity all those people, all of them without exception, running like little ants across the concrete arc down below. It was all a continuation of his half-waking, half-dozing semidelirium of last night's thoughts. He said, "Know what? You'd do better to feel sorry for *me*."

"I do, too." She stroked his cheek. "You're so restless, a kind of lost soul."

He began to visit the Ganchuks almost every day, sometimes to see the professor, sometimes Sonya. Before, the professor had called him "my dear fellow" and "Vadim Alexandrovich," but now he began calling him by the affectionate form of his first name, Dima. He invited him to join him on his evening walks. Whenever he donned his black Persian-lamb hat, slipped on his white Caucasian cloak patched with chocolate-brown leather or put on his long-skirted overcoat lined with fox fur, he looked like a nineteenth-century Russian merchant in one of Ostrovsky's plays. But that merchant, strolling along the deserted evening embankment with measured, unhurried steps, would describe the Polish campaign, the difference between the Cossack trooper's and the officer's saber-stroke, the relentless struggle against petty-bourgeois counterrevolution and anarchistic elements, and would discuss Lunacharsky's theoretical errors, the delusions of Pokrovsky, the vacillations of Gorky, the mistakes of Alexei Tolstoy: Ganchuk had known them all, had drunk tea with them, stayed at their *dachas*. And although he spoke about all of them with respect, even when discussing such famous men as Gorky, his tone of voice also carried a hint of hidden superiority, as though he possessed some additional knowledge: "If only Gorky had fully understood . . . ," he would say, or, "As I once explained to Alexei Tolstoy . . ."

Glebov listened to Ganchuk with great attention. It was all interesting and important. Sometimes Nikolai Vasilievich staggered Glebov with an astonishing remark. For instance, when describing his *dacha* out at Bruskovo and the troubles getting to it (the village Soviet had taken a disgracefully long time over asphalting the road), he ended quite unexpectedly by saying: "In five years' time every Soviet citizen will have a *dacha*." Glebov was amazed at this statement but made no objections.

There were evenings of fierce 25-degree frost, when sensible people preferred to stay at home, but sharp at nine Nikolai Vasilievich would wrap himself in a scarf, ram his hat down to his eyebrows, envelop himself in his merchant's fur coat and demand: "Are you coming with me?" How Glebov wanted not to go out into the cold! To slip through sheltered backyards to his house was one thing, but to stroll along the windy, icebound embankment . . . Glebov would answer with doomed acquiescence: "Of course, of course. I'm ready." He shivered and hunched himself up in his thin student's overcoat (cut down from an old one of his father's), restrained himself from breaking into a run and made himself keep a steady pace alongside the old man, who huffed and puffed pleasurably in his warm fur coat. "What a selfish, inconsiderate old brute," Glebov sometimes thought with annoyance. "It never occurs to him . . ." And another thought crossed his mind: Perhaps the professor was taking him out of the house on purpose, so that he wouldn't be left alone with Sonya?

Another guess was suggested to him by Vasyona. The crafty old peasant woman, who noticed everything, one day asked him sympathetically, "Why does he always drag you out with him? I think it's because he's keeping a kind of eye on you. . . ."

"Is he guarding me, or am I guarding him?" asked Glebov. Vasyona whispered, "I don't know, but there are people around here who don't like people like that who wear fur coats."

Occasionally Sonya, too, would come walking with them, and they would be joined by Kuno Ivanovich, or Kunik as he was known; a close friend of the Ganchuks, he was Nikolai Vasilievich's assistant in his work at the Academy. This Kunik was treated by the Ganchuks almost like a relative. Glebov noticed that Nikolai Vasilievich was not very fond of taking Sonya with him, and whenever Kuno Ivanovich insisted on coming he paid no attention to him. The reason turned out to be quite simple: when only Glebov was there, Nikolai Vasilievich would blossom into eloquence, told stories and reminisced without drawing breath, but when Sonya was with them, he was bored and silent. She was always liable to say crossly, "Be quiet, Papa. You mustn't talk when it's so cold." Or, "Papa, you're repeating yourself."

Yulia Mikhailovna, however, did not like the streets, the cars, the wind and frosts. She had stenosis of the coronary arteries. She was often too unwell to go to work: Yulia Mikhailovna taught German at the same institute in which Glebov studied and where Professor Ganchuk was chairman of a department. Although she had lived in Russia for several decades, Yulia Mikhailovna remained in some ways a tough, unbending German woman and spoke Russian with a noticeable accent. Her father had died during the Hamburg uprising. Yulia Mikhailovna still kept contact with several old anti-Fascists—Germans and Austrians—who had survived many hazards and hardships and who now and again appeared at the Ganchuks'. Kuno Ivanovich came from this milieu. His mother, who had died before the war, had been an old friend of Yulia Mikhailovna from their days together at the University of Vienna, and the Ganchuks had for years acted as Kunik's guardian, having known him since he was a boy. Kunik. It was like the name of a dog—a small, spoiled little lap-dog with intelligent little eyes.

"Kunik has to be fed," Sonya used to say.

"Ask Kunik . . . Call up Kunik . . . We must send Kunik to get tickets, but very tactfully . . ."

Thin and stooping, he held his head a little low and to one side as though he were permanently listening to something, although he never listened to anything and often failed to hear when people spoke to him. Now and again he would twitch his bent head—he probably suffered from a tic—throwing back his long, pale-reddish hair. At first Glebov thought he had tuberculosis.

Glebov disliked Kunik. He was so very taciturn, unfriendly, secretive and wily. Kunik lived alone. The Ganchuks were perpetually worried about him—was he sick? did he need anything? For some reason they had the idea that he always needed help and that he was unhappy. Indeed, the words "I am unhappy" were written on his mournful, desiccated little face with a thin-lipped mouth. But why was he unhappy?

One day at dinner Glebov cautiously started a conversation about an article that Kunik had published in a journal. He had heard for a long time that the article was in preparation, that the editors were demanding amendments to it, that Kunik was being obstinate and showing an unheard-of adherence to principle, that in his fight with the editor he had found allies in high places and had succeeded in getting the article into print despite all obstacles. In the scholarly world this was being talked of as a major event. Yulia Mikhailovna, in particular, had been closely involved in the whole business. When he had read it, however, Glebov realized that this article was thoroughly mediocre in quality and in no way outstanding, except that it was obvious, from a number of subtle, intangible clues, that Russian was not the author's native tongue. The writing betrayed a general sense of woodenness and lack of vitality. This was, in fact, the topic that he raised at dinner: that unfortunately works on literary history were often written in a language that was far from literary. Nikolai Vasilievich agreed with him, making many slanderous accusations on that score, and only then, after much discussion, did Glebov very gently introduce two or three examples from Kunik's article. The quotations were indeed striking in their lack of understanding of the spirit and style of the Russian language.

Nikolai Vasilievich laughed, Sonya smiled, but Yulia Mikhailovna remarked coldly that if people were going to make such malicious criticism, "they should make it to the author's face." Glebov insisted that there was nothing malicious in his comments, but Yulia Mikhailovna objected: "That is not true, Vadim. Don't be disingenuous. You haven't yet said what you think of Kuno Ivanovich's article as a whole."

Shrugging his shoulders, Glebov muttered, "What do I think of it? To be honest . . . I'm not exactly thrilled by it, but on the other hand I'm not . . ."

"Ah! In other words, I was right." Proudly, Yulia Mikhailovna raised a threatening forefinger. "And may I ask you . . . ?"

But Sonya interrupted her mother: why didn't Glebov have the right to his own opinion, which might be different from the opinion of the Ganchuk family? Why must she immediately attack him? Nikolai Vasilievich remarked that the Ganchuk family by no means shared a single opinion. Yulia Mikhailovna retorted that charging into the attack was the privilege of Nikolai Vasilievich, as a one-time Red cavalryman, and she was not given to wielding a sword.

"But you do wield a sword," said Sonya, "and sometimes very fiercely."

Glebov wished that he had not started the conversation. The delicate and apparently very weak and sickly Yulia Mikhailovna with her thin little hands and parchment-white face was, it must be said, unusually obstinate. She could argue and insist on her point of view *bis zum Schluss*—until, in fact, she had a heart attack. She said that criticism should above all be objective and should assess the work as a whole, and only then proceed to nit-picking. Kunik had written a splendid article. Minor comments should be confined to small print. He had written about an important topic—the danger of spontaneous petty-bourgeois counterrevolution. It was now in particular, when people wanted to relax and rest after the exhausting victory over nazism, that petty-bourgeois emotions, hitherto repressed, could flare up again. It was a danger that must not be underestimated.

Glebov had read nothing of the sort in Kunik's article. Timidly, he allowed himself to object: "Excuse me, Yulia Mikhailovna, but if I made a few comments about the language, that doesn't mean I underestimate the petty-bourgeois danger."

"Precisely!" said Nikolai Vasilievich, and banged his fist on the table. He tended to reduce most things to a joke. "The one doesn't follow from the other, for heaven's sake."

"No, you underestimate the bourgeois danger," said Yulia Mikhailovna, who was in no mood for flippancy.

"And where do you see it, Yulia Mikhailovna?"

"I'll tell you. Do you want me to be frank? For a long time I've noticed it in you, Vadim . . ." And here she launched on a catalogue of such staggering, unbelievable nonsense that Glebov was struck dumb with amazement. It appeared that he had always examined everything in their apartment with particular interest, that in the kitchen he was unduly fascinated by the refrigerator and the door of the elevator. Once he had questioned her in great detail about the family's *dacha* in Bruskovo—how many rooms did it have, was there a piped-in water supply, how big was the surrounding property in square meters—just as if he had been thinking of buying it.

"Mama! What are you talking about?" exclaimed Sonya in alarm.

"I'm talking about what I notice in the young people of today," said the obstinate woman, whose heart condition was already making her short of breath from the energetic statement of her principles. "And it doesn't only apply to Vadim. I happen to like Vadim, and don't want to offend him in any way. Don't worry, Vadim, you and I will still be on the best of terms. But I notice in so many people such a passion for things, for comforts and possessions, for what the Germans call *das Gut* and the Russians call 'goods' . . . Why? What does this apartment have to offer you?" She raised her shoulders and looked around the room with an expression of disdain, almost of abhorrence on her face. "Do you think you can't work just as well in your little room in that little wooden house of yours? Can't you be happy there?"

"But I haven't noticed you abandoning this place so that you can go and live in a little wooden house," said Sonya.

"Why should I? It's all the same to me where I live, in a great palace or in a log cabin, if I can live according to my own, inner standards."

Yulia Mikhailovna was right in that her attitude toward Glebov remained unchanged after these strange accusations. Glebov was determined not to be offended. He had guessed what was behind it all: Sonya's mother harbored a particular sympathy for Kunik, apparently seeing him as an ideal son-in-law, but Sonya had other views on this matter. Without knowing it, Glebov had hit a sore point.

Not without a certain concealed self-satisfaction, he felt that Yulia Mikhailovna's irritation, her digs and verbal attacks were only a sign that the advantage was *on his side*. Her remarks about his alleged petty-bourgeois sins seemed even more enigmatic. He did not for one second feel himself to be guilty of them. Could she really have been serious in what she said? Was it perhaps a carefully staged joke? It could have been significant that Ganchuk himself had made just one remark and then just grinned. And what about the elevator, paneled in fake mahogany, with its full-length mirror? Yulia Mikhailovna, after all, never walked upstairs to the ninth floor but rode up and down in that elevator, admired herself in the mirror and breathed the aroma of expensive cigarettes, expensive dogs and expensive everything else. Downstairs in the lobby, it was true, sharp-eyed elevator men in uniforms and caps no longer scrutinized you up and down, but there was an old woman in felt boots sitting there in a broken armchair, and in a lazy, husky voice she asked everyone who entered, "Which apartment are you going to?"

If the Ganchuks' apartment in Moscow could make any pretenses of luxury, their *dacha* was a slovenly, almost derelict house, with a rotting roof, an unfinished second story in which the windows were boarded up with plywood, but even so this house with its grounds of about an acre, its fence, its fir trees, the wild vine around the porch and its little kitchen garden was that same detested private property, that very *"das Gut"* in which petty-bourgeois values flourished like the onions that grew in the vegetable beds.

In spring, when the *dacha* season started again, the Ganchuk family would go out to Bruskovo for a so-called "working Sunday" at the *dacha*: they worked in the yard, in the house, in the kitchen garden—if you could call it work. Because of her general ill health, Yulia Mikhailovna only fluttered helplessly around and annoyed the others with her muddled instructions; Sonya was lazy and rather clumsy, while Nikolai Vasilievich went straight into the study and disappeared among his old books and papers. All the real work was done by the ancient Vasyona, helped occasionally by Anikeyev the chauffeur, who spent most of the day tinkering with the Ganchuks' car, a Pobieda. This Anikeyev, an elderly morose man, had been some sort of minor official before the war but had gotten into trouble. He did everything very slowly, never went anywhere in a hurry, skillfully avoided hard work and chose the easier jobs: he would spend half a day fixing a lampshade or nailing a new plank into the fence. Once when Glebov was pushing a wheelbarrow full of garbage to the far end of the yard—he had eagerly offered his help to Nikolai Vasilievich, being consumed with curiosity to see what the *dacha* was like—Anikeyev whispered to him: "Let the old woman move the garbage herself. Didn't you fix a deal with her?" He took Glebov for the hired help. . . .

That summer they were parted. Glebov went to the Kuban to do farm work in remote Cossack villages, and he found himself—unexpectedly—missing Sonya. It was then that he realized the thing was serious.

Around New Year, the winter being mild, a horde of their student friends descended on Bruskovo; they heated the *dacha* and decorated a fir tree in the garden with little colored electric lights. It was splendid.

It was then that Lev Shulepnikov joined their crowd for the first time; he had been at the institute for a year, then had gone his own way, no one knew where. "I'm like Kipling's cat," he said, "I walk by myself." He arrived at Bruskovo with a very pretty girl named Stella, a dancer in the then new and ultra-fashionable Beryozka folk-dance troupe.

For some reason, a very long and noisy argument took place. People shouted and yelled, until eventually a fight broke out. The unwitting source of it all was Astrug, a lecturer in linguistics, whom they used to bully and rag mercilessly in class. The argument started as a joke: what was the color of Astrug's underpants? The underlying cause was, of course, something different—quite, quite different!—and it even had nothing really to do with the wretched Astrug, who belonged, incidentally, to Professor Ganchuk's entourage, although on this occasion that had nothing to do with the argument either. It clearly resulted from the buildup of a kind of volcanic pressure of angry frustration, which had been gathering force below the surface, hidden from the casual glance, and now suddenly burst out. Lev Shulepnikov was, as always, the irritant that sparked the explosion, although he was too frivolous to be aware of what he was doing. There was, of course, a great deal of vodka and nothing to eat—the usual student binge, aggravated by ravenous hunger, tiredness, pre-semester nerves and that more sinister volcanic force that was seething deep down inside them.

It all began with a certain Cheremisin, an unpleasant youth who wasn't one of Glebov's friends but had simply shown up along with the others, the gang being a very mixed bunch (whoever put a bottle or two into the kitty was welcome), all in all about twenty people. They had thought beforehand that they could easily fit twenty into the big *dacha* comfortably, but in the event it seemed overcrowded and ended in a fight. When someone started talking about Astrug, Cheremisin told a story about him. It seems that during a test As-

trug had asked him, "What is a morpheme?" Cheremisin
didn't know. Astrug said, "How can you know a language if
you don't know what a morpheme is?" At which Cheremisin
asked, "What does *salazgan* mean?" Astrug, of course, shrugged
his shoulders. Cheremisin then asked, "And what is *shurdyburda?*" The lecturer didn't know that either. "How can you
know the language, Professor, if you don't know such simple
words? Where I come from, every old man and every little
kid knows them. *Salazgan* means something like riff-raff. And
shurdyburda means what happens in your classes—chaos and
confusion." Astrug just laughed, waved his hand and gave
Cheremisin a "C."

"But on the whole he deserved to be chucked out," Cheremisin added in conclusion. "He admires foreign bourgeois
scholars too much. He doesn't show it, but he does. That's for
sure. He may know the literary language, but he doesn't know
a damn thing about the language that real people speak."

A girl said, "I don't know, and I don't care, what he knows
or doesn't know, but I'm very glad he's going. He makes me
sick: sits down on a chair, crosses his legs, swings his foot, and
somehow his pants always manage to get hitched up so far that
you can see his long blue underpants tucked into his socks.
Ugh, disgusting." The girl pulled a face of revulsion. "I
couldn't bear to look, so I shut my eyes . . . and nothing that
he says goes into your head."

Cheremisin roared with laughter. "That's it. Right on the
button. But they weren't blue, they were white. I don't remember that they were blue."

"Well, now that he's been fired he can sit at home and
swing his leg," said the girl.

They began to get heated and quarrelsome not just because
they had drunk too much but also because it wasn't a gathering of friends, rather just a random collection. Sonya's classmates and their boyfriends made up one element, Glebov's
friends comprised another, on top of which there were the
gate-crashers and casual hangers-on, such as Cheremisin. The
whole bunch hummed, bubbled and boiled, as people met
new faces, became instant friends and equally instantly found
reasons why they disliked each other. The arguments were

shrill and furious. Some of Sonya's girl friends started to tease
the girl who had talked about Astrug's underpants. Lev Shulepnikov rudely interrupted Cheremisin: "You used to lick
Astrug's ass and now you sneer at him. That's pretty cheap."
Lev wasn't really as high-minded as he sounded and he didn't
give a damn about Astrug (Glebov knew Shulepa inside out),
but evidently Cheremisin had annoyed him in some way,
either by his impudence or by something else—probably because he had tried to make a pass at the pretty Beryozka girl.
Why did he do it? As the subsequent argument revealed, it
was simply to annoy Lev. Cheremisin hated Lev. And he
wasn't the only one. "None of us," shouted Cheremisin, his
prominent, high cheekbones turning white with fury, "give a
God-damn for you with your cars, and your daddies and mom-
mies. To us you're just a nothing—zero! Pfoo!" And to ram it
home, he spat at Lev. He might not have actually spat, but at
any rate he pretended to spit. The beautiful Stella shrieked.
Lev crawled over the table, ready for a fight. People held him
back, but it was obvious that there was going to be a big row.
Cheremisin had come with two friends from his dormitory.
Glebov knew them well; one was a decent, harmless kid who
belonged to Glebov's crowd—but everyone was so terribly
drunk. Up until about two o'clock in the morning, while they
were sitting at table, things were still more or less under control, but later, as chairs were pushed back and overturned,
people began scrambling out from behind the table; they
spread all through the rooms and up to the second floor, tumbled out of doors into the snow—that was where the real
trouble began, out in the snow. . . . Then they surged back
indoors, around the rooms, all over the floor, smashing chairs
to a background chorus of screaming women and the tinkle of
breaking glass. Glebov, feeling he was in a way the host, tried
to separate them, but he didn't do it firmly enough and suffered for his pains: somebody jabbed an elbow into his face,
giving him a massive black eye. The wretched Lev's nose was
broken, and he went around with a crooked nose for at least
six months. People said that the beautiful Stella behaved
heroically in defending her boyfriend—she took off a shoe and
lashed out at the attackers with the heel, aiming to smash the

spectacles of anyone who came within range. The damage and the wounds did not come to light right away—because by dawn anyone who was still on his feet was running hurriedly and shamefacedly to catch the train back into town and Glebov found practically nobody at the *dacha* at breakfast—but became apparent three days later, when they all gathered at the institute for sessions with their supervisors before the next exam.

Back in Bruskovo, however, when the others had all gone and Glebov and Sonya were left alone, something very important happened. The temperature was above zero, with only a gentle snowfall fluttering down. They went out with shovels and cleared the driveway. There was never more than twilight all day, and they turned the lights on early. For several hours they worked hard to get the house back into shape, until they were dead tired—Sonya was in a hurry to tidy it up, because she was afraid her parents might arrive—then they sat down in the kitchen and drank tea out of earthenware mugs. Her parents didn't come. The mugs were heavy, chocolate-brown in color, and the tea was unusually delicious. They remembered those earthenware mugs forever. There was also a moment when Sonya had gone over to the neighboring *dacha* to take back some borrowed crockery, and he was alone in the loft, the warmest room in the whole house; the window on to the garden was open, letting in the aromas of snow and fir trees and the smoke of burning lime wood, and he lay on the divan, an old-fashioned one with bolsters and a tasseled fringe, put his hands behind his head, stared at the ceiling with its striped wallpaper darkened with age, at the strips of insulating felt that poked out between the planking of the walls, which were adorned with photographs and a little engraving of a scene from the Russo-Turkish war, and suddenly—like a rush of blood to the head, making him dizzy—he had the feeling that all this might become his house. Even now, perhaps— no one had guessed it yet, but he knew—these yellowing boards with their knotholes and photographs, the squeaky window-frame, the snow-covered roof *belonged to him!*

He felt an urgent thirst for something to drink, even if only a mouthful of yesterday's flat beer. He went downstairs, looked everywhere but found nothing. Snow was falling soundlessly. When Sonya returned, he felt a sudden surge of strength. Sonya's eyes were sparkling, her cheeks wet with snow. He kissed her cold lips and cold fingers, murmured that he couldn't live without her. He was seized with real desire, which he had never felt before with Sonya, and this thrilled him. Sonya burst into tears and said, "Why have we been wasting the whole day?" Although it was still early, only about seven o'clock in the evening, they made up a bed on the divan in the loft, put out the light and fell upon each other naked, unwilling to wait another second. After a little while there suddenly came a knock downstairs, first at the front door, then at the side door on the verandah. It was probably some of their friends, coming back to carry on the party. The knocking was very insistent, and they could hear two or three people walking around the house in the snow, talking and conferring. Someone shouted: "Vadim! Open up, you sneaky bastard!" Then a girl's voice: "Sonya, it's us!" Someone else shouted cheerfully: "Hey, what are you two doing in there?" There was a burst of laughter. Glebov could not recognize them from their voices. Sonya wanted to go down and open the door, but Glebov would not let her: "Lie quiet!" His arms were around the thin, submissive, soft body, thin shoulders and thin back. There was no weight in this body, but now it belonged to him—or so he felt; it belonged to him along with everything else: the old house, the fir trees, the snow. And he kissed it, caressed it, did whatever he wanted with it, but tried to do it without any noise, while down below they knocked, buzzed like a swarm of bees, swore and went away.

It became unbearably hot that night in the *dacha*. Not knowing how to deal with the furnace properly, he had stoked it with too much coal and created such an inferno that they couldn't sleep. They opened all the windows, but it did little to help. There was a thaw outside, the crust of snow creaked as it began to melt and run down from the roof, and there was a continual melting, dripping and tinkling outside the window. Glebov and Sonya threw off the blanket, lay naked on the sheet, groaned at the heat and stuffiness and talked in low voices. They were now completely unembarrassed by each other's bodies. Sonya asked, "When did you fall in love with me?" This put Glebov on the spot: he truly could not answer with any exactitude; it seemed to have happened quite recently, but he decided not to say so.

He replied, "What difference does it make? The great thing is that it has happened."

"Of course," she whispered, contentedly. "I just asked because I remember very well when it was. . . . And you may have forgotten . . ."

"And when," he asked, "did it happen to you?"

To his amazement he learned that she had fallen in love with him way back in sixth grade, when he had first come to her home with the red-haired Yarik and Anton Ovchinnikov and told them about the very intelligent cat he had found sick on the street and how since then the cat had always walked with him to school along the embankment. They had all gone to see the cat at Glebov's apartment. Glebov had completely forgotten the whole episode.

"And I remember when I felt another burst of love for you. . . . It only lasted a second, but it was intense and painful but somehow sweet, I remember it clearly. . . . You came to school wearing a brown jacket with a belt. It wasn't new, but you never wore it as a rule, that was why I noticed it. I observed you very carefully, you see. And so when you were standing by the window I saw on the back of your jacket a large, carefully sewn-on patch, about as big as the page of a school notebook. You can't imagine how much I loved you at that moment."

He was offended. Why should she love him because of a patch? He didn't admit that this upset him, but just murmured, "My grandmother was a genius at sewing on patches."

Sonya, keenly interested, at once asked, "Oh, your grandmother did it? And for some reason I imagined that it was your mother who was such a good needlewoman."

Later, Glebov frequently noticed that Sonya had an insatiable interest in every kind of trifle about his childhood, about life with his parents, and was constantly questioning him on all kinds of silly details about his past. The surge of love for him evoked by the patch on his jacket had merged with a secret dream of hers: to raise enough money from somewhere to buy him a new jacket and send it to him with a note reading: "From an unknown friend." There had been another unusually strong impression connected with him: love and horror that for a second had fused into one. It had happened once when she had seen him out of the window: Chemist was standing on the narrow ledge of the balcony outside the railings, right over the abyss. And Glebov's face was frozen into such a look of horror, as though Chemist had already fallen and was lying down there on the sidewalk. Oh, that was a terrible moment. Did he still remember it? Of course he remembered it; that kind of childish madness stuck in the memory for a lifetime.

"And there were a few other minor agonies," said Sonya. "For instance, when you were so crazy about that little fool Tamara Mishchenko . . ."

At this he burst out laughing. Who was Tamara Mishchenko? Not that enormous fat girl? They both laughed until they ached.

Next day—which was Sunday—Sonya's parents arrived with Vasyona. Glebov was afraid that they were bound to guess what had happened to their daughter and prepared himself for the worst; it did not, in his view, require any great gift of intuition. Sonya, however, behaved so coolly and naturally, met them so joyfully, looked after them so lovingly and attentively that Glebov was secretly amazed and her parents suspected nothing. Anyway, they were a couple of old fogies. That was the explanation: two nice, decent old fogies—what's more, both of the same sort—completely preoccupied with their own affairs. But what about Vasyona and her sharp eyes? She didn't pick up any clues, either. Later, however, she was the first to guess.

Nikolai Vasilievich was out of sorts that day, gloomy and unaware of anything around him. Lunch passed in an uncomfortable silence. Glebov wondered whether the Ganchuks felt unable to talk freely because he was there. He whispered to Sonya: "Should I go?"

Sonya shook her head. "No, of course not. He's just worried about something. It's nothing whatever to do with you."

After lunch he and Sonya went for a walk. That evening, after taking a nap for a couple of hours, the old man was more relaxed, started talking and explained that he was worried about the business of Astrug's being fired from the institute. He and Yulia Mikhailovna had been unable to come out to the *dacha* yesterday because the Astrugs, Boris Lvovich and his wife, had suddenly asked to come around and see them. They could hardly refuse them. The Astrugs were utterly crushed—no one had invited them for New Year—so how could they not have them come around? Nikolai Vasilievich had been absent from the meeting of the Faculty Board that had decided on Astrug's expulsion and where, effectively, the rest of the plot took shape.

"Do you realize, Vadim, what a dirty trick they played? I was away on a trip!" said Ganchuk, growing more and more heated, while Yulia Mikhailovna, by gesticulating, making faces and adding irritating little remarks, tried to make him talk more calmly or, preferably, stop talking altogether. "You remember I was away for three and a half weeks in Prague, working in the archives, and they took advantage of my absence . . ."

"But Papa, why should they need to have you out of the way?" asked Sonya.

"What d'you mean 'why'? Ridiculous question. Because if I had been there I would have spoken out loudly and firmly against the whole thing."

"Exactly what they wanted you to do," said Yulia Mikhailovna.

"Please don't interrupt. You don't understand."

"No, I do understand. You're the one who doesn't understand what's going on, because you're hardly ever there, whereas I go there every day. It would have suited them very well if you had intervened in this business."

"Then I shall intervene!" barked Ganchuk.

"There's no longer any point. Absolutely *sinnlos*."

"We shall see!"

He relapsed into gloom, got up from the tea table and went to his study. Sonya and Glebov climbed the creaking stairs to the loft. Locking the door, and without switching on the light, Sonya flung herself at Glebov, began kissing him and whispering:

"Oh, I feel so sorry for Astrug. My poor, poor, poor, poor Astrug . . ." Each "poor" was accompanied by a kiss.

"So do I," he whispered, kissing the tender little hollow above her collar-bone. "I feel very sorry for him too. . . ."

"I simply can't tell you . . . how much I pity Astrug."

"Me too . . ."

She clasped Glebov with all the strength in her weak arms. He stroked her back, her shoulder-blades and her hips, everything that now belonged to him. They could hear people talking downstairs while Vasyona and Yulia Mikhailovna clattered the dishes. Then Yulia Mikhailovna called out: "Son-ya!"

Sonya pulled away from Glebov and whispered, "We're fooling around, but I really do pity him. Don't think I'm kidding. If he comes, you'll get to know him better."

Glebov wondered what she meant by this. Another shout from below, this time angrily: "Sonya, what's going on?"

She kissed Glebov and ran downstairs, heels clattering on the staircase. Still without switching on the light, Glebov went over to the window and pushed it open with the palm of his hand. Mist and cold forest air blew over him. From right outside the window the smell of pine needles wafted in from a heavy branch under its grayish covering of snow.

Glebov stood by the window, took a deep breath and thought: "That branch is mine too!"

Next morning at breakfast, when Anikeyev had already arrived with the car to take the three of them back to Moscow—Ganchuk and Vasyona were to stay for a few more days—the talk turned again to Astrug. Yulia Mikhailovna said, "All right, but you haven't said a word so far, Vadim. What is your opinion of Astrug? What's he like as a lecturer?"

"It's hard for me to say. He's only been teaching us for six months. An optional course on Dostoyevsky. . . ."

"That's exactly what I meant!" Yulia Mikhailovna announced with a certain triumph. "An indecisive assessment says a great deal. Only six months! But six months is a long time. Sonya, you're always biased about people and you like to overestimate."

"What do I like to overestimate?"

"You like to overestimate unpleasant things and injustices. Why should there not be a *single* particle of truth in the criticism of Boris? Is he an ideal, infallible man without any failings at all? I think he has faults, and not little ones either. To be frank, I think he has some rather big faults."

When Yulia Mikhailovna grew nervous or excited, certain gaps in her command of Russian became noticeable. It was still correct; she made neither grammatical nor lexical mistakes, but a barely detectable loss of accuracy crept in. As she became more nervous, she began to describe Astrug's shortcomings: he was unable to make people like him; he had made no impression in six months. She herself taught, and she knew for certain—she was prepared to have a bet on it—that she could win the attention and sympathy of an auditorium of young people in two hours of teaching. She needed no longer than that, and they would be coming to see her at home, calling her up and giving her flowers at holidays. After two hours!

As she said this, Yulia Mikhailovna put her arms akimbo and gave her husband and Glebov a slightly patronizing look. What she had said was indeed no more than the plain truth. The students loved her. Then Yulia Mikhailovna mentioned another of Astrug's failings: he liked to brag and show off his knowledge. Both he and his wife Vera—especially she—were occasionally prone to give themselves airs. They had a high opinion of themselves. Now what cause had they, one might ask, to put on airs and graces in front of Ganchuk? It looked ridiculous. Now, of course, one felt sorry for them. Without a decent job he could easily go downhill and fade away. And she would fade away, too, without the chance of queening it among the faculty wives.

Smiling gently and sympathetically, Sonya listened to her mother in the way that grown-ups listen to the chattering of children. Nikolai Vasilievich did not want to continue the argument. Turning to Anikeyev, who was standing in the doorway and impatiently jingling the car keys, he said, "Ivan Grigorievich, you at least don't put on airs, do you? Sit down and have some tea . . ."

But Yulia Mikhailovna was determined to have the last word. "No, my friends, we must take a broader view. The fact is, they were hoping to get rid of Ganchuk. Boris Astrug, unfortunately, is vulnerable to criticism and therefore represents an ideal target; that is also a fact."

"Nonetheless, I will intervene in this affair," said Nikolai Vasilievich briskly. "And that's that!"

In the car, Yulia sat in front beside Anikeyev; Glebov and Sonya sat in the back, between them a bundle of dirty laundry wrapped in a tablecloth. Yulia Mikhailovna kept up a ceaseless flow of stories and comments about matters at the institute, which were extremely involved and of which Ganchuk had no conception; she, however, understood them only too well. The principal didn't like Ganchuk—Yulia always called her husband "Ganchuk," both to his face and behind his back—because Ganchuk was independent; he was too great a figure to be ordered about, and Dorodnov, the director of studies, was a nonentity who would never forget that Ganchuk had refused to support him in his dubious maneuverings over his doctoral dissertation. And that wasn't all. They had old scores to settle. They were hoping to unseat Ganchuk as chairman of his department—but just let them try! It wouldn't be so easy: Ganchuk was, after all, an old Communist who had fought in the Civil War, author of a hundred and eighty published works, translated into eight European and seven Asiatic languages. And Boris Astrug, his pupil, was a very convenient tool with which to . . . Glebov and Sonya listened to Yulia Mikhailovna with less than complete attention. They were occupied with each other. All the way they caressed each other with their fingers, he with his right hand and she with her left. With his left hand he kept a hold on the bundle of laundry. Glebov saw that Sonya's cheeks were glowing and heard her voice tremble very slightly when she said now and again: "Yes, Mama . . . Of course, Mama . . . You're right . . ."

"All the same, Sonya, I would prefer Ganchuk to resign from the institute. . . . Well? What do you think of that idea?" Yulia Mikhailovna turned unexpectedly around and seemed to see something in Sonya's expression that surprised her. She turned around again and was silent.

Sonya said nothing to her in reply then, but just as they were approaching Moscow, she said, "No doubt you're right, Mama. But Papa will never leave of his own accord."

That night at the *dacha* when everything had happened, when the melting snow had dripped and it was too stuffy to breathe . . . Sonya saw it all in her mind's eye as she sat in the car. Glebov remembered it even now, twenty-five years later, although it would have been better to forget it. Then there were other nights, despite the fact that it was January, exams were looming and there was a sudden, violently cold spell that made it difficult to move about. They rode the train out to Bruskovo, because no one would disturb them there, and it was allegedly a more convenient place to study for exams. Running through the frostbound woods, they burst into the *dacha;* it was icy cold, but in two hours they had warmed it up. Glebov kept thinking that surely her parents had guessed what was going on? They were, after all, preparing for different exams at different times. What they were doing was really absurd: rushing out of town, spending two hours on the way and then sitting around in an otherwise empty house boning up on different subjects. They told her parents that several of their friends went out there with them. But it was unbelievable that they didn't notice how Sonya had changed. Yet they didn't see and noticed nothing. Sonya asserted firmly that they hadn't guessed.

Even when Sonya failed some test and laughed when she told about it—it was unusual for her both to have failed and to laugh about it—neither her father nor her mother were put on their guard. They were unshakably convinced that Sonya would pass, and with straight "A"s. It was in her genes, like her pale complexion. And in this they were right. They knew their daughter well. She even passed in the subjects that she managed to read up on only the morning before the exam, because examination candidates usually revise at night and Glebov and Sonya were otherwise occupied at night. Quite a few gaps were left in the work that Glebov was supposed to be doing, too, but he considered that what happened between him and Sonya during that January was his chief exam, immeasurably more important than anything else.

The first to find out was Vasyona—her thin, bony, yellow face reminded Glebov of medieval engravings of Death with a scythe—and it was she who took a swipe at Glebov, as though with a scythe. One day she said to Sonya, when she knew that Glebov was standing within earshot: "That fancy man of yours never wipes his feet when he comes in . . . acts like he's in some bar. . . ."

"What was that, Vasyona?" Glebov asked, going up to her. "And what does 'fancy man' mean?"

"How do I know? It's just a word people use . . . ," grumbled Vasyona.

Turning even paler than usual, Sonya embraced the old woman. "Vasyona dear, why do you talk like that? You're good and kind . . ."

At the end of January, Sonya told Glebov there had been a calamity: her mother had unexpectedly driven out to the *dacha* with Anikeyev to collect some things and had found certain unmistakable evidence that they had carelessly left lying around in their hurry to catch the train back into town. Although she used to blame Ganchuk for being naïve and unable to see what was going on under his nose, Sonya's mother was, if anything, even more naïve and had a habit of mentally brushing aside anything that distressed her. It was an unconscious reflex, like an ostrich putting its head in the sand, and on this occasion it resulted in an imaginative interpretation of what she had seen:

"Sonya, I have something unpleasant to tell you. Strangers broke into the *dacha* and spent the night there. They didn't take anything; they just came and slept there."

"Really?" said Sonya, terrified.

"Yes, unfortunately it's true. They left behind some rather nasty traces to prove it. I won't tell your father, because there's no point in upsetting him when there's nothing to be done about it."

After some thought, Glebov said, "What if Yulia Mikhailovna is perfectly well aware of what's happening and was obliquely letting us know this?"

He saw no great harm in it. They didn't have to keep it an absolute secret: they had, after all, decided to get married; nothing could alter that and it was just a question of time— now, in six months, in a year, what difference did it make?

He believed this sincerely, because it seemed absolutely firm and final and it could never be otherwise. They grew closer all the time. He couldn't spend a day without her. Now, when so many years have passed since that winter, it was possible to analyze it calmly: What had it been? True love that had matured slowly and naturally, or the physical infatuation of youth which had suddenly struck them like a disease? Probably the latter. Something blind, unthinking and heedless and so unlike his usual self. Another point was that she, too, turned out to be quite unlike the girl he had grown used to in those earlier years. Her taciturnity, shyness and anemic appearance—all that was left behind in the distant past. And only her kindness and submissiveness remained.

I remember the pain he caused me and how I still went on liking him. He would phone up in the morning—Father and Mother knew it was he calling and made a point of not picking up the receiver because I got angry when they did that— and I would rush headlong from wherever I might be at that moment: in the kitchen, where I was finishing a plateful of disgusting, sticky, lumpy semolina; in the bathroom, and even in the place from which, as I heard the phone ring through the door, I would rush out with my fly buttons still undone. "Hello!" I would shout. "Who's speaking?" I wanted to hear his name. He never gave his name, but always thought up something witty or absurd: "Sir," he would say, "I shall await you at eight-fifteen precisely under the clock in the central courtyard, and kindly come wearing your sword. I shall skewer you like a rabbit. You will make a splendid joint of roast meat, sir!" "And you, sir," I shouted, breathless with happy laughter, "you, sir, will make some very good meat balls! Yes indeed, sir! Juicy, tasty, fried meat balls, sir!"

It was awful—I could only copy him. Nothing original came into my head, and if it did, then only much later. I was at the meeting place five minutes early and waited for him, dying with impatience. In all my long life I cannot remember ever having waited for anyone with such trembling and such an agonizing fear of being let down, because Anton Ovchinnikov, as befits a true scholar and a great man, was incredibly absent-minded, forgetful and unreliable. Having made some arrangement with me, he was quite capable of immediately making a different arrangement with Walrus or Chemist, and I would suddenly see him calmly walking across the other side of the courtyard, heading for the other gateway and paying no attention to me whatsoever, just as if I didn't exist. As if he hadn't just called me and ordered me in conspiratorial tones to meet him under the clock.

When this happened the first time, I threw myself at him in fury: "What does this mean, sir? I was standing there like a fool, waiting for you, and you walk through the other gate." He looked at me with what seemed cold contempt and said, "My dear fellow, did we ever agree that I should go to that particular place? I am entitled to cross the courtyard by any way I choose and with whatever companions I may choose, and it is your business to observe my movements and, if you so wish, to join me precisely at the agreed time. . . ." He rapped out this high-flown nonsense in a dry tone that brooked no objection; Walrus and Chemist giggled, and I was reduced to silence. I lacked the skill to argue with him, and I lacked the will to be angry with him. Hanging my head, I slouched along behind him. Chemist, thin as a rake, and fat, podgy Walrus walked along on either side of the stocky Anton Ovchinnikov; despite the frost, he was, of course, bareheaded, his flaxen hair flapping, and he wore short pants and gaiters, the bare white gaps between gaiters and pants tinged with blue; passers-by grinned as they turned to stare at him. He was telling some endless story as Walrus and Chemist listened, open-mouthed.

That winter he developed an enthusiasm for paleontology. He acquired several large albums in which he drew dinosaurs and pterodactyls and told everyone all he knew about them. I could find nothing better to do than develop an interest in the same thing. I too started an album, I also tried to draw, or rather copy, or, to be more exact, copy with tracing paper all kinds of antediluvian monsters from books, but the results were so bad and I ruined the books by cutting out the illustrations. I was the one to whom he should have been talking about dinosaurs; yet he wasted his energy on trying to enlighten Walrus and Chemist, who were both, to be quite truthful, a couple of "crap-eaters." Anton and I gave the name "crap-eater" to anyone who limited his knowledge to what was in the school syllabus, and those who got top grades were called "super crap-eaters." These were absolutely hopeless cases, mostly girls, but some of them were boys—two or three miserable shrimps. There were not many "octopuses"—this was our name for those pure and honorable devotees of knowledge who were interested in all sorts of things, regardless of whether they were taught in school. There was Anton Ovchinnikov, perhaps myself, one or two others, and the only female octopus—Sonya Ganchuk, who studied mystic literature, such as the stories of Edgar Allan Poe. Besides, Sonya's father had a most splendid library—at least as good as Captain Nemo's library—and we often went to Sonya's to find out information.

It was Anton who conceived a marvelous idea—to create the SSTW, the Secret Society for Testing the Will. This happened after a gang beat us up in Deryugin Street. When Anton had recovered, we decided to go there again. The group consisted of Anton, Chemist, Walrus, Lev Shulepa and myself, but there at once arose the problem of Vadim Glebov, nicknamed French Loaf, who lived in Deryugin Street. Should we invite him to join the secret society? Once long ago he had brought to school a long French loaf of bread, which he ate in class and shared with those who wanted some. And there were plenty who did. It seemed like nothing special: he simply brought a French loaf, which anyone could buy at a bakery for fifteen kopecks; but only he, and no one else, thought of doing it. During break everyone asked him for a piece and he doled it out to them like Christ feeding the five thousand. However, he didn't give it to everyone; he refused to give it to some people—those, for instance, who brought cheese or salami sandwiches to school, and who wanted a hunk of fresh bread just as much as anyone else. For a long time Vadim Glebov interested me as a somewhat enigmatic personality. For some reason, many people wanted to be friends with him. He seemed to fit in with everybody: he was like this and he was like that; he got on with this bunch and that bunch; he wasn't bad and he wasn't good; he wasn't very selfish and he wasn't very generous; he was not exactly an *octopus* and not quite a *crap-eater* either; he was no coward, yet not noticeably brave; he didn't seem sly or cunning, yet at the same time he was not a simpleton. He could be friends with both Lev and Manyunya, though Lev and Manyunya couldn't stand each other. He was on good terms with Anton, went visiting with both Chemist and Lev, while managing to keep on the right side of the Deryugin Street gang, who hated us; he was simultaneously friends with Anton Ovchinnikov and Minka Bychkov.

So we were faced with a problem: how should we treat him? Should we tell him our secret? Lev Shulepa stood up for him warmly; he said that French Loaf would never give us away. Anton, too, was inclined to accept French Loaf into the SSTW, because he might be useful. I don't remember all the arguments and discussions—I only remember that the chief pleasure lay in the fact that we were deciding someone's fate. Would he suit us or not? I do remember, though, that the decision about French Loaf worried me particularly. I very much didn't want him to join our secret society, but I could not bring myself to say this aloud or to explain my reasons for it. And this was because a girl was mixed up in it. Well, of course that was the real reason. Sonya Ganchuk was in love with French Loaf, this insignificant, colorless creature who was neither one thing nor another. What did she see in him? His ears stuck out, half his face was covered in freckles, he had gaps between his teeth, and his walk was an ungainly shamble; his hair was dark and shiny, combed over to one side, and so slick that he looked as if he had just climbed out of the river and brushed it down. I never could understand what attracted her to him, but it was obvious to everyone: she blushed when she talked to him, tried to stay in the classroom whenever he was class monitor, asked him stupid questions and laughed when he tried to make a joke. He was one of those people who can't tell jokes; his attempts at humor had more sarcasm than wit. For instance, he was fond of sneering at Yarik, and would make spiteful remarks about him. Ah, what the hell—maybe I imagined all this simply because he annoyed me. The fact was that even Yarik had a soft spot for him and wanted to be friends with him. . . .

The thing about Vadim Glebov was that he was a *nothing person*. Later, I realized that to be a *nothing person* is a rare gift. People who have the ability to be *nothing* to the point of genius always go far. The whole essence lies in the fact that anyone who comes into contact with them projects onto that background of *nothingness* whatever is suggested to them by their own desires and fears. *Nothing people* are always lucky. In my lifetime I have come across two or three others of that remarkable breed—I only recalled French Loaf Glebov because he was the first to reap such obvious rewards for effectively doing *nothing*—and I was always surprised at the way they were carried onward and upward by the kindness of fate. After all, in his particular sphere even Vadim French Loaf became a big wheel, although I don't know exactly what it was, because it was of no interest to me; but whenever someone talked about him and his successes, I wasn't surprised: that was how fate meant it to be. And in those days—it seems like a century ago—when five little boys were trying to settle the burning problem of whether or not to initiate him into our secret, he was, of course, lucky as usual. We decided to tell him the secret and accept him. Anton said the war with the Deryugin Street gang would be a long one, a war of attrition, and we needed to have our man in their camp. So one day after class we took Vadim to a secluded spot and told him all about it. He had already suspected something and was obviously thrilled to be asked to join the SSTW. But his answer . . . Oh, it was a most remarkable answer! At the time we didn't appreciate it properly, but years later it suddenly came to one in a flash of comprehension: that was a classic example of the power of the *nothing* personality.

He said he would be glad to join the SSTW, but he wanted the right to leave it whenever it suited him. In other words, he wanted to belong to our society and simultaneously not belong to it. After a while, we tumbled to the extraordinary advantage of adopting this position: he knew our secret, while not being wholly with us. By the time we had grasped this, it was already too late. We were in his hands. I remember that we planned another march down Deryugin Street and named the day, but Vadim said the day was unsuitable and we should postpone it for a week—then for another week, then for three days, refusing, with an air of great mystery, to give his reasons, and we agreed, because he was one of us, though not completely, and at any moment he might drop out of the game. "If you want to, do it today, but without me. . . ." We began to fear he would warn Minka Bychkov, and the whole plan of a sudden raid on the street would collapse. Our aim was simply to walk up and down Deryugin Street, where the resident gang had previously injured and robbed the kids from our house, and if they attacked us, to fight back. Lev Shulepa promised to bring the German pistol that fired blanks and made a bang as loud as a real revolver.

At last French Loaf said: "Today's the day." We set off at five o'clock in the afternoon. As we approached the Deryugin house, we saw French Loaf's pale face at a second-floor window; he saw us too, and waved. We walked down the whole length of the street and no one attacked us. No black dog appeared. There were some kids sledding down a mound of packed snow in the middle of the pavement, but they paid us no attention. We stopped at the gateway into one yard, and at another, but still no pirates showed up—neither Minka nor Taranka Bychkov, no one. Shulepa fired into the air, we waited a little longer and then went home. Everyone was disappointed. No testing of our will had taken place. We went there a couple more times, still without any results. What had happened? Where had they all gone? We never did find out, or maybe I have forgotten after all these years. I can remember nothing except a feeling of annoyance and a strange hunch that Vadim Glebov had fixed it all, to our displeasure and to his own advantage. . . .

Later there were various ordeals, fears, nocturnal expeditions to the crypt and underground passages beneath our little local church. And the balcony of Sonya's apartment over the abyss. That balcony. And the deathly cold that gripped our hands. And Sonya's face, white, with that mad stare. Four of us were left. French Loaf refused to say yes or no right up to the last moment, and the fat Walrus backed off in an agony of shame—he suffered from dizziness. We had to choose the most suitable apartment. Chemist's place was no good, because his apartment was full of people and we would never be sure of being alone on the balcony. Lev's apartment was also swarming with people—relatives, hangers-on—and Lev's mother tended to stay indoors for days on end. Anton lived on the first floor, and I lived on the third floor. There remained the poor invalid Walrus. His home was ideal: on the eighth floor, with a mother who was away at work all day and a deaf old maid who could be locked in the kitchen if one gave her a copy of *Pioneers' Pravda* to read. The old woman loved reading this children's newspaper. Walrus, however, suddenly objected. He objected in general to this particular ordeal, saying that it wasn't a test of will but a test of health. It was then that I remembered Sonya. To be honest, I never forgot about her for a moment.

Sonya lived on the ninth floor, and her parents happened to be away just then. The maid was at home, but she went out at times and Sonya was alone in the apartment for hours on end. The ninth floor: it was, of course, incredibly attractive. Exactly what was wanted. The higher the better, the tougher the ordeal. We agreed on this, although our stomachs were churning with fear. The only thing that worried Anton was that a girl had been initiated into the secret; he was categorically opposed to women: "I haven't even told my mother about this, and normally I tell her everything."

It was true that Anton's mother was always right up to date with his plans and projects. If you called her up and asked what Anton was doing, she would reply: "Right now he's finishing the third part of his album of paleontology. Flying lizards. And he's already halfway with his Italian album. It's turned out very well, especially Vesuvius. . . ."

Oh God, how I longed for Sonya to be present at this latest test of will. I suggested we could conceal from her what we were going to do by saying that we octopuses had to go and talk in secret on the balcony and ask her to stay in her father's study for a half-hour. If she gave her word of honor as an octopus that she wouldn't leave the study, then she wouldn't upset our plan. Anton hummed and hawed, but finally agreed: "All right. Sonya, of course, is at least different from other girls because she understands Verdi. She even sang the Grand

March from *Aïda* once, although admittedly with a few mistakes." Coming from Anton, this was praise indeed. Mankind was divided into those who understood Verdi and those who didn't; the former were the best people, the latter were an ignorant rabble. A day was chosen, and we went up to Sonya's place. I can't say that we went bravely and willingly. My legs felt slightly weak, and ants seemed to be running up and down the bones inside them. None of the other members of the secret society looked much better either. I very much wanted French Loaf to funk it at the last moment and not to come; he had the right not to come, and we wouldn't have said anything—but he came, damn him. His face had a greenish tinge, like a corpse. Chemist kept giggling stupidly and trying to make inappropriate jokes.

We planned it to look as if we had come to consult one of the encyclopedias in Professor Ganchuk's library; suddenly Anton said to Sonya: "Sonya, you must swear an oath here and now that you . . ."

Disconcerted by all this mystery, Sonya suspected that something funny was going on. She began nervously to try and worm it out of us: what are you up to? Why does it have to be on the balcony, of all places? Were we planning to throw someone off? She had no idea how close she was to the truth. That "someone" might be any one of us. As I heard Sonya's half-joking questions, I felt tears of self-pity start to my eyes; fortunately no one noticed them.

As I took a few steps around the room I felt my knees trembling and my feet quivering as they trod the ground. Suddenly my legs became a serious cause for alarm. With legs in this state there would be no question of climbing over the parapet of the balcony and around the railings at the height of the ninth floor. I looked furtively at the others. When we each went to the toilet in turn, I noticed that they were all walking rather unsteadily. Only Anton Ovchinnikov didn't go to the toilet.

He remained sitting on the chair where he had sat down on arriving, without moving, until the moment came to get up— no sooner and no later. He was short, stocky, broad-shouldered, with a yellowish face and high, prominent cheekbones that made him look like Buddha. When Sonya finally went into the study and locked the door behind her—as Anton had demanded—he was the first to get up and stride firmly into the next room, divided off by heavy drapes and from which a glass door opened to the balcony. We followed him. The door to the balcony was not locked and not yet taped up for the winter, although the frosty weather had already started. Sonya's father used the balcony every morning to do his exercises. As everywhere else in the apartment house, the balcony was divided in two by a set of iron railings, the other half belonging to the neighbors—and here lay a source of danger: at any moment somebody from the next apartment might come out onto the balcony and—oh miracle!—save us.

Nobody came out, however, and there was not the slightest sign of life behind the neighbors' window. As I stared at the railings, at the jars, pitchers and saucepans standing along the wall and at the curtained glass door, I thought: "Why don't you look out, just for a second, damn you? It's so easy to hop over the railings and rob your apartment. . . . What idiotic carelessness on your part . . ."

No, the neighbors were clearly not planning to save us. We were doomed to carry out the test of will. It was about ten degrees outside and we were not wearing coats or caps. My teeth were chattering. Anton went over to the left-hand end of the balcony, where it butted up against the concrete wall, and where the window of the room in which we had just been sitting with Sonya looked out onto the balcony. Anton shook the metal handrail with both hands, using all his strength; it was absolutely secure. Everything was in order. I thought: "We must all be crazy." But even if I had wanted to go away at that moment, I couldn't have done it: my legs wouldn't obey me. Down below everything was normal—calm, quiet, snow, black sidewalks, white courtyards, car roofs—but all of it unattainably far away. We could no more reach the yard below than fly to another planet.

The only way of getting there was to fall.

Anton swung one leg over the parapet, then the other, and slowly moved along it, gripping the handrail with his back turned to the abyss and his face toward us. By this means, moving sideways and very slowly, he reached the next-door balcony and started to come back again, all the while humming a tune; I think it was the Grand March from *Aïda*. We followed him on the other side of the parapet, ready to help him at any moment. I wonder what we could have done? When he reached the wall, he put his bare knee—he was still wearing short pants—on the windowsill, rolled over the handrail on his stomach and fell in a heap at our feet. Immediately after Anton, Chemist set out; he couldn't help showing off, and leaning backward with outstretched arms he looked down and spat.

At that moment, I saw Sonya's face, twisted into a rigid look of horror, looking out of the window at the end of the balcony.

In a second she was out there with us. Her mouth open soundlessly, she grasped Chemist under the armpits and started to pull him back over the parapet—he told us later that she pulled him with inhuman strength—with her mouth still open as though shouting, but uttering no sound. Chemist tumbled down onto the balcony. We crowded back into the room. We were all frozen, dirty, stained with rust, our faces blue. Sonya seized Vadim Glebov by the hand and wouldn't let him go, afraid that he might pull himself away and climb over the handrail, whispering mechanically: "Oh, you fools, you fools, you fools . . ." French Loaf frowned with annoyance. He looked offended, as though something had been taken away from him. Later I discovered what had happened. Unable to contain himself, he had secretly blabbed to Sonya—no doubt when he had gone to the toilet—and advised her to watch the entertaining spectacle. Miserable little sneak. But he saved Lev Shulepa, himself and me. He saved us! My legs were completely useless. People who are neither cowardly nor brave, neither one thing nor the other, sometimes save people who are too much of either. I hated him even more. He snarled at Sonya and said something nasty to her. Then she fainted. We were terrified and called the doctor. . . .

And what happened afterward? Oh, long, long afterward, you mean? The house emptied. My friends disappeared, all in different directions. Walrus, who had suffered such pangs of shame because he couldn't take part in our tests of will—he couldn't even walk along an ordinary beam in the gymnasium—vanished first of all, probably that same winter. Anyway, we needn't have been in such a hurry to test ourselves: the ordeals came to us soon enough, during the war, and there was no need to invent them. They poured down upon us like heavy rain; some they knocked to the ground, others they soaked to the bone, and some of us perished in that flood. But I do remember this: Anton's mother, Chemist's father and someone else were sitting in our apartment, locked in the dining room, where Anton and I were forbidden to enter. However, we listened at the door. Some people's voices can be heard easily, especially when they are talking angrily. I could hear my father saying loudly and angrily: "See here—have you consulted a doctor?" And Anton's mother's voice in reply: "What for?" "Maybe your son is mentally not quite normal." Anton's mother laughed, "My son? What nonsense. My son is quite, quite normal." Then they all started talking at once, while Anton's mother went on laughing.

That winter, when Glebov's love affair with Sonya began at the *dacha* in Bruskovo, at his home on Deryugin Street the hopelessness that marks all life on the wane thickened into a dense mass. For the life of the Glebov family was fading away: Grandma Nila could hardly walk and could scarcely cope with all the household chores; after his wife's death, Glebov's father had aged and grown bent, eaten away by some disease, and on top of it all he had started to drink. Everything was disintegrating, moving toward the end. Glebov didn't like being at home. His father did not arouse his pity, because this confused, disheveled old man could not find the courage to accept the end with dignity; instead, he kept hoping for something, dodging and playing sly games with life, dreaming of wheedling from it a few last crumbs of comfort. He also succeeded in wheedling Aunt Paula: after her sister's death she started coming to visit more often, out of family feeling; she helped poor old Nila, and gradually, as though unthinkingly, moved into the place in bed where Glebov's mother had once slept. Where else was she to go? After serving his prison sentence in the far north, Uncle Volodya had left her and gone to Tashkent, where he started a new family. Glebov shrugged it all off. Let them do as they please. He felt a constriction in his chest and the blood thumping in his temples from a premonition of the change that was about to take place in his own life. . . .

Aunt Paula had a daughter, however, named Klavdia, who strongly objected to all this. She would not forgive either her mother or Glebov's father. Aunt Paula's son, Yurka, two years older than Glebov, had died in the war, and Klavdia was married with a baby. She and her husband lived well, and she should have been glad that her mother was no longer lonely and was able to live with Nila and ease her old age, but Klavdia hated her mother. Whenever she came to Deryugin Street, she made it painfully obvious that she had only come to visit Grandma Nila. She hardly said a word to her own mother, and with Glebov's father she was curt and sarcastic.

Klavdia took after her father—she was heavily built, big-boned and ugly. For some reason she was regarded as a good person—it was the same sort of family legend that regarded Aunt Paula as beautiful. Glebov was irritated by the mocking tone in which Klavdia talked to his father, which flustered the old man and made Aunt Paula so nervous that she could only rush about and talk nonsense. With some annoyance Glebov noticed in Klavdia a totally different, alien cast of character, and a nasty streak of cruelty in her nature.

One day she said to Glebov, "You amaze me: how can you swallow it all so calmly? You seem to have a unique character."

"In what way?" asked Glebov.

"In your ability to accept all this without batting an eyelid. Or maybe it's just a staggering degree of indifference."

Glebov grinned. "And what am I supposed to do? I'm a grown-up person, they are grown-up people . . ." He looked at his cousin's face, distorted in a grimace of bitter ill-will, and thought it was better to be indifferent than malicious. Aloud, he said, "I wish them no harm."

"My God, who wishes them harm? But it makes me suffer, it's torture to me—yet you don't seem to feel anything. That's what is so extraordinary."

"I find something else extraordinary: How can you hate your own mother so intensely? Why are you so pitiless?"

Klavdia covered her face with her hands and went out. On

a later occasion, however, she confessed to Glebov that she would like to soften her attitude and forgive her mother, but she could not find the strength to do it. Because her mother was the cause of all the family's misfortunes. It had all begun before the war, and got worse during the war. The reason why everything had gone to pieces was that Uncle Volodya hadn't wanted to go on living with Paula and it had broken Glebov's mother's heart. Glebov himself had somehow not noticed any of this, or rather had not understood it. As she told the story, Klavdia suddenly burst into tears and began to curse herself, saying that she was a horrible person, that she shouldn't have said all that to Glebov and begged his forgiveness.

"Now can you understand me, even just a bit?" she said, now weeping, now clutching Glebov by the hand. "Yes, I am a nasty, bitter, evil-minded woman and I didn't have the right to talk to you like that. What devil gets into me, pig that I am?"

Glebov was amazed, but said calmly, "Well, what of it? I guessed it myself. I don't blame Aunt Paula."

"But I do blame her," Klavdia whispered, and let her head fall to the table. "I blame her, I do, I do. She deprived me of both mother and father."

Glebov reflected in silence. Naturally the revelation was painful, but the worst of it had already happened, there was nothing to be done about it, and his only feeling was an increased desire to break away and start everything afresh and on his own.

Sonya began visiting him at home. She wanted to get to know all his family and loved them all even before she met them. Glebov, however, found these visits painful. She saw how pathetic his father was, listened to his futile, ingratiating remarks, saw the poverty, the overcrowding (in his schooldays none of this had bothered him at all, friends were constantly coming to see him; but now his own home was becoming more and more of an embarrassment)—and in particular he feared Sonya's bewilderment when she faced the most ticklish question of all: who was Aunt Paula and just what was her place in the *ménage*?

Once Sonya turned up when they all happened to be at

home, including Klavdia, who had come to visit with Nila and had brought some vegetables from the market. It was the end of May and the weather was hot. Glebov introduced Sonya to Klavdia, then quickly took her into his own little cubicle, which was now, thank God, well insulated from the rest of the room in which his father and grandma lived, and where Aunt Paula slept whenever she came to "help out." After a half-hour or so, they were invited to drink tea. Glebov was unwilling, but Sonya was eager to see her new friends: this time she particularly wanted to see Klavdia and her four-year-old daughter Svetlana, in whom Sonya was very interested. Sonya and Svetlana liked each other on sight, and at once began chattering and playing some game, which set them apart from the rest of the company. Meanwhile a wearisome family quarrel was in progress, which rarely happened—Klavdia avoided contentious topics in this house. This time the row seemed to break out suddenly, and Klavdia was unable to restrain herself. The cause of the argument was, in fact, little Svetlana, whom her mother wanted taken out of town for a spell of fresh air in the country.

With a disapproving glance at Sonya, who had arrived amid the heat of the argument, Klavdia said in a sharp, quarrelsome voice: "Now, Mother, give me a definite answer: Will you go with Svetka or not? If not, then I'll make an arrangement with Kolya's aunt, but I don't want to, because she's not well . . ."

Aunt Paula said that the *dacha* they rented was uncomfortable and inconvenient, it was a long way out of town, and she had to go to work in Moscow three times a week. (She was then working for a cooperative, where she wove safety nets that protected workers using machinery.) Anyway, how could she leave Nila without help in the house? At this Klavdia lost her temper: "Don't use Grandma Nila as an excuse. We'll take her with us to the *dacha*. It'll be even better for her there than here."

"You don't really think you can drag your granny all the way out there, do you? You must be crazy."

"Is it so good for her here?"

"She needs the doctors here, you fool! She has to go regularly to the clinic. You're not thinking of her—you only want her as a nanny. She's done enough nannying for one lifetime, thank you very much."

Grandma Nila objected, saying that she wasn't as sick as all that. Aunt Paula returned to the attack: "Why don't you put Svetka in a kindergarten? The kindergarten takes all its children out to a *dacha* in the summer. There's a very good kindergarten at your factory, I hear."

"Who says it's good? You just want to get the child off your hands. Call yourself a grandmother!" said Klavdia in fury. "God, the number of times I've vowed never to ask you to do us a favor . . ."

Glebov's father mumbled something; no one could understand what he was muttering through his toothless gums. The women went on quarreling, not exactly swearing at each other but in an intolerably nasty tone, and, worst of all, totally uninhibited by the presence of Sonya. Klavdia accused her mother of being selfish, saying that she never gave a thought to the little girl and never considered anyone but herself, so what was to be done? If there was no one to go with Svetlana, they would lose their deposit on the *dacha*. Of course, if she had known this in time, she would have fixed her up in a kindergarten, but now it was too late. Aunt Paula said, "And that's because you never talk to your mother. You keep everything to yourself, like the secretive little brute that you are. What harm have I ever done you?" And she burst into tears.

Suddenly Sonya broke in: "Can I offer you our *dacha*? There is a summerhouse in the garden, which is very comfortable, with electricity and water. Would you like to come to my *dacha*, Svetka?"

"Yes, I would!" cried the little girl, leaping up and down.

Nobody paid any attention to Sonya's remarks, just as if they had not heard them; they simply went on quarreling. Glebov's father brushed the offer aside with a gesture, and said to Klavdia, "Don't worry, she'll go; she can quite well manage it."

Weeping, Aunt Paula shook her head. "No, I can't go so far out of town. In any case I don't want to go with her; she doesn't want to know me . . ."

Sonya whispered to Glebov, "Tell them about the *dacha* at Bruskovo. My offer was absolutely serious."

Klavdia suddenly turned to Sonya: "Kindly don't interfere in our affairs, young woman. Thanks for the offer, but we couldn't afford your *dacha*. And anyway it is unsuitable."

"How rude!" said Glebov. "Come on, Sonya."

They went back into Glebov's little cubicle and sat down on the bed, covered with a flannelette bedspread. Glebov locked the door and switched on the paper-shaded wall-lamp over the head of the bed. How many evenings and nights had he lain sprawled on this couch under that lampshade, reading and dreaming. He lay down with his shoulders and the back of his head propped against the partition wall—one of his favorite sybaritic poses, which was evident from the greasy mark made by his head on the wallpaper—and Sonya sat alongside him, sinking deep into the sagging middle of the old couch, snuggled up against him with her head on his chest. He embraced her with his left arm, while with his right hand he stroked her thigh, which was encased in a stocking. Above the stocking was an expanse of bare skin. The tedious argument dragged on behind the partition; they could hear every word. Glebov was afraid that Klavdia would say something awful and irreparable, something that Sonya ought not to know. With the palm of his hand he stroked the entirely accessible piece of slightly chilly flesh, which belonged to him, and said that his cousin was arrogant, and uneducated; she had left high school at fifteen and taken some courses at a technical school, and he and she had absolutely nothing in common. She worked as a forewoman in a knit-wear factory, and Kolya, her husband, was a machine-adjuster in the same plant.

"And I felt sorry for that woman. She's so hard and embittered, it's painful to look at her," said Sonya. "And I feel so sorry for your aunt. I think she's a good woman, and beautiful too. The little girl's sweet, but rather weak and not too healthy. . . . I'm sorry for all of them, all of them. That's bad, isn't it? I shouldn't feel like that, should I?"

"No, why not? It's a good thing. You *should* feel like that," said Glebov, continuing to caress the skin through her stocking. Then he unfastened the clip and pushed the stocking down. He could do anything he wanted. She took hold of the fingers of his left hand and pressed them to her lips. The voices behind the partition droned on; this caused him mild irritation; yet over and above it all he felt a great sense of unruffled pleasure—because this woman was submissive, and because she was not just any woman but remarkable, and intelligent with it. He had always suspected that this was the source of her attraction, and now he mentally ordered his hand to derive the utmost possible pleasure from caressing the thigh of an unusual and remarkable woman who belonged wholly to him.

The summer passed, and there began Glebov's fifth and final year at the institute. In the fall—it was already cold, almost about to snow, probably in November—something happened when Glebov was working flat out on the last stages of his dissertation.

He received a request to report to the dean of studies. The dean was a man by the name of Druzyaev, recently appointed, whom Glebov hardly knew. He inquired about the progress on the dissertation. Glebov was writing on Russian journalism in the 1880s; it was a vast topic, and he was positively swamped in material, mostly straight quotations amounting to several thousand newspaper pages.

Druzyaev's questions showed that he obviously knew the subject, and he even quoted from memory a little satirical verse of the period, a lampoon on Pobedonostsev, the notoriously reactionary Procurator of the Holy Synod. Perhaps, thought Glebov, Druzyaev had purposely learned it in order to impress him at this interview. Glebov glanced with surprise at this weary-looking man with the telltale signs of heart disease on his flabby face and, as is often the case with heart sufferers, with a kind of dim, hidden melancholy in his eyes, and he wondered why the dean had sent a messenger to the lecture hall to demand his immediate presence. Druzyaev was wearing an officer's tunic and the pants of an ordinary civilian suit, under which were military boots that squeaked incessantly. All this conveyed a somewhat incongruous impression: the creaking, government-issue boots and the tunic hardly fitted in with the sadness in his eyes and the conversation about liberal editors of the late nineteenth century, spiced by some daringly unorthodox praise for the right-wing journalist Suvorin: "Just between ourselves, Suvorin was a remarkable character. Enormously talented."

One fact, however, stuck firmly in Glebov's mind during their talk: until recently Druzyaev had been a military prosecutor, and had been demobilized only a year previously. Another graduate student, Shireiko, glanced into the room. He stuck his black-haired, bespectacled head around the door as though just looking in for a second, but on seeing Glebov he decided, for some reason, to come in. He walked over to the dean's desk and sat down in a relaxed and familiar manner as though at home. Glebov took note of this and immediately saw the implications of his obviously close relationship with Druzyaev. At that time Shireiko was making remarkably rapid progress up the academic ladder while still only a graduate student. He was lecturing to the final-year students on Gorky, having replaced Astrug. Druzyaev asked Glebov: "Is Nikolai Vasilievich Ganchuk your supervisor?"

As in the children's game of Hot and Cold, Glebov suddenly sensed that his question was "warm." Druzyaev had not said "Ganchuk," which would have sounded brusque and hostile, nor had he simply said "Nikolai Vasilievich," which would have been the most natural way to refer to Professor Ganchuk, if not the normal and friendly contraction of name and patronymic into "Nikvas"; instead, he had chosen to use the precise, official, full version—"Nikolai Vasilievich Ganchuk"—as though at an awards ceremony prizegiving or in a funeral announcement. At the same time this form of the name was also respectful, and in some indefinable way it separated the professor in question from the faculty as a whole. Did Glebov have full and satisfactory contact with his supervisor? No problems? Glebov confirmed that there were no problems.

It was then that Druzyaev took on a quite different look, a prosecuting attorney's look; his unhealthy appearance seemed to vanish instantaneously, he straightened up and somehow filled out inside his tunic.

"Now, Glebov, the situation is a ticklish one. . . . Why did I send for you? I will tell you—only this must remain strictly *entre nous,* as the French say. Shireiko here is fully informed about this little problem of ours." Druzyaev nodded toward Shireiko, who was listening attentively. "So don't be surprised that he has joined us. We are all somewhat embarrassed. Did you know that Nikolai Vasilievich Ganchuk has included you in the preliminary list of seniors who are being recommended for graduate studentships? You didn't know? It's news to you? And good news, too, I should imagine. Anyway, apart from that, he is your supervisor. And then in addition you are, as it were, his future, er . . . son-in-law, are you not? Excuse me for mentioning this—my spies have reported it, as they say. And as a military man, I am accustomed to believing the information supplied by intelligence sources."

Here Druzyaev seemed to unbend slightly; he relaxed, leaned back and even smiled, although the smile was not directed at Glebov but at Shireiko. Glebov mumbled something and shook his head in a vague, noncommittal way, all of which implied that he did not deny the information provided by Druzyaev's "spies."

"You see, Glebov," Druzyaev went on, "we are not against your graduate studentship, nor do we have any objection to Ganchuk supervising your dissertation. And of course we cannot possibly object to any future family connection between you and the professor. Nor has it ever worried us—I'm new here, as you know, but my colleagues tell me that this point has already been raised more than once—that Ganchuk's wife, Yulia Mikhailovna, should also be working here in the Modern Languages Department, where she is in charge of the teaching of German. I hope you see where the difficulty lies: each of these things is perfectly admirable in itself, but taken together they add up to rather more than is strictly ethical."

"In other words, it doesn't look good," said Shireiko firmly, and added: "From the point of view of *moralité.*"

Glebov asked, "Well, what do you propose to do about it?" His attitude was even slightly challenging, because he realized that he was not the target. They explained that it was difficult to talk to the old man; he was accustomed to being above criticism, his old colleagues refused to raise the matter with him, but he must somehow be made aware of the position. Otherwise it would soon be too late; rumors would reach the competent authorities. Would Glebov agree to talk quietly and confidentially to Ganchuk, as a close family friend, and outline the situation to him? Let Ganchuk himself choose another supervisor for Glebov's dissertation; he need only submit his proposal in the usual form, giving whatever reasons he liked. All that was a mere formality, anyway. And that was all the secrets of the Spanish court amounted to. Well then—was comrade Glebov prepared to help them, and in so doing primarily to help himself?

The whole thing seemed perfectly clear and simple to Glebov and he said that he agreed to do as they asked. And on that day there began the chain of deception, confusion and despair that baffled him and finally tore his life into shreds.

If only he had known where it would all lead! But in some things Glebov was a little slow-witted, somewhat lacking in foresight. To him, the complex situation in which he was later embroiled remained a mystery sealed with seven seals. Besides, no one could have foreseen what eventually happened. Druzyaev, himself, for instance, who so audaciously and cunningly started digging his long-distance tunnel under the walls of the mighty fortress, was not to know that in exactly two years he would be flung out of the institute and suffer a stroke, after which he could only sit in a chair by the window, his clawlike hands shaking, and ask his wife in a pathetic whine to light a cigarette for him; and that a further year later Glebov, as a graduate student, would read a short announcement in the newspaper: ". . . with profound regret . . . after a grave and prolonged . . ." He heard from others that only eight people turned up at Druzyaev's funeral. Everyone was still disturbed and shattered by Stalin's funeral—it happened in March 1953—but even that was not the real point. The fact was that Druzyaev vanished as meteorically as he had arisen; and he had arisen, it seemed, simply in order to carry out one short, hard-hitting mission. He had descended on the institute, done his job and disappeared.

For the first few hours, as he reflected on Druzyaev's proposal, Glebov genuinely thought that it was prompted by the new dean's concern for the successful completion of his,

Glebov's, dissertation. How naïve of him! As far as he could see, it was simply a question of finding a colleague of Ganchuk's who would be prepared to put his signature to work which would actually be done by Nikolai Vasilievich himself, who would thus effectively continue to be Glebov's supervisor. A pure formality, in fact; they were always afraid of trouble caused by formalities.

He decided he would talk to Ganchuk the next day, when he went to see Sonya. The only thought that worried him was something that had not occurred to him at first: how was he to explain to the old man the situation to which Druzyaev had referred so rudely and directly? Although Sonya and he had decided everything, they had said nothing openly to her parents. An unfortunate situation had arisen: to announce this serious decision to Ganchuk simultaneously and in close connection with Druzyaev's proposal would be somehow stupid, and no matter how he might try to phrase such a delicate conversation, Glebov suddenly felt that it would inevitably sound tactless. It would mean artificially accelerating events that ought to develop smoothly, at their natural tempo.

The best thing would be to postpone it; with any luck, the authorities would either forget the whole business or it would somehow sort itself out. It was Glebov's favorite principle: Leave it alone and hope for the best.

Next day he did not go to Sonya, nor for the two following days. He was not purposely avoiding her; his reasons were that he was trying to earn as much money as possible by doing a series of odd jobs, including the most menial kind—chopping firewood with a friend in various Moscow backyards, and at that time of year, just before the onset of winter, there was plenty of such work—but subconsciously he was guided by the wish to put off an awkward encounter in the hope that it would go away. But it refused to go away! After a seminar, Shireiko asked him: "Have you spoken to him?" Glebov pretended not to understand: "To whom?" "To your supervisor. Your future father-in-law." "Oh, yes. No, not yet. I haven't spoken to him. There hasn't been an opportunity." "Well, please find an opportunity," said Shireiko coldly. "We've got to register you somewhere, if not under one supervisor, then under another."

This Shireiko was only a graduate student, yet the things he allowed himself to say! Glebov began to get seriously worried, realizing that the mood was exceptionally uncompromising and that leaving it to die a natural death was not going to work. He called up Sonya. What had happened? Where had he been for the last three days? He explained that he had been working to earn money. She was immediately alarmed: "You didn't overwork yourself, did you? You're not sick?" That evening Glebov went to see her and told her everything about Druzyaev and Shireiko. It was all too stupid for words—but whose help could he count on in a situation like this? She was dismayed; she could think of nothing to say but "You must do as you think best."

It was then that he first noticed that look of hers—a look of total amazement.

"Maybe I shouldn't have told you?" he asked.

"Maybe you shouldn't." And again she stared at him, smiling and amazed. "This is a trap. Do you know what I would have said to them if I had been in your place?"

"What?"

"I would have said: 'Listen, this is extremely indelicate. Don't you think it's indelicate?' "

"I tried to make them see that," he lied.

"How did they find out about us? Why do people say such things?" Her voice trembled and tears started to her eyes. Impulsively, he tried to embrace her, but she slipped out of his arms with a quick, agile and uncharacteristically coquettish movement. "What has happened between us concerns us two, and no one else."

"Honestly, I was completely thrown off balance . . . I tried to explain," Glebov muttered, continuing to lie, "how tactless it all was."

"You tried to explain? Did you say that it was just idle gossip?" Sonya smiled again. "I tell you, it's a clever trap. No, Dima, it's all a nightmare. We must not let father's problems mess up our relationship. Mother is having her troubles right now, too: she was called in to see Dorodnov and he said that she had to take some exams, in order to get a Soviet degree and so have the formal right to teach. She has a degree from the university of Vienna. She's been teaching for twenty years.

Ridiculous, isn't it?" Sonya took him by the hand. "Dima, I want to tell you: you are absolutely free. Do as you think you should. And for God's sake don't do anything rash or violent. Do you understand?"

He nodded glumly. At dinner Yulia Mikhailovna, in a state of extreme indignation, described her talk with Dorodnov: how Dorodnov had been courteous and kind, how he pursed his lips into a Cupid's bow, called her "dear Yulia Mikhailovna" and generally made it all sound as though he had nothing whatever to do with this intrigue, as though certain bureaucrats, faceless and nameless, were demanding that the formalities be observed. Formalities again! Dorodnov was very distressed and constantly apologized. But when Yulia Mikhailovna had remarked that although Sima, the other lecturer in German, had made a précis of the whole of Engels' *Dialectics of Nature,* she still did not know the German language half as well as Yulia Mikhailovna did and never would, Dorodnov suddenly opened his eyes wide in simulated amazement, clasped his hands and said: "Yulia Mikhailovna, surely you can't be denying the fact that language is a class phenomenon?" Yulia Mikhailovna laughed as she told the story. Ganchuk alternately laughed and frowned. Nothing else but the hilarious news that Yulia Mikhailovna had to take exams was discussed at the dinner table. There was much noise, conjecture and laughter and there were many suggestions; Yulia Mikhailovna revealed a gift for mimicry and gave a comic imitation of Dorodnov, Kunik told them of things that were happening in the academic institute, Yulia Mikhailovna's sister, Elfrieda Mikhailovna—Aunt Elly as Sonya called her, who was quite unlike her sister, a fat, self-confident peroxide blonde—loudly and indignantly denounced bureaucracy. Elfrieda Mikhailovna was a radio journalist. She recalled Lenin's words to the effect that the struggle against bureaucracy would take decades, that the success of this struggle required universal literacy and a universally high standard of education, and that bureaucracy was, of course, a manifestation of the petty-bourgeois spirit, something that should never be forgotten. Whenever Ganchuk was present, Aunt Elly talked in a categorical, didactic tone of voice, as though not he but she were the professor. On the whole, Glebov did not like this woman very much, perhaps because—or so he felt—for some reason she didn't like him. He usually repaid people in their own coin. She was a snob; sometimes she ignored him when he greeted her or merely nodded with arrogant haughtiness. She habitually interrupted him if he said anything at table. Anyway, what did she have to be so conceited about? An unsuccessful journalist, a failed foreign correspondent. It particularly annoyed him that Aunt Elly was regarded as the family hero—because she had spent two weeks in Barcelona as a reporter during the Spanish Civil War. Then she had been recalled. No doubt because she was so stupid. Aunt Elly asked, "I wonder what your Dorodnov's class origins are? I'm ready to bet they weren't proletarian."

Yulia Mikhailovna said she didn't know about Dorodnov, but she knew for certain that Druzyaev was the son of a mill owner: "*Voilà!* They spout all these Marxist phrases, but just scratch them and . . ." Ganchuk said they should not flatter themselves: Dorodnov came from a good, working-class background; his father had been a railroad engineer. ". . . so it's not all so simple as you like to think, my dears." "Are you sure you're not mistaken?" Aunt Elly asked obstinately. By the end of dinner they had all cooled off a bit, the comic potential of the Dorodnov episode was exhausted, and Yulia Mikhailovna and Aunt Elly sat down at the piano to play four-handed. Ganchuk and Kunik went off to work in the professor's study.

And Sonya was so unlike her family! She saw everything in a different way from them, and quietly laughed at them. She suddenly whispered to Glebov, "Do you know what Mama's and Aunt Elly's father was? The son of a Viennese banker—although admittedly he was ruined . . ."

She alone, it seemed, had noticed the absurdity in their ridiculing of Dorodnov, and there was sadness in her smile.

Late that evening, as Glebov came out of Sonya's room, he walked through the darkened dining room and saw the two sisters—one slender, with thin legs, the other fat with a big bottom and a little head, like a traditional tea-cosy in the shape of a peasant woman—standing by the window, each with an arm round the other's shoulders and draped with a single large shawl, looking out at the jeweled mosaic of lights down below and swaying slightly as they sang together, softly and beautifully, in German.

I still remember what it was like when we left that house on the embankment. A wet October day, the smell of mothballs and dust, the corridor piled high with bundles of books, bags, trunks, sacks and packages. All this junk had to be brought downstairs from the fifth floor. Some kids came to help. Someone asked the elevator man: "Whose is all that junk?" The man replied: "Some people from the fifth floor." He wouldn't say their name, he didn't nod at me, even though I was standing right beside him and he knew me perfectly well; we were just "some people from the fifth floor." "Where are they going?" "Who knows? I did hear tell it was somewhere out of town." Again he could have asked me, and I would have told him, but he didn't ask. As far as he was concerned, I might not have existed. People who leave that house cease to exist. I was overcome with shame. I felt it was shameful to have to display the pathetic innards of our home life out there on the street, for all to see. All the furniture in the huge apartment was government-issue, so it stayed there. We had sold the piano a year ago. We had also sold the carpets. But I had grown so used to those tables and chairs, with their metal inventory-tags, to those heavy square armchairs and sofas, covered in rough material that smelt of disinfectant. I had grown used to the doors with knobbly frosted glass in their small panels and to the wallpaper, which, now that the pictures were taken down (leaving patches of unfaded color) had taken on an oddly grubby and naked look. It was still almost ours, yet already not ours. I hovered indecisively in front of a map of Spain. Should I take it or not? Seven months ago, Madrid had fallen. My passionate concern over the Civil War was ended, the little flags all removed. "Take it!" said Anton. "We can still find a use for it." "Give it to me," said Vadim French Loaf, who had shown up without being asked. He followed Anton around wherever he went, like a sucker-fish following a shark.

Grandmother came in and said, "If you don't want to take the map, I'm going to wrap the meat grinder in it." No, I'd take it. I pulled out the thumbtacks, took down the map and folded it into eight, so that it looked like a fat brochure. I could put it into the pocket of my overcoat. I still have that map to this day among the books in my bookcase. Many years have passed and I have never once unfolded it. But the fact that I absorbed so much suffering and passion—even if they were only childish sufferings and childish passions—could not have just vanished without trace. It must be of some value to someone. At the time, in drizzling rain, standing beside the pile of our junk, waiting for the truck to come . . .

"What's it like, the apartment you're going to?" asked French Loaf.

"I don't know," I said.

"But I know," said Grandmother. "It's a very nice place, right alongside a park, lots of greenery, splendid air. True, it will be a long way for me to go to work. First by streetcar to the city limits, then by bus, about an hour's trip altogether. But fortunately I get on to both the streetcar and the bus at their terminus stops, so that the cars are empty. We shall be living in one small room in a shared apartment. It's a sunny room, looking out on the yard. A very good room."

I didn't want to tell any of this to French Loaf. I wasn't in the mood to talk to him. If only he knew how miserable I felt! They had all come running up, fooling around, joking, helping to carry our stuff. They were in an excellent mood; didn't any of them realize that we were probably seeing each other for the last time? It was all right for them—they were staying together. But I was going off to an unknown life, unknown people. Where would I find such friends again—clever ones like Anton, funny ones like Chemist, kind ones like Yarik? And most important of all—where would I find someone else like Sonya? Of course, nowhere on earth. It was pointless even to look or to hope. Naturally there are girls who are maybe prettier than Sonya, who have long braids, blue eyes and long eyelashes, but none of that matters. Because not one of them can hold a candle to Sonya. The minutes passed, the day grew darker, the truck would soon be here and still no sign of

Sonya. After all, everyone knew I was leaving today. Why couldn't she show up, if only for a second, if only at a distance to wave goodbye? But she didn't come and didn't come. French Loaf asked, "How many rooms? Three or four?" "One," I said. "And no elevator? Will you have to walk up?" It gave him such pleasure to ask these questions that he couldn't stop himself from grinning.

Suddenly I saw her on the far side of the courtyard, under the concrete archway. Quickly, skirting the black, wet courtyard, she came toward us where we stood outside the door. As she ran up, she asked breathlessly: "You haven't gone yet? Oh, that's good! There's something for you . . . as a keepsake . . . ," and she gave me something wrapped in newspaper, looking as if it might be a book. And she smiled around, not at me, but at everyone.

It was a traveling chess-set, with little holes in the squares to hold the miniature chessmen steady. I had seen others like it in her home. But now nothing pleased me. We were leaving—for a lifetime, forever! Why didn't they realize how terrible that was: Forever? I couldn't utter a word, but just looked at her pale, slightly freckled face, saw her smiling with those kind lips, the kindly look of her nearsighted eyes in which there was nothing but cheerfulness, sympathy, warmth—for everyone. . . .

"Well, goodbye," I said, holding out my hand to her. The truck drove up. People shouted, grandmother fussed around and got annoyed. We threw all our junk into the back of the truck. Grandmother sat beside the driver, while my sister and I clambered over the tailboard and settled down among the baggage. My sister was pressing our cat, Barsik, to her chest. It was still raining, thank God, so practically no one was there to see us go. Only the elevator man in his black peaked cap came out onto the porch and stood there with his hands clasped behind his back, looking not at me and not at my sister but at the truck, nodding his head very slightly: either he was nodding goodbye to us or he was thinking about something and nodding to his own thoughts, or he was glad to see us go. The rain-darkened asphalt courtyard, where I had spent my life until that moment, was rolling away from us. I saw my friends of that vanished life waving their hands. They no longer looked cheerful but they didn't look very sad either, and the girl was smiling at someone. I guessed she was smiling at the person who had been the real reason for her coming to see me off.

I t was like the impossible situation symbolized by the knight at the crossroads in the fairy story: go straight on and you will be slain; go to the left and you will lose your horse; go to the right and you will meet some other form of disaster (although in some stories it said: go to the right and you'll find the treasure). Glebov belonged to a special breed of knight: he was prepared to hang around at the crossroads until the last possible moment, until that final split second, when others are prone to fall fainting with exhaustion. He was a knight who could temporize, a knight who could stretch the rubber of patience until the very instant before it snapped; one of those who never decide anything themselves but leave the decisions to their horse. What was it? Was it mental laziness, thoughtlessness combined with a Micawberish hope that "something would turn up," or was it a hopeless perplexity at life's perennial tendency to place one, day in, day out, at major or minor crossroads? Now that so many years have passed, and one can at last clearly discern all the roads and little pathways radiating out from that dim, distant and forgotten crossroads, there emerges a strange and semi-intelligible pattern, one which no one in those far-off days could have guessed. It is the same process by which ancient cities, long since vanished and buried beneath the dunes, are rediscovered amid the sands of the desert by their contours, visible only from an airplane at a great height. Much of our past becomes covered with sand, smothered by the dust of time. But what seemed simple and obvious at the time is now suddenly seen from a new angle of vision; we see the bone-structure of our deeds, their skeletal pattern—and it is a pattern of *fear*. What, in those days, did heedless youth have to fear? Impossible to understand, impossible to explain it; thirty years on, no one can ever dig it all up again. But a skeletal pattern does emerge. . . . They *rail-roaded* Ganchuk out of the institute. And nothing more. Absolutely nothing more! But there was also fear—utterly despicable, blind, formless, like a creature born in a dark cellar—fear of making a false move, fear of defying . . . what? Nobody knew. And that fear was embedded so deeply, under such dense layers, that it was hard to believe anything of the sort had ever existed.

At the time it seemed to be just a case of incomprehension, simply a lack of sufficient love, mere unthinking foolishness. During half-time at an ice-hockey match in the stadium, where Glebov had gone to see Lev Shulepnikov (the bastard had carelessly blabbed to people at the institute about Glebov's affair with Sonya, so to make up for it he ought now to help him with some constructive advice), Lev suddenly said spitefully: "Look—you don't need Ganchuk; he's bad news." "Why don't I need him?" But somewhere deep down, semiconsciously, he was already half-guessing at the reason. Of course he didn't need him if Lev said so; through his stepfather, Lev had access to certain kinds of information that never filtered down to ordinary mortals. Shulepnikov rammed it home mercilessly: "You don't need him because I say so! Listen to me, you idiot. I'm telling you for your own good." But Glebov stalked away, unwilling to listen.

He had come to see Lev in order to find the answer to something that was worrying him to distraction and seemed more important than anything else: can a person know with certainty whether they are really in love or not? Where other people were concerned, he somehow always knew for sure: yes, he or she is in love; there was never any doubt. But what about oneself? He must find out; it was vitally necessary because he was standing at a crossroads. He sometimes felt that he was genuinely attached to her, that it was really serious and no fooling, that he was miserable if he didn't see her for a day or two, but then at other moments he would suddenly realize that he hadn't once thought of her for a whole evening. Then when he suddenly, as it were, regained his memory and started thinking about her, he felt a start of self-reproach, like a naughty schoolboy: "What's the matter with me? Why, that's really horrible!" Then at once he could be overwhelmed by an almost passionate desire to see her as soon as possible and he would call up, make arrangements about where and how they could meet. That winter his friend Pavlik Dembo, who was a lighting technician in a movie studio, gave them a key to his apartment on Kharitonovsky Street, so to be together Glebov and Sonya no longer had to take the train all the way out to Bruskovo, which took up so much time and energy. In any case, in that second winter he might actually have lacked the necessary enthusiasm to make constant trips out to Bruskovo. The amount of effort it required was really appalling; it needed almost a whole day, and usually meant spending the night there as well, whereas in Pavlik's apartment it took only a couple of hours. Admittedly it was much better at Bruskovo; there he was not plagued by doubts about the true nature of his feelings. On Kharitonovsky, in Pavlik's dark, nasty little room, where it always smelled of food—there was a restaurant underneath and the smells seeped up through the floorboards, and sometimes when the restaurant staff mounted a campaign to exterminate the cockroaches, the place reeked of disinfectant and the apartment was threatened with a plague of cockroaches fleeing from destruction—in that grubby bachelor's pad Glebov experienced the first attacks of loss of self-confidence, of inability to understand his own feelings, or, put more simply, of post-coital depression. Suddenly he would develop an aversion to her touch, her caresses, even to her voice; he would turn away in an access of gloom—there was absolutely nothing he could do to fight off the gloom, which gripped him against his will—and he would wonder miserably: "Can love really vanish just like that, in a second? This must mean that it's not love at all, but something else." Of course he was being a fool, reacting like a little boy; yet in some important respect, when he was trying to grapple with this vital problem, he was not being a fool. Who has not been tormented by the riddle: Is this true love? Most people try to guess the answer to this in other people, but Glebov obstinately insisted on conducting the inquiry on himself, because although he did not know it from experience he had either guessed it or read about it in some book—there is no more perilous union than one founded on pseudo-love. It would lead to nothing but unhappiness, ruin, or a gradual, tedious descent into a frigid state that was the very negation of life. But how was he to discover the truth about his feelings? He was particularly alarmed by one shameful, intimate fact: in Pavlik's apartment their lovemaking was occasionally not so good as at Bruskovo. There were times when he couldn't come, despite protracted and exhausting efforts. Sonya couldn't understand what was wrong, and almost wept with pity for him. She thought it was her fault, as she always blamed herself for everything: "You need another woman!" Naturally he hotly denied this, but in his heart of hearts he couldn't help thinking: "Perhaps I do. . . ."

But then, perhaps he didn't! There were other, good times on Kharitonovsky. There was never any doubt about her love, her kindness and devotion. At the time, like a fool, he undervalued these gifts. And she had another gift: an inability to conceal either her thoughts, her feelings or the slightest movement of her heart. Oh, she could be devious with other people! But only in order to share with him the pleasure of the most ruthless frankness. One day she told how she and Kunik almost lost their heads—and how she had hurt and offended him. She was eighteen at the time, it was summer in Bruskovo, the war was just over, the train service was frequently interrupted and they were stranded together at the *dacha*. That night there was a thunderstorm, lightning was flashing and thunder cracking all around, several panes of glass were broken on the verandah and rain was falling in torrents. She was so afraid of thunder that she almost went crazy, and in this state of mental turmoil she rushed into Kunik's room. Being partially deaf, he did not hear the thunder and was asleep, but he did his best to calm her down, wrapped her in a blanket, cuddled her, put her to bed on the divan—and in the process went out of his mind with desire for her. Through the fright, which made her shiver as though with freezing cold, she suddenly realized that this man had gone crazy. He was ceaselessly babbling some gibberish about "Your mother and my mother . . ." She hadn't the strength to lift a finger, let alone shout or scream; the crashing of the thunder had petrified her. He no longer had the strength of will to control himself. He crawled over on all fours, and tried to climb up onto the divan from the floor. He seemed to be moving like someone in a nightmare, when every movement requires a colossal effort. When he was lying alongside her and put his arms around her, she pushed him away, he fell to the floor and silently crawled back like a beaten dog. Her agony was indescribable—it was what you feel after you have punched someone in the face. What made it worse was that he was such a kind, weak person who was so close to her family and whose only fault was that he had momentarily lost his head. She agonized, not knowing what to do, how to smooth over this awful episode. And what must *he* have been feeling! Out of pity for him and from her own pangs of conscience she was prepared to do anything. But of course next morning nothing was said about the previous night, as though it had never been.

"Why don't you say something?" asked Sonya, and she began kissing Glebov. He was silent because he was slightly shattered by the story, but not so much as to admit it. "And what should I do? Challenge him to a duel?" Suddenly, and as though through a smile, she quietly began to cry: "No, no! Never, don't do any such thing. It's just that I've never told anyone but you."

To have told him this story—in reality it was a trivial matter, because after all nothing had happened—was for her a heroic feat, a purification. She wanted not a scrap of her life to be hidden from him. In any case, what did she have to hide? Not much had accumulated in her twenty-two years— adolescent friendships, other people's problems, the dubious experiences of her girl friends who came to share them with her and seek her advice. She advised them. But when the real thing overwhelmed her, she kept her mouth shut and said not a word to anyone. Her classmates, who had once been drawn to her house, to the fun and parties, to the generosity and the cakes from the special Academy store, had now all disappeared from her life. She no longer needed any of them—and not out of hardness, jealousy or selfish greed but simply because her whole being was filled by him and there was no room for anyone else. How could such a girl be made unhappy? She was threatened by something terrible: unrequited love. . . .

But above this cluster of painful dilemmas there secretly

hovered—invisible at the time, though now its outlines are clear—a nasty little skeleton called *fear*. For that, if nothing else, was genuine, even though one realized it only much later. The decades pass; and when everything has long since been hushed up and buried, and there is no way of understanding it all except by exhumation, no one will undertake that hellish piece of spade work. Then, gray as slate, suddenly from the darkness steps the skeleton.

Glebov was told: "You will come on Thursday and speak at a meeting."

After an instant's thought, he was just starting to make up some lie about someone at home being sick when he was interrupted by three words: *"more than essential."* He then realized that he had make a mistake; he shouldn't have tried to get out of it on the ground of family sickness, because if the matter was *"more than essential"* the institute authorities would take measures to ensure his attendance: they would contact relatives, or engage a nurse, and then if some real ailment suddenly happened to strike, say, on Wednesday . . . But there was nothing to be done about it now. He said that he would certainly come, although he did not believe for a moment that he would. It was really quite out of the question. "You must not only attend—you must also speak," was the firm amendment to the original summons. "Repeat briefly what you said to us. You will not be required to make any general statement or express an opinion. Just a few factual details, but these are vital. Without them, the business won't hold together. . . ."

That sentence drove itself into Glebov's mind like a nail. For hours he pondered on it, repeating it mentally with the same intonation that Druzyaev had used, trying to work out whether this was a threat or a statement of fact, whether the words applied to him, to Ganchuk or to the administration. Whose "business" wouldn't "hold together"? Several days previously, when talking to Druzyaev and Shireiko (these two were the prime movers in the railroading plot; the other lecturers submitted unwillingly or were even secretly opposed to it), Glebov had let slip a remark about the wretched little plaster busts that stood on top of the bookcase in Ganchuk's study. Druzyaev said in a kindly tone, with a charming smile, "Vadim, please describe Nikolai Vasilievich's study, if you can. What books does he have, what pictures, what photographs are there on the walls?" The question implied a kind of verbal police-search of the room, rather as someone else might request a verbal portrait. He decided not to mention certain books and pictures that he remembered, such as a photograph of Ganchuk in the Civil War taken with the now proscribed poet Demyan Bedny, both of them wearing pointed cloth-covered "Budyonny" helmets, and an inscribed photograph of Solomon Lozovsky, a trades-union leader of the 1920s; although Lozovsky was still in official favor, Glebov nevertheless showed a prescient caution. He had merely mentioned the little plaster busts, standing like a row of toy soldiers just below the ceiling, half-jokingly, as a minor detail. Shireiko, however, at once assumed a stern look and asked in a grating voice: "Which are the philosophers that Professor Ganchuk keeps on his bookshelf?"

Glebov could not remember them all. He recalled Plato, Aristotle, and, he thought, Kant and Schopenhauer and possibly one other German. "And what about the materialist philosophers? Do you remember if any of them are included?" Glebov thought hard, trying to remember. He believed Spinoza was there, but he wasn't sure. "Ah, Spinoza! Of course," said Shireiko. "But Spinoza was not a true materialist. And what about the materialists of antiquity—Democritus, Heraclitus? Perhaps some of the French encyclopedists? And Hegel? Ludwig Feuerbach?" Glebov had already realized that it was a stupid mistake to have mentioned the plaster busts; God knows what idiotic conclusions they might draw from this, so he insisted he couldn't really remember who they were. Then they asked him about the supervision of his dissertation, what advice he was given, what sort of comments or recommendations he received. Did Ganchuk's methodology perhaps contain any traces of past political unorthodoxy? In particular, for example, the influence of Pereverzev? Glebov firmly dismissed the idea, but his inquisitors persisted. An insufficient awareness of the significance of the class struggle? Overemphasis on the subconscious? Camouflaged Menshevism? He fought hard to ward off all these accusations, aware that once they made even one of them stick both he and the professor would be in trouble. Unfortunately, when a person is fiercely intent on hearing a particular *something*, it is hard not to acquiesce even slightly, not to admit to just a particle of that *something:* "Glebov, you are contradicting yourself. Just now you said . . ." "Well, perhaps in some small degree . . . minimally . . . I didn't give it any significance. . . ."

As he was saying goodbye to Glebov, Druzyaev asked him half-jokingly, with a smile—throughout the interview he had alternately frowned like a prosecuting attorney or smiled and chuckled, whereas Shireiko, never letting up for a second, had bored into Glebov with a steely stare—if he would, just for fun, find out the exact names of the philosophers on Ganchuk's bookcase. Glebov promised to do so, thinking to himself: "What nonsense! Idiocy of the first order. What on earth do they think they can make out of a row of little plaster busts? Whatever they're up to, they must be desperate if they have to stoop to such *fuflo.*" (*"Fuflo"* was a word he had learned from Pavlik Dembo; it was racetrack slang meaning garbage or nonsense.) Suddenly Shireiko said in a harsh voice: "I beg to disagree with you, Vikenty Vladimirovich. This is not meant to be done 'for fun' but in the cause of truth, in order to discover who are Ganchuk's real idols. This is not just idle curiosity but a matter of real significance." And Druzyaev, the dean of studies, instantly changed his tune and squirmed in front of this mere teaching assistant: "No, no! Of course not, Yury Severianich. I fully share your point of view. . . ."

Glebov turned cold as he listened to this revealing little exchange, and at the same time he felt an awful desire to laugh. "Idols"! All this solemn talk—and about sheer trivia. Why, no one had so much as dusted them for twenty years, these "idols." They just sat there, a row of ornaments on the top shelf, and no one knew or cared who they were. Very well, if they were really so interested, he would find out.

That evening he joined the Ganchuks for tea. In an unconcerned voice the old man asked whether it was true, as he had heard in the rector's office earlier in the day, that he, Glebov, wanted to change his supervisor?

"What? What?" Yulia Mikhailovna broke in with amazement. "Dima wants to change his supervisor? He doesn't want *you* any longer? That is remarkable!" And she laughed.

"I thought it was amusing too."

"Well, he's certainly chosen the right time."

"Yes, he couldn't have chosen a better time. By the way, an article by Shireiko is appearing on Saturday or Sunday. You don't know him; he's one of our graduate students, a rogue. The title of his article is 'Lack of Principle Elevated to a Principle.' My people have told me. Across all six columns of the bottom half of the front page."

"Who is it about?" With a look of horror on her face, Yulia Mikhailovna covered her mouth with her hand.

"Well, it's not only about me, but I am the chief figure in it, apparently. The queen on the chessboard. Of course it is a caricature, distorted out of recognition, but what is particularly disgusting is that I am made out to be lacking in principles."

"Oh my God . . . ," goaned Yulia Mikhailovna.

Very pale, Sonya stared questioningly at Glebov, but Glebov had frozen, unable to move or utter a word.

"I don't know the details, because I haven't read it yet. There's something in it about persistent traces of Menshevism, which surprised me, because as it so happens I have fought against Menshevism all my life. That is one obvious error; he should have taken the trouble to make even a cursory study of my biography. But on the whole . . ."

"Why don't you say something, Dima?" shrieked Yulia Mikhailovna, banging her fist on the table.

"I don't know . . . Sonya had better tell you . . ." Glebov muttered as he got up from the table. He went out, almost at a run, to Sonya's room.

Sonya was not long in coming. He was pacing the room from corner to corner, from one bookcase to the other, smoking furiously, cursing himself for not having had it out with Ganchuk sooner, and cursing Druzyaev. That was a really mean trick—to tell it prematurely to the unsuspecting Ganchuk. They had obviously done it on purpose, in order to force Glebov into making the decision and simultaneously to ruin his relationship with Ganchuk. What if he were to thumb his nose at Druzyaev and refuse to change his supervisor? Who would support him, whom could he rely on? What right had they to put this pressure on him?

Sonya ran into the room and rushed over to him.

"Dima! You look terrible!" Impulsively, she put her hand on his shoulder. It was such a comradely, schoolgirlish gesture of encouragement. "How do you feel? You're pale. I've told them everything, absolutely everything. . . ." She looked at him with alarm. He was startled by her appearance, her lifeless pallor, and by the trembling of the hand on his shoulder. "Papa understood at once. Mama didn't understand at first, but then she understood too and said, 'Well, perhaps he's right . . .'"

"And did you tell them about, you know . . . about us?"

"Yes. I told them everything. Including the talk we had about this horrible trap, when you came and asked my advice and I couldn't—no, I wouldn't—give you any advice . . ."

Then Ganchuk appeared, purple in the face and looking somewhat perplexed. "I understand and I forgive you . . . anyhow, what am I saying—understanding means forgiving. But in future you might remember to mention such things in good time."

He embraced Glebov and patted him on the back. Sonya wiped her eyes. All three were worried and keyed-up, but each in a different way. Ganchuk proposed that they should all drink a glass of Kagor; he always kept a bottle of this cloyingly sweet drink in the sideboard. He used to say that his grandfather, his mother's father, a country priest, had been very fond of this wine, known as "church wine," and had bequeathed this predilection to his daughter, so that Kagor reminded him of his childhood in a remote village in Chernigov province—the smell of a commode, the feel of rough pinewood floors, cows mooing in the evening—and although Glebov could not stand the muck, he naturally agreed.

They went back into the big dining room, told Yulia Mikhailovna, who was noisily clearing away the tea table (Vasyona went to bed early, and the evening meals were served without her), that they all wanted to drink a glass of Kagor, to which Yulia Mikhailovna, without interrupting her house-wifely chore, replied that she had a very bad *Kopfschmerz.* After this she carried out a tray full of dirty crockery and did not come back. She did not once look at Glebov, and her behavior was generally rather strange, as though Sonya had told her nothing.

Ganchuk explained to Glebov—to whom he now showed the confidence due to a member of the family—the reasons why this campaign had been mounted against him. No one had expected such a turn of events. There was, of course, a pretext: he had defended Astrug, Rodichevsky and certain others who had been criticized in an impermissible manner. When people were being undeservedly humiliated, he could not stand aside and be silent. And Dorodnov—one must bear in mind that he was the prime mover in this whole affair, the rest were just pulleys and cogwheels—had been hoping that he, Ganchuk, would maintain an aloof, Olympian silence. And he was an Olympian—a corresponding member of the Academy of Sciences. But his restraint had snapped. Incidentally, that was part of their plan too: to provoke him. Yes, he had pitched in—he had written letters, taken the matter to higher authority. In a word, war . . . What else could he have done? Boris Astrug had been his pupil, Rodichevsky was a man of enormous talent. . . . He had not hoped to reinstate them in their jobs, neither of them would return to the institute, but at least he wanted the smear removed from their names: excessive veneration of Western scholarship and culture, rootless cosmopolitanism—a particularly disgusting and hypocritical cover for anti-Semitism—and God knows what else, a whole ragbag of fabricated nonsense. Boris Astrug had served as a front-line officer through the whole war and earned several medals; yet they had the effrontery to accuse him of "excessive veneration of the West"! Well, Astrug had made a few mistakes in his time—there were some methodological lapses in his book on Gorky—but what of it? Who didn't commit a few methodological errors? Dorodnov himself, for instance, had piled up a whole heap of blunders in his book on romanticism, and what's more the book was worthless. Nothing but other people's ideas, cooked up together to make it look like original work. But none of the people who had been hounded out of their jobs were ideologically hostile; they were not enemies. He, Ganchuk, knew what it meant to strike down enemies. His hand had never trembled when the revolution had ordered him to shoot. In Chernigov, before he had gone away to study, he had served in a "special detachment" of the *Cheka*. In those days, the name of Ganchuk had struck fear into the hearts of the enemies of the revolution. Because he had never shown any hesitation or pity. When one day his own father, who was then a very sick man, had interceded to save the life of a certain priest (he was suspected of being linked with a gang of terrorists), Ganchuk had refused to spare him. The priest was eliminated along with the gang; he was a wolf in sheep's clothing who had the blood of several Red Army soldiers on his conscience. For that Ganchuk had broken with his own father and the quarrel was never made up for the rest of the old man's life. That was how they settled such problems in those days.

"And nowadays? Who is prepared to destroy comrade Dorodnov? The reasons, of course, go a lot deeper. Once again I am amazed at the genius of Marx, who in every phenomenon, every fact of life was able to discern its dialectical and class essence. And it is just that, my dear Dima, that you too must learn if you are going to stand firmly on your own two feet. Back in the twenties, Dorodnov caught it really hot. He was a fellow traveler, naturally not a Party member, and he used to churn out some garbage in the spirit of those bourgeois writers who tried to come to terms with the Soviet regime—in other words, a typical petty-bourgeois faker, slightly cam-ouflaged under fashionable slogans and attitudes, at a time when all sorts of private and cooperative publishing houses sprang up like mushrooms, little cliques and little maga-zines with half-baked political ideas, and it was then that we should have smashed Dorodnov. But we didn't. He slunk away out of sight, changed his colors, crawled into the wood-work, as so many of them did, in order to reemerge now in a new guise. What a joke: *he* tries to teach *me* Marxism! A high-school dropout with an old-regime right-wing psychology ac-cuses me of underestimating the role of the class struggle. . . .

He can thank God he didn't fall into my hands in 1920. I would have smashed him as a counterrevolutionary! That was a cardinal error: we failed to stamp out the petty bourgeoisie. Now that the regime has stood the test of time, the great ordeals are behind us and the hour has come to garner the harvest. They have come crawling out of their little holes, in various disguises—the vermin that we failed to exterminate in those days. . . . I grant you that they look and sound like superrevolutionaries. They pride themselves on quoting Marx and Lenin wholesale, make themselves out to be the builders of a new world, but their real essence—their stinking bourgeoisness—will always leak out and show through. They grab, scrounge, grow fat, fix themselves up with comfortable jobs, so that they are now in a position to settle old scores with the people who gave them a bashing in the twenties. The swine is hoping to have his revenge. But they're so ignorant and uneducated! They don't understand the simple truth that the bourgeoisie as a class has been liquidated, that there isn't and never will be a place for them on Russian soil. Incidentally, Sonya has told me about a certain important decision. Is it really going to happen? A plan for the revolutionary transformation of the Ganchuk family? In that case we must drink another glass in honor of this great event. . . ."

"Yulia! Come here, the young people insist that you join us!" Nikolai Vasilievich called out loudly, excited by the conversation, the wine, and the fact that his wife was exhibiting some sort of vague displeasure.

He could not appreciate what was going on in her mind, if only because Sonya's announcement in itself had not made any particular impression on him. Other matters were tormenting his heated brain: newspaper articles, friends, enemies, the academy, books, the past. Also old age and the nearness of death. His face, which a short while ago had been blotchy with worried perplexity, was now suffused with an even deep-pink flush brought on by the wine—the color of the little marzipan apples that people hang on Christmas trees. Yulia Mikhailovna was still laid low with *Kopfschmerz*. Sonya looked happily at Glebov, who took Ganchuk by the arm and led him into the study; the professor wanted to show him an album of photographs taken during the Civil War. "I'll show you a boy who packed a *very* heavy punch. I wouldn't have advised you—do you hear, Dima?—to let that boy catch sight of you in those days. Ah, how he hated learned young men in spectacles. He cut them down straightaway—ha! ha!—without asking who their mama and papa were."

Glebov remembered that he, too, had something to look for in the study—the names on those damned little plaster busts.

"More than essential," Druzyaev had said. *"On Thursday, the day after tomorrow."* He had also said, in that same conversation—the two remarks were continuous and inseparable, like two different-colored pieces of Plasticine rolled into a ball between your hands or into one long, soft, sticky sausage, and when you rolled balls of it between your palms you suddenly remembered the weakness and submissiveness of childhood, when other hands took hold of you like a piece of Plasticine and kneaded you, squeezed you, compressed you, flattened you and made what they wanted out of you—he had said, as though by the way, in a subordinate clause of the same sentence as the one in which he had discussed *Thursday*, that a provisional decision had been made about the award of the Griboyedov Scholarship. To him, Glebov. On the results of the winter semester. Glebov had not reacted, had kept silent, playing the same game—as though this news, so casually dropped into the conversation, was really insignificant and unworthy of attention—although his whole body had flushed for a moment with a hot thrill. The Griboyedov Scholarship! He would only hold it for his last few months at the institute, but even so, it was a blessing. It at once occurred to him that it was not the extra money that was important but the moral boost—onward and upward. The news, however, also contained its dose of poison—the sad realization came to him a second after his initial excitement—because it was inseparably linked with *Thursday*. It was either both together, or nothing.

"To go and speak against Ganchuk—it's unthinkable!" That evening he went to see Lev Shulepnikov, again with an insane hope—unshaken since childhood—that Lev could work miracles. What could he do? How could he influence them? Glebov imagined that Lev—well, not Lev himself, but his stepfather—only had to say to the institute administration, "Stop harassing Glebov," and they would immediately back off. How much more of it, he wondered, could he stand? There was a limit to human tolerance. First he was ordered to change his supervisor, then to tell them about Ganchuk's ideological deviations and God knows what else, then name the books in his bookshelves. And he had gone along with this sickening business; he had agreed to it and told them what they wanted to hear. As if that were not enough, they wanted him to speak at the meeting. Wasn't that the last straw?

Lev appeared to listen sympathetically, grinned and nodded while twiddling the knobs of a hitherto unknown piece of apparatus: a television set. In the little whitish window something flickered and twitched vaguely, and singing was heard in snatches—an opera was being transmitted from the Bolshoi Theater. It was said that there were only seventy-five of these television sets in the whole of Moscow. Obsessed with this new toy, Lev swore at it as the picture suddenly went fuzzy and temporarily disappeared. His mother and aunt had stayed home specially to see this program, and as a result Glebov could not have the confidential talk with Lev that he had wanted. But this was his only chance, so Glebov had to bring it all out into the open with the two women sitting there. Lev's mother said impulsively:

"Lev, you absolutely must help Dima!"

"Do you think so?"

"Yes, I do. I remember Sonya very well—she's a sweet girl. I don't know her father. But really, how disgraceful—to exploit the feelings of two young people . . ."

"Oh, feelings-schmeelings . . ." Lev dismissed the notion with a flip gesture.

"You, of course, wouldn't know anything about feelings," said Alina Fyodorovna sarcastically. "For someone who has no musical ear, all music is noise."

"Alina, please don't upset yourself," said her sister.

"Did you come to see an opera on television or did you come to lecture me?" asked Lev.

"What's the use of talking to you!" Alina Fyodorovna gave a sharp wave of her hand, which was exactly the same gesture

that her son had just made. After a silence, she whispered to
no one in particular: "Making such a mess of his life—and at
his age . . ."

The television screen grew brighter, the figures of singers
could be seen on the stage and for a while there was silence
while everyone watched the screen and listened to the singing.
Lev sat on the floor in front of the set. Turning to Glebov, he
said cheerfully, "The picture will be better. We need a new
antenna. Jan is getting me one. Everything depends on the
antenna."

"Lev, I repeat—you must do something for Dima and
Sonya!" There was a note of sharp irritation in her voice.
Glebov did not like this; he was afraid that she might make
Lev lose his temper. There was always some kind of discord
between him and his mother. "Tell me, why can you never do
anything for other people? It's mean of you. You really must
not be so arrantly selfish. An old friend comes to you and asks
you for help . . ."

"But what can I do?" Lev burst out. "Who am I—the principal? The deputy minister of education?"

"You could do something. We know. You've surrounded
yourself with such a gang of scoundrels that you practically . . ."

"Mother, leave my friends out of this—all right?" Lev shook
his finger at her, but quite good-naturedly. The whole conversation was somehow unnatural: his mother attacked him more
out of habit than from a generous impulse to stand up for
Glebov; he listened to her with only half an ear; and both
had somehow agreed in advance that the outcome of the contest would be a draw. "Why are you making such a fuss about
it, French Loaf? I don't quite understand."

Glebov repeated that he merely wished Druzyaev and Company would stop twisting his arm. Couldn't they do their own
dirty work without him? Was it really essential to humiliate
people to such a degree? "No, Glebov, you must come to the
meeting and say your piece; your opinion is of great value because of all the people in the institute, you are the closest to
the professor." But what would happen afterward? How could
he ever look Sonya in the face again? "Say your piece!" That

was easily said. What hypocrisy! They didn't mean "Say your piece"—they meant "smear yourself with shit." Come to the meeting and pour shit over yourself in public.

"Listen to Miss Purity!" Lev suddenly snapped at him in fury. "It's all right for other people to get their hands dirty, but I prefer to stand aside—is that it? Is that it? You're a nice one!"

Glebov said that it was easier for others, because they didn't have such close relations with the Ganchuk family. He realized that Lev couldn't, or rather wouldn't, do anything. He shouldn't have come at all. Lev had changed a lot. His mother was right: he had developed an attitude of monstrous indifference to everything. Hence, no doubt, that sudden, inexplicable outburst of animal spite. Something like guilt must lie behind such spite as a reaction to anything mildly unpleasant or inconvenient, such as being asked to call people up, ask people favors. In an irritated tone Lev continued to hold forth, asserting that there was nothing terrible in going up to the rostrum and saying a few words if one had to. He, too, was going to speak at the meeting, although this embarrassed him because he had known Ganchuk since childhood, and in any case he didn't have the time or the inclination—his mind was occupied with other things. He was in the midst of preparations to make a six-month trip abroad; he was up all night boning up on English—books and dictionaries were strewn around to prove it. But if they *had* to speak, then there was obviously a good reason for it; the old boy was getting senile anyway; he had long outlived his time but didn't realize it, he was making an undignified fuss instead of bowing out gracefully. Still, there was no point in going through all this oriental ceremonial; it only meant trouble. They ought to know that if you try to sit on a hedgehog like Ganchuk, you get your ass scratched.

When he repeated: "I shall speak—and I shall put the knife in!" Glebov asked, "Why?"

"Why?! For his unethical behavior, for forming cliques. And for being too fond of foreign writers and scholars. . . ."

"Garbage."

"Why garbage? I can prove it to you quite easily."

"Of course you can!" Glebov suddenly yelled at him. "It's easy enough for you to talk. You're not Sonya Ganchuk's fiancé, God damn you!"

"Are you her fiancé?" Lev gave him a crafty grin, winking with one small, red-rimmed eye. "I bet you a thousand to one in rubles that you're not. Is it a bet?"

"Lev! What are you saying? You ought to be ashamed of yourself!" said aunt and mother indignantly, without turning away from the television screen, which was still flickering and jerking. While he was talking, Lev now and again leaned forward to twiddle the knobs.

"I'm going," said Glebov, getting up. "Goodbye!"

But Lev sprang to his feet and seized Glebov by the arm. "Wait! Sit down! We'll think up something right away. Know what? Let me call up Yury Shireiko."

He went straight to the telephone and called Shireiko. The conversation was amazing: these two were obviously as thick as thieves. Glebov now realized how far Lev had drifted away from him: he no longer knew who his friends were at the institute, let alone in the world at large.

"What are you doing? Burning the midnight oil? Bent over a large-scale map? Still planning the great battle?" Glebov shuddered in advance as he wondered what Lev might say about *him* in that horrible, sneering tone. "Hey, listen—come over here. We've just got a television set. By special order. Come and watch it. We've just switched it on—there's an opera from the Bolshoi. . . . Yes, Dima Glebov's here, your godson. He sends his regards. Thanks, I'll pass it on to him. . . . Well, how about it? There's a case of Georgian wine here, *Khvanchkara;* the old man sent it yesterday. . . . No? You can't? You can't—or you won't? . . . Listen, there's this little problem—I didn't really want to discuss it with you on the phone, but since you're so busy . . ."

"Don't say anything about me!" whispered Glebov, making negative signals with his hands.

Lev waved him away: sit down and shut up.

"Here's the problem. There's this meeting on Thursday . . . Yes, of course we've read it. Powerful stuff, your article, very powerful." He winked at Glebov. "We're sitting here right now, discussing it. It's excellent, right on target. Exactly, exactly. Yes, yes . . . quite right. Exactly."

Holding the receiver out at arm's length he said through gritted teeth: "He dreams up all that filth *and* he wants to be complimented on it, the shit! . . . Yes, it is a very successful article. Congratulations. Splendid article. So look, what are we to do about Dima Glebov? It's embarrassing for him to have to speak at the meeting, you understand . . . What? Well, so what? I'm calling you to ask your advice . . ."

Then followed a long and barely intelligible exchange of cryptic remarks, at the end of which Lev flung down the receiver, sighed and announced, "He doesn't seem very pleased with you. He says no one is forcing you to speak, so you have no reason to make yourself out to be such a sacrificial victim. And he asks why you're running around to everyone and complaining. 'He's a whiner, your Glebov'—that's what he said."

Glebov was too depressed to reply. He'd had a premonition that this phone call would bring nothing but trouble, and he had been right. Lev, on the other hand, was smugly pleased with himself, looking as though he had won the contest and had just dragged Glebov back from the brink of disaster.

"Now you're a free agent: you may speak or not speak—suit yourself. The decision is yours. And I fixed it for you, all right? He respects me, the slimy brute. All they want is for me not to touch them. Now I'll bring in the Khvanchkara. And there's some real *lavash* from the Georgian store. This is going to be some party."

Before Glebov had had time to decide whether to go home, to go to Sonya or to stay in this weird household, Lev appeared clutching to his chest four large, dark bottles. The women had already set out the tablecloth, and glasses were tinkling.

There were two days left. Glebov still did not know what he would do on Thursday: both to go and not to go were equally impossible. On Tuesday, after his visit to Lev Shulepnikov, which ended in appalling scenes with everyone blind drunk, he was so utterly knocked out that he simply couldn't get up and go to the institute. He came to his senses around noon, sprawled across his bed like a corpse—he had staggered home at dawn, senseless, and collapsed as he was, fully dressed—and when he opened his eyes he saw a doctor in a white coat. The doctor had not come to see him, however, but his grandmother. Old Nila had been badly sick for several days and unable to get up. Through the buzzing and intolerable clatter in his head, as though someone were waving a sheet of corrugated iron by his ear, he heard the doctor talking to his cousin Klavdia. "And what if you give him an injection?" Klavdia was asking, and her expression was full of hatred. The doctor boomed: "The decision is yours." They bared an arm and gave him the injection. As he left the room the doctor, quite young and good-looking with pink cheeks, looked hard at Glebov and said: "The decision is yours." Glebov felt a clutching sensation around his heart and the cold wave of a minor heart attack surged through his body. Klavdia sat down beside him, bent her angry white face forward and whispered: "Grandmother's really bad, I haven't slept for nights, because I've been sitting here looking after her, and you"—there were tears in her eyes—"turn up like a pig. Where have you been? You've made such a disgusting mess, everything will have to be cleaned . . ."

He felt sorry for Klavdia because she was crying, but he couldn't think of anything to say in explanation, and with an enormous effort all he could do was to croak: "The decision is yours." Then fragments of the previous night began to come back to him. What had begun as a respectable domestic evening, with Lev's mother and aunt, a white tablecloth and tinkling wineglasses, had ended up, God knows where, as a hideous binge. In someone's attic apartment with semicircular windows, under the eaves. There was an old-fashioned phonograph with a horn. They had to walk along the hallway on tiptoe; someone kept falling down and the others picked him up, roaring with laughter. There was a blond woman, rather fat, white-skinned with big pores, who kept asking, "How much do they pay for a dissertation?" When they sat down with Lev's aunt and mother at the round table and drank Khvanchkara, Lev suddenly and very quickly became drunk. Glebov wondered, with some surprise, why he was getting smashed so quickly.

His mother drank glass after glass. Their faces grew more and more alike, so that it became strikingly obvious that they were mother and son. Her little round, birdlike eyes reddened and glittered, and Lev's eyes, already red-rimmed, flashed like sparks. And they quarreled, punching each other with their knuckles. Lev roared, "What right do you have to talk like that? What are you? You're nothing but a witch!" Alina Fyodorovna nodded with great dignity and said, "Yes, I'm a witch. And I'm proud of being a witch." Her sister agreed: "Yes, she's a witch, it runs in the family." Being a witch was regarded as almost a virtue. At any rate, both women hinted that it implied belonging to some kind of élite. We are witches and you are scum.

Glebov knew that he shouldn't have gotten involved with Lev Shulepa again. Things were bound to get noisy, or a fight would start, or somebody would do something monstrously stupid. It always happened that way. "Oh, so I'm just scum, am I? And what, may I ask, are you?" Then there was someone called Avdotyin, wearing an army-style tunic, who was also sitting at the table and drinking Khvanchkara. He had a long, droopy, despondent face like a cow's udder. He muttered: "Everyone pays for himself!" For some reason this phrase stuck in Glebov's memory. There were eight bottles of Khvanchkara. He wanted to get up and go, but his legs wouldn't obey him and he could not stand up. "If I'm a non-entity, then I'm going to leave them," Lev said to Glebov. "What do I want with a couple of witches? Even if she is my mother, I don't want her. To hell with them all—I'm going!"

Avdotyin would not let him go, so Lev punched him in the face. Then Lev and Glebov took off. Some car drove them through the dead of night. They lost their way and couldn't find the right house, while the driver swore at them and wanted to throw them out on to the street. But in the end they got there. It was here that there was the old phonograph with a horn. What did they talk about? How did the row start? Oh, yes, that was it: he tried to persuade Glebov to leave Sonya. "Sonya's all right, but why do you need to marry her? Don't be an idiot." And then he said, "Why don't you just be friends with her? That's perfectly honorable. I'm friends with her, too, and I will be for the rest of my life. Tell her everything, ask her advice. That would be perfect—to have a woman who was a friend . . ."

By now, Glebov realized that Lev was right: it would be perfect to have a woman who was a friend. But Lev's vitality and drive seemed so irresistible, so shattering. Do you need a woman? In the middle of the night? To console you, caress you, say tender, heart-warming things to you—and not for money, but just out of infinite feminine generosity—when you're unhappy, lying in the gutter, and your own mother curses you? Nothing can be so consoling as a woman in the middle of the night. The blonde with the white porous skin, who babbled such nonsense, could offer him only an unreal and intangible sort of happiness—like the bottle of beer which Pomrachinsky was suddenly holding, a man who never drank beer, and whom Glebov bumped into as he crawled around half dead in the corridor, and the beer had been bought by Pomrachinsky's wife to wash her hair with—but even the blond woman failed to induce total forgetfulness. Because he was unceasingly tormented by the painful thought: What would he do on Thursday?

The affair grew more and more complicated. Ganchuk's supporters—and there were still plenty of them in the institute, including such aces as Professor Kruglov, Simonyan the lecturer in linguistics, and some others, now forgotten, together with various undergraduate and graduate students— were getting ready for Thursday, burning with the desire to defend Ganchuk. Not all of them, however, were allowed to speak at the meeting. It was to be an expanded session of the Faculty Board, to which the active members of various student associations were to be invited. Glebov was supposed to attend as the vice chairman of the Student Academic Society. The notification came in an official blue envelope: "Your attendance is obligatory . . ." On Tuesday evening he was approached by Marina Krasnikova, one of the activists of the Society, a loud girl in a perpetual state of excitement as though mildly intoxicated: her passion for student politics was somewhat excessive. Whatever became of her? This fat girl showed all the signs of heading straight for the Academy of Sciences, or perhaps the Committee of Soviet Women. In fact, she sank without a trace, like a stone dropping to the bottom of a pond. . . .

"You must speak on behalf of the Student Academic Society, because Lisakovich is sick," Marina twittered. "Here are some points that you should make. Lisakovich dictated them to me over the phone."

"And what's the matter with Lisakovich? What's he sick with?" said Glebov suspiciously. It seemed that Fedya Lisakovich had cunningly forestalled Glebov, forcing him to attend. Lisakovich was chairman of the S.A.S. Marina said that he had quinsy, with a high temperature, but he was keen to attend, and hoped to be better by Thursday. The doctor had categorically forbidden it. Glebov asked dubiously what his temperature was. Marina said it was apparently around 101 degrees. The points to make were as follows: Ganchuk was the founder of the Student Academic Society; all the best things that the Society had achieved were due to Ganchuk; Ganchuk's errors were typical of the majority of the faculty, so if Ganchuk were removed, all the rest should be fired too. His merits and the services he had rendered far outweighed his mistakes. Not a word to be said about Shireiko's newspaper article. If it couldn't be avoided, then say that it was insufficiently concrete and unconvincing. Assert firmly that we should be proud that Nikolai Vasilievich worked here.

As he read this, Glebov was surprised: Fedya Lisakovich was showing real bravery. One of two things: either he was brave to the point of folly by speaking out so strongly against Druzyaev, Dorodnov and the rest of them, or he knew something. It was turning into a really serious battle. Marina said that Professor Vasily Kruglov, the folklore specialist, a good and much respected old man, had been driven to fury by Shireiko's article and was threatening to resign from the institute if the persecution of Ganchuk didn't cease. "Well, let him resign," thought Glebov, putting himself in Druzyaev's place. "He can't frighten us. No one here is indispensable." A girl graduate student had met Shireiko in the courtyard and when the latter had said good morning to her she had demonstratively turned her back on him. Apparently Shireiko went red in the face and asked loudly: "What does this mean?" She said nothing and walked away. And almost all the first-year students, for whom he ran a seminar, had failed to turn up to his last class.

Marina Krasnikova had never come to see Glebov at home before. Her arrival signified that passions were at white heat. Marina's eyes burned with noble sympathy for all honorable men and with joy that she too was a member of an honorable society. "You must speak out! You must speak for all of us. It's a disgrace if students can't defend their own professor." This onslaught, those flashing eyes and wagging finger reminded Glebov of Druzyaev's "more than essential." In effect it was one and the same thing, the same use of terror.

Marina seemed not to notice that there was a very sick woman in the house, a nurse with a black bag, the place reeking of medicines, and Klavdia was pacing up and down the corridor with a tear-stained face. And when Glebov, after some hesitation, nevertheless managed to say, "You see, my position is rather difficult. My grandmother is sick and we don't know what may happen from one hour to the next . . . ," which was a weak and almost hopeless attempt to wriggle out of the net, Marina at once said, "You can count on me. I'll sit here for an hour, two hours, a whole day, as long as you like. But you *must* attend. . . ."

That evening someone else came—Kuno Ivanovich. This visit was quite astounding. Glebov's relations with Kuno were distant, and the latter had never been to Glebov's apartment before. Whenever Glebov was present, Kuno Ivanovich became infected with a strange form of nervousness: he would get excited, make sarcastic jokes and his voice would begin to shake. Glebov had once visited Kuno Ivanovich at his apartment on Gnezdikovsky Street (Ganchuk had sent him to fetch some papers). Kuno's apartment surprised Glebov by its cleanliness, tidiness and a quite unbachelorlike degree of comfort. There were lots of flowers in pots and vases standing on tables, on the window ledge and on shelves, all arranged into a very picturesque total effect. The shelves alternated with photographs and reproductions of pictures; each wall was a carefully thought-out work of art. It was all so refined and museumlike, unmasculine and dubious. While Kunik collected the papers, Glebov sat on a pouffe and gazed around at the room. On the wall between two shelves, on which were some muscular-looking cacti in pots, he saw a large photograph of Sonya. There were lots of other photographs, but Sonya's was somehow significantly enlarged. "How he must suffer," thought Glebov sarcastically. He firmly and patiently put up with the tone of nervous, didactic superiority which Kunik always adopted when talking to him as a way of stressing his seniority. Glebov in return stayed resolutely calm.

On that evening, too, seeing the frail figure of this little man in his long overcoat, his head permanently inclined downward and to one side, although Glebov was astonished, he remained calm.

Dispensing with any greeting such as "good evening," Kunik at once started talking as though they were continuing a conversation that had only just been interrupted.

"My first condition," he said as he crossed the threshold, "is that Nikolai Vasilievich mustn't hear anything about this."

Condition? What was he babbling about? Glebov gestured to this enigmatic creature to follow him down the corridor. Klavdia happened to be coming toward them at that moment.

"Grandmother's asking if you're at home."

"You can see I am."

"You haven't been to see her once all day. She's worried that something may have happened to you."

"Our grandmother is sick," Glebov explained to Kunik, who appeared not to hear and went on with his speech:

"Because if he finds out, he'll tear me to pieces. He's so proud and touchy. I hope you understand his character: proud, impetuous, naïve and helpless, all mixed together." They went into Glebov's room, and Kunik, without taking off his hat and coat and without so much as a glance around him, with the air of a sleepwalker, sat down on what was nearest—Glebov's bed. "For other people he will fight like a lion, go anywhere, lock horns with literally anyone. That was how he fought for that nonentity Astrug. But he is absolutely incapable of fighting for himself. Wouldn't lift a finger. So it is we, his friends, who must act now . . ."

"What on earth can *we* do, miserable Lilliputians?" thought Glebov.

"I insisted to him: 'You must reply to Shireiko immediately. Write a letter to the editor, and make it tough. He must not be allowed to publish such beastliness with impunity.' He said he wouldn't dream of doing any such thing. He quoted Pushkin: 'If someone spits on the tail of my coat from behind, it is my valet's job to remove the spittle.'"

"Of course, one can certainly play the role of valet," said Glebov. "I have no objection. But what does that mean in practical terms?"

"I am not calling on you to speak out in the role of a valet but in the role of a friend. In the role of an honest man. The fact that he quoted those particular lines from Pushkin only shows that he doesn't understand what is going on. He thinks someone has spat on his coattails from behind, whereas in fact they are armed with spears and mean to run them through his gut. That is what is happening. They are out to finish him off."

"What do you suggest, Kuno Ivanovich? What can we do?"

"What can we do," muttered Kunik, as he shrugged off his overcoat with its black rabbit-fur collar, which fell back onto the bed with one sleeve lying across the pillow. "I have already taken steps. I have written a letter to the editor of eight typewritten pages. Six other people have signed. And now I'm writing to the authorities. I'm not asking anyone else to sign that letter, because it is too vitriolic and I wouldn't like anyone else to get into trouble. But I have nothing to lose, so I'm not afraid. As for you, dear Dima Glebov . . ." For a moment he stared searchingly at Glebov as though in some doubt, one ginger eyebrow twitching. The effect was slightly comic. "Forgive me for asking you: Can we regard you as a true friend of Nikolai Vasilievich?"

"Why not?"

"Excuse me, but I want an answer. Please answer me."

"But of course."

"Of course. Good. In that case, why are you acting so strangely?"

"Excuse me, I don't understand what you mean."

"Why don't you raise any objections to the way you are being used in this disgusting campaign of persecution?"

At this Glebov was completely dumbfounded. How was he being *used*? Had he, Glebov, read Shireiko's article? Yes, he had, but cursorily, skipping lines as one does when reading something repellent that you would prefer to throw away. In it, apparently, there was the following sentence: "It is not by chance that certain final-year students have decided to dispense with the services of Professor Ganchuk as their supervisor." Kuno Ivanovich explained that in fact there was only one of those "certain final-year students." He had at first not even bothered to go over to the institute and look with his own eyes at comrade Glebov's application to change his supervisor. When he had been told Glebov's name by telephone, he could not believe his ears, so he went over and checked it out. It was unbelievable.

"But do you know what's behind that?" Glebov shouted, "No, you don't know anything! You don't know the whole background story."

"Yes, I know, I know." Kuno gestured with impatience and disgust, as though afraid of hearing something unpleasant. "And even if I didn't know, I could guess. But I'm not interested in the background story. The important fact is that you are being used, yet you remain silent. You haven't said anything, Dima. Why not? How can you keep silent and at the same time go to their house, talk to Nikolai Vasilievich and other members of his family. You must agree that it is somewhat, well, what shall I say, less than morally irreproachable . . ."

Glebov glared sullenly at his inquisitorial visitor. At first he wanted to shout: "And creeping into a terrified young girl's bed during a thunderstorm—how does that rate on the moral scale?" Then he was seared by a feeling of shame and was ready to do anything, to go to any lengths if only he could make up for what had happened. But he could only mumble: "I really didn't see that sentence in the article . . ."

"As though the sentence itself mattered! Suppose," roared Kunik, "a man was attacked and robbed on the street before your eyes, and the muggers asked you, a passer-by, to lend them your handkerchief so that they could gag their victim . . ."

"Will you be quiet?" Glebov implored him. "Please talk more quietly; there is a very sick woman on the other side of this partition."

"No, you listen to me! What are you, may one ask? A chance witness or an accomplice? All right, don't answer; there are reasons, there's a background story . . . We'll allow that . . . But what are you going to do *now*? How will you go on living? Wait and hope for the best, as you've done up to now? There's no time left. On Thursday you will be going to your execution, Dima. I can see, though, that you haven't the guts to stand up and say: 'It's not true! It's an injustice!' So your execution it will be—It's inevitable. Sometimes you can put the rope around your own neck by keeping silent."

Glebov burst out: "That's not true! I shall speak on Thursday and I'll say everything!" The pale, gingery-haired little man got up from the bed and threw his long overcoat around his shoulders. He flung back his little crooked head and stared at Glebov, frowning intently, and although he was shorter, he seemed to be looking down on him. He did not say goodbye but flew off down the hallway with his fluttering, lunatic gait and out of the front door. As Glebov shut it behind him, Kuno at once knocked again:

"Dima, my dear fellow, one thing I beg of you . . . ," he whispered, his pale, anguished face leaning even more heavily over to one side, "do as you like, but don't tell the old man a word about any of this. Promise? Nothing about my letters, nothing about our conversation. He must not know!"

Thus inexorably Glebov was drawn ever closer to that agonizing crossroads. He could no longer feel his legs beneath him, such were the tension and exhaustion; he might fall at any moment. Where could he find refuge? He was being carried away by a powerful undertow. Although he was apparently standing still, he was being swept along. Only, he still didn't know where. Another day flickered past, equally vague and confusing, full of domestic worries, running to the pharmacy, irrelevant conversations. Klavdia was again quarreling with her mother and weeping in the kitchen. She loved Grandma Nila very much. And so did Glebov.

Who else was there to love, if not old Nila?

He sat beside her, holding the old woman's pale-blue hand, as light as a handkerchief, and told her a story—she had asked for it, like a little girl—while his imminent fate boomed in his head like a tolling bell: that way you will lose your horse, that way your wife—and this way, life itself. He was asked to go to the institute for some kind of discussion with the first-year students. But what was there to discuss? So why go? He didn't go. Then Afonicheva called up, the secretary at the dean's office: "Glebov, you haven't forgotten, have you? Tomorrow at twelve." The voice rapid and urgent: she had obviously been given a list of twelve people to drum up by telephone. "No, I haven't forgotten."

"Come on time, don't be late."

"Yes, I'll come."

He tried to reason calmly: there are four possible variants, let's think them all through. First variant: to go, and speak in Ganchuk's defense. Well, not straight out, but let's say with qualifications, mentioning certain shortcomings, but in general making it be a speech for the defense, even if only in the form suggested by Kunik, namely, by analyzing that sentence in Shireiko's article and explaining its provocative intention. What would be the outcome of that variant? It would infuriate the administration. Goodbye to the Griboyedov Scholarship, the graduate studentship and all the rest. Because it meant making an unexpected change of front, and they wouldn't forgive that. Ever. It would be regarded as treachery. Their vengeance would be swift and terrible. And since Dorodnov now had all the power in his hands—the principal had been absent for months, somewhere in Korea, or it may have been China, or maybe in hospital—he could do exactly as he pleased. He was determined to settle accounts with Ganchuk. What positive gains would result from that variant? The gratitude of Ganchuk and all his family. Sonya's even more boundless love. A few people, such as Marina Krasnikova, would pump his hand for a full half-minute and congratulate him on an excellent speech, and Kunik would say with a grin: "You surprised me! I'm delighted for your sake!" And that would be all. After that, a life as a minor clerk God knows where. On Sundays, with him loaded like a mule, they would take the train out to Bruskovo. The losses were crushing, the gains dubious.

Second variant: to go and to criticize Ganchuk. Or, put more simply, to bring up the rear of the mob as they attacked him. Naturally he wouldn't do it aggressively or rudely; he would even speak warmly, sympathetically, with profound regret that he was obliged to admit, etc., etc., finishing with an appeal for moderation and to remember Professor Ganchuk's great services, but . . . exactly the kind of thing that Druzyaev had asked him to say. Something about the pernicious influence of Pereverzev and RAPP—it didn't matter which. A passing reference to the plaster busts. Maybe he might forget the plaster busts altogether, or perhaps just make a gently regretful comment. The main thing would be not to say a word about that little sentence in Shireiko's article, as though it had never been. After all, if he put his hand on his heart and was quite sincere about it, was Nikolai Vasilievich perfect in every respect as a teacher and mentor? Might there not even be a grain or two of justice in those cannonballs that were being hurled at this fortress? Secretly one had to admit it: there was. . . . His books were boring. Glebov had never been able to read a single one of them through to the end. To be honest—they were unbearably tedious! People wrote like that twenty years ago, but now something different was needed. They all showed ineradicable traces of vulgarized sociology like a hereditary disease. (But not a word must be said about that; he would ever admit it only to himself, in secret, when confessing to his own conscience.) And the accusation that he ran his department like an autocrat was not so far from the truth either. Lecturers were only appointed with his personal sanction, and graduate studentships were given only with his approval. Nor was he nearly as "unworldly" as people thought; he was observant and discriminating where people were concerned, and by no means a paragon of impartiality: on the contrary he was highly partial, loving some people and hating others, sometimes for no discernible reason. His tastes appeared old-fashioned, his predilections rooted in the past, in those decades of rebellions, struggles and skirmishes. He was obsessed by certain chimeras whose chimerical nature had long since been obvious to most people, but to which he was as attached as a hungry baby to its mother's nipples. And there were the phenomena of recent years—the purges and terror that had taken place in the years before and immediately after the war—which his mind was simply incapable of accepting. Was Dorodnov capable of it? But none of that really mattered; the whole point was that Nikolai Vasilievich was an absolutely honest and decent man, and to attack him implied an attack, as it were, on the very standard of decency itself, because Dorodnov was one thing and Nikolai Vasilievich Ganchuk was something else. Sometimes ill-informed people would ask: What is the difference between them? They had simply changed places for a time. Both of them were flourishing their swords, the only difference was that one was now showing signs of flagging, and the other one had only recently been given his sword. Therefore to attack one, it might seem, was equivalent to attacking the other, too; they were birds of a feather. But that wasn't so. The two men made different movements, like swimmers in a river: one did the crawl, another did the breaststroke. Oh God, was there really any difference between them after all? They were both swimming in the same river, in the same direction. No, it really came down to one thing—parting with Sonya and her love forever. And that was so irrevocable, such a bitter wound to the heart—to deprive oneself of the love of even one person . . . And that wouldn't be all. He would feel it from all sides: people would revile him, would hold their hands behind their back lest they sully themselves by shaking hands with him. Someone, no doubt, would send him a telegram: "Congratulations on your Griboyedov award of thirty pieces of silver." None of that would upset him, because his career would suddenly accelerate so fast that he would fly far, far away; all these people would vanish from his horizon and disappear forever with their sneers, their contempt and the blinders on their eyes which prevented them from seeing that Ganchuk's goose was already cooked before the meeting took place and that nothing Glebov might say would make any difference to the outcome. To try to save him was like swimming against the current in a flood that carried everything before it. You could thrash away until you were exhausted and still be flung lifeless onto the shingle. For fear is the most intangible and the most secret motive force of human self-consciousness. Steel fingers were already noticeably beginning to push him, and he was ready, firmly and finally ready; yet some invisible force was barring the way. Was it Sonya? Whom he didn't love? And who was the best person he had ever met in his life? No, it wasn't Sonya, but the things that made up Sonya's nature: her warmth, her goodness . . . It was those essential qualities within Sonya which constituted the obstacle and which were an impassable barrier.

Therefore if the first two variants were impossible, there was the third. To go and not to speak, to remain silent. That would please nobody. Both sides would hate him for it. Out of the question! So that left the fourth and last variant. *Not to go at all.* But was that possible? He had been warned that his presence was "more than essential." Any excuse, therefore, had to be of positively cosmic significance or the result of some near-fatal accident, such as being run over by a car on his way to the meeting. Or perhaps he might kick a stray dog to make it bite him, necessitating an immediate antirabies shot. There were countless possibilities—but all of them absurd. If only the loss of consciousness and the heart attack that had happened two days before, after his night out with Lev Shulepnikov, could happen now; but Druzyaev, a former prosecuting attorney, would undoubtedly set up an investigation and find out that the cause of the attack was alcoholic poisoning. No, it was impossible not to go. And to go was equally impossible. Everything was impossible. Stalemate. Not one piece on the board could move.

It was this dilemma—though briefly, jerkily, in a tired voice and with many pauses for reflection—that he described to Grandma Nila, when she asked him to tell her something about his life.

"I love hearing about what you're doing," she had said.

Nila herself had never worked in her life. Or rather, she had worked all her life, only at home, in the family. Naturally she understood nothing about his problems, but he told her all the same; he had to talk about something, and he had only one thing on his mind.

Suddenly old Nila herself started to tell him some of her memories of the distant past, which she remembered well and in great detail. One summer Grandpa Nikolai, Glebov's great-great-grandfather, had taken her out to the country. He was a merchant, and the family used to live on the Varvarka, near the Salt Market (they had sold that house before the revolution and moved to Shchipok, across the Moscow River), but in a village in Venevsky District there was a house which Grandpa Nikolai had built for his mother-in-law, who had refused to move to Moscow. As a little girl, Nila used to love driving out to the country in summer. Grandpa Nikolai was not popular in the village, where he was nicknamed "Mr. Skinflint," although to Nila he always seemed kind. On the way out to the village, he would buy her a "raffia horn," a cone-shaped container made of clean, yellow raffia full of cheap little gingerbread cookies, nuts and raisins. The mixture was known as *yeralash;* in the store they would ask for "two horns of *yeralash,* please." All the little village girls would be there, waiting for them, as soon as their carriage drove into the yard, and then Nila would distribute the contents of her cones to them: some nuts for you, some candy for you, some gingerbread for you. Nila's old great-grandmother loved sugar candy. Grandpa Nikolai had built her a cottage there, although she refused to live in it because it was built like a town house, without a proper porch and with a huge living room full of city-style furniture. So Great-Grandmama lived in an ordinary peasant's cottage with her daughter, and the "proper" house was always empty until Nikolai brought his family there in the summer. He would ask her: "What shall we bring you from Moscow, *mamasha?*" She would invariably reply: "Sugar candy, Nikolai Efimovich, if it's not too much trouble." Of course, they always sent her some for Lent, too, as it was one of the things you were allowed to eat during the Lenten fast; then in summer they would never fail to bring her two slabs of sugar candy—it was sold in slabs in Zaitsev's grocery store. The slabs were not very big, about the size of the small drawers in a writing desk; the candy was displayed in the store stacked in two layers, each made up of different colors and flavors—lemon, raspberry, apple, plum, as many flavors as you could wish.

So they sat there telling stories to each other, Glebov and his Grandma Nila, and afterward everyone had the impression that the old lady was feeling much better. She even felt strong enough to offer Glebov some advice on his problems:

"What can I say to you, Dima?" She looked at him with pity, with tears in her eyes, as though he and not she were dying: "Don't upset yourself, don't aggravate your heart. If there's nothing to be done about it, then don't think about it. It will all sort itself out, you'll see, and whatever that may be, it will be the right way. . . ."

And strange to say he fell asleep that night easily, calmly and free of nagging anxiety. At six o'clock next morning he was suddenly awakened by a low voice, or it may have been by something else, and he heard someone say, "Our Grandmama Nila has gone. . . ."

Klavdia was standing in the doorway, black against the brightly lighted hallway. The low voice, which he had taken for a man's voice, was hers. Quietly, for fear of disturbing the neighbors, Aunt Paula was sobbing on the other side of the partition. The sound she made was strange and chilling, like the clucking of a chicken whose neck was being wrung. Glebov's father came in, muttering something about the doctor, a death certificate and the need to go somewhere. So began that Thursday. And Glebov was unable to go anywhere on that day.

I came back to the house on the embankment three years later, in September 1941, three months after the German invasion. School hadn't started yet. The nights were cold, but clear and starlit. I remember those nights; we lived a nocturnal existence. The day was spent rushing hither and thither: working at the riverside docks, at the lumber stacks, or delivering draft notices from the district military commandant; in our spare time we learned how to control the pumps on a fire engine, how to unreel a fire hose or operate a street fire hydrant. Although amateurs, we were firemen. At the same time we helped out with any job that came to hand. We un-

loaded cargoes of ammunition at the docks, and at the lumber
stacks we unloaded logs from freight trains. Everything had to
be done in a hurry; we didn't stack the lumber in neat piles,
but simply threw it off the flatcars in untidy heaps. The important thing was to clear the track as quickly as possible.
That is what I most remember—the mad haste. And I remember how I strained myself trying to lift those gigantic logs. But
our real life began at night, after Levitan's voice on the radio
had broadcast an air-raid warning. We did our turns of duty,
we blundered around in attics, ran over roofs in search of
those hellish incendiary bombs, which we would heroically
seize with long tongs and throw off the roof; but above all we
breathed the deathly chill of those nights.

They were bright, with a kind of ashen glow. The antiaircraft guns flashed incessantly all around and deafened us with
their noise. I shall never forget that smell of powder smoke
above the roofs of Moscow, the clatter of shell splinters falling
on sheet iron and the sad smell of burning, coming from somewhere beyond Serpukhovskaya Street. . . .

The station house of our fire company—its full title was
something like "The Komsomol Youth Company of the Lenin
District Fire Brigade"—was on the Yakimanka, over the
bridge. The house on the embankment did not belong in our
sector, but one day we found ourselves there all the same; I
forget what we were doing there, or why we were sent there.
On the roof, I remember, I met Anton and three other kids;
then we ran down to Sonya Ganchuk's apartment, and Vadim
French Loaf was there; it was his last day in Moscow before
being evacuated. He had come up to say goodbye; their train
was leaving at dawn, but they had to go to the station hours
beforehand, because the business of getting on the train was so
chaotic. I had already seen off my aunt on one of those trains,
and I knew what it was like. French Loaf had grown up a lot;
he now spoke in a deep bass voice and had even sprouted a
thin black mustache. It appeared that he had not only come
to say goodbye to Sonya but to fetch a trunk which she had
promised to him. I remember him as he stood standing in the
middle of the kitchen, drinking a cup of tea, while Sonya
cleaned the extremely dusty trunk with a brush, when sud-

denly the lights went out, we started looking for candles or a flashlight, and at that moment the air-raid alarm sounded. For the second time that night.

When the lights came on again soon afterward, I saw Sonya's face wet with tears yet smiling. By then I had almost forgotten about Sonya, and my feelings for Vadim French Loaf were of complete indifference. All that was in some long-distant childhood, whose pain has faded with the years.

I remember something else from that night. An enormous Caucasian dagger was dangling from Anton's belt. He and I were standing on the roof beside the thin metal railings and looking down on the black nocturnal city. There was not a gleam or a flicker of light to be seen down below; everything was murky and indistinguishable except for two pink, quivering wounds in the blackness—a couple of fires burning on the left bank of the Moscow River. The city was endlessly vast. It is difficult to defend something so immeasurable, and there was no way of disguising the river; its shining surface reflected the stars, its bends marked out the districts of the city. It hurt us to think of the city, a living creature that needed help. But how could we help it? There was a moment of paralyzing silence. We stood on the edge of an invisible abyss and looked up at the sky, where everything quivered and merged in a gamut of moving colors, tense with the expectation of a change in the city's fate: stars, clouds, barrage balloons, the slanting blades of searchlight beams tirelessly cutting into that fragile universe. And then Anton uttered a murmured remark that surprised me:

"Do you know who I feel sorry for? Our mothers."

By this he meant that our previous selves no longer existed. A violent break had been made in our lives. Time, like the sky, had broken apart with a deafening crash.

Later, we were waiting on the landing for the elevator, in order to take Sonya's sick mother downstairs to the air-raid shelter. French Loaf had just said that I had done well to get out of this house in time. The Germans were aiming at it; the building was surrounded by near misses—on the bridge, on the Kadeshevka. I wasn't sure whether he was paying tribute to my cunning or my good luck, but whichever it was, I sensed an undercurrent of spite in his remark. I said nothing to him in reply, because I was quite indifferent to him. Doors were slamming on every floor. All around there was noise, people shouting to each other, footsteps clattering on the staircase so hard that the stairs shook. Everyone was listening to what was happening in the sky. For the moment, all was quiet above us. Anton said, "Perhaps it's just a lone plane, some bastard on his own?"

The door of the apartment opposite the elevator opened, and a man came out, an overcoat thrown over his nightshirt, followed by a woman carrying a fat little girl with long legs. From far away came the banging of antiaircraft guns. Speaking to no one in particular, the woman said:

"Every damn German should be thrown out of this house." (This remark was aimed, of course, at Sonya's mother.) Then she looked at her husband and asked, "That's right, isn't it, Kolya?"

When the elevator door opened and Sonya's mother made a move to go into it, the woman adroitly pushed her aside with the little girl's legs and said, "No, you can wait," and went into the elevator first, followed by her husband and someone else. The elevator went down. Professor Ganchuk asked: "Who are they?"

Sonya said they were the new neighbors, and added hesitantly: "They're not bad people, but a bit strange."

Anton and I linked our four hands to make a "chair," put Sonya's mother on it and carried her downstairs to the cellar. Then we had to go back to the Yakimanka. The antiaircraft fire was getting nearer and louder. When I ran out of doors, the firing was thundering all around and in the intervals between salvoes one could clearly hear the fragments of exploded shells thumping violently into the asphalt. So amid haste and noise I parted from all of them, without a chance to say goodbye.

No—there was one more meeting. I met Anton for the last time at the end of October, in a bakery on the Polyanka. Winter had suddenly hit us with frost and snow, but Anton, of course, wore neither hat nor coat. He said that in two days' time he and his mother were being evacuated to the Urals, and he asked my advice on what to take with him: his diaries, the science-fiction novel he was writing, or the albums of his drawings? His mother had weak arms, so he was the only one who could carry heavy things. His question struck me as absurd. How could anyone be worrying about albums or novels, when the Germans were at the gates of Moscow? Anton drew or wrote something every day. A notebook, folded in two, was sticking out of the pocket of his jacket. He said, "I shall make a note of our meeting in this bakery. And our conversation too. Because it is all of historical importance."

Many years later I came back to see Anton's mother—she was the only one who returned to live in the house on the embankment, to the same little apartment on the first floor—and she gave me the six notebooks that contained Anton's diary. They were his diaries for the last year before the outbreak of war; for some reason they had remained in the Moscow apartment and so had survived. All the rest of Anton Ovchinnikov's work, his albums and his scientific studies, had sunk in the Iset, when the barge in which they were traveling capsized. Anton and his mother barely escaped with their lives.

Something that Glebov tried particularly hard to forget was what Kuno Ivanovich had said to him when, by an absurd coincidence, they met on the Rozhdestvensky Boulevard, and how he, Glebov, had behaved when he heard it. The times were different by then (it happened only eight years ago), but somehow there was still a nervous, keyed-up feeling in the air which affected them—it might have been on the eve of the so-called "doctors' plot," or it might have been when he was in the process of moving from the institute to his present job— and on top of it all he had to bump into Kuno Ivanovich on Rozhdestvensky Boulevard. It was in the depth of winter. The central avenue of the boulevard had been swept clear of snow, so that the yellow sand showed through, with deep heaps of snow piled up on either side. Someone fell into a snowdrift. Glebov was not the only person walking there at that moment; that was the trouble—it was all said in front of other people, and Glebov lost control of himself. If the passers-by had not pulled him away, it could have ended very badly, because he was unaware of what he was doing. He almost managed to strangle the little man, after throwing him to the ground and gripping his throat. For the rest of his life he tried to forget about it, and nearly succeeded; his memory almost suppressed it—he could not remember, for instance, what Kuno Ivanovich actually said to him—but it persisted in the form of a faint pain in his chest, like the feeling induced by recalling an escape from some horror in the distant past. Whenever he recollected that little man, which occurred very rarely and for no explicable reason, it made itself felt by nothing more than a slight constriction in his chest.

He also did his best not to remember the look on Yulia Mikhailovna's face when she was walking down the hallway, leaning on a girl's arm, having come out of Druzyaev's office. Glebov felt a moment's confusion, not knowing what to do— whether to nod, to say something, or simply to bow in silence— and in his perplexity he simply froze stock-still. Her face, too, froze into a mask as she went past him. He tried very hard indeed to forget those petrified features, because memory is a net which should not be subjected to too much strain by making it bear heavy loads. All those great cast-iron lumps of horror should be allowed to break the net, fall through and disappear. Otherwise we are obliged to live in a constant state of stress. He did forget her bloodless, frozen face, but not for long; it reappeared whenever he heard some news of her, such as her death. She died soon afterward, when he was still a graduate student. But then, she had suffered from a chronically weak heart. No one could understand why she tried so hard to get her job back. In her condition, it was out of the question for her to work. She couldn't work, couldn't judge others, couldn't make trouble, couldn't seek revenge—she could do nothing but lead a quiet life out at Bruskovo amid the shrubs and the flowerbeds, but she refused to accept such a passive existence, and in any case Bruskovo was taken away from them. She brought her death on herself. He never did know in detail what happened; he only knew that her face suddenly appeared in the institute. All the rest he tried to forget. Such as, for instance, what Ganchuk said at the editorial board when it met to consider an article that had been submitted. Nothing insulting was said, and no one else who heard him understood the implications of his remarks. The old man was so sick as to be almost unrecognizable: something had happened to the right side of his face, which made his speech very indistinct, and no one paid much attention to what he was saying. Although he had been reinstated and his chief enemy, Dorodnov, had been crushed and consigned to oblivion—the last few years had been taken up with this struggle—something important had irrevocably gone, and it was not particularly interesting to listen to an old man who was no longer up to par. No one but Glebov listened to his mumblings, but he caught a note of spite in what Ganchuk was saying. He was both piqued and surprised: apparently those scraggy old muscles still had the ability to contract. All that had to be forgotten, as did that September day in Riga, in an open-air café not far from the central department store, when he had seen Sonya sitting at a nearby table. The times were by then quite different, not even like more recent times, but quite, quite different; he could have safely assumed that no one would recognize him; that nothing that might reach him from the unpleasant past was any longer capable of stirring any emotions; and that it had all peeled off and fallen away. He had once heard that Sonya had been taken to a hospital somewhere out of town; this might have been expected, as she had a bad family history: Yulia Mikhailovna's mother had died in an asylum and Yulia Mikhailovna herself, of course, had never enjoyed the best of health. One of the people who had visited Sonya in hospital said that her illness expressed itself in photophobia and a desire to be in darkness all the time. That, apparently, was all: only fear of the light and a longing for the dark. Then, it seemed, she had gotten better, although he knew nothing definite. There were no more people left to form a link between him and Sonya; he had lost contact with everyone from those days. Then came that meeting in Riga. He was renting a house near the beach, and had come into town for the day. Marina had dragged him around the stores, and suddenly there was Sonya sitting at the next table. Beside her was a tall, strange-looking, big-nosed woman in spectacles, dressed untidily like a tourist in sloppy pants and sneakers. Sonya looked at Glebov; it was because he felt her glance that he turned around. At once he made an involuntary movement toward her and said something like "Sonya!" or "Hello!" or "Is that you?" Something warm, expressive of the wave of emotion that overwhelmed him for a second. She had aged and put on weight, half of her hair was gray, but she had kept her ability to turn instantly pale; she paled now, looking frightened; then the woman with the big nose took her by the arm, raised her from her seat and led her away. It stuck in his memory that the sneakers the woman was wearing were huge, outsize. Marina asked, "Do you know those women? Who are they?" He said they were old acquaintances from Moscow, but he couldn't remember their names.

Maybe it wasn't quite like that, because he was trying to forget it. Whatever one didn't remember ceased to exist. None of it had ever happened. There never had been that second, crowded meeting in March, when there was no longer any point in reproaching oneself; he had to go anyway, and even if he didn't speak himself, he was at least obliged to listen to the others. He did, it seems, say something at that meeting, something very brief and of very little significance. It had completely escaped his memory. So what? It no longer mattered. Ganchuk's fate had already been decided. He was to be transferred to an obscure teachers' college outside Moscow, ". . . to strengthen the faculty there." Some people objected, somebody clucked in protest like an angry hen, but that was all uninteresting and now forgotten—*it had never happened*. Or had it? One thing, though, was undoubtedly real: the café in Gorky Street. He remembered that for the rest of his days. That *had* happened. But all the rest, the shouting, the excitement, five hours of idiotic talk with breaks for those who wanted to smoke, Lev's drunken babbling, Shireiko's triumph (he had seemed to be heading for the front ranks, marked out as an up-and-coming big wheel, but somehow his progress went no further than those meetings and there his advancement stopped), all the stupid, incomprehensible fuss that was created around Ganchuk, with stamping of feet and twisting of arms, with tears, heart attacks and rejoicing—all that vanished as though sunk in a swamp. No, it didn't happen; nothing of the sort happened. Glebov was staggering along the street, his head muzzy and heavy, and beside him Lev, who was totally smashed. He had managed to stay on his feet in the meeting, and had still looked pretty good when he was on the rostrum. Lev was muttering: "We're all bastards, pigs . . ." He had to be helped home, or he might have collapsed on the street. It was then that his downfall began. Several years later, when his life really started to go downhill, his second "dad," the one who looked like a bewhiskered Ukrainian Cossack, turned out to be not up to his job. The apartment went, the car vanished, his mother was left alone but managed by a miracle to cling on to something, and Lev turned into a minor administrator in some soccer club; he traveled with the team from town to town, fixed up the hotel bookings, looked after the boots and the balls, arranged unofficial matches, and he drank, for which he was soon fired. After that he did God knows what, and when the police picked him up dead drunk on the street he would sometimes say his name was Glebov and give Glebov's address. No doubt he gave other names and addresses as well. The police brought him to Glebov twice. But even that was long in the past, about fourteen years ago. And then the waves closed over his head, and Glebov heard nothing more of him until his sudden reappearance now in the furniture store, when neither of them had any strength left for sentiment about old times—for anything, in fact, except harsh reality.

But back then, after the March meeting and before the deluge, as they swayed and circled around the Moscow streets, neither had any premonition of what was to come: Lev didn't know that he would soon be on the skids, slithering from side to side, like an empty sled shooting down an icy hillside, and Glebov didn't know that the time would come when he would try not to remember everything that happened to him in those days, and no doubt he didn't know either that he would come to live a life that *hadn't happened.* And suddenly, through the window of a café on Gorky Street, near Pushkin Square, Glebov saw Ganchuk. He was standing at one of the little tall tables where you drink coffee, and was greedily eating a Napoleon, holding it in its paper napkin with all five fingers of his hand. His fleshy face, with its pink folds of skin, expressed pure enjoyment as it moved and twitched like a well-fitting

mask, the whole skin from jaw to brow vibrating with pleasure. Ganchuk was so absorbed in the sweetness of the cream
and the thin crispness of the strips of pastry that he noticed
neither Glebov, who was frozen into immobility in front of
the window and for a second stared at Ganchuk in amazement,
nor Shulepnikov, swaying on his feet beside him. Yet a half-
hour ago this man had been destroyed. Later, Glebov often
told the story of seeing Ganchuk in the café. Yes, he would
say, you might think the old man had plenty on his mind at
that moment—this, that and the other, all of it forgotten
now—yet there he stood eating a Napoleon with the greatest
possible enjoyment.

Other things, too, imprinted themselves on his memory,
some with all the nuances, some in great detail, some blurred,
such as his first visit to the Ganchuks after his grandmother's
funeral, and after the Faculty Board meeting which he had
been lucky to avoid, but before the second meeting that took
place in March. It was one of those well-meaning but stupid
things that he was prone to do. Inwardly he had already made
up his mind. The stupid part of it was that he still felt the
need for Sonya to give him by some indirect, oblique means,
her permission. That is to say, he imagined her saying:

"Yes, you're right, my dear, you should leave me. It will be
better that way for me, for you, for Papa, for your work and
for everyone."

Of course she wouldn't say any such thing, but he wanted
her nevertheless to see him and share his suffering, to realize
that there had been no alternative. Somehow he was convinced that she would understand; that was after all her greatest quality—she always understood.

The door was opened by Yulia Mikhailovna. Glebov had
the impression that when she saw him, Sonya's mother momentarily and very slightly swayed, and there was a barely detectable pause before she said: "Oh, it's you. Come in." He
entered. There was something in the atmosphere that he had
never felt before. With a casual gesture Yulia Mikhailovna
pointed to the coatrack: "You can hang your things there,"
as if this were his first time in the house. The message was:
The house you used to know doesn't exist any more. "Sonya

will come soon. Please wait in the dining room." With a similar careless wave of the hand he was shown where to sit—on a little divan alongside the piano. Yulia Mikhailovna went out of the room. He sat there alone, feeling fairly calm although sensing a chill in the air and with a foreboding of painful encounters to come, as though in a dentist's waiting room. This visit, however, was essential; the aching tooth had to be pulled out, and so he was prepared to be patient. One thing puzzled him: why was Yulia Mikhailovna so obviously cold toward him? It was incomprehensible. The March meeting had not yet taken place. Surely she couldn't read his thoughts, when he had himself only just made up his mind? He decided that as soon as Yulia Mikhailovna appeared again he would ask her, with genuine surprise: "What has happened? Why do you seem to be so angry with me?"

Still Yulia Mikhailovna did not come back. Sonya had not yet returned home. He could hear Yulia Mikhailovna's quick little footsteps pattering down the hall, heard her talking to Vasyona; then the study door was opened, followed by the rumbling of Ganchuk's voice and Yulia Mikhailovna saying: "That is not what I want!" To this Ganchuk made some inaudible reply, after which there was silence. No one came into the dining room. The door opened noiselessly to admit Maurice the cat, who walked past Glebov without looking at him, as though he were a chair, and stalked across the dining room into Sonya's room. By the time Glebov had been sitting on the divan for about a half-hour, he began to get nervous. What sort of way was this to treat him? What grounds had they for this behavior? There were none. He had, after all, had a very good reason for not going to the Faculty Board meeting—a more than good reason: the death of a close and beloved relative was more important than troubles at the institute. A gradually mounting sense of hostility toward Yulia Mikhailovna rose in him—he had always felt there was something small-minded, egotistical and unpleasant about this woman—and he also began to resent Ganchuk, too, because he always gave in to her. For the first time Glebov experienced a certain malicious pleasure in the thought that these people were being made to suffer a certain degree of unpleasant pressure and even hardship. They couldn't go on forever looking down on others from their ivory tower. It was significant, what's more, that so few people had come to their defense. When Yulia Mikhailovna suddenly came in, she was carrying—no tea, no bowl of cookies, not even an ashtray—a table lamp, and Glebov said to her, with a hint of challenge in his voice:

"You seem to be angry with me for some reason, Yulia Mikhailovna."

Yulia Mikhailovna gave an odd grin but did not immediately reply. She put the lamp on an occasional table in a corner of the room, plugged it in and switched it on. "Yes, would you believe it? I am angry with you."

"But why, Yulia Mikhailovna?"

"I can't explain it briefly. We haven't time for a talk. Sonya will be here in a moment. It's rather dark in here, don't you think? I must put the light on. *'Mehr Licht,'* as Goethe said before he died."

She switched on the chandelier and went out again. It was four o'clock in the afternoon and not particularly dark. Suddenly Yulia Mikhailovna reappeared and firmly shut the door behind her; her eyes were flashing, her movements hurried. She sat down on a chair facing the little divan and fixing Glebov with a piercing look she said rapidly, in a low voice:

"All the same, I'll try and explain before Sonya comes. I'm talking quietly, so that Nikolai Vasilievich won't hear. I didn't want this conversation, but you asked me, so . . . Do you know what I think of you? I hate you. Yes, yes, there's no need to look so surprised . . ."

Then she started to spout a stream of unbelievable nonsense. There was something about how hard it was to understand a person, but that there always came a moment (for some reason she said "a moment in the night") when people revealed themselves. Then something more about her mother, who had been clairvoyant and able to foretell the future. This, he remembered later, had given him a nasty fright: was she clairvoyant too and had she been able to guess his intention to break with Sonya? But as though in answer to his unspoken question, she said that she lacked her mother's gift; she had no idea of the state of his relationship with Sonya, she did not want to interfere, but it did seem to her . . . It filled her with alarm to think . . . She cursed the day that . . . What an extraordinary rigmarole it all was, what an outpouring of malice, absurdity and madness! Obviously the woman was sick. Sonya had once told him that whenever her mother's blood pressure went up and an attack of stenosis was on the way, funny things were likely to happen to her mind. Feeling an urge to get out of the room, Glebov leaped to his feet and said, "I'll fetch you some water."

She seized him by the arm and would not let him go. Her fingers held him in a firm grip of unexpected strength, and he felt a momentary chill of anxiety: only a madwoman, he thought, could show such strength. But Yulia Mikhailovna was not insane; she simply hated Glebov and was in a hurry to tell him the reason. Again, as though reading his thoughts, she said rapidly, "Don't call anyone, I can explain everything before Sonya comes, and then we'll have some tea. And—do you hear?—I haven't said anything to you. . . ."

After that, with the same haste, in a half-whisper, gulping between words, she told him that he was intelligent, but that his intelligence was ice-cold, ungenerous and inhuman, an intelligence that was totally selfish, the intelligence of a man of the past . . . and similar remarks that were close to clinical delirium.

"You don't understand how *bourgeois* you are!"

He had, apparently, simply made use of everything: her house, her *dacha*, her books, her husband and her daughter. What could one say in reply to all this? There was no point in arguing with such an unhappy woman. He got up from the divan and asked, "May I get you a glass of water?"

"Yes, you may," she said calmly.

He went into the kitchen, Vasyona gave him a glass, which he filled with boiled water and took back into the dining room. Yulia Mikhailovna was sitting on the same chair and staring in front of her.

"Do you know what I think?" she said slowly, as though coming to her senses, as she took the glass. "It would be best of all if this conversation remained between ourselves. The best thing would be if you would leave this house . . ."

He asked, "What have I done wrong?"

"Nothing—so far. You have not yet been able to. But why wait until you do? Go away now . . . I ask you, I implore you." Indeed, there was entreaty in her look. "Sonya will never know about our conversation. I swear it. Do you want me to give you money?"

"Money? What are you talking about?"

"But you need money, don't you? You love money, isn't that so? And you don't have any. How much would you like me to give you?" The delirious ramblings started again. "Tell me quickly, before Sonya comes. Go on, tell me. I'll give it to you and then you can leave immediately. . . . No, wait! I'll give you something else." Here she dropped into a whisper. "I'll give you an antique ring, with a sapphire. You love bourgeois things, don't you? Gold? Gems?"

"If you are so anxious for me to go," he said, "then I won't object . . ."

She waved her hands, whispering, "Just wait a moment and I'll bring it. I don't need it, and you can make good use of it."

She ran toward the door of a neighboring room, which was her bedroom, but fortunately she was stopped by Ganchuk, who was coming in. There followed a strange, obscure, jerky conversation about, of all things, the works of Dostoyevsky. Ganchuk said that he had hitherto underrated Dostoyevsky, that Gorky had been wrong about Dostoyevsky and it was time to reassess him. He would have a lot more spare time now and he proposed to work on the subject.

Yulia Mikhailovna stared at her husband with sad intensity. He said that the thought that had tormented Dostoyevsky—if man's last refuge is nothing but a dark room full of spiders, then *all is permitted*—had hitherto been interpreted in a wholly simplistic, trivial sense. All such profound problems had, in fact, been distorted into pathetically inadequate form, but the problems themselves were still there and would not go away. Today's Raskolnikovs did not murder old women moneylenders with an ax, but they were faced with the same agonizing choice: to cross or not to cross the line. In any case, what was the difference between using an ax and any other method? What was the difference between murder and just giving the victim a slight push, provided that it removed him? After all, Raskolnikov didn't commit murder for the sake of world harmony but simply for his own ends, to save his old mother, to get his sister out of a tight spot, and to secure for himself something or other in this life, whatever it might have been. . . .

He was thinking aloud, oblivious to whether anyone was listening to him or understanding him. Suddenly Sonya came in, just as Ganchuk was saying, "And you, Dima—why did you come here? It is completely inexplicable in terms of formal logic. But perhaps there is a reason of another kind . . ."

"Papa!" Sonya shouted, rushing toward Glebov. "Don't be horrible to Dima. He's suffered enough already . . ."

She stood in front of Glebov, shielding him as though Ganchuk might throw something at him, but Ganchuk was so absorbed that he neither heard nor saw her.

"Perhaps," said Ganchuk, "there is a metaphysical explanation. You remember how Raskolnikov was drawn again and again back to that house . . . No, that's not it." With a brisk, professional gesture he dismissed his own hypothesis. "In the novel everything was much clearer and simpler, because there was a state of open social conflict. . . . But nowadays people don't fully understand what they are doing. Hence the arguments within themselves . . . they are trying to convince themselves. . . . The conflict is *internalized*—that is what is happening."

"Papa, dear," said Sonya, "I beg you!"

"All right, my dear. I'm sorry. Excuse me." For the first time Ganchuk now looked attentively and understandingly at Glebov. "And I want you to know that I do not bear him the slightest grudge. Absolutely none at all."

He went out. A short while later, however, when Glebov had followed Sonya into her room and was lying on the rug-covered couch, as he usually did at moments of tiredness, while she sat beside him and stroked his hair, Ganchuk suddenly put his head around the door and said in his old, familiar voice:

"Do you know what our mistake was? We spared Dorodnov in 1928. We should have finished him off."

Hearing this reassured Glebov; he realized that Ganchuk hadn't changed, that he was his former self again. So everything that had happened had been right. Glebov spent the night with Sonya. They hardly slept but dozed off just before dawn. Glebov had a dream: in a little round tin box that had once held candy was a collection of old medals, orders, crosses and badges and he was sorting through them, trying to do it quietly in order not to waken somebody. Later in his life, this dream about the medals and badges recurred more than once. Next morning during breakfast in the kitchen, as he sat looking down on the concrete arc of the bridge with its toy people and its toy cars and the grayish-yellow palace with its cap of snow in the Kremlin across the river, he said he would call her up after class and come again that evening. He never went back to that house again.

All this was what Glebov remembered—partly by exerting his memory, partly by involuntary association—during the night after that day on which he had met Lev Shulepnikov in the furniture store. One thing, however, puzzled him, and by the time he fell asleep in his study on the second floor with its window on to the garden he had still not solved the riddle: why had Lev refused to recognize him?

In April 1974, Glebov traveled by train to Paris for a congress of the IALCE (International Association of Literary Critics and Essayists, in which he belonged to the board of management of the essayists' section), and on the train he met Alina Fyodorovna, Lev's mother. She was also going to Paris at the invitation of her sister, who had left Russia fifty-three years before. Alina Fyodorovna had turned into a gray, bent old woman, but Glebov recognized her at once: the same hooknosed, terra-cotta-colored face, the same sharp, glittering look and the same cigarette between her teeth that he remembered from childhood. She stood for hours in the corridor by the window, smoking. Glebov approached her and reminded her who he was, but the conversation failed to get started. Suddenly, as had happened long ago, he sensed the existence of a wall of haughty superiority that surrounded this woman. What reason could she possibly have for acting like this now, for God's sake? Her world was destroyed, her life had fallen apart, her son had disappeared and she had no wish to talk about him; yet the old lady screwed up her eyes as though looking at Glebov through a lorgnette and asked with aristocratic indifference: "Oh really? Essayists' section? Is that interesting?" After Warsaw she had become slightly more talkative, and he learned that she was getting a pension due her as the widow of her first husband, Prokhorov-Pluhnge, an old Communist who had been posthumously rehabilitated, that she had a nice one-room apartment on Peace Avenue, not far from the metro, where she lived alone and had no wish to see anyone—neither her dear son nor her ex-daughter-in-law (who had left Lev eight years ago because no one could bear to live with him), nor her grandson, a seventeen-year-old punk who remembered her only when she was about to visit her relatives in Paris. Then he would become the best grandson in the world and visit her, ostensibly to see how she was; he would also casually give her a little order, which he just happened to have typed out, for a pair of jeans, a belt, a cigarette lighter, a blue denim shirt with sewn-on pockets and a fitted waist (the kind to be worn outside your pants)—all very efficient and carefully thought out. All her life she had lived for others; now she wanted to live for herself. After Berlin she became even more loquacious and frank: "They say the Russian nobility has degenerated; I heard that said in Paris. But I tell you the opposite: we are a very tough breed because we have been through everything and we have survived."

At the station in Paris, Glebov saw another hook-nosed old woman who looked somewhat like Alina Fyodorovna but was frailer and fussier in her behavior; there was nothing Parisian about her clothes, and she wore a voluminous, old-fashioned cloak. With her were a young man and a girl who twittered around Alina Fyodorovna, speaking half in Russian and half in French. As the crowd surged around them, Glebov stood there for two or three minutes, expecting Alina Fyodorovna to look around and say goodbye to him. But Alina Fyodorovna did not so much as glance in Glebov's direction. Instead he heard an insinuating voice say in broken Russian: "Welcome to Paris, Monsieur Gleboff! Let me take your baggage. Is this all?" The young, tanned, red-cheeked, wet-lipped young man with a thin mustache, named Seculot, whom Glebov remembered from the congresses in Oslo and Zagreb, picked up Glebov's only suitcase, nodded, pointed somewhere with his left hand and led Glebov away through the crowd.

The familiar smell of a Paris station, a heady, bittersweet fusion of aromas, enveloped Glebov like humid air on a hot day. Forty minutes later he was darting briskly back and forth in his rather gloomy hotel room, which looked out onto a narrow street not far from the Place Pigalle. Humming under his breath, he unpacked his suitcase, slammed the wardrobe doors, and almost ran into the bathroom, where he laid out his washing and shaving things under the mirror.

When I was working on a book about the 1920s, I came across the name of Nikolai Vasilievich Ganchuk, who had played a notable part in the discussions of those days, especially in the noisy arguments which had raged around the journal *Literary Outlook* in 1925 and 1926. Someone told me that Ganchuk was still alive. With considerable difficulty I managed to find him. He was living alone in a tiny one-room apartment jammed full of books—there were even bookcases in the kitchen—in a new, slablike apartment house near the Riverboat Station. He had voluntarily given up his old apartment (which as a boy I had visited, though he had of course forgotten this and I remembered it only vaguely) because he had not felt able to go on living there alone after Sonya's death. His new place, he assured me, had an excellent climate, the air was made fragrant by the surrounding pine forest and it was a good place to go skiing. He was eighty-six years old. He had shrunk, he stooped and his head had sunk between his shoulders, but his cheekbones still glowed with healthy, undimmed Ganchuk rosiness. When with an effort he stretched out his bent right arm, elbow first, and gripped your hand with his tenacious fingers, you felt a hint of his erstwhile strength. "I am!" said his handshake, although his eyes were watering and he had difficulty with his speech. A pair of skis stood in a corner of the foyer. An old woman with a sharp, pointed nose and a head of neat gray curls came to help with the housework. One day I heard her singing softly in the kitchen.

Several times I visited Ganchuk with a tape recorder, in an attempt to extract from him some details about the noisy, abusive literary quarrels of the 1920s—there are almost no witnesses of those semilegendary years still alive—but unfortunately I couldn't get much out of him. And not because the old man's memory was failing, but because he didn't want to remember. He wasn't interested any more. The events of those days were far more interesting to me than to him, and once he said with amazement and even some irritation: "Good Lord, do you mean to say you found *that* article of mine too? I can't see why anyone wants to rummage around in all that nonsense. . . ." On the other hand, he would talk with great enthusiasm about some mind-numbing soap opera that was running on TV, or about an article he had just read in *Science and Life*. He subscribed to eighteen different newspapers and magazines.

In October, on the anniversary of Sonya's death, we went to the cemetery. Sonya was buried in the grounds of the old crematorium, near the Donskoi Monastery. The crematorium had been closed eighteen months before; Moscow now burnt its dead somewhere else, out of town. People said that it was too far out, too inconvenient, too grim and forbidding. By contrast, the burial ground by the Donskoi Monastery was positively cosy. The cemetery was open to visitors until seven P.M., and it was ten minutes to seven when we arrived. The taxi waited for us in the little square in front of the gates. There was a mist on the ground, the trees and the cemetery wall were coal-black, but the sky still had a twilight glow and the place was alive with the cawing of rooks. We walked up to the entrance just as the gatekeeper was rattling an iron chain preparatory to locking the gates. I was leading the old man by the arm. The gatekeeper didn't want to let us in, and we started arguing in the darkness. We threatened, begged, tried to give him a tip, but the gatekeeper simply got ruder and more obstinate. Ganchuk pointed out that he was a state pensioner, that he was eighty-six and might die at any moment, but the gatekeeper shouted in a hoarse, angry voice that he was human too and wanted to get home on time.

"But you have no right, it's still ten minutes before closing time . . ."

"The grocery stores shut at a quarter-to!"

"How can you compare the two things? Have you no conscience?"

"Don't you lecture me. I can compare what I like. Anyone would think comparisons were forbidden."

"Tell me your name," shouted Ganchuk weakly. "Give me your name at once. I shall write a letter."

"Prokhorov!" barked the gatekeeper. "Lev Mikhailovich, if you want to know. So what? Where will you write to? The other world?"

"Shulepa," I said quietly, "let us in."

The man, unrecognizable in the gloom, fell silent and stepped back from the gates. We walked in. Amid a silence broken by the noise of rooks, my heels crunched and Ganchuk's rubber overshoes shuffled over the asphalt. We moved very slowly; no doubt he traveled at about this pace when he went skiing. When we were about twenty paces past the gates, I said to Ganchuk, "I think he used to be in our class. To hell with him."

We skirted the black, inert crematorium and began looking for the grave, which took some time to find in the dark. The old man bent over and felt the gravestones. At last, breathing hard, he said, "Here it is. . . ."

He squatted on his haunches and spent a long time in that position, brushing, tidying, making the dead leaves rustle.

There can be nothing more terrible, I thought, than dead death. The extinguished crematorium was dead death. And Lev Shulepa at the gates of the cemetery . . . Suddenly I understood why the old man no longer wanted to recall the past. The rooks made a deafening noise as they circled and circled over our heads in great anger. It was as if we had invaded their kingdom. Or perhaps their hour had begun, the hour when we should not dare to go there. There were very many large, solid nests in the surrounding trees.

The old man whispered, as though talking to himself, "What a pointless, idiotic world it is. Sonya's lying in the ground, her classmate refuses to let us in here, and I am eighty-six. Why? Who can explain it?" He gripped my arm with a prehensile claw. "And yet how we long to stay in this world."

A half-hour later we shuffled back to the entrance. The gates were wide open and the gatekeeper had disappeared. The taxi was still waiting for us. We drove in silence. It was not until we reached the square and turned into the tunnel leading to Sadovaya that Ganchuk leaned forward to the driver and asked him in a barely audible voice to go faster: there was a TV program that he didn't want to miss. The traffic lights flashed, the lights began to come on all around, the city that I loved, remembered, knew, and tried to understand stretched out to infinity. . . .

Soon afterward, dressed in a worn-out leather jacket with a sheepskin collar, of the kind that airmen used to wear in the late forties, the gatekeeper came out onto the avenue leading past the monastery wall, turned left and emerged onto a broad highway, where he got on a trolley bus. Several minutes later, as he crossed the river by the bridge, he looked up at the long, squat, ugly house on the embankment and out of habit located the windows of his old apartment, in which he had spent his happiest years, and he wondered whether some miracle might happen and another change might take place in his life.